Rosie Chapel

D1339941

First printing 2015
ISBN   978-0-9945053-1-6

Ulfire Pty. Ltd.
P.O. Box 1481
South Perth
WA 6951
Australia

www.rosiechapel.com

Cover artwork by H.E. Rodgers

To 'my Max,'
thank you for your love and encouragement,

and to Glen,
who inspired my passion for ancient history.

The Pomegranate Tree

Hannah's Heirloom ~ Book One

Chapter One

It was the shimmering heat that started it all, making me aware of a subtle shift in the air. It was quite hot that day, warmer than any day we'd had so far and unusually so for the time of year. It was hot enough for the odd mirage, cobweb like, to form and dissolve in front of me. Sitting on that desolate outcrop, letting my imagination run riot, taking in the ruins, the majesty of what remained, voices from the past whirling around me, I understood why people think they see ghosts.

Perched on a stone ledge, the wall behind pressing into my back, sheltered from that blazing sun, the wind soughing across the top of the plateau and down into its cracks and fissures, I felt that I could just call them up, that the long dead souls of this place would simply manifest from the dust beneath my feet, so close did they seem. Absently fingering the crumpled letter spread across a rather dog-eared book in my lap, I began to wonder why I had come here in the first place and what on earth did I think I was going to find.

But I get ahead of myself; you don't even know who I am, or why I'm rambling about a lump of rock. My name is Hannah, the rocky outcrop is the Herod's great desert fortress of Masada, the dog-eared book is Josephus' *The Jewish War* and my Gran wrote the letter. Ok, so its a strange mix and, I hear you say, not really all that compelling - you could be right - but something was stirring, as if all these, seemingly unrelated, things had to come together, at this one place for a reason. I just had no idea what that reason was, still, I had the uneasy feeling that I couldn't stop it and by the time it was over I would not be the same.

Yes, I know what you're thinking - its the sun and the heat messing with your mind - I agree, its possible, even as a child, my parents worried that I had too vivid an imagination. I overheard one of my aunts telling my mother that I was fey, which, as a child I thought sounded very important. I loved reading about swashbuckling heroes and damsels in distress, often losing myself in their world, I assumed that's what all children did, especially as my heritage, typical of so many born in Britain, blends the romance of the French and the Celts with the pragmatism of ancient Germanic tribes.

This sensation was different, more tangible, as if the past was about to come into the present revealing its secrets and that nothing in my imagination could prepare me for what I would uncover, I admit I felt rather disquieted. When I think about it, it does seem rather implausible, but we'll see where the days take us. More to the point, back to how I got here in the first place. My life has been quite ordinary, first school, then university, after which, I was lucky enough to land a job with a museum in their classical antiquities department. A dream job, I spent my days cataloguing ancient artefacts and got to help in the preparation of new displays and exhibitions. I have a lovely group of friends and enjoy an active social life, pretty much your typical single girl.

Then about six months ago I received a letter from my Gran, which threw me a little, as she had been dead for about ten years, but apparently, this date for its delivery had been at her instruction. I had read the letter hundreds of times and still didn't really understand it, the words didn't make sense, but one thing was clear, I had to come here, to this stark corner of the world, to Masada. Yes, I know, who just hops on a plane and travels to a remote ruined fortress in the middle of an Israeli desert, on the strength of a few sentences in a ten year old letter, I bet you are thinking I'm an idiot. Well maybe I am, but I need to unravel this.

Maybe it's nothing, just a letter from an old lady, so what have I lost? I will have had an interesting holiday at a world heritage site - but what if it *was* something, was I prepared not to take the risk? No I was not? You want to know what's in the letter? Well it's probably for the best, then you'll know what I mean;

My darling Hannah,

As it has been with all of us, you will have received this on your twenty fifth birthday; the age at which you are becoming quite the adult, yet retain some of your childhood wonder and imagination. I hope you will never lose that part of yourself.

Said to have been a gift from a grateful soldier during the siege at Masada, this clasp has been passed down through the generations of our family. Created in ancient times as a talisman, whispers of enchantment have always surrounded it, although, personally I think this was more likely a way to protect it from those whose curiosity may have got the better of them. I believe the power of the clasp is in its history, it is your turn now - guard it well.

Your loving Gran.

See, what was I supposed to do with this information 'guard it well' - it was just a brooch! More than that, who would know the history of this brooch or clasp or whatever it was and how on earth would I be able to trace it with nothing more than a letter, oh and the clasp itself? Masada - really - how is that even possible? To be fair, the clasp is gorgeous, an unusually shaped deep red stone, not quite a teardrop and not quite an oval, something in between. It looks like a ruby but I'm not really sure, set into a finely wrought design of some precious metal, with a pin on the back to hold it in place. I'd like to think that the metal is gold, but I can't imagine how it would have survived without being sold, stolen or melted down, it has a burnished look and I wondered whether it was more likely bronze, that could explain its longevity. I remember playing with it as a child, Gran let me use it when I played dress ups with my sister and I used to rub the stone pretending it was magic, now I'm not sure I dare even hold it.

Sorry, I got distracted there - back to the trip. Having decided that I probably needed to go back to where it all started, the timing of my visit to Masada was prompted further by the fact that my best friend, Max Vallier, was going over to spend some time on the current excavations. He'd been out two or three times before and loved it, reckoning that it was one of those sites that gets under your skin and you just have to keep coming back. Max, an engineer by profession, also loves archaeology and has found, to his continuing delight, that what can be discovered through the excavation of ancient structures can be useful in modern engineering. It seemed too good to be true, that he was already planning to come over here, when I got the letter.

What else can I tell you about Max? His family are very wealthy and claim to trace their history back a long way, right back to the Romans if I recall correctly, but, although from old money, are not snooty or snobbish. We have known each other most of our lives, I think I was fourteen when we first met and, we really enjoy each other's company. I'd say he's probably my best friend. Max suggested that since I wanted to visit, why not tie our trips together, giving us someone to travel and share spare time with. He even managed to get me a room to myself (ok, more like a bunk, with a desk, but it had its own bathroom) in the digs, where he and the other archaeologists were staying - how could I say no?

So, six months later, all that planning and organising done, here we are, actually on the top of the rock at Masada. We've been here a few days and, already I've helped out on some of the plots, done my fair share of exploring the whole of this fortress as well as the remains of the Roman camps below. If I move just a little, I can see Max, carefully uncovering a mosaic in one of the rooms; the other archaeologists are spread out all over the site.

Their work is often interrupted by tourists, who are wandering the plateau examining the excavations, asking numerous questions and gasping in astonishment, while snapping away with their cameras. As I said, it is warmer than usual, it isn't unbearably hot, but although the sun is high and I can see more heat mirages across the ground, the breeze keeps the temperature almost comfortable and I am in the shade.

From my vantage point I can see the Dead Sea glistening in the distance, teasing the parched traveller with its blue waves, yet entirely undrinkable. This land, which seems so hostile, is able to produce bright flowers, of unknown origin, which are scattered all over the rock, the result of an unusually stormy winter. The archaeologists tell me that in ancient times, the water from these rare wet winters not only filled the massive cisterns carved into the rock, but could also support all manner of growing things, from vegetables to flowers, even small fruit trees, an incongruous thought given the dry arid landscape spread out around me.

Several pomegranate trees, providing welcome shade, somehow manage to survive the harsh conditions on the plateau, planted by a group of archaeologists during a Jewish festival, in the early days of excavation. I lay back against the wall, soaking it all in, the incredible view and its ever-changing colours and the long history of this rock called Masada.

I think it was the shimmering heat that started it all!

Chapter Two

As I relaxed, I shut my eyes, my thoughts drifting, the sunlight and shadows playing across my eyelids. The heat was making me feel sleepy and I probably dozed a little. Then voices startled me, it had been so quiet, even those who had been with the morning tour group had wandered back down to the shady areas, or the cool of the information centre, under the fortress to wait for their bus. Glancing around, I couldn't see who had been talking, and, shrugging I closed my eyes again. It was so lovely just sitting there, letting my thoughts roll around, going back over Gran's letter in my mind and everything that had brought me to this point, all quite incredible really.

The voices, although muffled, shattered the quiet again, standing up I looked properly, no one was there. Must be some of the archaeologists, maybe a new discovery I thought and, feeling quite excited, I set off across the plateau to see what was happening. Reaching the edge of the wall, I peered over, nothing had changed, the groups were all working quietly together with an occasional burst of chatter, but nothing as loud as I'd just heard, so, deciding I must have imagined it, I returned to my bit of wall. It felt as though I had just sat back down, when I heard the voices again, only this time they seemed to be coming from in front of where I was sitting, however, as far as I could tell there was absolutely no-one there. Must be the sun I thought, too much sun and I'm not used to this heat. Fanning my face with the letter, I contemplated catching the cable car back to the bottom of the rock, the thought of its air-conditioned coolness almost irresistible.

Slowly I became aware of a shift in the air and noticed a group of people walking towards me, the dust from their feet creating a haze, making them difficult to distinguish. As they approached, I realised that it must be a group enacting some of the history of this plateau, probably something they put on for the benefit of the tourists. It was their chatter I must have heard earlier, made sense now, they would have been getting ready out of my line of vision in one of the more suitable parts of the ruin where they could leave their gear, or maybe they'd got changed down at the information centre and come up in the cable car.

Closer and closer they marched, their uniforms becoming clearer, definitely Roman soldiers, a frisson ran through me, this was turning out to be a very interesting day. The dust from their feet obscured one of the pomegranate trees and I remember hoping it wouldn't damage the fruit. Then, just as they were about to reach me, they disappeared - no way - what? I rubbed my eyes, where did they go? Not possible! They were right there in front of me, I could have touched them, they were so close.

I dashed along the escarpment to where Max was working, watching him for a minute while he gently brushed away dirt, slowly revealing coloured tesserae in a geometric pattern, part of the original floor. Such delicate work and such a beautiful result, I barely wanted to disturb him. Whispering his name, I dropped to my knees next to him. He looked up and smiled.

"What's up?" He whispered back.

"Where did those guys go," I replied, "the ones dressed like Roman soldiers? I would have loved to watch their re-enactment it would have been amazing."

"What soldiers?" Asked Max, puzzled.

"The ones who were over on the plateau silly, you must have heard them, there was at least thirty of them, is it something they do once or twice a week, for the tourists? Strange I haven't seen..." I trailed off, as Max glanced across at me, an odd expression on his face. "What? Why are you looking at me like that?"

"There are no re-enactments Hannah, its just us and the visitors up here, they'd never be able to get people to come up here even once a week to act out the siege, or the battle, its too hot and too far. You were probably dreaming, go drink some water, get some lunch and find something to read other than that tatty old book, its making you see things."

I stared at him in bewilderment.

"But, they were so real, the dust was kicked up and everything, are you sure?"

"Course I'm sure, I've been coming here for the last few years, never had anything like that and I'm pretty sure we'd know if they were, as we'd need to let them know which areas we are working in."

"I guess you're right, must have been my imagination, it would have been so interesting though. Never mind, sorry to disturb you, I think I'll go back to the bunks, maybe have a snooze 'til its cooler, see you later." I patted him absently on the back, smiled and ducking my head to avoid banging it on the protective sheet erected over this room, wandered back out into the sunshine. Max grinned, shook his head and went back to brushing, immediately forgetting that I'd been there, his work absorbing him completely.

Still puzzled, I strolled back along the top of the fortress, looking out at over vast expanse of desert and went to collect my bag from where I had been sitting. As I turned towards the cable car, I saw them again, no doubt about it this time, they were right in front of me. Then I realised why Max hadn't heard them, except for their voices, which were muted, there was no other sound, their feet made no noise on the sandy floor, their armour did not clink, their weapons did not clatter.

14

It made no sense, again I rubbed my eyes, hoping that it was just part of the mirage, but no, they were still there. A trickle of fear rippled across my shoulders, how was this possible? I must be dreaming, pinch yourself Hannah, I thought, that's what they (whoever 'they' are) say to do, so I did and no, that made no difference. I froze as they bore down on me, then right at the last minute, they swung away, marching along the side of the wall and turned into what had been a doorway.

Grabbing my stuff, I followed them, determined to find out what they were doing, was it some sort of initiation for new Israeli soldiers, was it a group of Uni students just having a lark…what? By the time I got to the entrance, there was no sign of them, assuming that they must have gone on through to the main body of the palace, I went across the doorway, still nothing, but there was another opening way across at the far side of the room, the walls, although ruined, were higher here and I could not see beyond them.

Mindful of Max's warnings about uneven floors strewn with rubble, gingerly, yet with as much haste as possible, I crossed the room and shot through the gap, crossing a courtyard and coming to a slithering halt as I realised that there were several openings and, that one of them led to the steps and hidden stairway, running between the three tiers of the palace. No way could those soldiers have gone down that way, it was too narrow, they would have had to have gone down in single file and with the number of men I saw, they would still be queuing to go down, so which of the other rooms could they have passed through. They were all ruined; I could see over some of the broken walls and into them, it wasn't as if they were enclosed rooms.

Where had they gone? Shivering a little, I retraced my steps, everything looked completely normal, no sign of strange goings on, not even a puff of dust, just another group of tourists meandering across the ruins chattering happily about the history of Masada. I sat down abruptly, catching my breath, I knew what I had seen wasn't possible, but I HAD seen it, surely I had? Glancing down, it dawned on me that there were no footprints, nothing to say anyone had walked passed me, just the marks from my sandals. Can't be, I thought, there would be a trail of footprints right across the plateau. I got up and walked out in the direction from which they had come, but there was nothing, not a single solitary marking of any kind.

Ok, I told myself, get a grip, its just a figment of your imagination, too much sun, not enough water, maybe still a little jet-lagged. Go home, get some rest and do something totally unconnected to all this ancient stuff. Too easy to conjure up ghosts here. I strode purposefully across to the cable car station, waited for the next one to come along, hopped on and rode it down to the base. My cab was empty save for me, cool and quiet was what I needed right then. I put the book and letter into my backpack and made sure the brooch was secure.

Arriving at the bottom, I stepped out, it felt cooler here in the shade of the great rock and, although it wasn't there quickest way back, I enjoyed the walk round to the accommodation block. Grabbing a bottle of water from the fridge and drinking deeply to quench my thirst, I made my way to my room then, having closed and locked the door, lay down on my bed and slept.

Chapter Three

I woke up to hammering on my door,

"Hannah, come on, get up, its dinner time, you've been asleep ages. Hannah!" Groggily, I called back that I'd be there in a minute and, swinging my legs off the bed, sat for a moment getting my bearings. It was falling dusk, the light fading rapidly and through my window I could see the clear sky turning soft purple at the edges. Evenings were so lovely here, even on the hottest days the temperatures dropped until it felt almost cold, the sky as clear as crystal, full to bursting with stars and astonishingly beautiful.

Trying to clear my head, I doused my face in cold water at the basin in the corner of my room, which helped a little. Glancing in the mirror to make sure I was, at least, presentable, I hurried down to the hall where all our meals were served. It wasn't a big room, there were only about twenty archaeologists at any one time staying here, most preferring to stay in Arad, about a forty five minute drive away, or one of the hotels on the shores of the Dead Sea. Max had saved me a seat; I slid in next to him and asked what was for dinner. Marinated chicken on a bed of couscous, with a roasted vegetable salad, the smell emanating from the kitchen was divine.

Our cook, Rafi, or to give him his full name Rafael Fisher, had been working at this site for years, seeing it grow from a small dig of a few hardy archaeologists, struggling to get funding, to the internationally recognised site it is today. Attracting archaeologists from all over the world, including amateurs like Max. Rafi, who must be clocking sixty, was English by birth, but had come out to a kibbutz back when that was the thing to do and had never gone home, eventually finding his way to this camp and becoming a permanent fixture. His cooking was legendary, every meal a mouth-watering adventure for the taste buds, it was worth spending time is this lonely place, just to savour his food. Even those staying away from the camp would occasionally drop in for a meal, declaring it was better than any hotel food and worth either the long drive home or bunking on the floor of some one else's bedroom for a night!

As we tucked in, Max asked me what I'd done after talking to him earlier. Unwilling to admit to seeing things I just prattled on about the site in general and nothing in particular, directing the conversation back on him by asking how his mosaic was coming on. Max launched into an enthusiastic monologue about the attributes of the mosaic and its importance in historical placement of styles or some such thing. Normally I could listen to Max all night, he has a lovely voice and his passion for this site was contagious, but tonight, I probably only heard about half of what he said, my mind kept wandering, back to the events of the afternoon. Had I imagined it, logic told me that I must have done, there was so much history connected to the, now ruined, fortress, thinking you'd had a vision of it was almost inevitable. That's why there was no sound. Ah but, the fanciful side of my mind countered, you heard their voices - explain that away.

Ok, Hannah, I told myself, that's enough, how could soldiers have appeared out of the dust, just for you? As far as you know, no one else saw them, Max didn't hear anything. Let it go. Wrenching my attention back to Max and his mosaic story, I pushed the events of the afternoon away and enjoyed the rest of the evening. The archaeologists, many who had been coming to this site year after year, hailed from all over the world, with a range of cultural and linguistic differences, which had often led to misunderstandings and, it must be said, occasional bust ups, which, admittedly, when between academics, is more like waving trowels at ten paces, than actual fisticuffs. However, because of these mix-ups, it had now become almost a tradition for them to attempt to best each other with stories of mis-adventures in digging, some of which, I grant you, went well over my head, but others were hilarious. So, I spent the rest of the evening listening to their tales, finally heading off to bed just before midnight.

Turning out my light, I stood for a little while at the window gazing at the stars, thinking of everyone else who might be doing the same thing. The air was cool and silent, undisturbed by even the hint of a breeze. Despite my afternoon nap, I was still tired and, ignoring my good intentions of jotting down my day, I hopped into bed, pulled the covers up and promptly fell asleep.

My dreams were fevered, hot dusty castles with too many corridors, people skittering away before I could reach them, pools of cool blue water just out of reach, soldiers scuffing through mosaics, uncaring that they were destroying their beautiful designs, always marching, marching marching. Enough, I bolted upright yelling at them to stop, then, worried that I woken everyone up, sat still for a minute, shivering a little in the night air. Nothing happened, no sound of anyone running to see what all the racket was about, phew - that yell must have been in my dream too. Although now I felt wide awake, there was no point getting up, it was still the middle of the night and my bed was warm. Rather than turn on the lamp to read, or finish the notes I'd managed to avoid completing earlier, I snuggled back down, watching shadows play across the room, images forming and fading in the moonlight.

Without thinking, I reached for the brooch, studying it, rolling it through my hands, caressing the cool metal, trying to decipher its secret while admiring the red stone in its centre, which seemed to glow in the soft light. Wondering what it was about such a small trinket that had allowed it to survive for nearly two thousand years and did I really believe that it had begun its journey here? More questions, and so far no answers, maybe I needed to go to one of the museums here in Israel, or see if I could get into the archives, but even if I could, there wouldn't be anything recorded about something so simple and innocuous as a brooch, it would be a pointless and fruitless task.

Sighing, I let my thoughts stray, hoping for a spark of inspiration. It was a trick I'd used while at University when trying to pin down an assignment, just let the ideas float and finally something would coalesce into a tangible thread and I'd have my plan. Tonight it wasn't working, too many threads jostling for the top spot. The shadow play on the walls was beginning to have a soporific effect and sleep was whispering its seductive melody. Placing the clasp carefully back on the bedside table, I plumped my pillows, turned over and sank back into oblivion.

I was standing on the edge of the fortress on a ruined section of wall, my back to the three-tier palace, looking out across the Judaean Desert, marvelling at the sheer ingenuity of this, Herod's most isolated of strongholds. It was late afternoon, the sky had paled to a soft pink, the sun was slipping down to the horizon and shadows had begun to cast their long fingers along the sides of the rock. Stealthy movement below caught my eye and gazing down I could see a horde of men, dishevelled but determined, scrambling up Snake Path.

More quickly than I thought possible they burst through the gate onto the plateau, spreading out towards the building complex between the two palaces, trampling across what looked like gardens or vegetable patches. Simultaneously, I noticed another band spilling through a gap at the opposite side, gathering round the Western Palace. I rubbed my eyes (this was becoming a habit) not again, what was going on? As before, when I had seen the soldiers, I could hear the murmur of voices, but no other sound, yet it seemed as though there were hordes of men, all carrying some kind of weapon, most of which looked as though they had been cobbled together from tradesmen's tools.

Their clothing was unfamiliar, yet recognisable, dusty from their journey, but definitely not the modern attire I was used to seeing in the local town. Then I realised, they looked like images I'd seen on the carol sheets from my childhood, on pamphlets we'd seen at Christmas from the Holy Land and in bibles, although illustrated by modern artists their inspiration had come from descriptions written down centuries earlier.

The first group ran past me, intent on pursuing their quarry, who I suddenly remembered from studying the history of Masada, was a Roman garrison, where was their watch, had they seen these men coming? Stomach churning and trying to calm my breathing, I ducked behind a pillar, which I noticed, inapropos of nothing, wasn't ruined - how odd. This was going to be a rout; these must be the Jewish rebels, Zealots led by Menahem and that they either massacred the soldiers, or at the very least drove them off the rock.

What was I supposed to do, I couldn't get close enough to warn the Roman soldiers and, as I was thinking it, realised how ridiculous it sounded, even if I could - would they hear me, was I visible to them? Neither did I want to get in the way of the rebels. Looking around for somewhere to hide where I would feel safe, I suddenly remembered the opening to the administration building not far off to my right just beyond the modern toilet block, I could hide under one of the protective canopies, but could I reach it without being seen? Edging round the pillar, I tried to work out what was happening, who was where and whether, if I ran really fast, I could make it along the front of the palace unnoticed.

The skirmish unfolding in front of me, across the open ground, was creating clouds of dust and, for the first time, as though from a great distance, I could hear the clash of weapons and the shouts of men. It was just a melee, with, as far as I could tell, everyman for himself, there didn't seem to be much, if any, organisation on either side. The Romans, taken by surprise, had had no time to either grab their weapons or employ their usual battle tactics and, although trying desperately to form a cohesive body, were failing miserably. The air was tinged with the metallic smell of blood and men were falling injured or worse. My eyes took in everything about the scene but my mind did not seem able to process it.

Everything slowed down, no one was looking in my direction and I could hear the thud of my heart beating, as I turned to run. Dashing across the same opening through which I'd followed the soldiers only a few hours ago, I hurled myself through the first entrance I saw along the passageway and pressed my back up against the wall through which the doorway was cut. The walls were quite high in this room, so anybody following would have to come right into the room to see me. After several minutes when I'm fairly sure I didn't take a single breath, I realised that the only thing that had followed me was silence, I sank to the floor feeling the chill rock seep through my clothes into my skin, cooling me down.

As I was trying to get my breath back and work out how to get off this rock and back down to the camp I registered that not only was I still in my pyjamas and had bare feet, but also, that the room I was sitting in, wasn't actually ruined. Slowly looking round, I noticed that there was a ceiling above me, not the protective cover or the night sky, that there was an intact tiled floor, not dirt and, that there were frescoes on the walls. It was also furnished, I could make out what looked like a bedroll, at least one chair, a sort of cupboard or wardrobe and a couple of baskets stacked against the wall. Then, I recalled with a sense of shock, that the pillar I had hidden behind, was not only complete, but also decorated and that the walls of the palace had appeared higher as I ran past them, but that the toilet block was still there.

This time my mind got there before my eyes - no way...yes way - I was witnessing the Romans being overrun by the Jewish rebels, but I was seeing it happen from my time - not when the event occurred, which also meant that maybe I was not physically in the fortress, for surely if I was, I would have thought to dress more appropriately. It must be an hallucination or something akin to it, the time periods overlapping and confused. Yes, I know its irrational, even as I was thinking it, I realised how ludicrous it sounded, but since nothing in the past day or so had really made sense, it wasn't totally without merit. I certainly did not believe I had been transported back in time, but it still begged the question of how I was going to get out, or wake myself up or whatever it was I was going to have to do to be back in my nice safe bed.

My left hip felt warm, strange, as the floor I was sitting on was quite cold. I reached down, half expecting to find that I'd cut myself on something during my headlong flight and that the warmth was my own blood. Surprised, I touched the brooch, drawing it out I noticed that the ruby seemed to be glowing and that the brooch itself was quite warm to the touch, warmer than was warranted simply from being in my pocket. Now I was definitely dreaming, this was the stuff of myth and legend, brooches, however old they might be, do not glow and get hot, plus, I remembered placing it on my bedside table.

Absently, I rubbed it with my thumb, buffing up the already polished surface, the glow seemed to be diminishing, had I imagined that as well? Quite probably, if this was indeed a dream. Putting it back in my pocket, I levered myself up, peered round the opening and, standing perfectly still, listened intently for several minutes. No sound and nothing to be seen, I tiptoed back up along the corridor, pausing every few steps to listen again.

On the way out, I noticed a dimly lit room to my right, one I hadn't seen it in my rush to hide, slowly, silently, I inched my way to the doorway and reaching it, peered in, making sure I was in shadow. It took a few seconds for my eyes to adjust to the gloom, from the darker corridor but as the room took shape I could see three people in various stages of collapse. All men and all bleeding profusely. One was almost prone on the floor, the other two standing over him as if trying to help, but prevented from being effective by their own injuries.

Part of me wanted to rush in and help, but the more logical part held me back, I was not 'there', I was 'here', nearly two thousand years in the future, aarrgghhh…this was doing my head in. Backing out, I stubbed my toe on the door jamb and, grunting in pain, turned to flee, noticing, as I did, that the taller of the two men standing over their comrade had lifted his head and was looking right at me, as if he'd heard my groan, which wasn't possible, was it? Our eyes locked and seconds ticked by as I was held, frozen to the spot, wondering what would happen if he called out.

Then it dawned on me, his clothing was that of a soldier, these men were Romans and injured, they must have sought refuge in this room, presumably hoping to escape later, after the battle was over. His eyes seem to implore me to stay quiet and as we gazed at each other, I felt a jolt of recognition, powerful yet fleeting. I nodded trying to convey my complicity and quietly left the room, still trying to remember where I'd seen his face before.

I reached the entrance and slipped out into the open, revelling in the fresh clean air. Daylight had waned, twilight was changing the sky from soft pink to dark blue, how long had I been down there? It only felt like a few minutes. I could see that the plateau was empty, save for the bodies strewn about, the long shadows, like grasping hands, threaded through the pomegranate trees. I wondered if the cable car was still running, then felt a hysterical laugh bubbling up, as I realised how incongruous that sounded after what I had seen, cable cars and an ancient battle do not mix. I really wanted to get home, and set off towards the station, hurrying in the fading light I missed my footing and tripped over some loose stones. Putting my hands out to cushion my fall, I felt the world tilt and woke up.

Chapter Four

Slowly, I looked around, everything was as it should be, I was in my bedroom, in the living quarters and could hear the sounds of people moving about. The days started early here, as occasionally it was too hot to work in some of the areas after lunchtime. My watch said it was 5.30, I didn't need to get up yet, but I wasn't sure I'd be able to get any more sleep. Grabbing my notebook, I propped myself up on my pillows and started to write down everything that had happened since yesterday.

Maybe if I committed it all to paper I would be able to come up with a sensible explanation. The more I wrote, the more fantastical it seemed - it had to have been a dream. After all, I woke up in my bed; I didn't walk back down from the fortress. Once more blaming too much sun and too much imagination, I closed the book and decided to get up. I remembered that some of the others were going down to the Dead Sea for the day and would be heading off before too long, I hoped there was room for me to go with them. A day away from all this could be all I needed, the chance to do something completely removed from massacres and sieges.

Suddenly excited at the prospect, I threw back the covers and swung my feet down, stopping mid-swing as I noticed that they were covered in dust and my left toe was all scuffed and bruised - what…whaaat? Putting my hand into the pocket of my pyjamas, my fingers curled around a familiar object and I slowly withdrew the brooch, no longer glowing, it felt cool and quiet, almost as if it was resting. How did it get there? I knew I had laid it on the bedside table and didn't think I was in the habit of randomly pocketing things in my sleep. I sat back on the bed, this was bizarre and, I have to admit, more than a little unnerving. Was I going mad, did I have some kind of virus or had I eaten something that would make me sleep walk and cause hallucinations? Did I tell anyone, who would even believe me?

Max! The only person I could even consider talking to about this was Max, who although would probably tell me it was just a dream, was understanding enough to listen to me and help me put things into perspective, without making me feel like a crazed lunatic. Problem was, I knew he was totally caught up in his work on the site and might not want to spare a day to come with me and if I stayed here, although he would try and concentrate on what I was describing, his head would be on what he was missing out on at the dig. I could only try. Shaking my head at the state of my feet, I headed into the bathroom to try and wash the muggy feeling away, along with the dust.

Twenty minutes later, I was in the dining room, the smell of bacon and egg wafting along from the kitchen making me realise how hungry I was. Max strolled in about five minutes later, looking very 'Indiana Jones' in his grey cargo pants and long sleeved pale green linen shirt. Tall, dark haired and green-eyed with an athletic build, he cut an imposing figure, but was actually quite reserved and, although fit, was more bookish than sporty. Happiest either involved in an engineering project, or immersed in archaeology in any of its forms. Piling his plate with breakfast delights, he came and sat next to me, his face lighting up.

"Morning sweetheart," he smiled, "sleep well?" Oh Max I thought, how little you know and started to laugh.

Oh, sorry, I'm not laughing at you," I spluttered, noticing his expression, "I had a terrible night, I feel and, probably look, like the wreck of the Hesperus and here you are all bright eyed and bushy tailed, looking ready for anything. I need more coffee." Topping up my cup, I sipped the coffee, inhaling the rich aroma, savouring the strong dark liquid and waiting for my synapses to respond to its caffeinated goodness. "Oh, that is nectar."

"Why didn't you sleep?" Asked Max "Too much wine last night?" I studied his face, noticing that despite his jovial question, his brow was furrowed; something in my expression must have raised his concern.

"I had disturbing dreams, at least I think they were dreams. Oh Max, it was really freaky and I need to talk to you about it. I want you to tell me that I'm an idiot, that its all in my head and I need you to convince me that I'm not going completely bonkers."

"Hey, slow down Hannah, there's nothing to get so worked up about, if it was a dream, then it's done, over. Too much wine and rich food, that's what'll have caused it." Normally, Max's calm certainty would have reassured me and, any other time I would have agreed with him, except for my dirty, scuffed feet.

"I know, that's what I thought and maybe it still is, but its really bothering me. This isn't something we can talk about over brekky; there isn't time to nut it out. I was thinking about going down on the bus today, I know you're busy, but would you be able to come with me?" I entreated him. Away from all the ghosts of this rock, it might seem less troubling and easier to explain. Max thought for a minute.

"I really can't make it this morning, but Rafi's going down this afternoon to get some supplies, I reckon we'd be there by about three, we could have a meal and catch the bus when it comes back up at seven. Gives you some time to potter about and we can talk later." It wasn't perfect but it was good enough and would have to do. I pulled myself together, ignoring the feeling of unease in the pit of my stomach and agreed. It was better than nothing.

"Sounds like a plan, looking forward to it."

Those of us lucky enough to be going down to the Dead Sea, set off about an hour later while the day was still cool, making the short journey down to the coast very enjoyable. No need for air-conditioning, we opened the windows and enjoyed the fresh air streaming through the bus. It didn't take long to reach our destination and we were dropped off at Ein Bokek, a resort area full of hotels, with shopping and restaurants, a great spot to be in after the limitations of our Masada accommodation.

I was a bit like a kid in a Christmas store for the first hour or so, wandering through the resort, letting the sounds of civilisation wash over me. Although quite touristy, it felt warm and welcoming, I found a coffee shop with a good view and just 'people watched.' After a very strong and very delicious coffee, I spent a little more time discovering the locale, but it was starting to get warm, I needed a cool spot to wait out the heat of the day and have some lunch. One of the hotels had a great souvenir shop with books on the history of the area, I chose three, one of which was by an eminent archaeologist. Then having paid for my purchases, I found a table in the beautifully cool restaurant, whose view over the Dead Sea was breathtaking. Time for lunch!

Remembering that I wasn't driving, I treated myself to a glass of white wine with my meal. Choosing hummus, baba ghanoush and tahini with pita bread and a side salad. I enjoyed the novelty of being on my own, with a table of beautiful food in front of me, without having to worry about a horde of hungry archaeologists descending on me to 'give it a try', which usually meant you ended up with an empty plate! The food was delicious, the wine chilled and the book fascinating, for me, an irresistible triple cocktail. Although I knew quite a lot about the history of Masada, it was refreshing to read about it from a different perspective and this was a very well written account. Moreover, the plethora of information within the pages confirmed why so many people wanted to be involved in uncovering its secrets year after year.

Situated at the edge of the Judaean desert between Sdom and Ein Gedi, Masada holds a commanding position, surrounded by deep gorges, its sheer rock sides falling about four hundred and fifty meters to the desert floor. Although today, the plateau is easily reached either by cable car at the east, or a fifteen minute walk up the western slope, in ancient times, access was challenging and dangerous, even via the 'snake path,' providing a natural defence and making it the perfect place to build a fortress. Our only detailed source of information about Masada comes from the writings of Josephus, a Roman citizen of Jewish origin, who, despite questionable affiliations, was granted his freedom by the Emperor Vespasian eventually becoming an advisor to Vespasian's son, the Emperor Titus.

Josephus wrote several books attempting to explain Judaism to the Romans and vice versa, probably his most influential being *The Jewish War* and *Antiquities of the Jews*. Notwithstanding his ambivalent role as an eyewitness to history, Josephus' work cannot be discounted, as was exampled when archaeologists, from a description by the author, were able to pin point the location of Herod's tomb close to Herod's palace of Herodium, south of Jerusalem. So even though historians accept that Josephus was writing after he had come under the protection of the Flavian emperors, his accounts are authoritative and, in most cases all we have.

Tying the original fortification of Masada to Jonatan the High Priest, Josephus describes how King Herod fled there with his family during the Parthian onslaught of 40BC, eventually reworking, rebuilding and fortifying the existing structure into two palaces surrounded by a wall twenty feet high and twelve feet wide. At the centre of the western casemate wall stood an opulent mansion which also acted as a working administrative centre and at the northern extremity a luxurious royal residence, distinguished by three cleverly engineered terraces hanging precipitously out over the cliff's edge. Situated within the walls were water cisterns and storehouses, a synagogue, barracks and an armoury, creating a self-sufficient fortress able to withstand a lengthy siege, which was attested to over half a century after Herod's death.

It is thought that a Roman garrison was stationed at Masada for about sixty years from AD6, until in AD66, at the outbreak of the Jewish War, a band of Zealots led by Menahem captured the fortress. Masada eventually became a safe harbour for Jewish rebels and, after the Fall of Jerusalem in AD70, was the only remaining pocket of Jewish resistance. Around AD72, a Roman legion led by Flavius Silva, marched on the outpost determined to quash the rebels, who refused to surrender. Laying siege to the fortress, the Romans constructed a ramp, up which they could attack much more easily than any of the existing access routes.

Despite several attempts to rebuff them, the Romans eventually overcame the rebels' defences. Rather than be taken prisoner and paraded through the streets of Jerusalem and Rome, those within the fortress decided their own fate. After setting fire to their personal belongings it seems, although not completely clear, that ten of their number were chosen to kill everyone else, one of the ten killed the remaining nine, then he himself committed suicide.

When the Romans stormed the plateau the next day, they were met with silence and dead bodies. Seven, two women and five children had survived, hidden in an underground cavern, their tale taken up by Josephus and, eventually shared with the world. After the Romans finally withdrew, Masada was abandoned until the fifth century, when, after an earthquake, which destroyed many of the structures, a group of Christian monks established a community there, building a small chapel in the centre of the plateau. After several decades the community was disbanded, leaving the site untouched and lost to time until the 1960s. Page after page I couldn't read it quickly enough, finding the author's style to be detailed and exciting without overdoing the tech-speak that often turns books into dry tomes.

With my head was spinning over the machinations of all those involved and the heartbreaking outcome, it took a little while to come back to the real world, so absorbed had I been with the tale of this isolated fortress. A place of infinite beauty, yet also one of horror and trauma, where civilisations clashed and so many lives lost with, ultimately, nothing really gained. It took me a moment to realise that my phone was chirping and by the time I picked it up, the caller had disconnected. Frustrated, I scrolled to the last caller…Max…was he here and looking for me, I glanced at my watch; it was only just after two.

Listening to his message, I felt my bubble of happy expectation burst - he wasn't coming down today. Seemingly an archaeologist, specialising in mosaics, had arrived on site and would be offering expert advice on their conservation and preservation. Although I understood that this was too good an opportunity for them to miss, I was unreasonably upset. I had been counting on Max to talk me through whatever was going on in my head and now I'd have to wait. Unwilling to speak to him, I simply texted back a brief 'ok, see you later', it looked stark, but that was as much as I could manage.

Deflated, I turned back to the book idly turning pages, not really taking anything else in. My concentration was lost, all I wanted to do was get back to the site, my lovely day at the Dead Sea spoilt. I pondered my mood, unable to put my finger on why Max's cancellation had up skittled me so badly. Idly twirling the stem of the empty wine glass, I decided that since I had been stood up, I would treat myself to a slice of something very decadent and another glass of wine. After all, I still had nearly five hours to fill in before the bus would be going back up.

Then I remembered what Max had said about Rafi coming down, he'd be in his own car. I quickly texted Max and asked if he knew whether Rafi had set off and whether he'd be happy to take me back up to site with him after he'd bought his supplies. Ten minutes passed, nothing, slowly the minutes ticked by…then my phone pinged. It was Rafi, 'Max has given me your number and I'll be there soon where are you?' I told him which hotel I was at and he said he'd meet me at the entrance in about an hour! What a relief, I relaxed with my wine and cake and simply watched the world go by.

An hour later, I was hopping along the kerb at the front of the hotel, when Rafi swung up in his dilapidated jeep. No luxuries in this motor, no air-con, or comfortable seats, I decided we were lucky just to have seat belts, something I was very glad of, as Rafi zoomed away from the resort, with little regard for the rules of the road. However, with the windows down (yes, we had those!) and the early evening breeze off the water, cooling the air, it was quite heavenly. Rafi chattered away about his day and what he'd bought and the plans he had with the ingredients. It sounded lovely and I realised he did not need me to respond, so I let his voice, with its lilting accent, wash over me like liquid velvet. It didn't take long for the wine, the breeze, the rocking of the car and Rafi's constant chat, to lull me off to sleep.

Chapter Five

I jolted awake as we screeched into the car park at our accommodation and it felt like I had slept for hours. In fact it had only been about forty five minutes, but I had certainly slept deeply. Pay back for my disturbed night I guessed. I tumbled out of the car and helped Rafi unload his stock. It took us about four trips and each time I put a box or bag on the counter in the kitchen, I noticed a group of people in the dining room seemingly very excited about something. Gathered in a loose group, some sitting some standing, they were all talking over the top of one another vying to be heard.

I finished helping Rafi and went off to my room; I needed a shower to clear my head of sleep and to wash off the dust from the drive home. It is all very well letting the wind blow through your hair, but there is always dust on the roads here, even on those properly graded and topped with tarmac. My clothes had ended up all the same slightly beige colour and my hair looked like I'd been dragged through a hedge backwards. Not the cool and elegant facade (one can always hope) I wanted to present to the rest of our company at dinner!

Stripping off my clothes, I got in the shower, turning the water on and just standing under the jets, letting the stream of water wash away the day. My head still felt a little muzzy, but it was clearing quickly, lathering my sponge in lightly scented shower gel, I scrubbed and rinsed and scrubbed again. Watching the water swirl away down the drain, I was hypnotised by the bubbles' dizzying demise. Finally, after what seemed an age, I felt clean.

Dressed in fresh clothes, I towelled dried my hair twisting it into a loose knot and put a little face cream on and a touch of lip balm. I have no idea why I needed to arm myself, but some instinct wanted me to look, at the very least, presentable, a little effort did no harm. I wandered back into the dining room just as the dinner gong rang out. The group was still there, yabbering away, but at the gong they began to move towards the food now laid out on the tables set against the long wall and, as they filtered away, I noticed a new face among them.

A tall woman was leaning against the back of one of the chairs, laughing at something, her head bent slightly, her hair falling over her face. As she lifted her head I got a shock, this must be the mosaicist, the woman I had assumed would be elderly and rather staid, turned out to be a stunner and not much older than me, definitely under thirty. She was absolutely gorgeous, so gorgeous I stopped in my tracks and must have looked like a gawking idiot. Long black wavy hair, barely restrained in a leather clasp, tumbled down to her waist, her skin was lightly tanned, but flawless (aren't they always) and her eyes a penetrating shade of grey. Oh no, I groaned to myself, this explained the gaggle of voices when I'd arrived; it was her attention they were competing for.

Feeling like a country bumpkin compared with this sophisticated beauty, I chose some food and slid into my usual chair, noticing that Max was sitting next to the newcomer. My light heartedness, achieved after my refreshing shower, evaporated. Not only had he stood me up, he also hadn't even acknowledged that I was back. I didn't necessarily want him to ignore the guest, but he could at least have said 'Hello'. Ok, yes, deep down I did want him to ignore this guest, but as I didn't really know why I felt like this I pretended it wasn't happening…I know…good one!

Although dinner looked very inviting, I just pushed it round my plate; it could have been cardboard for all the notice I took.

Poor Rafi, he'd gone to a lot of trouble, as always, but I could not finish my helping. Thankfully, everyone else was hoeing into their meals, so he wouldn't even register that I'd left most of mine. As soon as was polite, I got up to go back to my room. The scraping of my chair on the tiles, as I pushed it back, caught Max's attention. He motioned me over to introduce me to the visitor.

Still unreasonably angry with him, I walked grudgingly round to where they were sitting trying to plaster a welcoming smile on my face.

"This is Naomi Cartwright," he said, "she's over from America on another dig and heard about the mosaics we've been uncovering, Naomi, Hannah, Hannah, Naomi." I shook her hand as she smiled a hello.

"So lovely to meet you, Max has talked about you all afternoon." I glanced across at him in surprise, he was steadfastly focusing on our hands, still clasped in greeting, but a telltale warmth washed up his face.

"Really?" I said in astonishment. "I, err, I…" flustered I let go of her hand and muttered something about hoping she had a successful visit and sorry to cut and run but I'd had a long day and was very tired. Then glaring at Max, I left the room, quickly, but with as much grace as possible.

Plonking myself down on the bed I wondered what on earth was wrong with me. Rather than try and work myself out - I dislike naval gazing - I opened my journal and settled down to note down the events of the last few days. Although I usually wrote it in it every day, sometimes I was too brief, just dot points. I liked to go back and flesh it out fill in extra things like the progress at the dig, the weather how I was feeling, light, colour, any plants or animals I'd seen. Some of it was superfluous, but if I didn't do it now, I would never be able to recall these moments.

My journal is a beautifully crafted book, bound in red-brown leather that looks truly aged, like an old Psalter. The pages are pseudo parchment, thick and lustrous, to write on them is a joy and I use old trusty ink pen, which never blotches or drips. The journal is refillable and there are leather pouches to slot the used pages into. It was a graduation present from Max and, of all my family and friends, only he could have thought of this. The leather creaks as I open it, the pages crackle as I flatten them down and start to write.

Words flowed out of me, not only did I describe the last couple of days, I also described the nights, my dreams and the odd circumstances surrounding them. When my pen finally slowed, I looked at the clock, it was midnight and I had been writing for over four hours. My shoulders were tight, my neck too. I needed to rest. Closing the book, I finished in the bathroom and stretched out on the bed, feeling my limbs pop and settle.

Pulling up the blanket, I fell into a restless sleep. My dreams, like the previous night, were confused and chaotic, involving lots of running, noise, dust and shouting. Thankfully, it seemed that I actually stayed in bed for once, no dusty feet when I woke early the next morning, the dawn just beginning to break. So, although my night's sleep hadn't gone any where near recharging my batteries, at least my feet where still clean, that in itself was a plus.

Before leaving my room, I gave myself a stern talking to, resolving to make the best of the Naomi situation. After all, I had no claim on Max, he was just a friend and Naomi seemed charming. It wasn't her fault I was feeling out of sorts, well, ok yes it was, indirectly, but that was my issue not hers. Shrugging into my grey cargo pants and a teal blue long sleeved cotton top, I tied my hair into a loose plait, noticing, absently, that my fringe needed trimming. Light footwear was acceptable for indoors and made a lovely change from the boots we wore when on site, and as

I slid my feet into my soft slippers my toes wriggled in this touch of luxury. Throwing a light wrap over my shoulders, I padded quietly down to the refectory, noticing that, with the exception of the kitchen staff who were preparing breakfast, I was the first up. The scent of Arabica coffee floated towards me, so rich that my mouth started to salivate.

I poured myself a large mug of the heady brew and went to sit outside, choosing a swing seat facing Masada and, glad of my wrap in the cool air, rocked gently back and forth, watching the glory of the sunrise. Pink and purple hues bled across the rock, illuminating the ruin bit by bit, it was utterly magical, as though life was being infused into its depths. As the sky slowly lightened, the colours mutated into golds and yellows, silence enveloping the scene, not even a bird called, as though held in thrall by this timeless tableau. Captivated, I too held my breath, the minutes ticked by until suddenly a flock of Dead Sea sparrows rose, gathered together and soared over the rock. Their joyful chirruping song filling the air, welcoming the sun, which in turn banished the last of the night. High, high above, a Barbary falcon in search of breakfast wheeled in a lazy circle, its sharp cry scattering the smaller birds and another day began.

Chapter Six

Placing my coffee mug on the arm of the seat, I wandered across the desert floor, taking care not to damage my delicate slippers on the sharp rocks strewn here and there. Standing underneath the massive outcrop, I tried to imagine how the Roman soldiers under Flavius Silva must have felt before the final onslaught up their newly constructed ramp. The people they were going to face were revolutionaries, yes, but how well armed were they? Had there been any secret reconnaissance, had anyone infiltrated the group bringing down vital information?

In view of the final outcome, it seemed unlikely, but the Romans were master strategists, they rarely, if ever, advanced on a target without garnering as much information about it as possible. Questions rolled around my mind as I visualised the sequence of events leading to that devastating finale. As the sun rose higher and the blue of the sky deepened, with the peace of the morning enveloping me, it was hard to imagine the horrors they endured, Roman and revolutionary alike.

Sighing, I retraced my steps, back to our little corner of civilisation, the sounds of people moving, breaking the quiet. Collecting my mug I walked back into the refectory, nodding a greeting to the few already seated. Breakfast was generally a fairly quiet meal, people still half awake, mulling over what they hoped to achieve that day, were not interested in spirited debate.

This morning, however, it was a little different, the arrival of Naomi had piqued their interest, to be fair, mainly in her expertise, that she was probably the polar opposite of every other female specialist who had visited the site in recent memory, was merely icing on the cake. It was like watching a group of peacocks out to impress the peahen, although in this case the hen was the one with all the beauty. Naomi took it all in her stride and treated all with the same generosity, including everyone in her conversation.

Watching from the sidelines, I realised that although she was a consummate performer, knowing exactly what to say to keep them hanging on her every word, it wasn't forced; she was naturally inclusive, effortlessly making everyone feel special. Now why did that irk me so much? Maybe because up until now I had been the youngest female on site, there were only a couple of other, older women, who were salt of the earth, totally engrossed in their own world, types. Was it because there was competition for attention? I wasn't comfortable with the direction my thoughts were taking me. While it was lovely that the other guys included me, I just felt like one of the gang, they weren't overtly attentive and definitely not flirty.

As a rule these men were, like their female counterparts, usually wholly involved in their work, the sort who would miss a meal if it wasn't provided for them, in fact they would probably even have stayed up on the site all night if it was floodlit. To them I was just one of the guys, it wasn't as if Naomi's coming had changed anything, yet I was still irritated. Oh for goodness sake Hannah, get a grip, be friendly, it can't hurt. I mentally shook myself, fixed a big grin on my face, placed some food on my plate and, surprisingly, as there was a free seat next to her took the opportunity to do just that.

"Hi, Naomi", I smiled, "did you sleep well?"

Oh Hannah, thank you, yes, it was very comfortable, much more so than I'm used to. Usually, it's a camp bed in a tent miles from any proper facilities, with just a hole in the ground. An actual bed and a bathroom with running water was bliss." She grinned back, her face taking on an impish quality, as she described some of the sites she'd been on, a clever storyteller, it wasn't long

40

before she'd reduced us to helpless laughter with her lurid tales. I was very glad that we'd ended up here and not one of the really isolated digs. I don't mind slumming it a bit, but I do like to have running water and some home comforts.

I sat back and watched the group; they listened happily to her, asking questions, both insightful and ridiculous, about her travels and her work. As quickly as they had been caught up in the fun, they became serious, moving into questions about the Masada mosaics and how they were going to deal with a knotty problem they were experiencing. It was fascinating and I'm sure any anthropologist would have got enough fodder in that one hour's breakfast to give them a decent academic paper.

Sipping on a second coffee, I noticed Max had joined us and was entering into the discussion; it was the mosaic he was working on, along with a few others that Naomi was especially interested in. It seems that they were so unusual in their style, detail and positioning that those uncovering them preferred to let the expert decide how they were going to record and conserve them, to ensure their already meticulous cataloguing did not miss something of vital historical importance. One in particular, was in a room in the Western Palace, which initially looked if it had been used for storing food and wine, but the discovery of this intricate mosaic belied this. As if the room had been allocated for a different purpose when the palace was used in Herodian times, but had then been earmarked as a storage area later.

Herod had used the Western Palace, when in residence, as his administrative centre, with rooms for offices, for guests, for political visitors and government officials. While at Masada the whole of Herod's government was run from here, he couldn't simply pop back to Jerusalem if he'd forgotten something, everything had to be available. The room looked as if it had been lavish enough to be used for formal business, but not so opulent as to be mistaken as one of the rooms used by Herod or his family for personal pursuits.

Determining the true purpose of this room and its mosaic was one of the more intriguing objectives of this season's dig. The chat went back and forth, suggestions and ideas poured out of those around the table. Eventually Naomi laughingly held up her hands in mock surrender and said that it would probably be best if they carried this on in situ, it would be much easier to gauge what they had to do if they were actually looking at the mosaics.

Good humouredly, everyone got up, clattering pots and cutlery together as they placed them in the kitchen and pottered off to their respective rooms to get ready, their noisy chatter floating cheerfully down the hallway after them. I grinned to myself, such a happy bunch of guys and they were like pigs in muck at the promise of an expert helping them for even a short time. As I was walking back down to my room, Max caught up with me.

"Hannah, you ok?"

"I'm fine, Max." My voice was flat and for the life of me I could not stop the chill in my tone.

"It's just that you rushed off last night and I didn't get a chance to ask how your day had been."

"My day…my day." I said drawing out the second 'my.' "Well, lets see…my day consisted of a dusty drive down to the Dead Sea, for a day of R and R to try and clear my head. Hoping that my friend would join me later as he'd promised to try and help me come to grips with what's been bothering me. Oh wait…" sarcastically, "…said friend didn't show, something much more important had cropped up, so I ended up getting a lift back with our chef who, by the way, seems to have a death wish and, then was pretty much ignored for most of the evening. Until said friend saw fit to introduce to me to the very beautiful 'something more important." I knew I sounded petulant, but I could not help it, just when I needed Max to be there for me, he hadn't been and I was obviously still more than a little cheesed off.

"I'm sorry sweetie, I know it was thoughtless, I hadn't realised you were in such a state." He said, searching my face for some sign of forgiveness. I was not ready for that quite yet.

"Max, I never ask for help, you know that, I hate feeling out of control and unable to handle stuff. I really needed to talk yesterday and you just blew me off." I was mortified to hear my voice crack and feel my eyes well up. Wimp, I thought to myself, bet Naomi wouldn't be this 'girlie'.

Max pulled me into his chest; I stiffened as he wrapped his arms round me, hugging me close. I could feel his heart beating as he laid his head on the top of my head.

"Oh, Hannah, please don't cry, forgive me?" He whispered. "I seriously did not realise how freaked out you were." I lifted my head to look him in the eye; he was gazing down at me with a look I could not interpret. I think I must be programmed never to be angry with Max for long, for after several moments, when I tried to glare, I gave up and relaxed into him feeling his arms tighten.

"'S'ok." I muttered, my head buried in his shirt. "Just don't do it again."

"I promise love." As I gave in and hugged him back, I felt his heart rate rise and his breathing quicken. A pleasurable quiver ran through me and, shocked at this new development, I tilted my head again so I could look at him. Our faces were nearly touching, his lips were so close to mine - did I want this?

Thoughts tumbled through my head as, in that split second, I assessed what would change between us if we actually kissed. Our friendship would never be the same; our easy camaraderie would probably be, at best totally different, at worst - lost. Did I want this...oh yes, with all my heart I did. Our eyes met, his darkening with an emotion I couldn't quite read and I fancied that our souls were reflected there, we were so close. Then, just as I was sure he was going to kiss me, a noise distracted him, a door along the hallway opened. Max slowly released me, brushing his lips across the top of my head and guided me into my room making it look like the most natural thing in the world. Smiling ruefully, he winked.

"See you later sunshine." And strolled off as though nothing had happened.

I sat down on the bed - well it was more a collapse than a sit - totally inelegant - touching my lips, those lips that he hadn't actually kissed, feeling like a giddy schoolgirl. As I tried to breathe normally again, I suddenly knew what had been messing with my mind and much as I wanted it to be true, those thoughts that had run through my head a few moments before, re-asserted themselves. Max was my friend, one of my oldest and best friends, he had seen me at my best and, quite often, at my worst. We had no secrets; we had shared and talked about everything since I was a bratty kid.

What if it was this place, that ruin, the isolation, what if it wasn't real? What if it wasn't real…my thoughts spiralled and ran out as I faced what I truly feared, no I couldn't be, but I knew I was. I was completely, irrationally, irrevocably, head over heels, in love with Max and was terrified that his reaction this morning was because we were miles from anywhere and I was, or had been until yesterday, the only female within a forty mile radius. But he started it this morning Hannah, I reasoned with myself, he didn't need to hold you close and brush his lips on your hair and gaze into your eyes 'til you felt your world rock.

Max wasn't some guy who flitted from one woman to another. In all the time I'd known him, he probably only had two or three girlfriends and they had never seemed particularly serious, more something he'd fallen into rather than sought out. His work and study had always been the most important thing and as it often took him overseas, long term relationships were too hard. The best thing was just to see what happened, don't question it, let it unfold in its own way, don't try to force the issue, because if I had misread it, I didn't want to spoil what we already had, our friendship was way too important.

Decision made, I hauled myself off the bed and finished getting ready for the day. I was helping up on the site today, we amateurs often got to assist the qualified archaeologists, it was fascinating especially in view of my own passion for anything connected to Ancient Rome. Making sure I had enough water in my backpack, a packet of biscuits (having been warned that biscuits were highly desired, I had brought over several different brands, much to the delight of the group), tissues, wet wipes and sun cream.

I imagined this is what it must be like taking children out for a picnic, all you need to keep them from being hungry, thirsty, sticky and sunburned and this was for adults. I would not have changed it for the world! Chuckling to myself, I gathered everything together, grabbing my large scarf and big floppy hat to protect my skin from the harsh sun and wandered back to the refectory, ready to face the rest of the day.

Chapter Seven

Most of the rest of the group were already there and, as we were close to the ramp, we usually walked up, everyone carrying a little bit extra in the way of tools or water to share the load. It saved driving round to the cable car and going up that way. Plus, so early in the day, it was still relatively cool. This morning there seemed to be more excitement in the air, the promise of expert assistance in the shape of Naomi, had heightened their normal enthusiasm.

I don't think I'd ever worked with a group of people who loved their jobs so much and never lost their excitement about what they might discover. Even if it was nothing more than a tiny patch of fresco, or a piece of pottery, or a few small tesserae, they reacted as if it was their first ever find. Yes, to use the vernacular, they were the nerdiest of nerds, but their exhilaration was infectious and I was so glad to be part of it.

I was going to be assisting Nate, or Nathaniel Robinson and anyone less like your archetypal image of an archaeologist I had yet to find. Around six feet tall, with a shock of blonde hair, blue eyes and very tanned, he looks more like a surfer than an academic, yet he was a lecturer at a prestigious American university and a world-renowned pottery expert. I loved working with him, because although totally focused on his work, he would talk about what he was doing while he was doing it, so anyone assisting him could make notes or if nothing else, understand what he was doing. I have been told that his classes were often standing room only and I could see why.

He was working in the Northern Palace, which also meant I would be away from Max and, a little voice whispered, Naomi.

Hopefully, I would be able to concentrate on the job in hand with no distractions. A glimmer of an idea had been percolating at the back of my brain, about the possibility of producing some kind of information sheet about Masada, to include its history and the archaeological progress made in uncovering its secrets. A way to enhance our display back at the museum, as although we had a substantial gallery dedicated to Ancient Rome, our section showcasing the Roman East was rather meagre.

Anything to increase interest was worth exploring and if I could include a way to hold the attention of our younger visitors, all the better. Photos and descriptions, even dioramas are fine for adults, but we also hosted school groups. Holding their attention is always a challenge and if I could create something like a worksheet version of those children's books about history in all its gory detail, it might just help. Plus, if they liked gruesome, the history of Masada had it in spades.

By assisting the other archaeologists, I hoped to gain an insight into how they approached their individual tasks, what tools they used and why, methods of preservation and conservation and so on. If I could combine the important historical and archaeological material with the fun stuff, it would be a great way of getting them to assimilate information without really seeming to.

I hunkered down and got on with the job in hand, letting all those other ideas roll around my subconscious, hoping that by the end of the day I'd be able to remember what I'd come up with. Nate was absorbed in some shards of pottery he was uncovering, he asked me to take photographs of their position not only in relation to each other, but also the room as a whole. There seemed to be an abundance of pieces in the two or three rooms we were working in, indicative, initially, of either a waste dump or a place where people had spent a lot of time eating or cooking.

Although, as yet, there was no sign of any utensils, or even anything resembling a fire pit, we were the first people to be working this area and there was a lot of ground to cover and uncover. The ceilings of this area had collapsed centuries ago, but previous excavation groups had erected a sort of temporary roof to protect what might be in the rooms from the worst of the winters and, of course the workers from the summer's scorching sun. It made it a bit darker, but much cooler.

We worked well together and were soon totally engrossed; the pieces of pottery taking shape as we gently removed the earth from around them, with me snapping photos as we went along. It looked as though some might be quite large pieces, almost whole jars or bowls, quite unexpected in a place where so much violence had occurred. We imagined everything would have been smashed when the Zealots destroyed anything the Romans might want. Then, when the Romans finally abandoned the fortress, they finished off anything the Zealots had missed; to dissuade anyone else thinking that occupying this citadel was a good idea.

We must have been working solidly for a couple of hours when suddenly Nate stopped and sat back on his haunches, stretching his back, looking rather puzzled.

"This doesn't seem right," he muttered, "I don't see how it can be."

"What do you mean?" I asked. "Be what?"

"It looks like several jars all stacked together, they'll take some removing, but they look fairly intact and some of them seem to have stuff in them."

"Stuff, Nate?" Glancing across at him, I was about to tease him about his use of jargon, when something in his face stopped me. "What stuff?"

"I don't want to say yet, might jinx it."

"Nate," chiding gently, "you're a scientist, surely you're not superstitious, what is it?"

Nate grinned sheepishly.

"Just want to be sure, it would be quite the find if I'm right. Let's tidy this up and take a break, I want to be able to concentrate on this little section properly and my stomach tells me it's coffee time!" Humouring him and realising he wasn't going to share any more, I took the last few snaps of what we'd done so far, logged the new pieces on the map we'd drawn up and stood up. As I did so, the room spun for a minute, images flooded my mind and skittered off before I could grasp what they were. I wobbled slightly and I must have made a sound, because Nate grabbed my elbow.

"You ok Hannah?" Concerned. I shook my head, it felt as though I had water in my ears, but the humming was already fading.

"I'm fine, thanks, must have stood up too fast, head rush…" I managed a weak grin, "…definitely coffee time."

We came out of the cool room along the passageway and onto the sun drenched plateau, Nate still holding my arm. Thanking him, I gently disengaged myself, opening the backpack to get the thermos. Placing our mugs on the flattest piece of wall I could find, I poured coffee, steam rising from the hot sweet nectar and rummaging deeper in my backpack, pulled out two packets of ginger biscuits. Archaeologists must have the hearing of dogs, because just I started to open the first packet, they appeared one by one from their various digs, unbelievable…so much for a quiet cuppa. Their actions conjured up the story of the Pied Piper and I started to giggle. Nate, who had stayed close watching me uneasily, relaxed and, tilting his head back against a convenient rock, soaking up the sun's warmth, coffee in hand.

As the others sorted out their drinks, helped themselves to biscuits and found somewhere relatively comfortable to sit for a few minutes, the conversation turned to what each of them was doing. We had been nicely spread around Masada today; besides the two main palaces, there were three small palaces, one of which had been used by the Zealots, a synagogue, the Byzantine church, an apartment building and a mosaic workshop also dated to the Byzantine era, as well as several structures butted up against the outer walls. I think there had been at least someone in each of the areas and several in some.

There was enough work left to do, at this most incredible of sites, to keep archaeologists coming back for years to come. It was so interesting listening to them, discussing their area, comparing finds, arguing over who's was the most important in the overall scheme of things. I let their voices wash over me as I sipped my hot coffee, it was late morning and the air was still. Not yet too hot, thankfully, as the afternoon breeze was still a couple of hours away. I let my thoughts drift, trying and failing to recapture the images that had fluttered through my mind before the break.

Gazing across the plateau, the pomegranate trees caught my eye, little pockets of cool shade under the ever warming mantle of the sun, the dappled light through the leaves creating crazy shadow dances on the dusty ground. On one or two of the trees, baubles of fruit, their soft skins beginning to harden, were darkening from pink to red. Their very existence testament to a hardy nature and the blessing of winter rains and, I wondered, idly, whether they would be ripe enough to eat before we had to leave this place.

As I pondered the delights of devouring those plump sweet seeds, the sticky red syrup oozing down my chin and covering my fingers, I became aware of something teasing at the edge my consciousness, what was it, what had I missed? It seemed to be important and it fluttered again. I ran over the last few minutes again, coffee, chatter, finds, pomegranates...WHAT? Frustrated that I couldn't trace it, I looked around the group, hoping for inspiration. Was it to do with someone here, or someone - I felt a cold trickle run down my spine as I recalled my dreams - from long ago?

Pushing my disquiet firmly to the back of my mind, I stood up, needing to move, stretch and feel the blood flowing through my limbs. The warmth was enervating and, I was sure, not conducive to my riotous imagination. Get on with the job in hand Hannah, I instructed myself, go distract yourself with ancient stuff. Shoving my mug into my backpack, I called over to Nate, still chatting with the others.

"Hey Nate, I'm going back to the plot, catch you lot at lunch, finish those biccies if you can." Like they'd find that hard, I waved at the group, setting off towards the room we'd been working in.

Nate raised his hand in acknowledgement, gathered his things together and started to follow me. The day had certainly warmed up while we'd been enjoying coffee and I hurried to get back to the relative cool of the palace, remembering what Nate had said just before we took the break. I think I was probably as excited as he was and had already got the camera and notebook out by the time he shambled in.

"C'mon Nate," I wheedled, "what did you think you'd started to uncover before we had coffee?"

"Ok, until we get this totally exposed, I want you to keep this between us, I haven't found anything like this and I want to be sure. Normally I wouldn't say anything at all, but you're here and I need someone to record this while I work."

"Ok, ok, no problem, now what gives?" Nate took a deep breath.

"I think I've found evidence of a treatment or healing room, or possibly the jars which held the ointments and balms and, I think there might be some pieces of material which look as though they might have been for bandaging, or at least covering wounds."

"Why is that so unusual?" I asked. "Surely if there'd been a garrison, who were routed by a mob of Zealots, all of whom were more than a tad feisty, then later on a community of monks, some sort of medical room would be normal, wouldn't it?" I recalled that the healers of antiquity, usually a priest or priestess, had prodigious knowledge about the curative properties of certain plants and herbs, oils, salts and other stuff, including the rather gory practise of reading entrails from a sacrifice.

"We have no record of it being here, even the descriptions by Josephus don't include what was in all of the rooms. Although from previous excavations, we know that there were several storerooms adjacent to this building, so there would be no need to store anything here unless it was being used regularly, you know, like in kitchens. It may not even have been searched if there was no one here when they glanced in. They were looking for the Zealots, and while I accept that plundering any treasures was part and parcel of that, a room with jars probably wouldn't have been worth looting. So had it been used as a healing room from the time of Herod, or was it an improvised 'hospital'?" Nate air-comma'd that last word, then continued:

"Was it used when the Zealots were here? If so, why would they have needed such a place, did they set it up after they overran the garrison, or did the Romans use it after they stormed the citadel? It seems too haphazard to have been a designated room under the Roman watch, they were much more organised. Plus, I think that the monks would have left things in a much neater fashion and probably closer to their chapel rather than all the way over here in the palace. Too far to be coming back and forth if you needed something regularly."

"Yes, I get that, but why is it so important that you want me to keep quiet 'til we know for sure? Might it not simply have been a small kitchen, or a sort of ante room where they stored a few easily accessibly things like wine, or oil?"

"Because there are other items here. I think there are remnants of cloth, which, if I'm not mistaken, are in strips, like primitive bandages, as well as what appear to be, wads of material. But I don't want to speculate yet, let's get on with it and see what I can uncover, I might need your help with the extractions as they look very fragile."

Eagerly, I moved over to where Nate was working and took a closer look at the area he'd been exposing. The shards were clearly visible, quite large pieces, amazingly and, darker on what would have been the inside of the jar or pot. Close to one pile, there was, what looked to my inexperienced eyes, like a sizeable lump of dried clay and this was what Nate was trying to lift away. How he had even been able to work out what it might be was beyond me, which is why I'm just the assistant. Gently, he worked around the lump, taking care not to get too close to the central mass, scraping away layers of debris built up over the centuries, it was a long and painstaking task.

Any dirt Nate pushed aside, I collected in a bag so that later, we could put it through the mesh trays, which would catch anything we had missed. I clicked endlessly with the camera, capturing as much as I could, then every once in a while, I'd draw the layer while Nate stood up to stretch his cramped muscles. Lunch passed, as did the afternoon break, neither of us realised how long we'd been at it, until suddenly a head poked through the doorway and a voice asked us whether we were intending on spending all night up here as well. Looking up, neck muscles groaning from being too long in one position, we both noticed that the light was fading.

"What time is it?" asked Nate

"Its well after half three mate." Replied the voice, whom I suddenly realised came from Geoff, who had been working in one of the rooms in the main body of the Northern Palace. Tall with very unruly dark hair that always looked like it needed a good cut, Geoff was a gentle giant of a man, with hands like spades and fingers like sausages, yet somehow he could work with the most delicate of tools on the most fragile of artefacts and, although he preferred to work on frescos, he was an expert in several archaeological disciplines and had a Masters in Anthropology. He was the 'go to' guy if you had curly questions or an unexpected find. It would probably be Geoff whom Nate would need to bring in on this material he thought he had discovered. Time, yet though, we still hadn't got it all out, a job for the next day.

"Thanks Geoff." I smiled. "We've been so caught up that we hadn't noticed the time"

"Well tell me something I don't know." He laughed. "Honestly you two, what is so enthralling that you missed the afternoon break? Did you even have lunch?" As Nate and I looked at each other, then back at Geoff, a distinct rumble was heard, answering his question and making me blush. "That would be a 'no' then. C'mon guys, gather your stuff and we can walk down together, the others have already set off, I'll wait for you at the ramp."

Quickly covering up the lump of dried whatever and anchoring the tarp with a few rocks, we collected the tools, camera and notebooks, shoving them rather unceremoniously into our backpacks. In mine, I found a couple of pathetic looking bananas, which we inhaled as we walked over to meet Geoff. The sun, although still quite bright was well on its downward trek toward the horizon, casting its long shadows across the landscape, its shimmering heat tamed by the afternoon breeze, fresh enough to lift my hair and cool my skin, but, thankfully, not strong enough to stir the dust on our path down the ramp.

We chattered about the day and the finds, Geoff had spent his day trying to determine whether three Corinthian capitals, found lodged against one of the walls had come from that space, or fallen through from the level above during or shortly after the great fire. They had discovered that one of them still had some coloured plaster on it, which should help in locating its original position, as it had been determined that the columns were decorated differently on each level. It was just a matter of deciding whether all three were from the same level and which level that actually was. Geoff's excitement was infectious and we spent the whole walk discussing his finds, it also meant, to Nate's relief that he didn't have to talk about what he had found and what its implications were.

Arriving at the digs, we split off to our respective rooms and I spent a few minutes noting down the day, for some reason Nate's discovery seemed vital, like a piece of a jigsaw turning up after being thought lost. As I finished writing, my mind went back to the thought that had been nagging me at coffee that morning, jigsaw puzzles…hmm, I ruminated…that's what it felt like, as though I was trying to find pieces of a puzzle for a picture I had never seen.

Turning to the back page and, in the hope of clarifying things somewhat, I began to jot down what I knew,

- Brooch or clasp, ancient or not?

- Masada, supposedly the place my ancestor received this clasp,

- Strange dreams, disjointed images of historical events - real or imagined?
- Dusty feet,
- Odd sensations - some familiar, some unexplainable,
- Nate's discovery,
- Pomegranate trees…

…my pen hovered over these last two words, unsure why I written them and, hesitating, I debated whether or not to erase them, wondering what on earth they had to do with anything. Yet, somehow, I felt that they were integral to what ever was going on, despite their part being unclear. My list wasn't very long, in fact it looked ridiculous, nothing tied in and if anyone else read it they'd think I'd spent too long in the sun - some jigsaw puzzle.

Frustrated, I pushed my journal aside and leaned back on my pillows, then remembering the clasp, rummaged around in my backpack to find it. I held it up to the window; the red of the stone was deeper in the centre, dark as blood, fading to a paler hue at its edge, strange, I hadn't noticed that before, so maybe it wasn't a ruby after all. I'd always thought it would be most unlikely - a gemstone as costly and desirable as a ruby, especially one the size of my stone, would have been sold or stolen at the first opportunity. The way the colour changed in my stone suggested, in my limited experience, costume jewellery and I actually felt better about it that way, carrying around something that could be worth several thousand pounds was rather worrying.

Settling back on my bed, I rolled the clasp around in my hands, feeling the cool of its setting around the warmth of the stone, it was very tactile, the filigree design giving the burnished metal a sensuality, a fluidity, almost as if it were a living entity, the red centre its pulsing heart. "Oh very poetic Hannah," I muttered to myself, "you need to stop over thinking things."

Dragging my poor aching body off the bed, I took a long hot shower, taking time to condition my hair rather than just shampooing, as was my habit. The water pressure was pretty high, the shower jets making my skin tingle. After rinsing my hair and soaping myself down, I simply stood, letting the water wash away all the tension, along with the dust of the day. Towelling myself off, I realised I felt much better, more awake and suddenly looking forward to dinner, especially since all I'd eaten since breakfast, was a handful of biscuits and a rather overripe banana.

Quickly dressing, I dried my hair, noticing that the sun had kissed highlights into its brown length, silently sending a prayer of thanks to the sun gods; I whipped it up into a loose knot and tidied my fringe. I could smell food and my stomach growled again, so after checking all was tidy and, where necessary, safely stored away, I closed my door and pottered along the corridor to the refectory.

Most of the others were already there; it was curry night and always a very popular menu. Rafi usually did several different styles accompanied by mountains of fluffy white rice and a variety of breads for dipping into the rich sauces. Tonight was no exception, the aroma in the refectory was heavenly, the combination of spices, fresh breads and coffee mingled to create a symphony for the nostrils. I piled my plate high with a goodly selection and, balancing a basket of mixed breads on the top of a glass of cold water, plonked myself at the table. I was probably half way through my dinner before I realised that Max wasn't there, odd, I thought, he loves his curries.

"Anyone seen Max?" I asked, adding half laughingly. "Don't tell me he's missing curry night. Never thought I'd see the day." No-one else had seen him, in fact no-one could remember him coming down from the rock, surely they couldn't still be up there, it was dark by now and trying to get down without a decent light would be madness. The cable car had stopped for the day and even the ramp wasn't safe, despite the fairly bright lights from our camp below it.

We were all mulling over what to do, when the door burst open and the two stragglers almost fell into the room, so full of excitement were they. Still dusty from their day, they cannot have been back down very long and, biting back a smart remark, I waited for one of the others to ask what was going on. They could barely contain their excitement and launched into a babble of explanations about the mosaic and how old it was and what it signified, talking over each other in their enthusiasm to tell us about their finds.

"Must be a room of luxury, the mosaic is so intricate, it has swirls of vine leaves surrounding colourful blossoms, with what seems to be a tree in the centre, we haven't worked out what the tree is yet, but its rather lovely. Its survival in such great condition is probably mainly because it's been hidden by something that might have been wooden, a large pile of broken pots and a heavy layer of dirt. The pots look as though they have been dumped there over many decades and they themselves will no doubt yield some fantastic information, but no one else seems to have bothered much with that area yet. I think because it was thought to be simply a storeroom or possibly a minor official's office, other areas were more important to excavate. Its quite likely that the pots have been left there from all over the site, which may make placing them in specific rooms or buildings quite difficult."

This information was delivered by both of them at the same time, words tumbling out at high speed until, finally they paused for breath and realised that we were all looking at them with expressions ranging from merriment to complete bewilderment.

"You might want to slow the heck down there guys, take a deep breath, get some food and start again." chuckled Nate. "We cannot understand a thing you're gabbling about, except that it was, quite obviously, an awesome day."

Max and Naomi looked at each other, than back at us and started laughing.

"Sorry guys, it was totally awesome." Naomi gurgled through her laughter, "Ok, food it is, I just realised how hungry I am." Having sorted themselves out, they tucked in to their dinner, while the rest of us either got second helpings, or descended on the dessert table. I decided to have ice cream, I'm not really a dessert person, but Rafi makes the most delicious pistachio ice cream and I defy anyone to resist its velvety lusciousness. Making sure I had a huge dish full, I sat back down, finding that Max had taken the seat next to mine. In between mouthfuls, he asked about my day and I told him as much as I could without giving away Nate's suspicions.

"Sounds like you two had a much more interesting day though, way to go on that mosaic."

"Oh its so fascinating, mainly because it suggests that some areas of the Western Palace were not quite as business-like as we imagined. You know about the whole this with this being the show piece for honoured visitors as well as a place where state business was conducted right?" I nodded.

"Well previous finds have confirmed that money was no object here and the mosaics that they found in the original excavations merely a testament to Herod's desire for magnificence. But we didn't expect to find such a beautiful mosaic in an area we thought was probably dedicated to the domestic side of life, like kitchens, laundries, small storerooms, or maybe even the offices of lesser staff members. Plus, it looks as though artisans brought over from Rome made these; they have marks, which can be traced to particular mosaicists. So on top of the obvious design choices such as the columns and frescoes, this was yet another way for Herod to link himself to Augustus and Rome, something he did in many of his building projects."

Max finally finished his meal and sat back, absently rubbing his belly in satisfaction. "Oh that was good, Rafi excelled himself tonight, mmmmm. What's for dessert? Is that his pistachio ice cream?"

"Take a breath Max, you'll get indigestion." Laughing at him. He glanced at my half finished bowl. "Yep, I'd go get some before it's all gone, you know this lot are like gannets. I'll get you a cup of tea."

"Thanks sweetheart." He grinned loping off to elbow his way through the throng of confectionary hunting hordes that had descended on the dessert trolley.

"Honestly," I ruminated, "they're just like kids." Going over to the hatch where Rafi kept the hot drinks, I brewed up a couple of mugs of tea, dash of milk in each, idly dangling the tea bag in the hot water, waiting for it to darken. As I walked back over to the table, I noticed Naomi deep in conversation with a couple of the guys and, without having realised that they were tense, felt my shoulders relax, I had Max to myself, for a little while at least. Smiling, I wandered back over to the table, noticing that Max was watching me, his expression hooded. My smile faltered and a frisson of anxiety ran through me. What was bothering him? He'd been so happy a minute ago.

Wordlessly, I handed him his tea, drinking mine while he devoured his ice-cream. Scraping his bowl, determined to get the last little bit, I swear he would lick it out if he thought nobody would laugh at him, Max very causally asked if I fancied a stroll. Looking towards the window I saw that night had fallen, seemed an odd time to take a walk, but I wasn't going to turn it down, maybe he needed to tell me something, the knot in my stomach tightened, get it over with Hannah. Not trusting myself to speak, I nodded and, quietly we left the room, leaving our half drunk teas on the table. Max didn't say anything, strangely, words weren't needed, but there was a tension between us that was palpable.

As we made our way out of the building, I looked up at the night sky, which was breathtaking. Whatever was about to happen, I knew I would never forget the beauty of that evening. The air, still mild after the heat of the day, was just beginning to cool; the sky was crystal clear, the stars twinkling like a gossamer blanket. We still didn't speak, just walked together towards the dark enormity that was Masada, the night wasn't silent, sounds which were now as familiar to me as those from home, wrapped around us like a shield, there was only we two, together.

Chapter Eight

I sighed, it seemed to come from a great distance and, without thought leaned towards Max, even my nagging unease couldn't stop me. Close enough to hear him breathing - I wanted everything and nothing. Away from the lighted buildings, the darkness was complete, yet not impenetrable, there was enough light from the stars, the moon had not yet risen, time slowed. We had still said not one single word. Max turned me to face him and curving his hand gently round the back of my neck, he tilted my head back, ever so slightly, so he could look down into my eyes, his gaze holding mine and, breathing my name, bent to kiss me.

I knew it was coming, I knew as if I had been waiting my whole life for this moment and I knew that once it had happened we could never go back. Scary as that was, I yearned for it. His lips, soft and cool, teased mine just touching, exploring, I could feel electricity sparking deep inside me, as I responded, my arms closing round him, my heart quickening, the kiss deepening as passion flared. I have never been one for believing all those trashy romance novels, where the hero kisses the heroine and fireworks go off, or she becomes putty in his arms, that's always been a bit too twee for me - great for a story, absolute rubbish in real life. Serves you right, a tiny corner of my brain gloated, as that's exactly what it felt like, a notion that was immediately doused, as my whole being was consumed by emotions that threatened to overwhelm me.

I was drowning in his kiss and my knees began to buckle; holding me close to his chest, Max prevented me from sliding ignominiously to the ground. Our hearts were beating in time and our breath was coming fast and short. I could not get enough; it was like a life force, this kiss. From a gentle touch, Max now plundered my mouth, almost as if he was punishing me and I matched him kiss for kiss, I knew where this would lead and I did not have the will to stop it, even if I had wanted to. Time stood still as delicious sensations rippled through me and still we kissed.

Without rational thought or conscious awareness we sank to the floor, unable to let go, passion rising with every second and although we were far enough for the buildings to be in darkness, we were not out of sight to anybody stepping outside and even that was not enough to stem this tide. Somehow we were lying next to each other, hands moving frantically over the other's body, touching, learning, the never ending heat rising.

One arm wrapped around my waist, Max slid his other hand under my top, making me gasp as his long slim fingers, chilled from the night, searched my hot skin. Tentative, yet firm, caressing every part of me and as he brushed my breast I was almost certain I'd caught fire...my body felt like molten lava and I simply abandoned myself to the feelings surging through me. Pain shot through my hips and back from the rocks I was lying on and still I couldn't let go, I wanted this to go on forever, fearful that I would suddenly wake up and find I'd dreamt it all...let's face it, that wouldn't be unexpected given recent events!

Even as this thought ran through my head, I felt Max loosen his hold on me and he shuddered as he slowly pulled away, the night air cut between our warm faces and I blinked in confusion.

"Don't stop Max, please don't stop." I whispered. Max looked down at me.

"I don't want to stop either sweetheart, but I have to, I don't want this to happen here, out on a dirty, rocky, desert floor. I want it to be where I can take my time and make love to you for as long as I can. Without worrying about some archaeologist coming out and interrupting us. Plus, you cannot possibly be comfortable lying there."

He grinned, his face close to mine, he kissed the tip of my nose and, after a minute or two, started to get up, pulling me with him. My body would not work and I stumbled. Preventing me from falling, Max held my arm, his finger catching my breast, causing liquid fire to shoot through me again and I gasped. His arm around me, I finally managed to regain some form of balance and began to brush the desert off my clothes. As I straightened up Max caught me to him and I could feel his desire pulsing through his taut body as he kissed me again.

"Oh God Hannah, I can't get enough of you." He breathed. "This is so hard, my need to possess you, all of you is only marginally outweighed by the fact that I don't want it to be right here."

"I can tell." I grinned tremulously, making him laugh sheepishly.

"Sorry, we men are not able to hide certain things very well."

"Hey, I like it. I like knowing I can do this to you…its kind of exciting." I wondered at our conversation. We had gone from friends to lovers - well almost - in the space of an hour…was it really only an hour since we'd stepped out into the night? This night that would be burned into my memory forever. What did we do now?

"What do we do now?" Max's question mirrored my thoughts. "Do we keep it between ourselves or do you think that's going to be too hard?" I pondered his question.

"I'd like to keep it just us, just for now. It's too new and tenuous to have everyone gossiping. I don't want to have to answer questions, when I'm still trying to get my own head round it. Weird though…" I left my words dangling.

"What's weird?"

64

"That this doesn't feel weird and I was so afraid it might. I didn't want you to stop kissing me, 'coz then we'd be back in the real world and we'd be all awkward and not know how to talk to each other. We've been friends for so long and let's face it we've just royally blown that. I mean, for goodness sake, you've known me since I was a gawky teenager, you've seen me at my very worst - like when I get angry over nothing, or burst into tears at the silliest things. I was terrified that once you'd kissed me and got what ever it is out of your system, you wouldn't want anything more to do with me and I don't think I could bear that, but I still wanted that kiss."

I gazed at Max as I was speaking and caught a flash of some emotion deep in his eyes.

"Oh Hannah, Hannah." His voice caught, was that a sob? "I have loved you pretty much since the day we first met, hissy fits and tears aside, I've just been waiting for you to catch up." Cupping my face with his hands Max kissed me again, a habit I highly approved of. His body trembled as our desire whipped up again, I circled his waist with my arms and let the feeling wash over me, totally uncaring, my life was complete, Max loved me.

"How long have you known?" I sighed, trying to catch my breath.

"Shuushhhh…don't interrupt." Effectively shutting me up for several more minutes. I struggled against his chest.

"No, tell me, I want to know, how long have you known?" Giving up, at least for now, Max looked at me.

"Known what?"

"Known that I would fall in love with you."

"How could you resist?" He teased; I nudged him in the shoulder.

"Seriously Max, c'mon, tell me."

"Ok." Resigned. "To be honest I wasn't certain, there's been the odd time when we've been together over the years when I thought you were about there, then nothing happened. Then occasionally I worried that you'd gone and fallen for someone else, especially that guy in college, you were pretty tight there for a while."

"Alex? Yeah, I guess, but none of the guys I dated ever seemed quite right, don't know why, well maybe now I do."

"Was that his name, Alex - I've blanked him." Grinning. "Then, suddenly you wanted to come here and I was coming anyway, it seemed there might be a chance. So I kinda hoped that being on this dig, since it was just you and me, no distractions, that things might have a better chance of sparking off, but I was only absolutely certain this morning."

"This morning?" Confused.

"Outside your room, when you gave me that serve about not meeting you yesterday. You were so mad and for a split second I thought I'd lost you, but when I was looking at you..." he paused and as he did so we spoke in unison, "...it was as if you knew what I was feeling..."

"That's when I knew." he finished.

"That's when I knew too...although I've been fighting the oddest feelings over the last few days and last night when you were so excited about Naomi's visit and then I SAW her. I couldn't work it out; I thought I was just mad coz she was taking my friend off me...I know - I sound like a petulant brat. I tried to talk myself around, but I could not get her expression, when she was talking to you, out of my head. It was only this morning when I thought you were going to kiss me that I realised why I was so confused, yet it seemed so obvious. Once I actually accepted what had been staring me in the face for so long, probably years, everything just clicked. But then you didn't...and we'd never…and there was Naomi and she's so beautiful and…" I dried up suddenly, unsure how to phrase what I was worried about.

Max put his finger on my lips.

"Hannah, you are and have always been, the most beautiful girl I have ever laid eyes on, I don't think you realise just how beautiful you are." He sounded quite astonished that I didn't know this.

"Me, beautiful, hahaha give over, I'm just me, Miss Average Everything - average height, average weight, average hair, average eyes."

"Well, Miss Average Everything, I love that your hair is soft and catches the light and that I can run my fingers through it like this," tugging my, now very messy, hair out of its loose knot, "I love that your eyes glow deep green when you're excited or happy or sad and most especially when I kiss you." Suiting his words to action, more minutes passed, then, a little breathlessly. "I love that I can rest my chin on your head and that we seem to fit perfectly together when I pull you close."

"Hmmm…ok sir, average does seem rather wonderful right now." I smiled, kissing him back with interest.

And in a dark corner of a dark pouch in a dark room, it seemed as though something glowed in satisfaction.

"I need to sit down." I murmured against his lips. In the shadow of a much larger boulder there was a flattish rock, giving us a kind of chair and, sitting down, Max leaned against the boulder pulling me close, my back against his chest, wrapping his arms round me. The night air was chill now and our bodies, so hot moments ago, were cooling rapidly, reaction causing me to shiver. Nestling into Max I rested my head on his shoulder and wrapped my arms over his, he was right…even like this we fitted.

"Right, what was it you wanted to talk about?" Max asked, business like all of a sudden, rubbing my cheek with his chin.

"Now, *now* you want to talk?" Trying to turn and look him in the eye.

"Ok…smarty pants, don't get all stroppy, you wanted to talk, we're both quite, errr, relaxed, why not now? No-one else is about, no-one to interrupt us, well unless they decide to come see where we are, perfect time…oh…and what do you mean Naomi's expression?"

"Haha - wondered if you'd go back to that, she was looking at you as if she might like to put cream on you and eat you. Although to be scrupulously fair, that might be her default expression, as she looks like that when she's talking to the other guys too." Feeling magnanimous, now I was secure in Max's arms.

"Hmm…hadn't even noticed, nice thought mind, but there's only one person I'd allow to slather me with cream." I blushed furiously, glad he could not see the telltale red flare in the darkness. Knowing me better than I realised, his body shook with laughter. "Sorry, that was too easy, now where were we…oh yes, perfect time, get on with it."

"I guess." I sighed, pressing my back into his warm chest, "I was rather hoping we could just continue where we left off."

"Hussey, you're leading me astray!"

"Me - leading *you* astray, hey…how d'y…what….." while I was spluttering in feigned indignation, Max turned my head, his warm lips once again, effectively shutting me up.

"C'mon Han, spill." His use of the diminutive of my name worked its spell, he's the only person who ever dared to, my parents hated it and only ever used my full name, yet somehow Max got away with it. I gave in and settled myself back against his chest and began to describe what had been happening to me. It took a bit of time and Max asked a lot of questions, trying to piece together my hallucinations or whatever they were.

"See, the thing is, I'd put it down to an over active imagination, or too much sun if it wasn't that my feet were so dirty when I woke up yesterday morning and look at my poor toe." I flicked off my sandal, wiggling my battered toe for him to admire. "That was not a result of my kicking the bed frame and there's another thing…" I hesitated not sure whether to disclose the last piece.

"What Han, what else?" Max turned me round to face him and as he tilted his head, I felt the same jolt of recognition of my dream rock through me again.

"The Roman soldier, the one who looked at me…I know who he reminds me of."

"Who?"

"You!"

Chapter Nine

I woke with a start, the sun was streaming in through the window, I rarely closed the curtains and I completely forgot last night, when I finally got to bed. I luxuriated in my secret for a few moments, as I remembered the rest of last night. We had talked a little longer, going back and forth over everything. By the time we'd hashed it out, Max was convinced that I was not imagining things, but suggested that maybe I thought the Roman looked like him because he'd been on my mind. Yeah, logical progression of thoughts, I know, but something still niggled at the back of my mind, it wasn't that it was Max's face exactly, not like looking at a photograph, it was more hints of his features.

In my head, this wasn't over and I thought Max was involved somehow; it was as though I needed to see this, whatever 'this' was, through to its conclusion. Only, I knew how it concluded, I'd read it two days ago and studied it while at Uni, there were books and movies about it. I'd only seen the start, if this was something I was to play a part in; there'd be more dreams to come. Strangely enough, this didn't bother me, discovering that Max loved me, made everything else seem bearable and secure in that knowledge, I'd be able to handle whatever happened. Oh grief Hannah, I thought, you sound like a trashy romance novel. Didn't care about that either!

After a very satisfactory interlude where we had re-discovered each other's lips, Max walked me back to my room, avoiding the refectory, too many questioning eyes, especially as we'd been gone the whole evening. Kissing me one more time, he'd hugged me close, pulling away just before our passion, resuming its slow burn, would have made it too hard to stop. Then as he'd done a little over twelve hours ago - had it really only been that morning? - he pushed me gently into my room, smiled his heart warming smile and strolled off down the hallway.

Moving into the security of my room, I sat for what seemed like forever, in actual fact it was probably only ten minutes, trying and, failing to come back to earth. My life would never be the same; things had shifted to such a degree that everything seemed a little out of control. How was it going to be around the others? How long would we be able to hide, what I felt was coming off me in waves? I have always had trouble trying to hide my emotions, everything I feel is right there on my face, or in my body language, up front and out there, good, bad, sad, happy, they just tumble out.

I didn't know how I was going to be able to cover up my love for Max, when all I wanted to do was shout it from the top of the highest tower on summit of the great rock we were working on. I'd just have to try, I was the one who'd said I didn't want to broadcast it, to keep it between us, so that's what I'd have to do. My worry was, that in my determination to seem casual, I might go to the other extreme and come across as cold or haughty…me - haughty…shock I know - who'd have thought it!

Glancing at my watch, I realised, to my total embarrassment that it was after 7.30, everyone would have set off up to Masada and I was here lounging in my bed, when I should be up there helping Nate. I was so excited about what Nate had found that I didn't want to miss anything. Diving out of bed, I noticed a slip of paper by the door, giggling at the image of someone stuffing a note under my door. It was from Max. 'Told the others you'd gone to bed early with a headache, said it was from not enough food or water yesterday, they swallowed it. Nate said just to go up when you're ready. Love you x.'

My first love note from Max, in fact my first love note ever and lets face it, it wasn't very mushy, but it warmed me and I felt a silly grin spread over my face. Hannah, you need to get a grip, useless you are, useless. By continuing to talk sternly to myself the whole time I showered, dressed and tidied up, I felt I had gained a modicum of control and went to see if there was any breakfast left.

Rafi smiled at me through the kitchen hatch as I walked into the refectory,

"Max said you might be a bit late, I've got some bacon and eggs ready to go here…hungry?"

"Yes, thanks so much Rafi, that would be heavenly." I smiled back, realising that I was really hungry, more like starving. All that kissing must work up a good appetite. Chuckling to myself, I went to get a cup of hot green tea, savouring the delicate flavour as I waited for the bacon and eggs to cook. Lost in my own daydreams, I was leaning against one of the tables, when the main door swung open and Max came in.

Startled, as I'd assumed everyone had already left, I could not for the life of me stop myself from blushing. Geez, so much for being in control Hannah. He winked at me, before glancing round to see if anyone else was around.

"There's just me, I think the other's have gone, thought you'd be with them, thanks for the note and talking to Rafi, did you sleep well?" The words tumbled out of my mouth far too quickly for coherence, as I gazed at him, drinking him in, hmm…way better than tea!

He smiled his slow smile and I felt my heart do an odd flip flop in my chest.

"Just wanted to be sure you were ok sweetheart and I slept very well." He said as he came over, pulled me to him and kissed me quick and hard. Electricity shot through me, I wanted to pull him down and kiss him, just kiss him 'til we had no breath left.

As he lifted his head I could see my desire reflected in his eyes, drawing a deep breath, he drew back and as he stood up we noticed movement in the room. Rafi had come in from the kitchen with my plate of food; his expression told us he'd seen everything.

"Err...umm...well.' I started to explain, wondering how I could make it sound less that it was.

"We were just..." Max spoke at the same time.

"About time you two, thought he was never going to get round to it." Grinning wickedly.

"What on earth do you mean?" Aiming for nonchalance and failing dismally.

"You two, from the first day you arrived I knew you should be together, plus as Max has talked a lot about you every time he's been here, it was obvious how he felt, even if he didn't know it.

"Oh, I knew it," Max seemed relieved, "...but please..."

"Don't tell anyone? No worries, it'll be nice to have a secret" Chuckling. Blushing again, oh dear, this would have to stop; I got up and gave Rafi a big hug, kissing him on the cheek.

"You are an absolute darling Rafi, thank you. It's just all a bit new and we don't want to have to explain it to the others yet, should have known you'd get it."

"My pleasure Hannah, mind you..." nodding at Max, "...you might want to take extra care round Miss Naomi, reckon she has the hots for you my friend."

"Naomi? The hots for me, don't be daft, she's only here for another few days and I can't think I'm her type."

"Oh, by 'type' you mean male and breathing?" Laughed Rafi. "Don't say I didn't warn you, she'll try to sink her claws in and if she does, she won't let go."

Although half jesting - Rafi could see how Max was looking at me - I couldn't help feeling a chill at his warning. So Rafi had noticed it too, it wasn't just my imagination, would she try something? Would Max be able to resist her? She was so incredibly beautiful. All my worries flooded back with a vengeance and I felt my shoulders droop. Then Max looked at me and smiled and I pushed them to the back of my mind, that smile. I kissed him, just because I could.

"Get your brekky, Han, it'll be getting cold, I'll wait and walk up with you, I told them I'd wait to make sure you were ok after last night's headache and Nate mentioned you'd had a funny turn just before coffee yesterday morning, so nobody thought anything of it."

"Oh that, it was just a head rush…not enough coffee in my system." Given our conversation of the night before, Max looked at me questioningly, but I just shook my head. "Nothing to worry about."

I polished off Rafi's offering with gusto, grabbing an extra slice of bread to mop of the egg yolk and, after pouring another cup of tea, felt ready to face the world.

"Not sure how good I'm going to be at keeping this hidden Max." I said, after I'd swallowed my last mouthful of tea. "Did you see my face when you walked in? Totally obvious to anyone watching us, or me at least, I'm rubbish at this. I still don't want anyone to know, but every time I see you all I want to do is ravish you. See what you've done to me, in the space of one night, I've gone from friend to floozy."

"Hmmm…floozy sounds ok with me." He drawled, draping his arm over the back of my chair and leering at me most unattractively. Spluttering with laughter, I pushed him back.

"Idiot."

"Well, you started it, telling me you want to ravish me, what's a guy supposed to do - turn you down?" I sighed.

"Why has it taken me so long to realise how I felt? We've wasted so much time."

"We'll make it up - promise. We're wasting even more time now gabbing about this, when both of us should be up on site. We'll have to take the cable car, it'll be too hot to walk up now."

"No, I think we'll be ok, most of the ramp will be in shadow a little longer."

"I was thinking if we took the cable car, I could have you to myself a little longer."

"Well...I could be persuaded...." letting the words hang. I was, most effectively, persuaded to take the cable car.

"C'mon then." I got up. "Lets do this, or we might as well not bother." A lascivious glint re-appeared in Max's eyes as I hauled him up out of his chair.

"Stop, seriously," laughing helplessly now, "we have to go." I took my plate over to the hatch, thanking Rafi, who grinned knowingly at me and nodded at Max.

"See you two later then."

"Count on it." I smiled back.

We walked out of the room, arms around each other secure that no one else was about, it was utter bliss and for the first time I didn't care about the dig, or my research, or the brooch, or anything. I wanted the world to stop just so that I could savour this feeling, a little longer. At my door, Max hugged me close, kissed the tip of my nose and released me.

"Go on, meet you at the main door in ten minutes, don't forget your water."

Reluctantly, I let him go, watching him as he walked down the hall, aware of my gaze, he gave a silly little wiggle as he arrived at his door, making me laugh. Turning, he winked and went in, shutting the door behind him.

The place was quiet as the grave, I couldn't even hear Rafi in the kitchen, the cleaning guys hadn't started yet and everything was utterly still. I went into my room and looked round, grabbing up things I needed for the day, making sure my water bottle was full and that I had biscuits. Using the bathroom, I took a minute to have a long hard look at myself in the mirror. Did I seem different? I couldn't tell, hopefully not. Shrugging, I tied my hair up into a ponytail, found my sun hat and a long sleeved, lightweight linen shirt…it didn't bode well if you walked around without some protection from the sun, even if you weren't out in it much. Then collected my backpack and, at the last minute dropped my brooch in its pouch into the back pocket of my jeans, locking the door behind me as I left the room.

Max was waiting for me at the door holding a bread roll stuffed with cold meat and salad.

"Remember to eat to day…you don't want another headache!"

"Oi…I didn't invent my headache, that was all you." We chattered as we walked along the path, glancing up, we noticed that the ramp was still shadowy; it was still early enough to risk climbing that route.

"I think we should go straight up honey." I motioned, "We're late enough, the guys'll be wondering what's up."

"Ok, ok" Max grinned, "I'm not one to knock enthusiasm when I see it - oh and now I'm your 'honey'?" I shoved him in the shoulder.

"Oh, well if you don't like it…." I winked and pretended to flounce off. Catching my arm, he pulled me back to him and with a quick kiss, attempted one last pull towards the cable car. Then, as I kept aiming for the ramp, finally gave up and we started the trek up. Despite his insistence on going up in air conditioned comfort, I recognised the signs, he was as excited as I was to get back up to the top of the citadel and, once clear of the digs, he started to hurry.

We made our way up the ramp, panting a little with exertion as we got there, going our separate ways as we came through the gate.

"Just watch her claws." I muttered as he squeezed my hand, both of us conscious that we were no longer alone.

"What?" Questioning.

"Her claws, Naomi's claws, watch them."

"Haha, don't you worry sweetheart, I'm taken, have been for a long time." Raising his hand he strolled off in the direction of the mosaic room.

I turned the other way, retracing my steps to the room Nate and I had been working in the day before. Entering the shelter of the building, I wondered why I hadn't registered this the day before; this was the room from my dream. Was that why I'd felt so odd yesterday lunch time? It had just taking my head longer to catch up with my eyes. It was the room the three soldiers had been in. Nate looked up as I walked in.

"You ok Hannah?" Concern edged his question.

"I'm fine thanks Nate, probably just not enough to eat yesterday, I slept it off." Feeling like a fraud for lying to him, he accepted my explanation, noting that he'd been a bit worried about me yesterday when I'd turned faint.

"You need to make sure you eat and drink enough you know."

"You're a fine one to dish out advice Nathaniel Robinson, you're just as bad." I grinned at him. "I'm ok, I've got a roll in case I get hungry and I've brought biccies again too!"

"Good on ya! Now let's get on." He waved me down to the pile of pots and that familiar lump of clay we'd worked on yesterday.

He'd made real headway in the hour before I'd arrived and several of the pots were now clear of the dust and dirt, which had anchored them to the floor. There looked to be at least a couple of dozen and more pieces could be seen jutting out of the ground, hidden until now by the layer we had just lifted. It was clear that there were jars of all different sizes. Smaller jars or pots could mean that what ever was in them was infrequently used, or needed, or was rare or costly, larger ones more likely held wine and oils, or fresh water.

The staining on the inside of many of them might help us identify some of what was stored. If something like garum was fermented by the Romans during their occupation of the site - the fish sauce which was apparently a favourite - it would not surprise me if we could still smell its extremely pungent odour on the inside of anything it was stored in. One of my lecturers had had a go at making some while I was at Uni and I can safely say it was one of the most disgusting smells ever, still makes me shudder when I think about it...ugh.

Nate had photographed and sketched in situ everything he had removed, so I quickly logged them into the record and we moved to the lump. Dissecting this would take a steady and very experienced hand, so I just clicked, recorded and drew, as Nate continued where we'd left off, slowly prying the bundle apart. Fragile pieces wound in a ball began to emerge from the built up dirt, eventually, it would need specialist attention, but they were obviously pieces of material, looked like a fine hessian or maybe linen to me.

Unwilling to use any thing like water to rinse the dirt away for fear it might damage what was left, it was a case of lifting and brushing, lifting and brushing, until the years of dust were removed and a piece could be levered free. The first segment that we were able to separate took over an hour, but as it finally came

78

away we whooped and as soon as we had laid it in one of the conservation boxes we high five'd each other. The relief was tremendous, no damage, and it was quite a substantial piece, stained with either years of dirt or something else yet to be determined. Geoff would be the best person to inspect it and Nate wanted to bring him in now, so we might get a better idea of what we were dealing with.

Standing up, slowly and stretching our cramped muscles after being hunched over for at least two hours was very painful and I felt my back twinge where the rocks had bruised me. That was going to be a pretty sight I thought to myself, might need to make sure I haven't scuffed the skin too. Good job I wasn't on a beach in a bikini, questions might be asked. Nate covered everything back up again, securing the sheet and we made our way across the plateau to join the others for coffee. The rest of the group was gathering in dribs and drabs, Geoff was following us over, so Nate dropped back and they chatted in undertones 'til we arrived at the spot we had adopted for our breaks. As I handed him his coffee Nate thanked me and nodded and I realised he had told Geoff what he wanted advice on and that Geoff in turn had agreed to come back with us afterwards to check it out.

As I passed out the biscuits, I suddenly felt rather shaky and, misconstruing this as hunger I helped myself to a couple, as well as one of the tiny lady-finger bananas someone else had brought up, washing them down with the hot sweet coffee. Waiting for the trembling to subside, I sensed, rather than saw, Max strolling over with Naomi and a couple of the others and realised it was anticipation I was feeling not hunger. Face shadowed under my ridiculously wide brimmed hat, I was able to watch them come towards us, without anyone else seeing my expression, drinking in his easy loping stride and animated countenance. I felt my heart beat rise and as they reached us, Max ran his eyes around the group, seeking mine out, as imperceptibly, except to me, he dipped his head. My heart settled and I closed my eyes, resting my head on the cool rock behind me.

"How's your head Hannah?" Naomi's bell like tones cut across the chatter as she sat down not far from me and, to my over sensitive imagination, seemed to cause everyone else to shut up while they waited for my answer. This was far from true, of course, most didn't even hear her, much less care, but there seemed to be an air of expectancy, as if my response was far more important than the question warranted.

"I am so bad at this, so so bad." I thought, taking a deep breath.

"Much better thanks Naomi, a good night's sleep seems to have sorted it out. I forgot to eat lunch yesterday so I think it was probably because of that and maybe I was a bit dehydrated." My voice sounded quite normal and friendly; those close enough to hear (and care) nodded accepting my explanation and turned back to their conversations.

Naomi held my gaze for a few more seconds, then,

"Nate did say he thought that's probably what had caused it, but Max seemed worried enough to wait for you." Was I being fanciful or had her voice taken on a cool edge?

"Max was just looking out for me, plus I'm the one with the packets of biccies, he'd want to make sure I remembered to bring them up." I tried for levity and think I convinced her, although why I felt I had to was a whole other issue. She nodded and struck up a conversation with Tom, who happened to be sitting next to her.

Tom was a third year archaeology student from Durham, on exchange at Ben Gurion University and, like most of the team, he was pretty laid back. In his late twenties he had come to his studies as a mature student and was loving every minute of his exchange programme. Clever with languages, Tom was teaching himself Hebrew and Arabic and was part of small team working in some of the rooms that had been discovered in the casemate wall, mostly used by the rebels prior to the last siege. Broken pieces of tablets covered with lettering had been found and his rudimentary knowledge was a real help in deciphering them. He was a great bloke, very gentle and unassuming and obviously smitten with Naomi, revelling in her attention. I was just happy she wasn't monopolising Max.

Unable to stop myself I let my eyes rove across the group, stopping as they reached my lover. Yes I'd decided to call him my lover - it sounded better than 'boyfriend' or 'my man' - even though he, technically, wasn't my lover, the title sat well with me, it warmed me and made my toes curl and sounded very grown up. Smiling to myself I let my thoughts wander relishing them, as, covertly I watched Max chatting to Geoff and Nate, thanking the stars I'd brought this behemoth of a hat, my expression totally hidden in its shade. Making sure didn't let my gaze linger, I shut my eyes again, just for a few minutes letting the noise of the chatter waft over me, inhaling the heady scent of coffee mixed with the slightly saltiness of the breeze coming up off the Dead Sea. I drifted off.

Chapter Ten

I was leaning against a tree trunk, glancing up, I could see the familiar leaves of the pomegranate, struggling to endure in this harsh landscape. Although very pretty, they are scrubby plants and it was only because I was small that I was able to stand upright under its canopy. The plateau was covered in gardens and vegetable patches delineated by paths wide enough for a cart to be pulled along. Were they the same garden beds I had noticed in my dream?

There was the sound of oxen to my left and as I turned I could see two walking along a bed of churned mud pulling what looked like a plough. Nearby a couple of baby goats skittered about, mewling calls catching the attention of their mother who was chewing on the stubbly grass a few feet from them. A large stone trough brimming with water, stood at one end of the planted areas. As far as I could work out the trough seemed to have a hole near the base, half way along allowing water to drain into narrow gullies, feeding the garden beds, although I had no idea how it was filled.

I looked down and saw that my clothing was unfamiliar. I was wearing a sort of tunic with holes for my head and arms, over the top of what felt like a thin under dress, with sleeves to my elbows. A belt made of twisted material cinched my waist. Running my hands across it, it felt like linen and, scouring my memory I knew that this was one of a higher quality than the coarser woollen garments usually worn by rural or less wealthy people. The under dress was soft grey and the tunic was pale pink in colour, my belt was in a darker shade. Sitting across my shoulders, I had a cream mantle with a fringed edge, clasped at my neck by a delicate pin, I felt that all these layers should make me hot, but I was quite comfortable. My feet were encased in soft sandals and I realised that my hair was a rich dark brown and quite curly, lying over my shoulder in a loose plait. Then I looked at my hands, noticing that my skin was darker too, more olive.

Confused I stood a moment longer trying to get my bearings, the Northern Palace was to my left, I was in front of the Western Palace, the Byzantine church wasn't there, wouldn't be there for several hundred years. The sun was high, the light breeze was blowing up little dusty willy willies and, over the high wall I could just see the sparkle of the Dead Sea off in the distance. The sounds of people going about their daily chores seemed normal, I almost forgot that I didn't belong here, what would happen if someone saw me.

"Hannah!" Startled I looked round, someone had seen me. "Hannah, quick we need you over here." I squinted in the direction from which the voice had come and saw a tall dark haired man approaching me from the Northern Palace. "Quickly!" The urgency in his voice compelled me to move and, without thought, I pushed myself off the tree and moved towards him, unconsciously lifting my tunic in case I tripped over its length.

"What's happened my brother?" Brother? I don't have a brother, I thought to myself, yet I knew his name was Aharon.

"The gravely injured one suffers, you wanted to save them, you need to help him, or we will have to finish him."

"No." Sharply. "You cannot do this, it would be murder. I have fought for them for this long, please let me keep trying." What on earth was I doing, I'm not a nurse and I usually throw up at the sight of blood. He nodded cursorily and, assuming that was a nod of agreement, I followed him into the cool of the palace, along a corridor and entered the room of my dreams.

It was quite large and spacious, something I hadn't noticed before, the floor was beautifully tiled and there were what looked to be rugs rolled up against one wall. Three men lay on makeshift cots, sort of wooden pallets, two of whom looked slightly less cadaverous than the one lying nearest the door. His skin was clammy and pale, his jaw clenched in agony. Shocked, I realised that these were the three men whom I'd seen when I stubbed my toe and, that the critically injured man was the one the other two had been leaning over. How long they had been here, I couldn't tell - they were all still alive, that was something - but it was obvious one of them was dying.

How could I help, I had no healing powers, no medicines, he needed surgery and clean sheets and intravenous antibiotics. Glancing round the room, I took in pitchers and bowls which looked like they might hold water, a sort of shelf with jars of ointments and herbs and, a large wooden cupboard like piece of furniture with doors, which, when I opened them held what seemed to be sheets, blankets and smaller cloths. On the top of this, stood more jars and an array of dowels and other strange instruments.

Not wanting to look to closely at them, I turned back to the other shelf. Ok, Hannah, get on with it. Finding a large bowl that held fresh water, I rinsed my hands, drying them on a towel I discovered was looped through my belt, I was prepared it seemed. Turning back to the sickest of the three, I felt his head with the back of my hand, he was burning up. I carefully peeled back the sheet and saw that his tunic was stained with blood and a yellowish substance I assumed was from an infection.

Holding his head in my hands I looked him straight in the eye,

"This will hurt." I said, not knowing what language he spoke, he seemed to get my gist and nodded slightly, gritting his teeth.

Gently, oh so gently, I lifted his tunic, thankful to note that his lower half was covered in another sheet. His worst injury was contained to his abdomen; a gaping wound which might well have been inflicted by something like an axe. It was oozing blood and pus and he must have been in absolute agony. He had other wounds but they seemed less devastating and some looked as though they might be healing.

"Oh God." I whispered. "Help me help him." Not one for praying, I needed all the help I could get and it felt like the most natural thing to do, he looked too young to be getting injured in battles. Reaching into the basket I ripped up one of the sheets, soaking pieces in a bowl of water to which I'd added some salt, and dabbing carefully at the wound, washed out as much of the blood and pus as I dared. I didn't want to start it bleeding gain, but the infection went deep and I knew it had to be cleaned properly. Moving to the shelf with all the jars, I removed the stopper from one of them - opium - it would dull the pain. How did I know it was in that jar? How did I know what opium smelled like? Was it even called opium? Dredging through my history, I recalled that it was called poppy tears, or poppy juice.

I mixed a small measure with some wine, poured from a flagon on the floor, in one of the little bowls. Going back to the man, I sat on the edge of the cot, lifted his head ever so slightly and held the bowl while he drank. He was familiar with my actions, I had done this before. Grunting with pain, he lay back on the lump of straw, covered with yet another sheet, that was acting as a pillow and slowly, very slowly, the pained expression started to relax. His face began to lose some of the waxiness I had noticed when I entered the room and his breathing steadied.

Going back to his wound I worked on it for a while longer, making sure that it was as clean as it could be, the edges were neat and not jagged, either from whatever inflicted the wound, or someone, possibly I, had cut it smooth. Without questioning my actions, I concocted another brew of herbs and oils, this time one that smelt rather pungent and, vaguely recalling that frankincense and myrrh were used widely for healing, I wondered if this is what I was mixing up. The result was a sort of salve that I pressed into and around the wound, leaving the swatch of cloth with the remaining salve covering the gash. Ripping up yet another sheet, I would need more, where would I find them? I fashioned a long bandage, wrapping it round his body holding the swatch in place over his injury.

It must have been excruciating for him, but he barely made a sound, hopefully the opium mixture had taken the edge of his agony. Checking his other wounds, cleaning them all, then re-dressing any that needed it, noticing that one or two appeared to have been stitched up. Had I done that too? Finally and with infinite care, I changed all the sheets on his cot, piling the dirty ones into a basket at the doorway, which seemed suited to the purpose. Filling a larger bowl with fresh water, I washed his face and hands, removing the dust and sweat, cooling his skin. Not sure that I was doing anything other than making him comfortable while he waited for the inevitable call of death, my gentle movements lulled him off to sleep.

The room was so quiet, the other two men simply watched me work and I realised I was in a rhythm, I knew what I was doing, whoever I was in this time, I was practised at healing. So I decided not to over think it, follow my instinct and continue what I had started. I turned to the other two, their injuries, while pretty gruesome, were nothing like as bad as their comrade's. More deep lacerations than critical wounds, but they still needed to be bathed and dressed. I repeated my actions with the wine and opium, the second man lay quietly, while I cleaned his injuries and washed his face, many of his less serious wounds were almost healed, how long had I been looking after them? When I had finished he was covered in little bandages but he seemed relaxed, the fresh bedding was cool and dry and he nodded off to sleep. By the time I was ready to treat the third soldier, I was hot and dusty and my clothes reeked of blood.

"One minute." I whispered to him and, leaving the room, I ran further down the corridor into the next room along, suddenly registering that this was the room where I had sat down in my dream and that it was as spacious and cool as the one next door. The walls were painted and a large rug warmed the tiles, a small oil lamp burned, shedding soft light across the space. A bedroll in one corner and on a wooden cupboard, next to a bowl and flask, lay a pile of neatly folded material that looked like clothes. Somehow I knew this was my sleeping quarters and, grabbing whatever garment was on the top of the pile, I changed more quickly than I thought possible, given that I had no clue how to dress myself in this fashion and hurried back.

"Sorry." I muttered. "You have enough problems, you don't need your wounds to get more infected by me dressing them wearing dirty garments." Starting to pour out some of the pain numbing draft, I was startled when he put his hand on my arm and I looked at him, properly, for the first time since I'd entered the room.

"Max." I gasped, yet it wasn't Max, but so much like him they could have been brothers. This man was harder, rougher, his hair longer and unkempt from being sick and in captivity. His skin, although very pale, was swarthy, but his eyes, his eyes were that same deep green and right now they held my gaze.

"You finally use my name?" He questioned quietly. How were we speaking the same language? I must have been speaking in Hebrew; if this were a Roman soldier he would likely have been speaking Greek or Latin. Pulling my arm out from under his grasp, I stared at him.

"Your name is Max?" Embarrassed, it seemed I should know this. I offered him the draft.

"Not Max really, Lucius Maxentius is my name, but that seems awkward for you, Maxentius is acceptable and I do not need this drink, my pain is not so bad as it was. Save it for them." Nodding at his comrades. His words were careful, stilted almost, as if searching for the right phrasing.

Not really knowing what else to say at this point, I busied myself mixing the saline solution and started to bathe his wounds. Like the second man he appeared less severely injured and luckily none of his wounds seemed to be infected, but he had massive bruising darkening his chest and back, which was rather a concern. Some of his wounds had begun healing and, again I wondered how long they had been in my care.

"You are lucky." I told him, "You will heal."

"How lucky? They will still kill me."

"Not if I can help it, I do not spend my days treating these wounds to have them kill you. Maybe they will use you to send a message to the Romans in Jerusalem, maybe they will allow you to go free." Not certain how much of this he understood, or how much I believed, I simply continued to clean and wrap his wounds and, as he was able to, got him to stand up, helping him over to the wall on which he leaned while I changed the sheets. Finished, I was about to help him back to bed when he motioned to the door.

"You want some fresh air?" Nodding, he slowly made his way out through the opening, stopping occasionally to catch his breath. I took his arm and although people were passing by, no one seemed to mind that I was helping this tall burly soldier, an enemy to our people, out onto the plateau. Well what could he do? One strong wind would blow him over, he was no threat and maybe we had done this before, maybe it was an everyday habit.

"Over there." He motioned to the pomegranate tree.

"You want to walk all the way over there?" It seemed too far for the injured soldier, he was still very weak.

"Yes, the shade is…" again searching "…nice." We walked very slowly over to the shade of the tree and I spotted an upturned urn, had I done that? Helping him to sit I made sure he could lean against the trunk.

"Are you comfortable?" He looked at me unsure of my words. "This…" pointing at him and the tree, "…this is good?"

'Yes, this is good." He smiled at me, the same slow smile Max has and, suddenly I warmed to this man, whom I should hate for what his country was doing to my country, but he was just one man and he did not appear to be a danger to me. We sat for a while in companionable silence, enjoying the air and the sounds of everyday life. As we sat, I realised that these actions were familiar to me; I had been doing this for many days, maybe even weeks. I knew these men and their injuries, I knew a little about their lives and I knew, without a doubt that one of them would not survive. I also knew that this man and I must have conversed before, it seemed as if this had become a routine. I would help him out into the fresh air and we would talk.

"Thank you Hannah." He said quietly. "Thank you for your kindness and your patience, you are a gifted healer. But how is it that you, a woman is allowed to do this? This is a man's calling."

"I used to watch my uncle, he was a great physician and I asked him to teach me his skills. He was a kind man and thought he was humouring me, but I learned quickly and soon wanted more than he could teach me. He knew it should not be, but I was good at persuading him. I used to dress like a boy and help in his rooms when he operated on sick people. I learned that fresh air is better than closed rooms; that everything needs to be clean and never to touch a wound unless you have washed your hands. Then we fled the city and my brother said we needed to come here, that there were others already making their way to this outpost because they wanted your weapons. Even though I did not want to get caught up in a war, I didn't have much choice, Aharon refused to leave me to fend for myself back in Jerusalem. Then it seemed I was the only one who had the skills to treat wounds and sickness, so they had to let me be the healer. It gives me a little status and I am allowed more freedom than many women. That's how…" I dried up, again unsure how much he understood.

"I understand Hannah and I am grateful to you. Do you know why they decided to let us live when they found us in that room?"

"That was me." Blushing a little. "You were all so ill, it was three days before we found you and how you all, especially your gravely ill comrade, had survived that long I do not know. After the ambush, the rest of your men were dead, or had fled, you three were the only survivors. I asked Aharon if I could try and heal you, I could not let them kill you too, it was not acceptable so many days after the battle. It could not be called a battle death, it would be murder. This I could not condone. They let you live, although…" hesitating, but needing to share my fears, "…I am afraid your comrade is gravely ill and may not last many more days. He needs better medicine than I can offer."

I spoke slowly and deliberately, hoping he understood most of my words. Looking around, making sure no one was close, he tentatively touched my hand,

"You could not have done more, if he dies it will be with honour and he will be among friends."

I knew I should pull my hand away, but I didn't want to. In this place, I was a Jewish girl talking to a Roman soldier, he could be killed for touching me and I should know better than to touch the skin of an enemy, but I liked the feel of his hand and I was still unsure how long I had been treating him - maybe he had done this before. Yet I knew that it couldn't be real, I was from another place, centuries after this time, I was sitting with my back against a rock drinking a cup of coffee.

"Your comrades, Marcus and Sergius is it not?" Stumbling a little over the unusual sounds. "How long have you known them?"

"We did not know each other until we were in this regiment, but we became strong friends, they have been loyal and hardworking, not shirkers like some of the scoundrels I have had charge of. I know many fled the rock, leaving their comrades to die, but their cowardice will find them and, what need do I have of them now? Marcus and I have been on this outpost for several years, Sergius joined us quite recently and he is still very young, hopefully his youth and strength will work in his favour. He became a trusted friend." He paused and took a breath, before continuing:

"We were to return to Rome as the year closes. I never thought this would…that this could…happen, that we would lose this rock, it was thought it to be impenetrable and we should have been safe. Sergius saved my life, I was being attacked by several men and losing ground, he took them all down, I don't know whether he killed them but before we could get the upper hand he was badly injured. Marcus and I dragged him away and we ended up in the room you now find us in, ironic really." Half smiling. "I still don't know how they got up here without us seeing them."

"They are a desperate people sir and desperate people will go to any lengths to get back what they feel is theirs. Also, they knew you had weapons, they need those weapons for the fight they are sure will come."

"Still 'sir'? When will you call me Maxentius," I looked at him. "You already call the others by their names why not me?"

Feeling that this informality was overstepping the boundaries of propriety, I hesitated.

"You are their commanding officer, it is not right that I should address you so casually."

"Please Hannah, I would be honoured if you would and, you called me 'Max' earlier, I haven't been called that since I was a child."

Looking back at him, I felt my qualms melt away.

"I will do as you ask." Still formal, yet we seemed to be almost comfortable, him sitting on an upturned jar and me leaning against the trunk of the pomegranate tree, shaded from the sun, which was beginning its downward journey. I had spent longer dealing with the three men than I had realised and the day was waning. Surely there were other tasks I should be doing.

"Will you be comfortable here for a little while, or do you wish to return to your room?"

"I am fine, the air is nice, where are you going?"

"I must put those sheets which can be cleaned into water to soak away the dirt and sickness and burn the rest. The wrappings I removed will also need to be washed, or I will have none to dress the wounds tomorrow. I will only be a moment."

As I walked away I was sure I heard him whisper,

"Hurry back my Hannah."

Odd, it made me feel warm inside, a warmth I was unfamiliar with. Confusion was running through my head, how could this be? Not wanting to deal with it, I hurried into the sick room, where the other two men were sleeping almost peacefully. Sergius' face was red, and touching him gently, I realised his fever was spiking again; his skin was dry and hot. Quickly soaking a rag in cool water I laid it across his forehead, leaving it for a moment, while I gathered the other sheets and bandages together and without knowing how I knew, took them across a courtyard, to a room at the opposite side.

It looked like a laundry room, there were large stone sinks, massive jars full of water, a huge wooden cupboard, which when I opened the doors found full of sheets, blankets, cloths and towels. A large fireplace built into one wall was laid ready and wooden racks, on which I could drape things, were stacked alongside, it was well set up. Trying to orientate myself, I realised that I was in the administrative building at the top of the Northern Palace, huge storerooms ran off to my left and somewhere among all the other offices and rooms surrounding this courtyard, there would be a kitchen.

Filling one of the stone sinks with water I shoved everything in it. Did we have anything like soap, or something to sterilise the material. I needed it to be clean and then I remembered smelling something lemony in one of the jars in the sick room. Dashing back, I found what I was looking for and opening other jars I found a liquid that appeared to be vinegar. Pouring them together into a smaller flask, I went back across the courtyard and tipped the whole lot into the sink containing the sheets and pounded the water till it was all mixed in, crossing my fingers that it would do the trick.

I recalled from the depth of my brain that something called *quali* was used like soap. A grey mix created by burning vegetable matter and adding water 'til it formed lumps but, as I had absolutely no idea how to do that, my option would have to do. I would leave it overnight and let them soak. Tomorrow I would work out how to hang them outside to let the sun's heat kill any bacteria lurking in the material. If not, these drying racks would do the trick.

Happy that I had done all I could with the sheets and bandages, I went back to the sick room and changed the cloth on

Sergius' head, he was burning up, I needed to stay with him. Brewing up another batch of opium and wine, I let it sit, while I went back outside to find Maxentius. He was standing now his hand against the tree, it was at high point on the plateau and from here you could just see over the casemate wall across the desert towards the Dead Sea.

"Its a beautiful view isn't it?" I came up behind him, startling him out of his reverie. "Desolate but very beautiful." He turned.

"Yes it is very beautiful." I had the oddest notion he wasn't talking about the view.

"I must get you back, Sergius' fever is rising, I need to sit near him and keep him cool." Letting Maxentius lean on me, we slowly made out way back to his room. "I don't think you should sleep here." I worried. "You could become more sick. You are healing well and infection can be spread though the breath." Suiting my words to actions, I lifted his pallet, which was quite light and, carried it down the hall to my quarters, setting it near enough to the door for him to hear me call, but away from prying eyes. Picking up my bedroll, I went back along the hall.

"You can sleep in my room, I need to be in here. I will not move Marcus as he sleeps soundly, it will be worse if I rouse him, but my room is quiet and you can rest undisturbed."

"Hannah, I can't expect you to leave your room, I will watch Sergius and call you if he gets worse."

"Too late, I've moved your bed and how would you know what to give him? Go, I will come if he asks for you." I helped him along to my room, he was very tired now, the exertion was telling and he needed to sleep. Settling him on to his cot, I covered him with a fresh clean sheet and found a blanket in case he got cold. Then back in the sick room, I mixed a draft of refreshing lemon, honey and water, with a drop or two of opium, he was going to have a proper sleep if I had to trick him into it.

94

Back in my room, he was already drowsy.

"Drink this, it is cool and sweet and there is honey which is good for healing." He drank deeply and settled back. As I moved to the door he caught my fingers.

"You will get me won't you?"

"If there is time or need, I will get you."

'Thank you my Hannah." Eyes drooping I watched as the opium worked its magic and sleep took him.

Chapter Eleven

Back in the sick room Sergius was not doing so well. He was muttering in his unconscious state, his skin was still burning up, but was becoming clammy as the fever took a tighter grip. I let my instinct take over again and ground more herbs and oils together with wine to see if I could get him to drink it down. Tenderly lifting his head I crooned a lullaby as I tried to get the liquid through his parched lips. I was losing him, but I wasn't going to let him go without a fight. I managed to get most of the mixture down his throat; he began to settle, his temperature dropping a little. Finding another sheet I soaked the whole thing in water, removed the dry sheet covering him and, wringing most of the water out, draped the cold wet sheet across the whole of his body.

I needed ice and knew there was no way that was available. Looking round I wondered if I could use small stones or pebbles dipped in cold water, would they stay cool long enough to have some effect. Without stopping to think, I ran back out into the open air, looking around for anything that would be suitable. To my left lay a few small rocks, would there be enough? I gathered them into my arms, using my mantle as a kind of bag as they were heavier than I anticipated - they might work.

Back in the room, I found a large bowl and placed the rocks into it, covering them with plenty of water, which was cold enough for me to think it must have been freshly drawn from the cisterns. Someone must be helping me, I had seen no one else enter this room, but all the water jars had been filled and the oil lamp trimmed. Grateful to whoever it was, I continued with what I was doing, making sure the rocks were clean, emptying the dirty water out, I rinsed the bowl and refilled it with clean water, putting the rocks back in, realising that they were cooler, much cooler, to my touch.

Glancing up at Sergius, his teeth were beginning to chatter; now he was cold. Whipping the wet sheet off, I dragged a warm blanket from the shelf, wrapping him in it making sure his hands and feet were covered. Wiping his face with a clean damp cloth, brushing his lank hair out of his eyes I had done all I could for now. Checking that the stones were indeed cooling, I stepped back outside for just a moment. Drinking in the fresh air, I stood looking across the top of the mighty rock thinking of all that had gone before and all that would come. This place should stand for ever, Herod's great citadel, for surely nothing could destroy it, surprised that I knew that it actually would be and in the not too distant future. My present and future self struggled with this knowledge, as I watched the sun sink slowly towards the horizon. Too soon it would be gone and night would cover the land, hiding the tragedies I knew would come.

Walking back to where I'd left them, I checked my two patients, Marcus was resting quite comfortably, although his colour was higher than I would have liked, his skin was cool and his chest rose and fell steadily. He would heal this soldier, his spirit was robust and he would be able to fight any infection that may lurk deep within his body. I touched his wrist checking his pulse; it was very strong and rhythmic, what I would give for my watch so I could be sure. I stood still and counted guessing that his heart rate was within an acceptable range.

His comrade on the other hand was hot again, this fever was going through him too quickly, it would reach crisis this night. Did I wake Maxentius, so he could sit with his friend, or let him sleep? Lifting the rocks out of the water, I laid them along Sergius' body, making sure they touched his skin. I removed the blanket and let the night air waft over him, a small opening high in the wall, reminiscent of the slit windows in medieval castles, allowed enough air to enter the room without cooling it too much. I had no idea whether it was part of the original building or was made later, after the Roman garrison took over and right then I didn't care, it was a very welcome draft and helped to cool both my patient and me.

In the throes of delirium, Sergius was wracked with seizures causing his wound to bleed again. I felt overwhelmed; whatever I did I wasn't able to help him. Had I been a fool to try and save him in the first place? Should I have let Aharon and the others kill him when they were first found? Would that have been the kindest thing to do? Had I just prolonged his agony for him to die anyway? Defeated, I slumped to the floor, feeling useless tears run down my cheeks. This is not helping Hannah, I pulled myself together, scrubbing my face on my sleeve, then wiped Sergius' face with a fresh cloth, dropping the warm ones back into the bowl of cool water.

Checking his body where the stones rested, I felt that he was cooling down again, his bout of delirium passed and his breathing settled. His skin seemed to regulate, not too hot, not too cold, but I knew it would not stay this way for long. Taking this opportunity to mix another draft, I decided to try and rub some honey onto his poor sore lips hoping it would soothe them. Gently, I smoothed a small drop onto each lip, making sure it covered the chapped edges. Carefully unwrapping his bandages, I lifted the swatch of material with the salve and noticed that the infection was oozing again. Tearing a small piece off the bandages I had just removed, making sure I used the clean end, I dipped the piece into the remaining salve and while that soaked in, I tore up the rest of the bandage to clean the wound again. Managing to wipe away excess blood and pus without disturbing Sergius, I placed the newly soaked swatch over the injury and tore another sheet up to bandage it in place. I would have to go and get more sheets; I was going through this pile like there was no tomorrow.

Job done for now, I sat on the floor, my back against the wall, just watching for any changes. Marcus slept peacefully on, blissfully unaware and I thanked God for it. I must have slept too for a little while, exhaustion creeping up on me unawares. When I awoke it was completely dark outside and I had no idea of the time. Confused at my surroundings, I stayed where I was, struggling to get my bearings. Then it flooded back, I was not in my bed in the digs, I was in a sick room, hoping a man in my care didn't die.

After a few minutes I walked quietly to the other room to check on Maxentius. He was still fast asleep, looking so vulnerable in repose that I had to curb an unexpected desire to kiss his forehead and smooth his cheek. It was not acceptable behaviour in this time. I was not a twenty first century woman with freedom of choice and expression - here ancient laws and rules bound me. Sighing, I went back along the corridor, but before re-entering the sick room, ran quickly over to the laundry room and, intuitively searching the large store cupboard, found a stack of fresh bandages. Collecting them and another pile of sheets, I hauled them back across the courtyard. It was dark, but the moon had risen, giving enough light so that I didn't trip.

In the few minutes I had been gone, someone had placed a bowl of food and bread in the room, with a flagon of wine. I hadn't even realised I was hungry until I saw it and devoured it gratefully. Sipping straight from the flagon, too tired to find a more suitable drinking cup, I thought about this day, this day that had started with the joy of knowing Max loved me and finishing with me trying to keep a dying man alive. As I sat, I realised that although my day did sound completely preposterous, and nobody, in either era, would ever believe me, I wasn't totally freaked out. I was beginning to take this in my stride, but just as I accepted it, I was chilled by the thought that I might never see Max again. How was I here, how was I able to think in two time periods, yet not able to see any of my friends.

A bubble of panic started to build and just as I was about to have a full-blown anxiety attack, Sergius moaned, breaking through the hysteria threatening to swamp me. Getting up, I moved to his bedside, watching his features contort in pain and the inevitable seizures start shuddering through his skeletal frame. I knew the crisis was close and I knew I needed to let Maxentius decide whether he wanted to be with him, but I also wanted to let him sleep as long as possible. The fever intensified, throwing him back into delirium, convulsions wracked his body and I knew I just had to let it run its course. It was severe and I was helpless. Giving up, I went to wake Maxentius. Shaking him gently, he came awake immediately; despite the sleeping draft I'd given him less than three hours ago. He grabbed my hand and started to rise.

"Shhhhhh, its just me, Sergius needs you, he is very sick, the crisis is on him."

He used the blanket as a wrap and was in the other room more quickly than his wounds should have allowed. I followed, standing at the door leaving them space. Sergius was unaware of Maxentius' presence; he was probably unaware of anything, descending deeper in unconsciousness, his body desperately fighting for survival, the infection winning the battle. He tossed and muttered in his delirium, spasms running through him like a freight train and his skin was on fire.

I was really scared, I had never seen anyone die and this man was in my care. I couldn't stand back and do nothing. Cooling his forehead again I got Maxentius to do the same to his hands with wet cloths. I lifted the sheet soaking in the bowl and without waiting to wring it out, laid it over his body, water dripping all over the floor. Maxentius held Sergius' hand talking to him all the while, talking to him about things they had done places they'd seen and battles they had fought together.

Sitting myself by my patient's head, I smoothed his hair crooning the same lullaby I had sung to him earlier, trying to reach something inside him that could hear and respond. Maxentius watched me while he was talking, listening to my voice calling to his friend. The crisis was taking him and all we could do was watch, I felt utterly powerless and the expression on the face of the man sitting alongside threatened to undo me completely. I needed to be strong for him as a feeling of foreboding was creeping up on me. I knew Sergius would die tonight, the fever was too strong and the subtle changes I knew would indicate that I was losing him were beginning to manifest.

I studied his features for what felt like a very long time singing quietly, hoping against hope that I was mistaken. Eventually, breaking off my lullaby, I looked across the bed.

"Maxentius." I whispered, "I don't think I can save him, I think he's slipping away, I think you need to let him go."

"No." Voice cracking. "I can't, he saved my life."

"You have to tell him its time to leave, that he's saved you and that you and Marcus are safe. I think he's fighting it because he fears for you."

"He's my friend." Helplessly.

"Yes, I know and I hate this too, but I can't save him, I can't save him." Sobbing uncontrollably now. "You have to let him go."

Maxentius looked at me reading in my face what he didn't want to believe. Turning back to Sergius, he spoke in undertones telling his friend how the battle was over, that they were all safe and that it was ok to leave. His voice was breaking, but he fought to keep it steady and strong. He talked and talked, it seemed to me that he talked for hours and, all the while I stroked his friend's face, soothing his fiery skin with my cool hands.

I removed the bandages that were restricting his movement and let the air touch his broken skin, what did it matter now, dropping the pieces onto the floor next to me, I told myself I would deal with them later, my patient was more important than some bloodied bits of cloth. After what, to my weary mind, felt like a very long time Sergius began to calm down, his seizures slowed and he stopped muttering. Slowly, oh so slowly, but surely his body stilled and cooled and all became quiet. Controlling my features, I moved down the side of the bed and held Sergius' wrist. His heart rate was dropping and I knew he was leaving us. I nodded to Maxentius,

"Time to say goodbye." His face broke my heart.

"Goodbye Sergius, honoured comrade and faithful friend, you will be missed."

The beat against my fingers faltered, slowed and stopped. It was very peaceful at the end; Sergius slipped quietly away. I checked his heart just to be absolutely sure, but he was gone. No longer wracked with pain he had gone to whichever heaven he believed in. Unable to vent my distress and anger, I balled up the bandages lying next to me on the floor, uncaring that I was getting blood and puss on my hands, I pummelled the cloth, twisting the pieces together trying to rip them into shreds. They stubbornly refused to tear and in my frustration I hurled the lump towards the cabinet, hearing a light thud as they landed against the wooden frame. It didn't help.

Maxentius' head drooped, his devastation was palpable and I couldn't bear to watch. Touching his shoulder, I started to walk out of the room leaving him to his grief. Grasping my hand, he stopped me and slowly stood up. Turning me to face him, he started to speak, gave up and kissed me hard on the mouth - my heart missed a beat. Ok, that was an unexpected, interesting response to grief and my body had responded in a way I also did not expect. Without thinking, I leaned into him, kissing him back, then pulling free, fled out of the room, along the corridor, out into the fresh air and let out a primal scream.

"Noooooooooooooooooooooo." Bending over and keening, the stress of the last few hours took over as, exhausted, I dropped to the floor. The world started to spin and as if from great distance I saw Maxentius come out onto the plateau, he reached his hand out and called my name,

"Hannah, Hannah, Hannah!"

"Hannah, come on wake up, you need to wake up."

...and I was back...

Chapter Twelve

Slowly, things swam into focus; I was lying on the ground in the shade looking up at six concerned faces. I giggled slightly hysterically; they looked very peculiar from this angle.

"Hannah, come on, what's going on, you fainted and we couldn't get you to come round." Max was looking at me fear darkening his eyes.

"Humph, gnerf, what…no…silly no faint, dead, lost."

"What are you muttering about, nobody's dead, or lost. C'mon Han, come back to m…us." Max's slip jolted me back, I tried to sit up, the world tilted and I moaned groggily.

"Sorry guys, I didn't mean to scare you." Finally getting into a sitting position, I waited until everything stopped spinning and looked around the group.

"What happened? Why am I lying down?"

"You fainted, well we think you fainted, we heard your coffee cup hit the ground and as we turned round you, very elegantly, slid off the rock you were resting on. We couldn't wake you up, then you started crying out and you sounded absolutely devastated."

"I can't remember, I have no idea what happened, but please get me up, I have get back to helping Nate." My words seem to come from a distance, stilted, disjointed and I was having trouble making my mouth form them, was I even making any sense?

"Not so fast young lady - go on you lot - I'll stay with her and either take her back to the digs, or walk her over to the room Nate's in when she's stopped being all woozy." Max flapped his hands at the other five, whose faces still reflected their concern.

"If you're sure?"

"Happy to stay."

"Maybe a rest would be better than work."

"I'll go with you if you need to walk her back, she might faint again." All speaking at once, their words lifted me, nice to know they cared. I smiled, albeit rather weakly, truth be told, thanking them as, reluctantly, they turned to go back to what they had been doing, before my antics so rudely interrupted them.

"Now madam, what was all that about? That wasn't just a cry - you were wailing just before we managed to wake you up - like you'd lost the whole world, inconsolable. What on earth happened? I was really worried there for a minute, we could not get you to come round." Warmed by his obvious anxiety, I rested my head against Max's chest and his arm snaked around my shoulder pulling me close. Suddenly I didn't care who knew about us, I needed him, this was way beyond anything I could explain and I was more than a little unnerved.

"I was just sitting here drinking coffee, my eyes were closed, I was day dreaming about last night and it was so lovely. The next thing, I'm back sometime in the first century AD, looking after three soldiers who had been injured when the rebels overran Masada. They were the three I saw in my dream, including the one that looks like you." I told him everything including that my wailing was because of losing Sergius. I started crying again, it was too close and to me it had only just happened.

"To you all here I have only been out of it for a few minutes, but in my mind I have been working non-stop for nearly twelve hours trying to save someone's life and I failed, he died..." my voice cracked and broke. "...I was so frightened that I would never see you again, that everything that happened last night was lost and that I was trapped forever here on this rock, but two thousand years in the past." Trying to master my sobs and get a grip, I hate weeping women; I straightened my shoulders and moved to stand up. Max held me tight.

"Just sit a minute longer, sunshine, its ok, you're safe with me." Giving up, I relaxed back into him, nestling my head under his chin, waiting for my sobs to subside. We just sat holding each other close, I breathed in his scent, feeling my horror start to dissipate. The world came back into focus; there were no oxen ploughing, no baby goats jumping around, no upturned urns under the pomegranate tree. Slowly, my heart rate settled and my head cleared.

"What do I do now? What if it happens again? I can't seem to control it." Panic gripped me, I broke out in a cold sweat. "Oh God Max, I can't lose you now, its taken so long for us to get here and I don't want to be stuck back there, besides…" aiming for levity, "…there are no decent shoe shops…" Max tightened his arms around me and kissed the top of my head. I looked up at him and before I could say anymore, he kissed me full on my lips, gently, deeply and as the now familiar spark of passion flared into life, I responded in kind.

Desire rippled through me and all the emotions from the last few hours, of my recollection anyway, spun and melded, absorbed into my need to make this man burn with the same fire that was consuming me. I felt Max shudder, his ardour rising to meet mine. The next few minutes were lost as we simply revelled in each other. Finally, Max drew away; we were both trembling from the strength of our feelings for each other.

"I love you Max, I love you, please don't ever let me go."

"I'm not going anywhere sweetheart, I love you too and it took you long enough to say so."

"What, no - I told you last night."

"No what you said was, 'how did I know you were going to fall in love with me,' not quite the same."

Ok wise guy, that's just semantics. I love you, I love you, I love you, that do?"

"For starters…you're a work in progress." Starting to laugh, I realised that he was distracting me from what had happened and I was grateful. I did not want to think about it anymore, it was too distressing. My life was here in the twenty first century, with Max and the rest of this motley crew. The other was just a dream, a terrible dream. We stood together for a minute looking out over the desert, then turned and walked towards our respective work areas.

"Are you sure you want to go back to work Hannah? I can walk you back to our accommodation if you like."

"Its ok, Max, honestly, I think I need to do something normal, if I go back to my room I'll just dwell on it."

"Sure?"

"I'm sure hon. Thank you." Smiling I gripped his hand and let go, he kissed me one more time and turned to walk over to the corner of the rock he was working on. Half way across he turned back and smiled that slow sweet smile. I grinned blew him a kiss and went over to find Nate.

Feeling much more human, I was smiling as I entered the room Nate and I had been working in.

"So sorry, Nate, I don't know what happened."

"Sure you're ok to work?

"Totally, lets do it, what did Geoff say?"

"He reckons that this was used as some kind of treatment space, maybe soldiers or rebels came here and were dispensed herbs and stuff, like a kind of pharmacy. Its close enough to the kitchens and laundry rooms, it would make sense, the cloth we are finding could just be pieces that were discarded or too dirty to wash clean and reuse."

Glancing at Nate, I wondered if I dared tell him, I knew exactly what this room was used for and the one next to it. I could describe it to him in great detail but I held back. He would laugh at me, he was a scientist and he would think I was going crazy. But, a small voice inside my head nudged, he does trust you, try him. No, not just yet, it was too raw and I could not bear it if he didn't take me seriously. Maybe one day, but not yet.

"Sounds feasible." I agreed. "What does he want us to do with the pieces?"

"Asked me to leave the rest of this large lump for him to work on back at the conservation room and continue to work here in case we can find any more."

"Cool, c'mon then, let's see how far we can get by the end of today."

We focused our attention on the area around where Nate had found the lump of what I now knew to be bandages. We found more bowls and a few of the smaller ones seemed to be intact, we would know better when we cleaned the dirt off them. Our finds trays were filling up. At one point Geoff stuck his head in, asked how I was feeling - how many people knew I'd chucked a wobbly? - and then checked with Nate to see how we are going.

"We'll have to take these down by the cable car Geoff, too many to try and carry down the ramp." Pointing to the rapidly growing pile of trays.

"Give me a yell when you're about to leave, I'll bring the barrow over and we can stack them in that, make it so much easier than having to make several trips over the plateau."

"Cheers mate, ok, that sounds like the best plan." Nate nodded and Geoff went back to his capitals, happy with how we were going. We worked steadily for another hour or so, until Nate said it was time for lunch.

"Not having you fainting again Hannah, what with yesterday and this headache you had last night and then this morning, I'm getting worried about you." Concern etching his features, I hadn't the heart to tell him that the 'headache' was pure fiction, but I had given them a shock this morning, fair enough and I hated being a bother.

"Sorry Nate." I said, hugging him. "Didn't mean to scare you. Max thinks it still just a bit of dehydration after yesterday...and yes, before you ask, I've got plenty of water left and had some more before I came back to the room."

We walked over to the same spot where we'd had coffee, was it really only three hours ago? It felt like a lifetime. Digging into my backpack, I found the roll, Rafi had made up for me and pulled a bottle of water out. Sitting against the same rock, I munched my food, chatting with the others as we ate. Several of them asked if I was feeling ok, thankfully, it seemed that most of them had already returned to their respective sites before my bid for attention. Embarrassed, yet warmed by their concern, I nodded that I was fine now, just one of those things, blah blah blah.

Max and Naomi were already there, sitting with the group who were working in the chapel. Max was facing me and, without anyone else noticing checked me over, his features smooth and untroubled, dropping a slow wink. I smiled back, uncaring who saw. Trying not to let my mind wander back into the events of last night, my last night at least, I thought about the room that had been my quarters and wondered whether there was anything left to find in it, had everything that had survived the fire and any subsequent damage from the Roman onslaught, been found.

I thought about those clothes I had been wearing and the soft mantle, the rugs on the floor and the bedding I had been using, so finely made, that it must have been from the time of Herod, or at the very least imported during the first Roman occupation. Was any of it, even a fragment left? Maybe I would ask Nate whether he would mind me conducting a brief search, for my own benefit, it too was covered by the makeshift roof so it would be cool and I wasn't sure he'd need me much longer in the treatment room.

Lunch finished, we made our way back over to our work area. On the way I floated my idea to Nate, who was perfectly happy for me to give it a go.

"Maybe tomorrow, if we've finished up here, I can give you a hand if you like." Smiling, I thanked him and we went back to work, I felt happier and more relaxed than I had done since leaving the digs this morning. By the end of the day we had a large set of trays, several calico bags and so many photographs, it would take weeks to title them all, but we had got as much as we could and dug further than we thought we'd be able to.

Several more 'lumps' had been unearthed, along with what looked like individual rags. It was hard, my knowing what they were and not saying. Let them work it out for themselves, maybe one day I would share my knowledge, it would certainly give them a different perspective, but not yet. Geoff came as promised, with his barrow and one of the other guys, Andrew, who had been working in the chapel, joined us to help carry any excess.

Between the four of us, we managed to get to the cable car and down to the bottom of the rock without any major catastrophes, where we waited for the bus to come and take us round to the digs. Once there, we carefully unloaded everything and carried them to the conservation area, which for us, consisted of two very long rooms with trestle tables down the middle, displaying finds in varying stages of treatment.

There were large, solid and secure metal cupboards standing like sentries at either end of the tables, places to store the most delicate and rare of artefacts. Everything else was locked up in cupboards which stood under the tables and along the sides of the rooms, still made of metal, but not quite so safe-like. The air-conditioning was running, not only maintaining a stable temperature twenty four hours a day, but also keeping everything in the same dry atmosphere that had protected them for nearly two thousand years.

Geoff directed operations, making sure we placed everything where he felt it most appropriate. He was going to start working on some of the lumps the next day, I wished I could assist, but it was probably not a good idea, who knew what that would do to my head. Eventually, we left him to it, sensing that we were getting in his way and, knowing Geoff, he would want to get a head start now, unable to contain his excitement over some of the artefacts.

Going back to my room, I showered quickly, it had been a very long day, in my mind almost two days and I felt unutterably weary and sort of wrung out. Putting on fresh clothes, I wandered back along to the refectory, which, at one end, had a few comfortable chairs and the odd sofa, giving the look of a student common room. Calling a hello to Rafi through the hatch, I made myself a cup of tea and sat down on the nearest sofa, stretching out like a cat and settling into the cushions. The others would be along soon, a few minutes peace was unexpected, but welcome. I was facing the windows, watching some of the others come down the ramp, when the door opened. It was Max; I knew it without needing to turn round.

"Hey there sunshine, how's it going?" Nonchalant.

"'S'ok, just having a cuppa and watching the world, such as it is, go by." Pouring himself a hot coffee, he walked across to where I was sitting,

"Scooch up." He grinned, making as if to sit on my legs.

"Not fair, I had this all for me." Making room for him anyway, Max sat at the far end of the couch, lifting my legs over his, massaging them gently, his touch sending pleasurable little waves up my body. He too had just showered, his hair still wet, clung to his scalp, the smell of his aftershave, intoxicating.

"Be careful Max, we aren't really alone now." I warned, not wanting him to stop but knowing where it could lead.

"I know." Sighing. "But I've barely seen you today and I've missed you."

He lifted my leg and kissed my knee, which had anybody else done I would have thought it weird, with him, totally natural, then pushed my legs off his and stood up, moving to the armchair. His sudden movement left me feeling bereft, as if he was pushing me away, then he leaned over and tickled my feet, which I hate, grinning as I jumped.

"Rat bag." I grunted wriggling to get away from those remorseless fingers. "You wait, I'll get you back!" Laughing he gave up tormenting me and sat back in his chair, drinking the hot coffee and letting me finish my tea.

Within minutes the room started filling up, what seemed like an army of tired hungry archaeologists marched in looking for sustenance. Rafi already had bread and hummus out on the table alongside platters of cold, sliced roasted vegetables, and shaved meats. They fell on it, piling their plates and stood in loose groups talking about their day. Max went to get me something before it all went and as he did so, Naomi came in. Spotting me, she came over and asked how I was feeling.

"Much better thanks, headache has completely gone."

"I was thinking more about your fainting fit at coffee time."

"Oh, you know about that?"

"I was the one who saw you go, we heard your cup bounce and I managed to catch you before you hit the floor. You were well out of it." Funny she didn't hang around long enough to make sure I was ok.

"Oh God, I'm so embarrassed, I've never fainted before and I have to go and do it for the first time in front of thirty odd people.

Thank you for catching me, a bang on the head would probably not have been a good thing."

"Those of us who saw it were all pretty worried, I think you were unconscious for about ten minutes. Max was frantic." Still friendly, but calculating now, watching for my reaction.

"Hahaha, Max didn't want to have to explain to my parents why their daughter ended up in hospital, when he should have been keeping her out of mischief." Keeping it light I laughed it off, but noticed Naomi wasn't convinced. Inwardly sighing, I thought she'd worked it out, she was a woman after all and not stupid, she'd recognise the signs which were probably radiating off me like a flippin' beacon...and did I really care? What was it to her anyway? Max came back with two plates, handing one to me.

"Do you want this one Naomi? I can just as easily go and get another one for me."

"No, its ok thank you Max, I can see Tom as got one for me, I thought he might, he's such a sweetheart..." smiling, although it did seem a little forced and she patted my knee, "...well, glad you feel better Hannah, try and get an early night, might help." She sauntered over to where Tom was holding plate for her and was immediately swallowed in a large group of noisy chatter.

Sighing with relief, I nibbled at the food Max had brought. My appetite seemed to have left me, Naomi's mention of an early night had set my stomach churning, I felt antsy and a little out of sorts. The events of the day were starting to bother me again, I realised I was afraid of going to bed, of something happening while I was asleep. Agitated I shifted in the chair; fear trickling down my spine, my breathing quickened and Max, seemingly attuned to me, knew instantly that something was wrong.

What's up Han?"

"I'm frightened." I muttered.

"What of?"

"Sleep." One little word, yet it filled me with dread, anxiety flared and I could feel panic building again. "I need air..." then, "...must not faint, must not faint." I instructed myself and as I attempted to regulate my breathing, spots appeared before my eyes. I tried to put my plate down but couldn't for the tremors in my hand. Max quietly removed it from me, put both plates on the table and very calmly pulled me out of my comfortable seat.

As I stood up, the room receded and the edge of my vision darkened. No, no, no, I would not faint. Gritting my teeth and taking a deep breath I waited 'til everything steadied. Then as casually as possible, with Max's arm round my waist - oh no this was in full view of everybody, more embarrassment - we walked out.

"I don't think they noticed Hannah, they're all too busy eating."

"Hope so, please, I need air, I can't breathe." Max got me to the door and I sank onto the bench just outside, dropping my head between my knees to try and stop the dizziness. The evening was quiet, the air mild with just a hint of a breeze.

Finally my head cleared but I remained with it bowed for several minutes, feeling totally pathetic. Eventually I looked up at the tall man sitting quietly beside me, holding my hand.

"Oh, Max, this is ridiculous, I can't even sit and have a conversation without chucking a wobbly, what am I going to do?" Helplessly, I looked at him. "I'm sorry, you don't need some useless female coming over all feeble and nonsensical, you go back in, I'll be fine." Max looked at me, just looked at me, long and hard.

"If you think you can put me off by throwing wobblies and chucking habdabs you mustn't think much of me..." serious now,

"...we're in this together sunshine, haven't you got that through your thick head yet."

My voice catching on a sob, I whispered.

"What do I do? It's like this thing is consuming me, I'm frightened to go to sleep, frightened even to shut my eyes in case I get sucked back there, I feel like its not over, that it doesn't matter what I do, it will run its course. This afternoon, I wanted to tell Nate about the lump we'd found, that I know want it is, that I put them there. Do you hear how crazy that sounds?"

"I'm not scared, not for me, I am worried for you, but I'm here, I'll keep you safe, trust me." I was crying again - oh geez Hannah, enough with the crying - not the deep wracking sobs of earlier, more a release of emotion, tears poured down my cheeks, Max just held me and let them fall, making no attempt to stem the flow. I wept, until I had no more tears and as they dried, I felt strangely calm.

"Thank you, funnily enough I feel better now."

"Its reaction love, what did you expect? Sounds like you've experienced more in the last day, than most people do in a lifetime. Don't be too hard on yourself. Now come on, I know it's early, but you're going to bed. I'll go get you something to eat, all that crying will have made you hungry." Suiting his words to his actions, Max stood, pulling me up off the bench. Night had fallen while we'd been sitting there, the light from a billion stars started to shimmer, the moon, beginning its long trek across the sky, could just be seen peeking over the distant mountain range. It was unbelievably beautiful. Taking one last look, I turned to follow Max inside; he walked me to my door and said he'd be five minutes, going back towards the dining room for my food.

True to his word he was not long, he knocked before entering and I was curled up on my bed. Placing what looked like a very full tray, including a bottle of wine and two glasses - where had he found that? - down in the middle of the bed, we tucked in. Max steered the conversation away from darker topics, keeping it light and the wine helped. I started to relax, even giggling at his outrageous tales, though I knew he was telling them as a distraction, it worked and at one point I was laughing helplessly. We finished the food, I was surprised at how hungry I was and, polished off the whole bottle of wine.

Slightly tipsy now, we continued to talk, the conversation, of its own volition, becoming about us. We just talked about our lives and what we would do when we got back to the real world, where we would live, our jobs, our relationship. I liked that we were cocooned here, no one in our families knew what was happening and it was delicious this knowing, I wasn't sure I wanted to go back where explanations might be demanded.

"I'm pretty sure Naomi has guessed." I said ruefully. "She didn't seem convinced when I said you were just keeping me out of mischief."

"Not sure I really care." Max replied. "I'd like to shout it from the rooftops."

"Idiot." Laughing. "I suppose it doesn't matter, especially after this morning's little display of nonsense, anyone who saw us after I came round, would have to be blind not to know what was going on."

"Maybe we just go where it takes us, I'm not suggesting I drag you onto the floor in the middle of the plateau and start making love to you, but holding hands now 'n' again and sharing the odd kiss or hug, they'd probably not even realise what was going on and by the time they did we'd be an established couple. What d'you reckon?"

"Actually, that sounds rather lovely, although being ravished on the desert floor would be much more fun." Smiling I shifted my legs, so I could sit against the wall, looking at Max as I spoke and, noting his darkening expression, felt my breathing quicken, the curl in my stomach tightened as the now, oh so familiar, spark ignited.

"Hussey." He muttered leaning towards me and in one fluid movement, pulled me to him somehow swinging me round so we were both lying on the bed.

His kiss scorched my lips, fierce and hot, he pinned me to the bed, plundering my mouth pressing his body hard against mine. My response was immediate and, clinging to him, I pulled him even closer, wanting every part of me to be touching him. Fire shot through me and I arched against him, feeling the answering throb from his body. His hands roaming, he touched and caressed, but it was not enough. I needed to feel his skin on mine and, as if of one mind, Max slid my t-shirt over my head and as his hand moved back along my body, he smoothly unclipped my bra, cupping my breast as the flimsy material slid off. I moaned, unable to stop myself, shuddering at his touch. Again, I couldn't breathe, but this was so different and I did not want him to stop. Frantically, I undid the buttons on his shirt, trying not to rip them in my haste to slip it off his shoulders and throw it into the corner, before running my hands over his warm skin, feeling his heart beat and the tremors that echoed mine, rippling through his body.

And…oh…what a body, lithe and taut and tanned, I kissed his chest, his neck, circling his nipples with my tongue, feeling him quiver as I did so, anywhere I could plant my lips, my behaviour was wanton and I did not care. Suddenly the bed wasn't big enough and we tumbled onto the floor. Fumbling with his belt, I tried to divest him of his trousers at the same time as he was trying to loosen the tie round the waist of my linen pants. He won, mine slithered down my legs as his hand curved round my bottom, drawing me back in, his other hand round my neck as he kissed me nearly senseless.

Not entirely sure how we managed it, but eventually we were both almost naked, I'm sure it would have been a vision of total inelegance, nothing like you see on the movies where clothes slide off in one silky smooth movement. Still I could not let him go, I was driven, abandoning myself completely to his touch, which, I may tell you, was masterly. He stopped kissing me for a moment and lifted himself up on one elbow, looking down on my flushed face.

This isn't how I planned it," he whispered,

"I don't care," breathlessly," I won't...I can't stop this, I want you too badly, I need to feel you, I need you to take me now. Please."

Smiling gently, he flicked the hair off my forehead and leaned down, kissing my eyelids, my nose, brushing my lips, making me lean up to catch him.

"Are you sure?" His eyes darkened as his passion flared, holding his gaze, I deliberately moved my hand down his abdomen, curling my fingers through the dark hair, sliding them under his shorts, feeling him catch his breath as I caressed him, yeah, I was sure. "Oh God Hannah." He ran his fingers down my back, catching the edge of my underwear and pulling me free, I sighed and pressed back against him, feeling the heat in our skin and the throb of desire slake through us. Pushing them down with one hand, I, very dextrously I thought, bent my leg round him and using my toes removed his shorts.

"Oh very clever." He muttered against my breast. "S'pose you want a medal for that move?"

"I can think of a better reward." I murmured, gasping as he teased my nipples, one after the other with his tongue, his free hand sliding between my legs, touching the sensitive skin hidden there. New sensations raced through me and just when I thought I couldn't take it any more, he entered me. I had expected a moment

118

of pain, but there was only an exquisite spasm, after which I exploded, wave after wave of pleasure crashing over me as I matched his movements. My legs curled round his back pulling him deeper and deeper into me, we became one pulsing, writhing mass of limbs. Rising towards a crescendo, which kept building and building, until at last we reached the climax and exploded all over again. We rode it down, gasping for breath, our bodies, shaking from the intensity of our lovemaking, hot and slick with sweat. Max kissed me deeply and tenderly, I ran my fingers over his back, gently letting them roll down his body, causing new tremors, waiting for our breathing to steady.

"Hannah?" Questioning gently. "Hannah, that was your first…" hesitating, "…time?"

"Yes." Shyly, bending my head, blushing and suddenly feeling rather gauche. "Is that ok?"

"Oh Hannah, you have no idea how ok that is, but I'm so sorry if I hurt you." Lifting my chin away from his chest, he kissed me tenderly, like the touch of butterfly wings and I began to melt all over again.

"You didn't." Smiling against his lips, I felt his kiss intensify, heat rippled through me. He started to shift position and I placed my hands on his waist and pulled him close, whispering.

"Not yet, not yet, don't pull away." I could still feel the throb of his desire, I wasn't ready to loosen my hold, there was a new flame building. I lay quietly for a moment savouring the feeling, then suddenly clenched my hips, moving ever so slightly under Max, his response was instant and we went back up the volcano, fire erupting. I arched my back, trying not to cry out, not sure whether I succeeded as Max was plundering my lips again. His tongue flicked inside my mouth, searching, I did the same to him, this intimacy was beyond my wildest imagination, not even the odd steamy romance prepared me for this. We rocketed up through the stratosphere, lingering for what felt like a lifetime, until finally we came back to earth, satiated and exhausted.

"Oh lordy." I croaked, still panting. "I am so gonna want to do that again."

"Your wish my dear, but it may have a to wait a few moments." I grinned into his chest, kissing him, using my tongue to lick the droplets of moisture gathering there. Drawing a shuddering breath, Max rolled me onto my back, lazily drawing circles on my stomach with his finger. We lay quiet for a long time, resting in each other's arms, occasionally kissing, mainly just talking. It felt so safe to be curled up together...I never wanted this night to end.

"Please don't leave me tonight Max, I don't think I could bear it, not after this."

"I'm not going anywhere love, might be a squeeze in that bed of yours mind."

"Like I could care less, if necessary we'll pull the rest of the bedding off and sleep on the floor."

"We could go to my room, I've got a huge bed." Invitingly.

"Hmmm...that could work...and how did you wangle that?"

"Luck of the draw I guess, are you complaining?"

"No, but if I'd had the bigger bed, we wouldn't have to move and we could stay here, while I do this." Letting my fingers glide down his chest, back to where I could feel his need for me beginning to pulse once more.

"Hannah, you will kill me, I don't think I have the en...ahhhh..." His words were cut short as I stroked him back to life, pushing him onto his back and stretching my body along his length, kissing him with fervour.

"My turn." I grinned and proceeded to discover the whole of Max's body, savouring the taste of him, loving that I could give him the same pleasure he'd given me, taking wicked delight in making him tremble with wanting me. Then, without warning, he curled round me, moving so that we sat face to face, lifting me onto him and burying himself so far inside of me I thought I would consume him, my legs curled back round his waist holding him there as we rocked together, frantically kissing, teeth nipping, arms gripping tighter and tighter. Once more I felt I was about to touch the heavens as Max quivered in release, which I met in an explosion of pleasure so intense I would never have believed it possible if I hadn't experienced it myself. Holding him against my chest I kissed the top of his head, pushing him slightly away from me, smiling with all the love that was suffusing me.

"Never...never in my wildest dreams..." My eyes held his reading the emotions in their green depths.

"Oh my darling Hannah, I'm not sure I have to words to describe how much I love you."

"Your actions were very eloquent I thought." Lifting my hands, I cupped his face, bending slightly to kiss him again. Sliding back down to lay full length on the floor, facing each other, I couldn't look away; I wanted to etch every facet of him into my memory. Grinning back at me, he pulled me closer, kissing the tip of my nose.

"Cutest nose ever."

"Silly." Snuggling in, we lay quietly for a while longer then, sighing I whispered. "I suppose if we're going to sleep in your room, we should probably think about making a move."

"In a minute, just let me...." For the next few minutes he just kissed me, tenderly, gently and deeply, passion was there but tucked away, just circling the edges. Tired now, I could feel sleep beginning to take hold. "C'mon sleepy head," reading my thoughts, "let's go to bed."

"Mmmmmm...that's one of the nicest invitations I've ever had." Max helped me up, my legs were all wobbly and I giggled slightly hysterically. "Best get dressed too, wouldn't do to be caught streaking down the hallway." Max spluttered with laughter at the image that conjured up.

"It'd give them something to talk about." We got dressed, tidied my room, after a fashion and, glancing along the corridor, saw that all was quiet. I had no idea how long we'd been…errr…involved, but the lights were still on in the dining room, so someone was still up. We walked along to Max's room and slipped in. He was right, he did have a big bed and it looked so inviting.

Undressing again, at a more leisurely pace, we slipped beneath the covers and curled up, my back against his chest, his legs curled round mine.

"Max?" I murmured just as I was about to drop off.

"Hmmm."

"Do you think you'd be able to help me up on the dig tomorrow? Nate said he'd be there, too, but just in case? I'm going into the room that I believe to be my quarters, next to the sick room and I don't know what'll happen if I find something."

"Sure sunshine, I'll come with you, be a nice change from mosaics."

Kissing the back of my neck, he sighed, resting his chin on my hair.

We slept.

Chapter Thirteen

My night was dreamless, nothing. I'm not sure I even turned over, safe in Max's arms; I slept the sleep of the just. Pretty sure Max did too, I never felt him move, not until the early hours when he decided that I'd had quite enough sleep and woke me up most effectively. Afterwards, we slept a while longer, this time facing each other and the next time I woke, he was watching me.

"Morning love." He whispered, stroking my hair, which after all our antics of the night before must have resembled a bird's nest. "Sleep well?"

"Oh yes." Stretching like a cat, I arched my back feeling odd aches in my muscles. "Oooof, mind you, my muscles aren't used to that much exercise." Grinning widely. "You?"

"Like the proverbial." He ran his fingers down my body...inviting.

"Is this wise? Neither of us will be able to walk before much longer."

"Probably not, but, I'm willing to take to risk...you?" Raising an eyebrow and wiggling it lasciviously. "Resistance is useless." Laughing now, I pushed against his chest.

"You idiot." Kissing him soundly on the mouth shutting him up but in no way distracting him from his intentions, I gave up and let him have his way. An extremely delightful while later, we finally dragged ourselves out of bed.

"I'll go shower in my room if you like, might give you some space."

What makes you think I want space, c'mon, saves water if you shower together." Glancing at the clock, it was only 6am; we had plenty of time, why not. Feigning reluctance, I allowed myself to be pulled into the bathroom, we showered, soaping each other down, letting the water run over our aching bodies, refreshing us for the day. Max proved to be most adept, managing to soap and kiss me at the same time, very enjoyable, I highly recommend it.

Thankfully he had two dry fluffy towels and we managed to get dry and dressed without further incident. He did spin me round at one point to check out the bruises, blossoming nicely in shades of purple, across my back from our adventure on the desert floor the other night. Sucking his breath in he gently kissed them.

"Oh Han, I'm sorry I didn't mean to cause that."

"Hey, what are you sorry for? You didn't bruise me that was the rocks on the ground. I could have said something, I didn't care, so what, they'll fade, it was very much worth it." I winked at him.

"Ok, are we ready for this? Oh hang on, I'm going to go dry my hair and pick up a couple of things, but I need to walk in with you just in case. I'll be right back."

"Will you get my shirt, I forgot it last night." Grinning wickedly. I kissed him quickly and went back to my own room. It didn't look too chaotic; we'd managed to leave it a decent state. I dried my hair, pulling it back into its usual ponytail. Studying my face in the mirror, I couldn't decide whether our hours of lovemaking were reflected in my face, my skin and my expression. I always struggle to hide my feelings and these were big huge enormous ones, not a little flirtation or a mild crush. This was mind blowingly, all consuming, incandescent, can't get enough of him love. Surely everyone would see it written all over my face.

Honestly, I could not tell. Grimacing, I added a touch of lip balm and went back to Max's room, locking my door behind me. Max was waiting, looking devastatingly handsome, as always, how did I get this lucky?

"Did you remember my shirt?"

"Damn, forgot it, I'll get it after brekky

"No worries, ready?"

"Ready." Deep breath. "Ok lets do this."

We sauntered down to the dining room; we were the first up, although I'd heard sounds of life as we'd walked passed other rooms. We wouldn't be alone for long. Rafi was beavering away in the kitchen, the tables already had fruit and cereal laid out.

"Morning Rafi." We called. "Ok that we help ourselves to cereal?"

"Go for it." Came a voice from the depths. "Hot food will be out in about half and hour." 'Going for it,' we filled our bowls with a mix of cereal and fruit, splashing ice-cold milk and yoghurt over the top. Max poured us two teas and we ate quickly, Max refilling his bowl and I picked at some more fruit. The tea was very welcome, its aromatic scent clearing my head, which was threatening to become a bit groggy. Related to lack of sleep, or over stimulation or something.

Smirking to myself, I stretched my legs out under the table and leaned back in the chair reliving the night before, revelling in those precious moments.

"What is that smile for? You look like the cat that got the cream." Max smiled, sitting back down.

"Well, I rather think I did." Topping up our teas, while he polished off his second helping, we were chatting quietly when the others started to dribble in, in twos and threes. I was rather interested to note that Naomi came in with Tom, both of them looking rather pleased with themselves. I hoped that this meant she'd given up on Max, but I still could not shake the niggling feeling I had about her, she just didn't seem quite true to me. Ok, it may have been the 'only other young single female' thing and I'm pretty sure jealousy may have been part of it, but I couldn't relax around her, she bothered me. I just wanted her to leave. Surely she had other commitments.

Rafi started bringing out the hot food but I couldn't face it this morning, the cereal had filled me up, so I decided to go back to my room and get ready for the day. I needed to fill in my journal, although I wasn't quite sure how I was going to describe the last twenty four hours, especially as in my head it had been more like thirty six, but I wanted to capture it, while it was fresh.

"I'm off to my room Max. I need to gather my stuff." I spoke in undertones.

"Ok, I'll be along in a minute."

"Don't forget you're helping Nate and me today…in case you need to give anyone else the heads up." And by 'anyone' I meant Naomi, but wasn't going to actually say it.

"Under control love." Flicking him a grin, I sauntered out of the refectory, pausing to chat to a couple of the guys as they were coming in for breakfast. Dawdling along, it was only when I actually reached my doorway that I realised it was standing wide open. Strange, I was sure I'd locked it. I looked along the corridor, no one in sight, then carefully peered into the room incase someone was still inside - no one there either.

Unsettled, I took a good look round, there was nothing of any value to take, just clothes and my books. Oh, the brooch, the brooch, pulling my bag off the bed, I rummaged through it, I couldn't feel it, anxiety shot through me, searching, checking every corner, no, no, no, I couldn't lose, it, it might have no monetary value, but in sentiment it was priceless, it was from my Gran. Taking a deep breath, I tipped everything out, opening every pocket, frantically checking every little corner.

Nothing, oh God, why would anyone take it? Just as panic was about to overwhelm me, I remembered - I had put it in my jeans, which were in the wash basket in the bathroom. Yanking everything out, I grabbed my jeans, fingers, thankfully, curling round the pouch with my trinket safely inside. I sat back on my heels, beginning to breathe again, rolling the little bag around in my hand and feeling its weight. Such an innocuous thing, why would any one want it, if this was in fact what they were looking for? I hadn't realised anyone else knew I had it with me.

Sitting back on my bed, absently repacking my bag, I took a good long look round my room. Whoever had been in hadn't left too much of a mess. My bedside drawers were open, some clothes were spilling out and my wardrobe door was standing ajar, so had they been disturbed before they'd managed to search properly, or was it the wrong room? My passport was still in my bag and my purse hadn't been emptied - weird. Tucked behind my bedside cabinet, hidden from view, my journal nestled safely and, dragging it out, I flipped the pages, they were all still there, nothing was torn out.

Relieved, I clutched it to my chest, feeling completely unnerved. I heard movement in the hallway, seconds later Max appeared and took in the chaos of my room in a glance.

"What happened Hannah?" I just sat there, not quite trusting myself to speak. "What happened?"

"Errrr, well, mmmm, well…" My words wouldn't form; I still couldn't quite believe it.

"Hannah, what's going on?"

"Well…" drawing out the word, "…I think…I think someone's been in my room."

"What d'you mean been in your room?"

"Exactly how it sounds, when I came along the door was open, someone had rummaged through my backpack, this top drawer and my wardrobe were open. My journal and my brooch are safe, I have no clue what they were after, but I know I locked my door this morning."

Back in control and feeling anger start to build, "How dare they, this is my room, who here would do this, coz it can only be someone who lodges here." My voice started to rise, Max came in and pulled the door closed.

"Hey, hey, calm down, we'll sort it out. How about we put your journal and the brooch in my room, I've a lock box under my bed which is screwed to the floor, nobody's walking out with that. Your backpack isn't secure, and you will be sleeping in my room from now on. I'm putting my foot down." Smiling weakly at his fierce expression, I nodded.

"Ok, ok." I put my hands up in surrender. "Sorry, but I thought my things would be safe here, you know behind a locked door and, what do we do about my door? The lock is probably bust." I gathered my stuff up while Max examined the lock.

"Its been jimmied, not sure what with, I'll speak to Bill and see if he has a new lock he can fix on. I'll be back in a jiffy, here's my key." Passing me the key to his bedroom, Max hurried off down to the caretaker's quarters. Bill, like Rafi, was another long term fixture here at the digs, he'd been here forever and there wasn't much he couldn't fix or make. Middle of nowhere you had to be jack-of-all-trades. I knew Bill would sort out my door, even if he had to put on a new one!

Tidying up the mess, I refolded my clothes, putting them back in the drawers and shut my wardrobe door. Turning to pick up Max's shirt I noticed that it wasn't where I thought I'd tossed it the night before. Odd, had I dropped it in my laundry basket? Checking quickly, it wasn't there, confused, I did another search, under the bed, nothing but my suitcase and a suspicion of dust, it wasn't behind my chair, in fact it was nowhere to be found. Not particularly bothered, I assumed Max had grabbed it on his way back out to find Bill. Making sure my room was as neat as possible, I gathered up my bag, grabbed my toiletries and made my way along the hall to Max's room.

Slipping in unnoticed, I locked the door behind me and waited. Good as his word, Max was only minutes behind me; quietly knocking when he realised the latch was dropped. I let him in and he gave me a quick hug, dropping a kiss on my head.

"Ok, so Bill'll have a look and do what ever he needs to, he'll have a new key for you this evening. He said he'd check round outside your window too in case they went out that way." I must have looked worried because he continued, "'S'ok Hannah, probably just one of those things, you were just the unlucky one."

"But they didn't take anything, my purse was in my bag, no money was taken, all my cards are still there, don't think they'd even opened it, or my passport holder, which was in the same pocket. Its bizarre, do you know whether anyone else's room was broken into?"

"No, I didn't ask, just went to see Bill, then came back here, oh did you get my shirt."

"Didn't you pick it up?"

"No, didn't see it, thought you'd already grabbed it."

"Well now that's just too weird, why would anyone want to take your shirt?"

"Maybe they thought it was a stunning shirt and they'd look better in it." Shaking his head. "Who knows? It'll doubtless turn up." Unfazed he took my brooch and journal from my hands, securing them in his lock box, which could only be opened with a code, no keys involved. I felt more relaxed when they were safely out of sight.

"Thanks Max, I appreciate it." Sighing, I sank onto the bed, this just seemed to be one thing too many and I felt overwhelmed again. "Can we sit here, just for a minute? I know we need to get ready, but I feel like everything's running way from me, out of control, I don't know what to do." Max came to where I was sitting and bending he gently parted my legs so he could kneel between them on the floor in front of me, his eyes level with mine, he wrapped his arms round me and held me close, not trying to take it further, just comforting me.

He seemed to sense that my need was for peace not passion and he just held me, stroking my hair and talking about anything that came into his head. To this day I cannot remember what he was gabbling about, but the words soothed me, like a lullaby. Lullaby - unbidden, an image flashed into my head, an image of a man lying on a cot, being calmed by my crooning. With a huge effort, I pushed it away, concentrating on Max's voice, letting his words flow over me, washing away my fears, eventually it worked and I felt better, ready to face the day. I rested my head on his shoulder, enjoying the scent of him, sandalwood soap and his favourite aftershave and, intoxicating though it was, today I found it calming, familiar and restful.

All too soon, it was time to go, but now I felt up to it, I wanted to get into that room, hopeful that I could find something, anything that would help me pin down what I had 'seen'.

"Ok." Repeating his words from earlier. "Let's do this." Relinquishing his hold, Max stood, pulling me up so we stood face to face - well, more like face to chest, but you get my drift - "I can hear the others, let's go see if anyone else's room was broken into." Kissing me gently, butterfly soft, he released me and, quickly, we finished getting ready. Hauling both backpacks off the floor, he held the door for me and we went to join the rest on their way up the rock.

Casually chatting, we discovered that mine was the only room that had been broken into, but didn't go into any details. As far as I knew only Max was aware I had the brooch and, as for the journal, well that was just a notebook, of no interest to anyone but me. The question as to why anyone would want either still nagged at me, but I let it go for now, filing it away for another time. We walked up, enjoying the cool of the morning, there were a few clouds in the sky today, I wondered whether we might get rain, not knowing really whether that was likely at this time of year.

When we reached the plateau, Nate and I found our way to the two rooms in the administration block of the Northern Palace where were we had been concentrating our search. Max followed after giving instructions to one of the other guys who would be assisting Naomi in his stead. After checking round, I entered the room I believed to have been my quarters in my vision, today it was just a ruin, hints of the paint on what was left of the walls could be discerned here and there, round the edges, but not much else. I worked out where the bed would have been, where the cupboard stood and where the rug lay. I could picture it, clear as day, but in front of me there was nothing but dust. Max came up behind me.

"You ok?"

"So far, what's Nate up to?"

"Totally engrossed in his pots, what is it?

"I wanted to tell you what I saw, how it looked, but I don't want anyone else to hear, they wouldn't understand."

"Go on them, I'm all ears, in fact I'm very intrigued."

So, I wandered through the space, telling him what went where, the cupboard here, with my clothes folded neatly, both inside and on top. My bed rolled up against the wall, and, in its usual space, a soldier's cot. A rug on the cool tiles, which warmed my feet. A shelf with bowls and, a large flagon full of water to be used for washing and drinking. A chair, which I recognised to be of Roman design. Something in my voice had captivated Max, he was riveted by what I was describing, I turned in the room, my words creating a picture of my other life, entwining themselves round his senses, ensnaring him, persuading him to believe.

Continuing, I told him about the room next door, the pallets for the injured men, the storage jars, urns and flasks full of herbs and balms and other exotic ointments. One large basket full of dirty linen for washing and a pile of bandages soaked in sweat and waste thrown in a heap on the floor to be burned. Another basket piled with freshly laundered sheets, cool and crisp to my touch and blankets, folded on the top of a wooden cupboard, for warmth on chill evenings, or to wrap around a dying man. My voice trailed off, I stood still, my mind two thousand years away in a dimly lit room.

"Max." It was barely a breath.

"I'm here. What do you need?"

"You." Simply.

He came to me, his cool hands held mine, then he held me close and we just stood together. In all honesty I didn't know whether I was there with my Max, or back with Maxentius, either way I needed their strength, my visions were close here, my worlds melding. I didn't want to fall.

Slowly I came back to earth, tilting my face up, so I could look Max in the eye I spoke quietly,

"So you see why I need to look, if there is anything at all left, I need to find it." And just as quietly,

"I understand Hannah, I'm here for you and I'll help in any way I can."

We began by mapping the room, making squares that we could work through logically. Delineating the spaces with twine, then drawing the same thing on a graph, photographing every step, I wanted to do this right, Max had far more experience and knew the process. Just as we began in the first square in the back right hand corner of the room, farthest from what would have been the doorway, Nate came along to check on us.

"Looking great guys, just be careful with that dirt, it has a tendency to stain items and if you're not careful you can miss the tiny things. If you're unsure bag it, we can run it through the screens later on." He looked over our mapping and diagrams with approval. "Very professional, we'll make an archaeologist of you yet Hannah." Grinning he went back to his pots, satisfied that we weren't complete amateurs.

Max chuckled,

"He's rather pleased with us methinks."

"Hahaha, had to happen eventually." Our mood had lightened, now we were focused on the job at hand, we worked together well, missing the coffee break, but taking time to stop for lunch and a hot drink. After my shenanigans of the day before, Max made sure I had plenty of water and, although I'm pretty sure dehydration was not the problem, it kept him happy. After lunch we got back to it, managing to work through the first ten squares by the end of the day. It didn't seem like much, but we were well chuffed, everything nicely bagged and tagged, drawn, photographed and logged. I really felt as though we had achieved something. It would take a few days, but we could map the whole room and maybe, just maybe there would be something tangible from my other life.

We finished the day tired but happy, strolling back down the ramp with Nate, who had also found some more interesting items in the room next door. Underneath some of the pots he had discovered seeds and nuts, causing him to second guess his conviction that it was some kind of dispensary. I caught Max's eye, he looked away before Nate noticed. Oh Nate, I thought, I could tell you, I could clear this up right now, but I'm too afraid, I know you won't believe me. Without letting him see my expression, I suggested they could have been in a bowl that was dropped by someone accidentally, bit like a false positive. He nodded, accepting the premise, but I could see that it would take more than that.

We arrived back at the digs taking our evidence to the conservation room. Geoff had spent the day there working through the trays we had brought down the day before and he looked happy as a pig in muck surrounded by shards of pottery and lumps of mud.

"How's it going Geoff?"

"Pretty flipping awesomely thanks for asking." He smiled. "You got more for me?"

"Several bags of stuff to be put through the trays and I think Nate might have some too." We placed our finds here and there at Geoff's direction and left him to it.

"Don't forget dinner Geoff." Was Nate's parting shot as we went to get sorted ourselves. Max and I went to check on my room, true to his word, Bill had put in a new lock, the room seemed as I had left it. Unwilling to spend any longer there than necessary, I grabbed a change of clothes, my hairbrush and a few odds and ends I might need before the morning and we went back to Max's room. We showered and ate dinner, doing the right thing by hanging around chatting with the others, catching up on their day, before quietly leaving the room when we didn't think they'd notice our absence.

Chapter Fourteen

On entering the bedroom, we got things ready for the next day, talking while we did so, ordinary, normal everyday conversation about mundane things, managing to ignore completely, the very large pink elephant in the middle of the room. It would still be there in the morning; we could deal with it then - if we absolutely had to. Finishing up, I sat on the bed, tired and very happy, but strangely calm, watching Max methodically packing things into his bag. In a very different mood from the night before, I didn't feel the need to pull Max down onto the bed and rip his clothes off, although the image made me giggle, making him raise an eyebrow in my direction.

He flipped the top over on his backpack and came to sit next to me. We stayed there sitting shoulder to shoulder for what seemed like an age, happy in each other's company, no talking, words weren't needed, relaxing in the quiet that enveloped us. I could feel my senses sharpening as we sat there, the silence lengthening, for a moment I thought that Max had fallen asleep, so steady was his breathing.

"Hey." I nudged him. "Am I boring you?"

"Yeah...think I need another girl." Dodging to avoid a thump to the leg. "Hey, no need for violence." Grinning wickedly, he reached round and got hold of my hands, while I made a feeble attempt to wriggle free.

"Oof...not fair, you're too strong, let me go." Laughing now we struggled and he managed to grasp both of my hands in one of his and started tickling me with the other. "Noooo...c'mon," squirming, "that's just cruel." Abruptly Max let go and I fell back against his shoulder laughing helplessly, I hate being tickled, its like my kryptonite or something, I just completely lose control. While I was catching my breath, Max decided to shift gears and lifting the hair off my shoulders, he bent close and very gently kissed the back of my neck, causing frissons of delight. His lips, cool and firm, barely brushed my skin and I felt my spine begin to tingle. Twisting to face him, I smiled against his mouth, gliding my fingers up his leg, feeling a quiver as I reached his thigh.

Instead of the frenzy of the night before, we went slowly, exploring each other's bodies, taking our time to undress each other, button by button, zip by zip. Kissing tenderly and deeply, caressing, nuzzling, stroking, feeling the slow burn of passion start to build. Finally, we stood, naked - nothing between us, nowhere to hide. Max lifted me, laying me on the bed and starting from the tips of my toes, kissed me all the way up to my head, leaving nowhere untouched, tremors were rippling through me. I leaned up to pull him down, needing his weight on top of me, marvelling at the feel of his cool body against my fevered one, my hands running over his skin, I kissed him until I felt his desire match mine.

"Oh no, Hannah, not yet." Lifting my arms above my head, he trapped them there while he continued to kiss me, grazing my breasts with his mouth, gossamer light yet enough to make me beg him to take me, the feelings roiling over me were so intense I thought I might faint. Smiling, still refusing to release my hands, or quench my desire, he continued his slow lazy journey across my body, tongue flicking, lips kissing, teeth nipping, it was exquisite torture and, just when I thought I could take no more, he whispered against my ear, "Now" and entered me in one powerful movement, pulsing deep inside. My hands freed, I pulled him to me, wrapping my legs around him, raising my hips as if to pull him into my very core, running my fingers down his back, trying not to dig my nails in, hearing him moan, a primitive, almost
136

animal sound, that seemed wrenched from the depths of his soul. I gave myself over to my desire, matching his movements; riding a wave of ecstasy so high I wasn't sure we'd ever come back down.

Shuddering, I tried to steady my breathing, Max held me close, nuzzling my neck, kissing the tender hollow, holding me close while our heartbeats resumed their regular rhythm. I never wanted this to stop, this feeling of euphoria, of oneness with this man who it seemed I had been looking for my whole life and who had been standing next to me the whole time. One step in the wrong direction and I could have missed this, it could have passed me by, lost forever. Oddly, I felt a tear roll down my cheek and, sensitive to my every mood, Max lifted his head to look at me.

"Hey baby," softly, "why the tears?"

"I came so close to missing this Max, how could I have been so blind?"

"You'd have got there, eventually." Slow smile.

"What if I hadn't, what if I'd decided Gran's letter was just some silly nonsense and let you come here without me?"

"Oh." Winking. "I'd've found a way of persuading you, I'd decided long ago that you would be mine, its only ever been you sunshine and, now I've got you I am rather enjoying demonstrating that in as many ways as possible. Now shut up and let me show you another way," and he began his exploration of my body all over again. Revelling in my response to his touch, he made delicious heady love to me, bringing me to peaks of pleasure again and again until, in the early hours of the morning, finally satiated, we slid into delightful slumber wrapped in each other's arms.

The next few days followed the same pattern. We worked hard during the day, excavating the room, me desperately trying to find something to tie me to another time, Max, I think, hoping we wouldn't and, our nights were spent making love. Sometimes with fervency, sometimes slow, tender and languorous, finding new ways to delight in each other's bodies. Becoming so familiar with each other's touch that it felt like we'd been together for a lifetime. Our stay here on Masada was about half way through, and it seemed to be running away from us. I didn't want to go back to reality, I was still happy to keep this romance, or affair or what ever it was, hidden from prying eyes.

The only fly in this particularly sweet ointment was Naomi, who had taken to making the odd comment, muttered under her breath, as she passed, nothing I could define, but enough that I was uncomfortable, I felt she was watching us too. I could not work her out, she was lovely and friendly in a large group, but if she and I were alone together she would drop not so subtle hints about Max and how well she knew him. I had mentioned this to Max who told me it was a figment of her imagination. He didn't remember ever meeting her before this dig, but she seemed to know him and certain comments alluded to parts of his life she shouldn't know about.

I tried to push it to the back of my mind and ignore her, but it was beginning to wear me down. It was interesting though that she never did it in front of anyone, why? What was it about Max that obsessed her so? Eventually, like everything else that was happening, I simply decided to let it run its course. I knew there was nothing in Max's past that connected him to her at the level she seemed to believe and I trusted him, no question, her on the other hand...not as far as I could throw her.

Four days after first asking Max to help me in the room, we were coming to the final few squares, we had moved heaps of debris, many pieces of broken pottery, a few shards that may or may not be charred wood along with mounds of dirt that would take weeks to scour through. Resigned now that I wasn't going to find anything to prove my story, to myself as well as to Max, we had at least found several items that the others seemed excited about, most especially pieces of coloured tile. It was late afternoon when we were finishing up in the last square, which was by what would have been the doorjamb. Max was brushing away at a fairly large pile of debris that had built up against a piece of wall.

Suddenly he called me over.

'Hey Hannah, come here a minute." Standing up and wandering over, taking care not to trip over the string lines.

"Whotcha got?" I drawled, leaning on the ruined piece of wall next to him.

"Just tell me I'm not seeing things here, does it look like there's something metallic in this junk?" Pointing at a thin point of something totally encased in grey dirt, which glinted dully when it caught the light.

"Looks promising." I answered, coming round to help him. "Should we take it back down for Geoff or see how far we can get?"

"Lets just try doing it here, the dirt is quite dry, we can probably dust it off." Max reached into his back pocket for his little brush and, very gently, began to sweep it over the lump. I grabbed a tray and held it underneath to catch anything that broke or fell off with the dirt.

Hardly daring to breathe, I watched him work, could this be it? Please let this be it. It took ages, the light started to fade and still he worked.

"Max, it's going to be too dark soon, we need to go, leave it 'til the morning, it's not going anywhere."

"Hang on, nearly got it." He worked for a few more minutes and then. "Here, its coming free…wow, this is so delicate, have you got a small finds tub?" Reaching around him, I pulled a small plastic tub from our dwindling pile and with infinite care he laid the piece onto the tissue lining - we both looked at it. It was so fine, part of a pin, fashioned from several lengths of very slender metal entwined down a central sliver and, what might have been the remains of a clasp at one end, ever so slightly bent as if it had been holding something too heavy for its fine design.

I felt the world tilt.

"Max…" My voice sounded as if I was parched, the words forced through dry lips. "…Max." Unable to continue, I just looked at him, my mouth hanging open.

"What, what is it? Hannah?" Sharply as I sat back abruptly against the wall, my face was pale and my skin clammy. "Don't you dare faint Hannah Wilson…" I instructed myself sternly, "…not now, get a grip woman." Taking a deep breath, I replied.

"Its mine."

"What do you mean its yours, don't be silly, if you'd dropped something it wouldn't be this damaged and how did it get stuck in all this…" Max stopped speaking mid sentence as he realised, how nonsensical he sounded at the same time as registering what the import of what I'd just said, "…yours?" Raising his eyebrow in question, I nodded not trusting myself to say any more. I held my hand out for the tub, he handed it me and I held it in nerveless fingers. The light was so low now, it was difficult to see anything, let alone make out this thin piece of metal, but to me it was as clear as if lit by the sun.

I ran my finger over it, feeling along its cool length to the tip, barely dulled over time, as I did so, I saw a mantle, with a fringe, clasped at the neck with a pin, the weight thrown over my shoulders as I helped a wounded soldier across the warm dusty ground to sit beneath a pomegranate tree. Trembling now, I handed it back to Max, who placed another piece of tissue over the top and sealed it carefully with a lid. Having stored it safely in his backpack, he held out his hand and pulled me up. I swayed and he moved against me holding me against his body, solid and comforting, until I steadied myself.

"I've got a torch, I think we'll need it before we get to the bottom, neither of us needs to take a tumble, especially with this little beauty in our care. Geoff will be stoked." Switching it on, we followed the bobbing beam as it lit our way. It wasn't really too dark, but the ankle breaking rocks were shadowed now and harder to spot, grey against grey. As we walked, I realised that I didn't want to give the pin to Geoff, the thought of it hurt my heart, a sensation I found hard to fathom. It was just a pin, the 'here and now' me had never owned it, touched it, used it. It was just a thing, an inanimate object, yet I couldn't shake the feeling that I was losing it again. We reached the bottom without incident and took our finds into Geoff, who was just packing up his things.

"Lucky last," he grinned, "what have you got for me today?" We handed over the few packets of dirt, and several tubs, then Max lifted out the small tub, with its precious cargo. Wistfully, I watched him put it on the table and everything seemed to slow down, while he explained what it was to Geoff, who opened the lid to take a quick peek. They talked a moment, their words, to me, distorted as I dragged myself back to reality, determined not to slip away again. Their conversation finished, Max put his arm across my shoulders and we walked out together, I could not help it, I looked back and saw Geoff lift the pin out of its box, his enormous hands cradling it gently as if it were cobwebs.

I swallowed a sob, refusing to let Max see how this was affecting me, especially as I couldn't really explain it to myself, let alone him. My lover wasn't fooled, not even for a second and the minute we got to his room, I barely even went into mine now, except for clothes, he spun me to face him and looked into my eyes for a very long time, trying to read their bewildered depths.

"Ok, give…" Coaxing.

"Not sure I can, it sounds so farfetched, even to me."

"Yes, you can, you have to, I need to understand, it's the only way I can help you."

"Ok, I'll try." Sitting on the bed, I explained about the mantle and how it was clasped and, as I was talking information slipped into my mind, information I didn't think I had.

That the pin had fallen off when someone pulled me away from the doorway, for what reason I didn't know, but I did remember a hand catching my cloak and ripping it off my shoulders. The pin snapped at the clasp and fell on the floor; I had tried to find it later but had been unable to. I recalled feeling deep sadness at its loss; maybe it had been a token from someone, my mother perhaps. I knew though, that I had been given a replacement, a piece given as a gift, but what it was, or from whom, was lost to me. As I talked, I watched Max, trying to discern what his reaction was going to be, but he remained utterly impassive throughout my tale, the only outward sign of emotion held in check, his clenched jaw and a pulse throbbing in his cheek.

As I finished, I bent my head, fearful that I would see disbelief in his face, in his eyes. Fearful that the man I had come to love more than life itself would look away, that this was too much, that what had seemed possible to explain away as dreams had suddenly become tangible. That the person sitting in front of him may quite possibly have been living in two different times. Come on, even I'd think I was crazy. Barely able to breathe, I waited, my heart beating a rapid tattoo against my chest, my stomach twisted into knots so large I swear you could see them under my shirt.

Several long moments passed, still I couldn't raise my head; in fact if anything it drooped lower. For the life of me I could not stop the tears from coursing down my cheeks - for goodness sake woman, Max will think all you do is cry. I thought my heart was breaking, why, why did I tell him all that, I should never have started this, my own stupid fault.

"Hannah…" His voice warm as the desert breeze, hand lightly on my chin, he lifted my head, "…oh my darling girl, don't cry, I'm here for you, don't ever forget that. I will never let you go, you're stuck with me, whatever happens." His eyes held the truth I was terrified I had shattered with my revelations; in fact as I gazed into them I felt that it was even stronger. Relief flood through me, I hadn't lost him and he wasn't going to hand me over to the men in the white coats, well not right this minute anyway, but did he believe me?

"Is this too hard for you to take Max? I know how it sounds, but I can't help it, I can't undo what's happened. I don't think that its me, this me, the person sitting in front of you, who watched that man die, or talked to a Roman soldier. I think it's more like an ancestor of mine, someone I am seeing life through, her actions are her own actions, I'm just witnessing it through her eyes. Oh, I know it sounds absurd, incredible, but that's the simplest way for me to explain it."

"No, its not too hard for me sunshine, bit mind bending, but not too hard. It's just difficult for me to watch what you're going through, without being able to help or go with you, or stop it. My biggest fear is that if you 'go back,' I would be powerless to bring you home, that I'd lose you somewhere out of time, that would be more than I could bear."

"I'm sorry, I didn't ask for any of this to happen either, but I s'pose on the bright side, if I hadn't chucked that temper tantrum with you the day after I got back from Ein Bokek, we might never have got together."

"That's all you know…I had a plan." Grinning, more relaxed.

"Oh yeah…like what?"

"Well, I'd already decided I'd waited long enough, by the time we finished here, come hell or high water, you'd be mine."

"Pfft…what makes you think I'd fall for it?" So he proceeded to show me just how I would have fallen for it and how he would have made me his.

Chapter Fifteen

The next day, we checked in on Geoff before setting off up to the fortress, he was surrounded by boxes and trays, but he had my pin - yes I was claiming some kind of tacit ownership - in front of him, turning it carefully, inspecting it thoroughly. He nodded at us as we came in.

"This is a beautiful piece guys, found in that room next to Nate hey?"

"Yep, just in the doorway, how damaged is it?"

"Pretty bad, but you can still tell it was a well made piece, just the amount of silver used in the strands and the central section, not as dull as I would have expected and with bit of work we might be able to bring it back almost to how it would have looked originally. It'll never be quite as shiny as it was when new, but we'll have a pretty good idea."

"I think its better that it's not all glittery." I said. "It would feel too much like a modern piece rather than something that's been under dust for two thousand years."

"My sentiments exactly." Agreed Geoff, smiling. "I like a bit of mystery to cogitate on when I'm conserving beautiful artefacts, keeps my mind busy when I'm working on more mundane stuff." I glanced at Max, who winked,

"You have no idea mate."

We left him to it, walked slowly up the ramp and began our day. Max, I assumed, was going back to his mosaics and I was going to be working in the storerooms, next to the large bathhouse in Northern Palace. There were several of us spread throughout these rooms so there was lots of chitchat going back and forth. Their camaraderie meant that I didn't feel lost without Max's presence although I did miss working with him. As the non-archaeologist, I offered to take photos and record any finds, this went down well with the guys, who had me running ragged. We worked until lunchtime after which, Sebastian, one of several research assistants, who had come over from the UK, asked whether I'd like to go take some photos of the three tiered palace including the hidden stairwell. Any changes that had occurred during the excavation needed to be recorded, plus, I hadn't been down to these levels yet, so I was pretty excited.

By the time I got down to the lower terrace I was the only one there and it was so peaceful. For a few moments I just stood as close to the outer wall as possible and admired this incredible feat of engineering. Even today, with all the other remarkable buildings in the world, this ruin could still take your breath away. Literally hanging off the edge of a precipice, I was totally in awe of the ingenuity and skill of Herod's engineers and builders. Here at the lowest level, I was standing on, what had been in antiquity, a peristyle courtyard, its fluted columns topped by Corinthian capitals and its lower walls decorated to look like costly marble, or painted with colourful geometrical frescoes.

A Hellenistic style circular building graced the middle terrace and the upper level had been the living quarters featuring a huge sweeping semicircular balcony. Black and white tiles in simple geometrics designs, popular in Roman Italy at the time, would have likely covered the floors of all these terraces. The two lower levels seemed to have been designed purely for pleasure and entertainment, with the main palace set aside for Herod's personal household and, the view from any of these levels would have been spectacular. A secret stairway linked the three terraces meaning servants and anyone who did not want to be seen could move between them unnoticed. Guests could stand and gaze out over the harsh, unforgiving, yet strangely beautiful desert, to the shimmering waters of the Dead Sea.

"Way to impress, Herod." I thought.

I pottered around snapping photos of everything I could see, I wasn't sure what had changed, if anything, but I reckoned it was better to have too many than not enough. The remnants of wall paintings were quite breathtaking and I spent quite a while just studying them, getting more photos, with my camera, purely for my own enjoyment. I may never have the chance to come back here and I would hate to think I'd missed capturing every moment. As I was wandering through the ruins, I came upon what had been the small private bathhouse where, during the original excavations in the sixties, skeletal remains had been found under the collapsed structure, including that of a young man aged around twenty two.

Initially it had been thought that they were Zealots, killed by the Romans when they retook the fortress, but recent studies had suggested that they might well have been Romans who had been killed during the rebel attack about six years earlier. I stood for a long time in this space, a young man, possibly a Roman soldier killed and dumped in a bathhouse, a shiver ran down my back and another explanation nudged at the edge of my consciousness. Could it be? Was there any chance at all that this would be possible? Surely we wouldn't have just dumped him? He deserved a Roman burial. Ah, but he died while in captivity, there are no such rules for a prisoner. Would Maxentius have allowed his friend's body to be treated this way? What choice would he have had? Did I have any sway? Had I even tried?

Moving slowly round the edge of the ruined room, I listened to the whispers of the past. I needed to know that after trying for such a long time to save this man, I hadn't allowed him to be discarded, like waste, on the steps of a bathhouse. Not today, today the voices of the past were muffled by the mists of time and

I could not hear them. Sighing, I moved away from the steps and made my way up to the middle terrace.

Very badly damaged from the huge amounts of debris that had fallen from the upper tier throughout the years, it did not look as if much had ever been done here, relative to the other levels. I wondered, idly, about the people who had walked this floor, who had stood and looked out over the desert, whether they had been entertained in lavish style and, whether during the different occupations, this space had been used and for what purpose. It seemed strange to think that anyone, either Roman or rebel would have been bothered to come down here, it was a few minutes walk from the main level and the other buildings on the plateau and, would have no real import to everyday life.

Roman soldiers while happy to relax and drink wine probably weren't interested in a couple of courtyards. Although I did remember reading somewhere that this end of the rock was kept very cool during the worst of the heat, as the cleverly engineered rooms were able to capture the breeze off the Dead Sea, so maybe they did use it. We would never know. It was fun just trying to picture their lives, until I remembered that I had actually been part of the lives of some of them. That brought me back to earth with a bump...and not wanting to deal with that part of me, I stopped daydreaming, finished recording this level and walked back up to the main palace.

I could hear the voices of the group I'd been working with earlier in the day still chattering among themselves, so hard at work they didn't even notice my approach. I watched them for a while before checking with Sebastian to see whether he needed me to record anything they were doing. He reckoned they'd be ok for about half an hour, so, returning his camera, I motioned to the other side of the courtyard and said I'd been over that way if they needed me. I was going to get some water and use the facilities.

148

Nodding absently, he turned back to what he was doing and immediately forgot I'd been there, so typical of these guys. Smiling I left them to it and, picking up my backpack from the corner where I'd dropped it, went to freshen up. Thankfully, the toilet block had cold running water, so I washed my face, hot from being in the sun, despite my large hat keeping the worst of it off me and, refilled my water bottle from the drinking water tap. Coming back out into the sunshine, I squinted across the plateau to see if I could see Max. Sure he'd be busy in the Western Palace again, I strolled through hoping he might have time to take a quick break. Walking past the ruins of the barracks and the Byzantine chapel, I reached the other palace, looking across the walls to see if I could see where people were working.

It seemed very quiet, no chattering here, although I could just hear voices drifting over from the casemate wall on the far side where many of the Zealots had made their living quarters. Moving quietly through the ruins so as not to disturb the archaeologists if they were hard at it, I was puzzled when I didn't come across anyone. Strange, they must be working somewhere else this afternoon. I hadn't seen Max at lunchtime and really didn't know where he might be. Retracing my steps I peeked into the chapel, its delicate mosaic floor now protected by a roof. Nobody there, but I did stop to look at the floor, it never ceased to amaze me, exquisitely designed, it was one of the most beautiful known from this period.

Continuing on, I checked the synagogue and, although a few people were working there, there was no sign of Max. Had I missed him back up at the Western Palace? I didn't think so, but I didn't know why they'd be working here. If Naomi were with him, they'd be with the mosaics. Then I remembered that over the other side between a building described as a small palace and the casemate wall was a mosaic workshop, made sense that Naomi would want to check that out, if she hadn't already.

Checking my watch, I saw that it was coming up on three o'clock, not too long and it would be time to head back down, could I really be bothered to go all the way over to the workshop? You need to know that this is not a small surface area, it is around six hundred metres in length and nearly three hundred metres wide - that's well over half a 'K' people - and it was a pretty warm afternoon. Realising that it was going to take me longer than the half hour I'd told Sebastian I'd be, I decided not to bother. Returning to the storerooms, I was quickly called upon to record the remainder of the work they had done and log any more finds.

Another half an hour or so whizzed by, the breeze kicked in and the light began to change, softening from the harsh blue of earlier to a gentler hue. I noticed shadows appearing here and there, darkening corners and passageways and, whimsically, I imagined that they were nature's shrouds concealing any secrets still lurking in the gloom. Gathering up our equipment we began to organise ourselves to set off back down the ramp. Still no Max, it was unlike him not to check in on me, especially after the last few days and I was unable to shake a feeling of foreboding, I had no reason to feel worried, but still it bothered me.

"I'll follow you down guys, I'm going to find Max."

"No worries Hannah. Take care if you're coming down on your own, watch those rocks." Sebastian waved as they trundled off down the ramp, still gossiping about their day, I grinned as I watched them and then turned to go and look for Max. I was methodical this time and as it was cooler, started off at the far side of the plateau. It took me a good while, as I checked every building, yet he was no-where to be seen. I rechecked the Western Palace, the chapel, the synagogue, the administration building even the storerooms, and I knew he hadn't been in there. I wandered through the main level of the Northern Palace and decided, since I was already in that direction, to check the lower two levels.

Maybe he'd come down after I'd left. There were mosaics there after all, who knew whether he and Naomi had decided to make a quick study of these. Leaving my backpack at the top, cautiously I made my way down the modern steps that led to the hidden stairwell. I'd need to be quick, the light was starting to fade and I didn't want to have to walk back to the digs on my own. As I reached the top of the secret stairs I heard a voice behind me and as I glanced back to see who it was, noticed that someone was hurrying back up the ramp. Geez these guys, couldn't keep 'em away!

"So, are you looking for lover boy?" Astonished, I realised that it was Naomi.

"What? What on earth?"

"Well, you can see he's not here." She drawled, sitting down on a piece of wall about three feet from where I was standing. "He's back at the digs, I told him I thought I'd seen you go down with one of the other groups."

"Well that's no worries, come on, let's go, I don't want to be here all night and I certainly don't want to walk down in the dark." I moved to go past her, but she put her hand on my arm, halting my progress.

"Naomi what are you doing? Come on, let's go." Trying to shake her off. "Let go of my arm."

"You need to listen to me girlie." 'Girlie,' who used that word? "He's mine and you'd better get used to it." She continued. "Back off and leave him alone, he's only humouring you, filling in time until we can be together." Her words, which made no sense to me anyway, seemed sluggish, as if she was drunk, but with an edge that made me think she was a bit crackers. I just wanted to get away from these stairs and off this rock - agreeing with her appeared to be the wisest option.

"Ok, ok, whatever…I'll back off, I'll tell him when we get down that he's all yours, that I don't want him." Banking down the panic in my voice, I tried to sound convincing.

"Hmmm…" considering, "…you say that, but I know your sneaky ways, you'll just start pestering him again. So, I'm not sure that's going to be enough, maybe you need to be out of the way altogether."

"What exactly do you mean by 'out of the way' Naomi?" Wary now.

"Well, if you weren't here, he'd come back to me." This woman was cuckoo. Trying to distract her I asked,

"Come back to you? He's been 'yours' before then?"

"Oh yes, many times, he and I. He's not interested in you at all, its just pity. Why do you think I came to the site, I knew he'd be waiting for me."

I peered at her face, her oddly glazed expression confirming my fears. She had totally lost the plot. Oh lordy, what had prompted this, something must have happened during the day and it had tipped her, probably already fragile, mind over the edge. Dammit, why had I decided to come looking for Max and how the heck was I going to get out of this? The only way back was up past her, but she still gripped my arm, I could feel it bruising, her fingers vice-like. The person scrambling up the ramp was getting closer, I dared not risk looking to see who it was, but I yelled out at the top of my lungs.

"Hey you, please, I need he…lp." The last word a screech as Naomi yanked my arm hard, pulling me towards her, wrenching my shoulder in, or possibly out of, its socket. She was strong this woman, this woman who had seemed so delightful on first meeting, this woman who thought she owned Max. Fear trickled down my spine and I felt suddenly very cold. The sun was slowly dipping over the distant horizon and soon night would fall. I really didn't want to be here in the dark. I sensed rather than saw movement behind Naomi, I still couldn't tell who it was but I also became aware that others were coming up the ramp, following whoever was already here.

Breathing steadying, I felt safer, it'd be ok, I just hoped they'd get down to us soon; Naomi was dissembling in front of me. Her hair was tousled, falling out of its usually tidy plait and her clothes dishevelled and, it was at this point that I realised she was wearing Max's shirt. So it was her, she was the one who had been in my room…if she'd she wanted something of Max's, why hadn't she gone into his room? Yanking me again, she began to laugh, a sound that set chills through me, her cackling was arrested as a soft voice spoke from above her on the steps.

"Naomi…" murmuring his words gently, "…Naomi, what are you doing?" It was Max, oh thank everything that's holy, it was Max. He was very carefully making his way towards us, the others having reached the plateau were also moving in our direction. His words were deliberate and calm. "Why do you hold this woman?"

"She is trying to steal you, she refuses to let you go."

"No, no." Trying to keep my voice calm. "I said I would, I told y…"

"Shut up bitch, you lie, you want him for yourself, you are trying to trick me, you are like all the other whores, always taking what is mine." Charming turn of phrase I thought.

"But I'm not Naomi, I do not lie, leave her here, she is nothing, come to me." So smooth and persuasive were his words that I was nearly convinced he actually meant them. He wasn't looking at me at all, he was trying to hold Naomi's gaze, ignoring everything else around him completely. "Come to me my darling, the night will be cold if you are not with me, I need you to warm you." Geez he was good.

"This cow needs to be taught a lesson, she has meddled where she shouldn't have done." This unravelling of a once refined and composed woman was awful.

Waving his arms at the guys inching their way towards us, hoping to get them to stay back, Max held out his arms.

"Well, why don't we leave her here on this rock, she cannot get down without help, it is nearly dark, by the morning she will know that she should not interfere, she will have been cold and alone and we will have had the night together warm and safe." Even though I knew he didn't mean it, the thought of being left here all night was enough to freak anyone out. I couldn't stop a moan of fright escaping my lips. "See she is scared now, it will be a good lesson." He crooned the words, soothing and tranquil.

I could see Naomi playing with this idea in her mind; she was beginning to believe she had the upper hand. I bit my lips to stop my teeth from chattering, terror roiling across my skin. The others stood quietly, not daring to move, we waited - stalemate. Max started to inch closer, very slowly and carefully, still talking to her in the soft sing song voice, lulling Naomi's broken mind. He nearly made it, he nearly reached us, when suddenly Naomi swung me round again, this time I knew my shoulder had come out of its socket and, unable to stop myself I screamed in pain.

"No!" She thundered. "It is not enough, this trollop must be gone."

Despite the fact that under any other circumstance, I would have burst out laughing at her words which were peculiar and way more dramatic than I felt this whole ridiculous scenario warranted, this time I panicked. I tried to disengage my arm, but the pain was too bad, fire shot though my shoulder and bright lights danced across my vision. Surely she wasn't serious? Surely her 'be gone' didn't mean what I thought it meant? Anyway I thought, inconsequentially, being 'be goned' wasn't in my plans for today. Hysteria bubbled up into my throat and before I could stop myself, I giggled, the sound echoing across the space and that did it - with a strength beyond anything I imagined she possessed - Naomi whirled round and shoved me down the stairs.

It was like slow motion, detachedly and in a split second, I saw Max push Naomi out of the way and dive down the stairs. As he moved towards me, the others rushed at Naomi, who was laughing uproariously, gathering her up and trying to pull her back up the walkway. It was all movement and sound. She screeched like a banshee when she saw that Max was not coming back to her and tried to wrest herself out of their grasp. At least two of the guys followed Max to get to me.

I felt like I was floating, I have no idea whether I hit any of the stairs on the way down, but the last thing I remember was slamming into the ground, feeling my breath knocked out of me and an excruciating pain in my head, then nothing. I didn't feel Max grasp my hand and check my pulse. I didn't hear him shout for someone to go find something that they could lay me on and, something else to staunch the blood. I didn't feel him running his hands over me to see if he could work out whether I'd broken anything. I was not aware that they lifted me gently onto some kind of stretcher and carried me carefully down to the accommodation block.

I was unaware that the doctor spent a long time examining me, of discussions about head and spinal injuries, of my head being shaved, treated and bandaged, along with my shoulder. Or of being connected to monitors and tubes. Of instructions being given about signs that would indicate whether I was deteriorating or coming round. I did not know about their concern that taking me down to one of the hospitals would risk further injury and that they preferred to keep watch on me in the medical centre here on the site. Neither did I know how long Max sat beside me willing me to wake up.

By this time, I was far away.

Chapter Sixteen

"Hannah, Hannah, wake up, come on wake up." Urgent voices were penetrating my consciousness; I could feel a hand clasping mine, a thumb rubbing on my palm. Vaguely I thought to myself that I was ok, that Naomi hadn't hurt me and Max had reached me before she pushed me down those stairs, relief swept through me. Fighting through layers of fog, I tried to open my eyes, but they were too heavy and I sank back into darkness. There were moments, when wakefulness seemed close, when I struggled to open my eyes, or tried to speak, but every time it was easier to stay asleep. Occasionally, I was aware of faces that swam across my vision, familiar and unfamiliar, of voices talking over my head, trying to rouse me and, still the pressure of someone's thumb on my palm. I didn't want to wake up, I was comfortable where ever I was and just wanted everyone to leave me alone.

I don't know how much longer I slept, but eventually I began to come round and, although wakefulness was taking some time to banish the fuzziness from my brain, I realised I felt quite normal. My head didn't seem to hurt so I presumed what ever I'd hit it on hadn't done too much damage. Thick skull I've got…not much to lose in there either, I grinned to myself.

"You're back with us." The voice seemed familiar, yet not quite. "You gave us a bit of a scare there." The words an echo of something I'd heard recently, but couldn't quite recall where.

"Uhuh." Running my tongue across my lips, which felt very dry. "Hummmm…what happened? Where am I?"

"In your room, the room you made me sleep in. Here wait…" a bowl was held to my mouth and a few drops of a cool sweet drink slid down my parched throat, "…this will help, no," as I tried to gulp it, "just a little at a time." The words didn't make any sense, who had I made sleep in my room? I hadn't been in my room much at all lately; I'd slept with Max in his. Still struggling to come round, I pushed myself up on my elbows, I felt hampered by too much clothing, or sheets or something, it was too hard, I flopped back against the pillow, which made me wince, it was quite solid and made my head hurt, maybe I had hit it after all.

"Come on Hannah, you need to wake up, we need you to help us." What? Now who was I helping? Everything was jumbled, I forced my eyes open, fighting nausea and looked up at the person watching me anxiously. It wasn't Max; it was his altar ego Maxentius. Oh no, no, no, no, not again, this couldn't be happening - grrrr…if I ever got my hands on that woman I'd knock her through next year.

"Maxentius?" Questioning. "Is that you?"

"Who else would it be Hannah?"

"I don't know, I wasn't sure, how long have I been asleep?" Realising that in this time I had patients to care for, one of whom was sitting next to me, I tried to get out of bed, pushing what seemed to be layers and layers of blankets off me. It actually turned out to be more like a heavy quilt and where it came from I have no clue, I didn't remember seeing one when I glanced through the things in this room.

It was still too hard, my body felt like lead, too heavy, I rested on my arm for a moment, panting a little. "What on earth is happening to me? What's happened to Marcus, to you? Who has been treating your wounds? Sergius what happened with Sergius?" Fear sharpened my voice, I tried to fight this lethargy, I had never known anything like this before, I had no strength in my limbs and felt that I would never be able to get up again.

"Do not worry Hannah, it has only been four days."

"Four days?" My voice went up several octaves as I squeaked this out, "Four days, oh no, your sheets, your bandages everything will need changing and washing, you both will need to be bathed, oh no, why did you let me sleep for so long?"

"We could not wake you, it was as though you were in a stupor. Ever since the night we lost Sergius. You went out on onto the plateau and suddenly collapsed, we had to carry you back here, we could not get you to respond to anything."

"We, who's we?"

"Me, your brother, one or two of the other men and a woman, she has also taken to watching you when we needed to sleep, I think she might be your brother's wife. We have taken it in turns to sit with you, trying everything we knew to make you awaken. You had us worried." His concern seemed to be much more than his quiet words suggested, his eyes were running over my face watching for any changes that might indicate I was going to go back to sleep. His hand was still holding mine, his grip firm, not too tight, but his thumb was still rubbing my palm, light dawned, oh - it had been Maxentius sitting with me, he had been the one holding my hand. I did not want him to let go, he felt like a lifeline, an anchor.

As we sat, the swimmy feeling began to dissipate. Slowly, very slowly I was able to sit up without my head lolling. It was such a strange sensation, I was the strong one, I was the one dispensing the help, not the one receiving it. I didn't like this feeling that I had no control. It took forever for me to want to risk standing, my legs felt very wobbly and sudden movements brought the nausea back with vengeance. Eventually, I managed it, Maxentius was unbelievably patient, I could not imagine too many men in this era, caring enough to help a woman stand, they'd just expect her to pull herself together and get on with it.

By the time I had done all this I was exhausted all over again, but I was determined to check on Marcus. After making sure my mantle was wrapped around my shoulders, Maxentius held my arm and we walked slowly along to the next room. To my delight, Marcus was sitting up, he was chatting to a woman, whom I assumed was the same one who'd been watching me. All at once, I realised several things. Her name was Raizel, which I knew meant 'Rose,' I knew that we were friends, that we had been friends before she had married Aharon and that I had introduced them. I knew that she and Aharon had recently had a son and, I knew that I had started to teach her the basics of caring for the sick. I felt a warm glow suffuse me. I had a friend, in this time beyond history, someone who cared about me.

They looked up as we came in, Raizel's eyes shadowed when she saw Maxentius holding my arm, but she smiled at me and, Marcus grinned.

"Finally up and about then? You've had everyone in a right flap, good job Raizel here knew a little bit about looking after the injured. We're thinking of taking her on full time, if you're going to while away the days snoozing." I had given up wondering how we all seemed to understand each other - that was way too much for my head at any time and especially at the moment.

"Oh, ha ha, you cheeky so and so. You wait 'til I need to look at your wounds, I'm sure I can find an ointment with a bit of a sting." Smiling back at him I was pleased to see the colour in his cheeks was not so hectic as it had been the night Sergius had died. It looked as if during the days I had been unconscious, he had turned the corner and was well on the way to getting better. Turning to face Maxentius who was still holding my arm, I looked properly at him for the first time.

"How about you sir, how are your wounds?" Behaving with as much decorum as I could muster, while his thumb, no longer on my palm had begun to draw little circular patterns on the soft skin of my inner elbow, sending frissons along my arm. It was all I could do to ignore them and in all honesty I wasn't sure he realised what he was doing, it seemed an absent-minded thing, like something you would do when trying to comfort a child.

"Pah, little more than scratches now, I'm doing much better." He sounded confident, upbeat, but I could see pain etched round his eyes and his skin was still too pale. Marcus, I no longer worried for, but Maxentius had taken a bashing, his ribs had probably been cracked or broken and, although most of the cuts seemed superficial, I wanted to check them properly. If only I didn't feel so weak.

"I really want to examine you both properly, though I'm not sure I have the strength to attempt it today. Raizel, would you be so kind as to help me out a little longer? They look to have thrived in your care, I cannot thank you enough." She smiled at me, and shook her head.

"I only continued what you had started, and of course I will help, as long as you need me. I think you were exhausted, until that night when you collapsed, I don't think you had had more than two hours sleep a night in over four weeks, that is enough to kill a man. We are not made to go without rest. Go, you should be properly rested, you will sleep a healthy sleep tonight and be even better tomorrow." She stood then and held me close; I felt tears trickle down my cheeks and cursed myself for such weakness.

"Thank you my sister, you are my comfort." The words sounded old fashioned in my head, but they seemed to hit the right note, she went back to talking with Marcus, while Maxentius helped me to my room.

"Right Hannah, you need to eat, nothing except a little sweetened water has passed your lips for the last three days, your body will have lost all its energy." Tell me something I didn't

161

know. "You are pale and weak." Made me sound totally pathetic and although I knew he was right, didn't mean I liked it and he was still holding my arm.

"Did I hurt my head?" Remembering the pain when I lay back on the pillow.

"What, no I don't think so, you just sort of folded in on yourself. Why? Does it hurt?"

"Not sure…" gingerly, I passed my hand over the back of my skull, fingers gently feeling for a bump or a cut, the injury I was pretty sure should be there, but couldn't feel. "…can't feel anything, its just that it hurt when I rested my head on the pillow, like there was a lump or something."

Maybe it was perception of the pain caused by whatever I hit when Naomi shoved me, my mind was registering an injury that hadn't really happened, sort of on the lines of a residual haunting in reverse. The sheer convoluted nature of that thought made me chuckle, it was a bit shaky, but definitely a chuckle.

"Oh, now there's a sound we've missed, you have the loveliest laugh." Embarrassed I dipped my head, not really sure how to answer that. So much had happened since I last talked to this man, Max and I had become lovers, my heart was his completely, yet the emotions I was experiencing while talking to this man were confusing me.

Thankfully I could use my lethargy as an excuse for not really responding, so I simply smiled shyly and let him help me to the chair he had used while I slept. He disappeared for a few minutes, returning with a bowl of something that looked like a stew or thick broth, whose aroma set my taste buds going and I realised that I was very hungry.

"Steady, don't gobble it, you'll be sick." Maxentius admonished, pulling the bowl away from me. "Honestly Hannah, you should know better, how many times did you tell us not to eat so fast…?"

"I don't remember." Without thinking - careful Hannah - Maxentius, not aware of my slip continued,

"…well it was plenty, you treated us as though we were greedy children, I'm surprised you didn't rap our knuckles." Appalled I looked at him.

"I should not have been so disrespectful, please, I am so sorry."

"You did what you had to do, we were very sick, too much food too quickly might have been contrary to our recovery, although Marcus and I were amused by your insistence." Sadly I remembered that probably Sergius had been too sick to see a funny side in anything, sighing I looked across at Maxentius and asked, very quietly.

"Where did they move him to?" Maxentius glanced at me from the bed where he was sitting.

"Don't worry about this yet, we will have time enough when you feel better."

"I need to know." Urgently now I leaned over and, without thinking, touched his hand. "Where is he? Please tell me." He turned my hand over and pressed my palm.

"They moved him somewhere private, I think. It was not hygienic to keep him in the other room."

"No, I expected them to move him, but I need to know where, there are things I must do to cleanse his body."

"I will find out, if I can, but they may not tell me, your brother's wife may know. She seems…" searching for the right word, "…understanding. Now do you wish to rest for a while, I think maybe you are tired again." I was unutterably tired, all I had done was walk a few yards and eaten a meal, but I felt like I'd run two marathons. My head felt groggy and my mouth wouldn't form words properly, this exhaustion thing was no fun, I was over feeling reliant on others, but I had no choice.

"Please…" haltingly, "…please will you help me outside later, I want to breathe fresh air and feel the breeze on my face, I think that will help to clear my foggy head."

"Foggy head, what do you mean?" Smiling at my use of jargon, I tried to explain. Goodness Hannah, you need to remember you're not in a modern world now. After several minutes of me trying to explain that the inside of my head was like a day full of heavy mist, or low cloud, he said he understood, which was belied by his perplexed expression. Unable to be bothered anymore, finding that sleep was about to overwhelm me, I slid down in the chair; quite ready to snooze where I sat.

"No, Hannah, come to your cot, you cannot sleep properly like that." Once again holding my arms, he pulled me carefully out of the chair and helped me to lie down. My strength gave out; I slithered inelegantly onto the bed, my legs hanging over the side,

"They'll have to stay there." I thought woozily, "They'll be fine." I was dimly aware that Maxentius gently lifted them on to the bed and tucked the coverlet over me warming my body. Just as oblivion enveloped me, I felt his fingers, feather light, brush the top of my head and saw that he had seated himself in the chair, guarding my rest, like a sentry. His presence was comforting, I was pretty sure it was not appropriate for him to be there unchaperoned, but it looked as if everyone knew he was and they were not perturbed. So I simply accepted it and slept, secure in the knowledge that my sleep would be undisturbed.

Chapter Seventeen

Again, I did not know how long I'd slept, but as I came round the next time, I felt much better. The nausea had dissipated and my limbs didn't seem quite as heavy, the lethargy that had overtaken me must be waning. I could only hope. I realised I felt well enough to resume my duties and get on with things. Lifting my head, I saw that my protector had slept in the chair, how many nights had this happened? My night had been disturbed; I had tossed and turned, unable to get comfortable, images of the last few days mingled together. My Mum would have called them temperature dreams, like the delirium you have with a fever. I was aware that someone pressed a cool cloth on my forehead and tried to calm me.

I worried about Max, two thousand years away, what was he doing? What was *I* doing? I wanted him to be with me, holding me and loving me, without him I felt bereft. What happened after Naomi pushed me? I had no recollection. Once, I thought I heard his voice calling my name, I woke listening, hoping it was real and that I was back with him, but the only sound was Maxentius' laboured breathing, something I made a mental note of to check as soon as possible, other than that, there was silence. Eventually, sleep reclaimed me, a deeper, more settled slumber, untroubled by dreams.

Daylight was shining through the high window, as I opened my eyes, I had no idea what time it was, but my room still felt cool, so maybe it was still morning. There was no sign of Maxentius and I hoped he had gone back to his own bed in the night. I could hear a quiet conversation in the next room and knew I really must get out of bed and go and look after my patients.

Raizel's best intentions aside, I needed to check, for my own peace of mind, that infections had not set in and that the pair of them were indeed on the mend.

Maxentius in his concern for me, had tried to play down his pain but even in my fuzzy state the last time I saw him - was it the day before or longer? - I had noticed that he walked stiffly and his jaw often clamped as if sudden movement caused him sharp pain. His ribs needed checking, I didn't think he had anything so severe as punctured a lung, but his breathing concerned me and I recalled the discolouration of his chest the first time I actually remembered treating him. Severe bruising of his lungs from the beating was a real possibility. The stab wounds would need a thorough clean and check, nasty little infections could hide for days without anyone being aware.

The fact that these things were running through my head made me believe that I was over the worst of whatever it was that had laid me low, whether it had been exhaustion, stress, grief, or the trauma of apparently slipping between the twenty first century and antiquity (yeah, I thought, pretty sure that would do it)! I had just started to get up, when I heard footsteps along the corridor and Raizel appeared at my door.

"Oh, you are awake, I was about to come and check on you. It is already into the fourth hour and we thought you might want to try and get up for longer today." The fourth hour, I tried to work out what time that was and decided it might be sometime after ten. I kind of assumed that the 'me' of this time period, would know all this, but maybe I was just rusty from too much sleep. Grimacing, I threw back the covers and stood up.

"Thank you Raizel, I do feel much better today, at least my legs can hold me up." Smiling at her. "How are my - well actually your - patients this morning?"

"They seem in good spirits, although I fear that the older one, Maxentius, is in more pain than he admits to."

"I fear the same my sister, he looked very stiff yesterday, and he requires a thorough examination of his wounds and bruises. I think I can mix up something that will dull the pain for a little while and let him rest properly. I woke in the night and his breathing sounded unnatural."

"I came and brought him back to his own cot, he has barely left your side these past few days and regardless of the fact that he probably should not have been with you alone, sleeping in a chair is not the way to get a healthy rest."

Sighing, partly with the effort and partly because I knew she was trying to censure me without actually saying so, I took her hand.

"Trust me Raizel, I will do nothing to dishonour the family." Although as the words left my mouth, I wasn't one hundred percent certain that I would be able to stick to them, recalling the warmth of Maxentius' hand as he held mine, the touch of his thumb on my inner elbow. Dragging my thoughts back to Raizel, I asked if she would help me dress, the effort still seemed too much. Quickly washing, I slipped into my shift and Raizel helped me pull my tunic over my head, then she tidied my hair, which felt a bit ratty to me. It was very soothing; having someone brush your hair, not since I was a child had anyone done this for me. After spending quite a bit of time trying to get the knots out, she finally tied it into a long plait and twisted it up onto my head.

"There, that should do you." She said, turning me to face her. "You look almost human again."

"Oh very funny." Grasping her hand I squeezed it quickly. "Thank you."

"Just be careful Hannah, your brother and his friends watch you, they know something has changed, please, please be careful."

"I will, don't worry." Trying to dampen the disquiet, knowing that now, not only did I have to deal with two Roman soldiers, it looked as though I was also going to have to deal with a brother I had no real memory of and his Zealot colleagues. Oh I wished I were two thousand years away. "Not helpful Hannah…" I told myself, "…nothing you can do, just get on with it."

Gathering myself together, still feeling a little unsteady, I walked along to the treatment room. The two Romans were sitting on their beds chatting to each other and they both looked up as I entered.

"Good morning you two, I am so sorry, I seem to have overslept." Smiling. "I think it's about time I gave you both a thorough check up."

"Hmmm…I am not sure that's necessary, we have had the best of care while you were not - how should I say it - available." Marcus chuckled. "Raizel has been doing a very good job and she doesn't hurt." I smiled back at him.

"Well, if your cheek is anything to go by, I'd say you were pretty much back to normal but I want to make sure. Infections can be tricky and I do not want a repeat of what happened to your comrade." My words, though gently spoken, brought them up sharp, Marcus stopped laughing and Maxentius looked at me with reproach.

"How could you bring this up?" He said. "While we still grieve."

"I am sorry, but you need to understand the nature of your injuries, you were both stabbed and cut with weapons that were not clean, probably covered in dirt and the blood and skin of others. You, Maxentius, were also beaten with fists, which are usually coated in dust and if the knuckles on these fists break your skin, infection can sit undetected for many days. I refuse to lose either of you to sickness like I did Sergius; please you must let me

168

help you. Raizel has been a blessing, she understands how to keep the bedding clean, and dry, that you needed to be bathed, but I am the one with the knowledge of medicine and of how to heal you, or at least I am your best and only chance."

A long speech, I tried not to sound like I was lecturing them, but I wanted them to understand how serious their injuries were. "Many of your fellow soldiers died simply from wounds that although did not appear, at first to be fatal, were so full of filth that nothing I did could save them." Again, I wished for those sterile hospital beds and some penicillin. I also realised, with a jolt, that I must have worked on other men too, both Roman and Jewish. Did I have a room full of injured men that I needed to check in on? How on earth was I going to work that out without looking like an idiot? Aiming for nonchalance and hoping they would blame my illness for my forgetting something as fundamental as a group of injured people under my care, I asked Raizel.

"How are they by the way?"

"They are…" waggling her hand, "…so, so. I have kept an eye on them while you were unable to, some are worse than others, but their wounds seem less savage."

Not surprising really, I thought, they were not the ones taken unawares. Many of the Romans probably didn't even get the chance to defend themselves since most of their weapons would have been stored away in the armoury. I felt sick at the thought of ambushing unarmed men and, probably women and children too, as I'm sure there must have been auxiliary and domestic staff as well as the men of the garrison. Not wanting to deal with the horror of that quite yet, I turned back to the two soldiers.

"Right who's first?" Without waiting for an answer I went over to the shelf where my ointments stood, checking the contents and, as before, letting my instincts take over. I asked Raizel to heat some water over the fire, I assumed was still burning in the room across the courtyard, while I filled several bowls and flagons with mixtures of herbs and oils. Remembering that I had opium, I mixed some in with honey and water and stood it to one side. I would only use it if necessary, hoping that the need for painkillers had passed.

Raizel returned with warm water in a large bowl and she had also brought some cloths. Turning to Marcus, who seemed rather embarrassed, by what I was about to do, I smiled gently and touched his shoulder.

"Do not be anxious, I will only uncover you bit by bit. I do not wish to make you uncomfortable." Asking him to lay back down on the bed, I pulled his sheet back over him, demonstrating what I meant. He began to relax and I turned the sheet back to uncover his upper body. Adding a large dose of salt to the warm water, I waited until it dissolved and carefully removed the bandages, then I covered his top half and examined the rest of his body, making sure not to be too obvious when I checked his groin area. Awkward as it was, for both of us, it had to be done. I examined every nick, scratch, cut and stab wound. Most were healing very well, but two or three on his chest and abdomen seemed rather more raw than I would have liked given the time lapsed since they were inflicted.

Talking to him the whole time I was working, explaining what I was doing, I used the saline to clean all the wounds, but spent quite a bit longer on those that worried me. I knew that there must be some infection, because Marcus winced when I squeezed the water into the injured skin.

"I need to debride these three wounds and it will hurt, but it is the only way to remove the diseased tissue, you will heal much more quickly if I do it."

"What does that mean?"

"I must either cut the dying tissue away, or…" thinking out loud, "…if there are any maggots about, I can place them into the wound and they will eat the infected area, leaving only healthy tissue."

As I was talking, I watched Marcus pale and quickly lifted an empty bowl, knowing he was about to be very sick. Holding him around his shoulders and letting him get over his nausea, I quietly continued to explain why this worked. Much as some things sound quite revolting, I think that the more information a person has, the better they are able to handle it.

"There's always maggots about." Interjected Raizel, who'd been watching from the other side of the room, in case I needed her help. "I can go and get a few if you like." I nodded over Marcus' head as a fresh bout of sickness overcame him.

"Even with the pain dulling drink, if I cut the skin away it will hurt, the soreness is caused by the infection. Though it sounds horrible, I am fairly sure that you will not feel the maggots because they will only eat dead flesh where there is no pain. How about we try it? Don't watch while I place them in the wounds, then they will be covered up, and if you feel them, I can take them off immediately." I looked at him encouragingly and then went in for the kill. "You are a soldier Marcus, surely after all you have been through this is a mere trifle." I could almost see him straighten up; it would not do for his commanding officer to see him quake like a baby.

He drew a shuddering breath and gritted his teeth.

"Do it, just don't say anything 'til its done." I winked at him.

"Deal." Raizel appeared a few moments later with a nice selection of maggots wriggling on a platter,

"I found them in the store room." I waved my hand at her.

"I do not want to know." I said. "That will set my stomach off too." Carefully, I placed several of them throughout the three wounds giving me most concern. I was fairly sure that the rest of his injuries were healing properly, but to be on the safe side, I added salve to some of the larger ones and re-bandaged all of them. Then I bathed him and even managed to wash his hair, after which, although still rather pale, he looked much better.

Between us, Raizel and I remade his bed, putting on clean sheets that smelled of fresh air and lavender, helping him to sit back down. Guessing, rightly, that he was rather tired by all these exertions, I asked him if he wished to have a brief rest. Nodding, he lay back on his pillow and shut his eyes.

"Can you feel anything Marcus?" I asked quietly.

"No, but I'm worried that if I think about it, then I may do." Laughing, I offered him a sip or two of sweet water, which he accepted, unknowing that it had a little sleeping draft added and I watched him carefully as he nodded off.

"One down, one to go." I motioned to Maxentius, who had watched these proceedings without a word. "Come, I must examine you too."

"I'm fine Hannah." Making as if to stand and leave the room. He would not look at me.

"No sir, you are not fine. I have seen your movements and watched the pained expressions cross your face. Discomfort has made you stiff and you suffer when you move suddenly. I know I can help, please let me." Beseeching him. He looked at me, glowering, I couldn't understand what was bothering him and I had treated him before, what was wrong?

"Max." Deliberately using the diminutive. "Max, you have spent many days watching me, protecting my rest and making sure I was cared for, please let me heal you. I could not bear it if anything happened to you..." the last few words were barely a whisper, knowing Raizel was within hearing range, although she seemed to be occupied folding bandages and cloths. I also knew my words to be the truth, that this man whom I had known for such a short time, had become very important to me, despite our different backgrounds. The thought of losing him tore at my soul. As quietly as I had spoken, he heard and turned to look at me.

"As you will." Abruptly, he sat back down; I helped him remove his tunic, leaving his lower clothing on for now. His stab wounds were not too bad, one was slightly yellower than I would have liked, it needed some attention, but it was the bruising that shocked me, the whole of his upper body was purple and green and black. He looked at me rather sheepishly, and listened as I talked myself through the damage.

Pressing very gently on each of his ribs, it was obvious that at least two were broken, but by the simple method of putting my ear to his chest and back and asking him to take deep breaths, I was fairly certain that his lungs were intact. His breathing, although laboured did not sound obstructed and there was no rattle. Without the aid of x-rays or ultrasounds, even a stethoscope, I had no way of knowing for sure, but to the best of my rudimentary knowledge, his chest was clear. His ribs would heal of their own accord, it would just take time and rest.

To be on the safe side and to restrict his movements, I wanted to bandage his chest. Before doing so, I rooted around my jars until I found one that smelt like it contained arnica, an extract known to reduce bruising and something which I assumed must have been purchased from a merchant who passed along the trade route near Masada, for it was grown in Europe. Never mind, how we had it, the fact was we did and I could use it. Mixing it with oil, I began to rub it in, my fingers gently massaging it into the skin across his chest and back.

Without thinking, I began so sing softly, a lullaby, like the one I had sung when I tried to soothe Sergius that night, a lifetime ago. Raizel watched us, anxiously, my behaviour with this man worrying her, but I didn't really care, he was in pain and I intended to fix it. I continued to smooth the mixture in until it was all used. Then I bandaged over the top of it, not too tightly, but enough to make him think before he moved, hopefully it would stop him doing anything too quickly.

Rubbing the oil off my hands using a piece of cloth, I proceeded to dress the infected wound. His gasp as I tried to clean it merely confirmed my suspicion that all was not 'fine' and, ignoring his grunts of pain, I managed to push some of the horrible smelling salve right into it, then wiped some more round the edges finishing by packing it with a fresh piece of cloth soaked in the same mixture. More bandages protected this and, finally I sat back, satisfied I done all I could. As with Marcus, I changed the bedding, Raizel coming forward to help me, the room felt better brighter and cleaner.

I gathered the dirty and contaminated cloths up into a ball and took them across to the laundry room, dumping them into some water that looked as if it was boiling hot. I noticed out of the corner of my eye a sort of kettle, or bucket on the fire, full of water. Raizel must have done this I thought gratefully; I will have clean cloths and bedding. Then it dawned on me that the night I had tried to save Sergius, all the work I had done on the three men, Raizel must have been the one who was working to keep me supplied with everything I needed, even the food I had eaten. Smiling, I walked back over to the treatment room and gave her a huge hug.

Thank you for everything, you are such a blessing to me." Touched, she hugged me back and said she'd be back shortly, she would go and check on the other men and would call me if I was needed.

Chapter Eighteen

I sat, suddenly weary, I had forgotten that this time yesterday I had not been able to walk let alone care for wounded soldiers. My hands were trembling and my legs felt weak. I had an absurd desire to cry, but refused to let the tears fall. I was just tired and I really wanted a coffee…hmmm, good luck with that Hannah.

Maxentius looked at me.

"You look fatigued." Stilted. "Perhaps you should rest too, now you have finished your examination of us." Confused at his tone, I stared at him. His eyes were hooded and I could not read his expression.

"What's wrong Maxentius?"

"Nothing is wrong, simply that I think you need to take some time for yourself, you have not been well." His voice was wooden and hard, I didn't understand.

"What have I done?" Tremulously, then with a little more force. "What have I done? I know I was disrespectful when I told you why I needed to examine you both and I know that during my care of you I hurt you, I am sorry, but your injuries had to be treated. I refuse to let any one else die." Especially not you, I added silently.

"Oh Hannah." His words were a sigh as if dragged from his very core. "It is nothing you have done, it is what I fear you cannot do."

"I don't understand, tell me."

"I cannot." Biting back my frustration, I stood,

"Why not, what is so hard that you cannot tell me, I have treated your wounds, bathed your fevered body, held you while you tried to stand, walked with you to the shade of the pomegranate trees and listened as you talked about your life. You picked me up after I collapsed, you helped to carry me to my cot, you watched over me while I slept and worried that I might not wake up. These things, we have shared and after all of that, you still refuse to tell me."

Forgetting that Marcus was sleeping, my voice rose in my anger and in my determination not to cry. I couldn't believe I was hearing this, what had changed? I knew that in this time, our friendship, or whatever it was that was going on, was complicated, ok, it was probably forbidden and dangerous, but it was my life. I had come here with my brother and his family, but only because they needed a healer. I was not a Zealot and I did not care about their cause. Despite my best intentions, my feelings for this man had become very strong and I thought he returned them.

I suddenly remembered the words that had followed me, when I had left him on sitting on the upturned jar under the pomegranate tree, to check on Sergius and Marcus and I flung them at him.

"'Hurry back my Hannah,' you said those words, 'hurry back my Hannah', *my* Hannah, not just Hannah, **my** Hannah and, later when I talked about the view, I had the strangest feeling that it wasn't the view you called beautiful. Or am I just a stupid woman with too vivid an imagination?" To my complete and utter mortification I was crying now, tears were pouring down my cheeks, although quite frankly, I was surprised it had taken me this long given recent events.

In my defence, I had been pushed down a flight of steps, presumably banging my head at the bottom, sort of fallen through time, where I was fighting off an exhaustion borne, apparently, out of taking care of several badly wounded people and the death of at least one of them, who knew how many others I had lost. Then finding that the one person who seemed to care anything about me was pushing me away was simply too much to bear. Nothing else mattered right now, not even that in my other life I was in love with a man, who could make me feel as though I was his whole world. I heard a sound and sensed, rather than saw, him move, my head now bowed, my eyes too full of tears, my voice trailing away as I felt my heart breaking.

"Don't cry, oh my love, please don't cry, I cannot bear it." Hang on, did I hear that correctly? Did he just say what I think he did? I was so distraught by now I wasn't sure what I was hearing. "Shhhhh." He whispered as, taking a huge risk, he pulled me to him. "Hannah please don't cry like this you are breaking my heart." His heart? Mine was the one shattered into tiny pieces all over the floor.

"I'm pretty sure you don't care about my heart." I muttered against his chest.

"This is what I cannot tell you and this is what you cannot do."

"Don't you dare start all that again." My anger was fighting my distress and gaining the upper hand, as I struggled against the arms pinning me to him. "If you don't tell me, so help me I will punch your lights out." I felt a rumble of laughter rock Maxentius' chest as he refused to let me go.

"And how precisely, are you going to achieve that?" I continued to wriggle; trying to free myself, the harder I tried, the tighter he held me. He was still, laughing when he finally let me go. "Come this way, we must not wake Marcus, your brother's wife would not be happy." I was still too angry to care, but allowed him to guide me to my room, where we were unlikely to be disturbed. We stood a moment and then Maxentius gently manoeuvred me so I was sitting on my bed. He came round and sat on the chair alongside it, the chair he had slept in while seemingly so concerned for my well being. Grumpily I looked at him, feeling my anger bubbling under the surface, my distress threatening to spill over again. He looked at me, watching all these emotions fight for dominance and me trying to damp them all down.

All at once I felt tired, so tired that everything else battling for control of my senses fell away, I slumped, defeated. Then, determined not to appear broken, I raised my head and staring at his chest, I could not meet his eyes, spoke in cold and haughty tones.

"If you refuse to tell me, you may leave, I am tired now and no longer care that you don't care. I was prepared to risk everything for you, because I thought maybe we had become more than just patient and healer. Obviously I was mistaken and I apologise for reading something into your behaviour that was not there. I see no reason for you to remain with me, please go."

Proud of my little speech and that my voice seemed to be quite steady, if chilly, I lifted my head and looked straight into his eyes. Eyes that were darkening, a face that was tightening, hands that were clenching and for one awful moment I thought he might actually hit me. A shiver ran through me, had I pushed him too far? Debating quickly with myself whether I was cruel enough, or brave enough, to hit him in those bruised ribs if he did take a swing. I couldn't breathe and in my agitation could not prevent a whimper of panic, which propelled Maxentius into action.

He stood, hauling me up off the bed in one swift movement, one arm pulling me close, the other one wrapping round my back and his lips descended on mine and, with a passion I was unable to withstand, he felled me. I was completely powerless, this tall, strapping Roman soldier was kissing me as if he had been waiting a lifetime to do so and couldn't wait a second longer. His kiss went deeper and deeper, his tongue tasting my lips, caressing my mouth, then moving his head slightly he kissed my face, my neck, my shoulder, I shuddered, tremors running down my body. Still

178

keeping one arm around me, his other beginning an exploration of my body, caressing my curves and my hollows, his lips never releasing me, I was undone. After several minutes and attempting to gain a modicum of control - I was still really mad with him - I pushed him away, trying to see his face, having to tilt my head, so tall was he.

"Maxentius" I breathed shakily. "Maxentius, please, just a second..." With a groan he halted the delicious progress down my back with his fingers and kissed my nose. Such a familiar action, deliberately pushing that memory aside, I shifted in his arms so I could see him properly. His eyes were so dark they were like pools of night and I was pretty sure if I stared into them for too long I would drown, then I continued plaintively, "...does this have something to do with what you wouldn't tell me?" I felt that rumble of laughter again.

"Oh Hannah, you do chose the most inopportune of moments."

"Not sure we're going to be able to get back to 'opportune' after that little exhibition." I muttered, still trying to gain control.

"Please, may I just kiss you again?" And did so without waiting for my answer, warmth coiled round my stomach, I needed to have this out before we went any further, as I had the feeling once I let go, there would be no stopping of anything for some time.

"I'm still angry with you, stop distracting me." Sighing and loosening his hold Maxentius took a deep breath and sat us both back down on the chair, settling me onto his knee. I knew that in this world, I had never sat on any man's knee before, at least not since I was a little child, and it felt very intimate. No Hannah, don't let him suck you in, not 'til you know what's going on. "Now give, or I will never let you kiss me again." Really? You're on his knee how the heck would you even stop him? Still it sounded good.

"Oh my love." Now that, I liked the sound of! "I am a Roman soldier, an injured man who is a captive and maybe doomed to death. You are a Hebrew woman, the sister of one of the Zealots and a healer of some repute. We are from different worlds, thrown together by circumstances, which may yet tear us apart. I did not want this to happen because I don't think I could bear to lose you. I did not want to tell you that I love you more than my own life, because if by chance you loved me too, I did not want you to risk everything for me. I cannot see how this can ever work for us, yet I am utterly in your power. You posses my every waking moment, you haunt my dreams, I shut my eyes and you are there, if I don't see you when I am awake I feel adrift. The days after you collapsed and we could not wake you were a nightmare, I knew that if I lost you then, I could not live. My Hannah, without even trying, you have seduced, ensnared and bewitched me and, even though I know that there was a time before I loved you, I find I cannot recall it. I am yours, my heart is in your hands."

His words were quiet, yet compelling. I had watched his face the whole time he was speaking, I knew every word was true and I also knew that it was mutual, that I returned every single feeling and emotion one hundred fold. How was I supposed to tell him - he'd used all the good words dammit. Hesitating, anxious that I do so without sounding trite, I started to speak, fumbled my words and stopped. Biting my lip I took a deep breath.

"There are things that have happened to me in the last little while that I am unable to explain, one of those was being confronted by three injured men whom I thought to be my enemies..." I hesitated, Maxentius opened his mouth to speak but I put my finger on his lips, holding his words back.

"...shhh...wait, I must say this. As time went by I realised that these three were not monsters, just men who believed in one cause, as much as my people believed in another. Spending time with them, trying to heal their wounds I became aware that one of these men had pierced my heart in a way I would never recover from. I tried to fight my feelings in the same way that I have just learned this man was fighting his, but I knew when you claimed me as 'your Hannah' that I could not fight it any more. Then I fell ill, but the last thing I remember before I collapsed, was you calling my name, you sounded so distraught and I wondered whether your distress was more than just friendship, more than just grief for a lost comrade, more than simple concern for someone who had been treating your injuries. When I woke, you were there, holding my hand, rubbing my palm with your thumb, such small gesture, but it sealed my fate. I don't care whether this is forbidden, I don't care whether we are risking everything, I don't care that we are from completely different cultures. My life is ruled by yours, my fate is bound up with yours; my heart has been and will always be yours."

Silence! Concerned that I hadn't worded things properly, I searched his face. Had I succeeded in making him believe me? Maybe I'd said too much or he hadn't understood. I began to speak and, echoing my actions, he placed his finger on my lips. Breathing my name and holding me as though I was about to shatter, he kissed me, pushing his hands into my hair, loosening it from the neat plait, running his hands through its curly length and gripping it while he continued to kiss me senseless.

Wriggling against him, trying to get comfortable, I caused him to moan, and I started to pull away, fearful of exacerbating his injuries.

"No, don't move."

"I don't want to hurt you." I murmured against his mouth. "Your poor body is bruised enough."

"Shut up woman." He growled moving his hands so they were roving across my body sending ripples of desire up and down my spine.

"This chair isn't working for me." I whispered, after a little while. "Do you fancy trying the bed?" I felt a quiver of laughter shake his body.

"Quite the little seductress aren't you?"

"Oh." Blushing. "No, sorry, I was only think…" I was not given the chance to finish my sentence, before he lifted me across onto my bed and joined me there. Lying alongside me, he continued to kiss me deeply and tenderly, his calloused fingers teasing along my arms, roving under my tunic to stroke the hollows round my neck.

I was in unknown territory here, I knew how I had behaved with Max was pretty wanton given the fact we'd only been together a matter of days, but it happened in a different time with different rules and we had known each other forever. In this time, there was strict adherence to traditions and tenets and, unless you were a prostitute, I was pretty damn sure any form of intimate relationship before marriage was totally off limits. Plus, this man here in my room, on my bed, was a stranger and an enemy and a captive. He might even be married. What was I thinking, how did I handle this? Lying next to him, luxuriating in the sensations he was creating throughout my body, listening to his ragged breathing and feeling the rapid tattoo of his heartbeat, I wasn't really sure I cared.

Wrapping my arms around him, I felt fire shoot through me as his kiss deepened and became more fevered, I responded with interest, letting my fingers wander over his body, touching, caressing, stroking, forgetting anything except that I could not get enough of him. Trying to be careful so I didn't hurt him, I somehow managed to get my hands beneath his tunic, brushing my cool fingers lightly across his hot skin, making him shudder. As our passion flared and escalated, I realised we were on a dangerous path, if anyone came along there would be no innocent way of explaining what was going on. Panic caught me and I knew we had to stop before it got out of hand, more frightened for Maxentius than for me, I stilled my hands, and pulled back from his kiss.

"Maxentius." Giggling as he nuzzled his head in my hair and then tried to kiss me again. "No, wait, hang on, we must be careful, this is dangerous, we need to stop before we are beyond caring."

"Think I'm already there." He muttered against my cheek.

"I know but if we are caught, retribution will be severe, the risk for you is too great. To be allowed into my bedchamber while I was sick was one thing, but this is pushing our luck. We have time, your wounds are still healing and we will work something out. Maybe we can find somewhere on this rock that no-one else bothers to go to, a place we can be close without raising suspicion, but we must be careful." Sighing, and knowing I was right, Maxentius leaned towards me and kissed me tenderly for just a few more moments, then lifted himself off the bed, wincing a little he stretched his bruised body.

Adjusting his clothes so that he looked a little less unkempt, he helped me up running his fingers through my thick hair trying, unsuccessfully, to tidy it, its length and richness distracting him, so that while I made sure my tunic looked presentable, he began kissing me behind my ear. Batting him away with a grin, I found a comb on the little wooden cupboard and used it to untangle my unruly locks, re-plaiting it so that I looked, more or less, as I had before we came into the room.

Finally sorted, our breathing a little calmer and the heat in my body a little less hectic, we stood, for a few seconds just holding each other. The hallway was quiet, I guessed we could risk it and, despite knowing I had to, I was finding it hard to release him. He was so tall, I felt like a child standing beside him, I tilted my head to look up into his face, his eyes, green and deep as a forest twinkled down at me, his dark wavy hair in the longer style I noticed all three of the soldiers sported, fell across his cheeks and I could not help but raise my hand to push it back.

"You are so tiny, my Hannah, I am afraid I will snap you."

"Pfft…I'm stronger than you think good sir, it will take more than a brawny Roman soldier to break me." Chuckling he swung me up into his arms, my feet dangling off the floor, he held me close to his chest. Squirming, I tried to escape, an absolutely futile attempt since he merely squeezed me tighter. I tried to kick him, but my feet were bare, so that didn't have any effect either.

Helpless with laughter, I entwined my hands through his hair trying to yank his head back, still writhing in his arms trying to get free, until finally he shook his head, my hands flew to his shoulders fearing I would fall, but Maxentius had no intention of letting me go, he lifted me still higher and swooped on my mouth, his lips hard, he kissed me 'til I lost my breath. Then, gently standing me on the floor, he relaxed his grip, kissed me on the nose then the top of my head and smiling his slow heart turning smile, walked back down the hallway.

Head whirling and body trembling, I just stood there, I have no idea for how long, anyone passing must have thought I'd lost the plot. I'm pretty sure I must have looked much more like a simpleton, than the 'healer of some repute' Maxentius had referred to me as. Eventually, my emotions settled and I felt able to face the outside world, vaguely recalling that Raizel had said she was going to check on the 'others.' I needed to do something to take my mind off what had just happened, straightening my shoulders,

I took one last look down at my clothing to make sure I looked presentable and went out into the daylight.

Chapter Nineteen

As with everything I had done since 'returning' to this place, I followed my instincts, which led me out over the plateau and towards what had been Herod's Western Palace. Feeling a little relieved because, if this was where the other wounded were, they were unlikely to cross paths with Marcus and Maxentius. I went in through an open doorway and, following the sounds of voices, opened another door into a very large and airy room, in which there were several cots. An opening at the far end, its door ajar, linked another room to this one and appeared similarly set up. I also noticed that there was an anteroom to the left side through which I glimpsed shelves and store cupboards. This must be my main treatment area; the other one was merely a temporary room to treat the captives. It made much more sense; it looked as though we had set this up purposefully, although how we had managed to do so in so short a space of time was beyond me, as I had no recollection of doing it.

Several people, all men, glanced up as I came in and all greeted me with smiles and questions.

"How are you feeling?'

"'Bout time you stopped lazing about in bed."

"What some people will do for attention."

"C'mon woman we've missed you in here, nobody to shout at us for not doing what we're told."

"Still look a bit peaky - hey - maybe we need a doctor in here."

Laughing uproariously at their own wit, the men obviously cared about me and as I looked round the room I realised that I cared about them. Many of them were men I had known a long time and whether or not I agreed with their actions or politics, I didn't like to see them hurt. Smiling ruefully, I went among them, checking pulses and temperatures. Some had very pale, clammy or waxy skin and I knew they would need a more thorough examination, but I wanted to get a feel for what I was dealing with before I went any further.

As I reached the second doorway, I noticed Raizel was tidying up bottles and jars on one of the ledges, I walked over to her and quietly asked if she would go and check on the two Romans.

"I think they might like to get some fresh air, but I want to get on and help these men before I go back to them, Marcus likes you, he will do as he's told. Plus, I'm not sure I have the strength yet to help them walk out and I would not want either of them to fall." Sounded a bit weak, even to me, but Raizel did not question me, merely nodded smiling and, quietly leaving after she'd finished what she'd been doing. Taking a deep breath, I went through the connecting door and glanced round, a similar number of men as were in the adjoining room, lay on pallets here. It was cooler and a little darker in this room, here and there oil lamps burned, lifting the gloom. The men seemed quieter; maybe they were more seriously hurt.

Washing my hands in a large bowl I spotted on the top of one of the cupboards I began to check each man thoroughly. Taking a smaller bowl filled with tepid water in which I had dissolved some salt, I started at the bed closest to the far wall. Many of these men were fevered, but it did look as though they were beginning to turn the corner. I removed bandages and cleaned wounds, leaving the air to circulate round their injuries while I went on to the next man.

Once I had completed my first check, I mixed up some of my pain killing draft along with the salve, which seemed to have done the trick on the wounds for the two Romans. Then collecting a pile of sheets, which I placed on a stool in the middle of the room, returned to the first man. Waiting until I had soothed the salve into worst of his injuries, before I offered him a sip of the draft, gave me a chance to monitor his pain level. Finishing up, I bound his wounds in fresh bandages, then changed his bed linen and sat a moment to make sure he was comfortable.

I repeated my actions on every man and by the time I had reached the last bed in this room, I was hot and tired, but the men were all clean, bathed, re-bandaged and lying on fresh bedding. One or two of the men had wounds that needed to be packed with cloths soaked in the salve and left open and they would need watching round the clock for the next few days until I was sure the infections had been erased. Patting the last man on his arm, I smiled down at his pale face. He grinned weakly back at me and whispered his thanks.

"My pleasure Eli, but just get better that's all the thanks I need." Watching as his eyes drooped, heavy with sleep, I stood up quietly, running my eyes over the rest of the room.

Some of the men were chatting together, others drowsed, I was happy that I had done all I could and made a mental note to come back in a little while to check on the few who really worried me. Gathering up the dirty linen, I pulled the door nearly closed, then carried my bundle over to the laundry room, enjoying a few minutes of fresh air. Dumping them into the trough I glanced around to see whether the fire was still lit. It was and was crackling away merrily. I hoisted a large metal bucket like object full of water right onto the flames, not knowing whether this was the correct way to do it, but not really having the time to think it through properly. I'd be back to check it soon enough anyway.

Making my way back over to my sick bay, I began to examine the men in the first room. They were much less badly injured than the other men and most would be up and about in a few days. One or two of them had stitches and my mind went back to those odd dowel like instruments on the cupboard in the other sick room. Stomach churning I realised what they were for and that I had used them to suture some of the larger wounds. Pushing that, rather sickening, thought to the back of my mind I continued my work. These men were much brighter, I chatted with several of them while cleaning and re-binding their cuts and lacerations. I had no fears for most of them; clean wounds, cool skin and clear eyes meant that any infection had been beaten. As in the other room, though, there were one or two who seemed listless and had trouble responding to my questions.

With infinite care I checked every tiny cut, scrape and nick I did not want to miss anything and although they could just be taking longer to heal, I wasn't going to risk ignoring the warning signs. Even if I couldn't see any yellowing, or smell any infection, every wound was covered in salve to which I'd added extra honey to be on the safe side. Finally, I persuaded them to drink a proper dose of the sleeping draft, so that they would rest without tossing, minimising the chance of further damage. My heart ached for these young men who were so helpless, the desperation they must feel to be prepared to gamble their lives in the hopes of seizing a stash of weapons. The gamble had worked, but I wasn't sure the cost had been worth it.

Eventually I had examined and treated every man, I think there were forty altogether. I really wished I had a notebook and pen so I could jot down their injuries and how I felt each man was responding to treatment. Hunting around the rooms close to the ward, I came across what looked like an office and on a wooden table stood a set of wax tablets and a stylus. It wasn't perfect but it was better than nothing. Excited that I could record the symptoms and treatments of the men in my care, I rushed back over to the sick room and began the rather painstaking task of writing names, details of wounds and what treatment I had dispensed to each man. I noted down which of them had taken the pain numbing draft and at approximately what time that had been.

It took me well over an hour, but finally, I had done them all. My hand was cramping from trying to use the unfamiliar stylus and I had used nearly all of the tablets, but I felt triumphant, my need to document my work was fulfilled and as I finished the last one, I sat up stretching my back to ease the tight muscles and did a little air punch. The man in the bed two down from where I was sitting by the open doorway grinned at me.

"Happy now Hannah? I wondered how you were coping without being able to record everything. You always were a stickler for detail." I smiled back at him, remembering that his name was Tobias.

"Hahaha, watch it Tobias, just because you're feeling better doesn't mean you can be cheeky. I'm sure I can find a nice diuretic amongst my potions that will wipe that grin off your face for a few days." He clutched his stomach in mock pain,

"No, no, anything but that...please, please, I beg you..." Laughing at his banter, I walked over to his bedside to check his pulse. He was one of the ones I was a little concerned about, not so bad that he needed watching constantly, but his skin was rather more pale than I was comfortable with and clammy to my touch. However, since I had redressed his wounds and given him a nice fresh goblet of water, he seemed to have perked up a bit. His pulse, while a bit fast, was steady and quite strong, so I just made a small extra note, to keep an eye on him. About to leave him to rest, he caught my hand.

"Sit with me Hannah."

"Tobias, I have work to do, I can't be sitting gossiping with you all afternoon." He gripped me tighter.

"Just for a few minutes, I've missed you." Uh oh, this wasn't something I needed to hear, just exactly what was my relationship with this man? I couldn't remember, I know I had been treating all of them for quite some time, but did I know him before then, was he a friend of Aharon's…an alarming thought hit me…of mine? No, surely if I had been involved with this man, I would have remembered, Raizel would have told me. My heart stopped hammering, Raizel, surely she would have mentioned something if Tobias and I had something between us. I needed to ask her what was going on.

"Would you like to sit outside for a while, in the sun? It will make you feel brighter."

"Only if you sit with me." Sighing, I nodded.

"Just for a few moments, I have too many things to do to be bothering with pesky patients." I helped him up off the cot and we walked out into the afternoon sun, I guessed it was sometime around three, but couldn't be sure. Time seemed the least of my worries right now. There was a long stone shelf along one of the casemate walls, which we walked over to and sat down. I made sure his blanket was wrapped round him properly and we sat for a while enjoying the view. A few men were pottering about the plateau, the inevitable oxen were still ploughing the soil over at the far side of the planted area, their handler making sure the lines were straight. Someone was picking vegetables.

The pomegranate trees were casting lovely shadows across the ground. Sounds of life came from every direction and it was hard to reconcile this with the horror I knew had occurred here not so very long ago and the terror I knew would come. It felt like home. Not wanting to think this way, I wrested my thoughts back. I had a home in another place and another time I did not want to get comfortable here and, not even knowing whether I could, I wanted to go back to my place in history, not be here with death and destruction.

As these thoughts ran around my head, I looked up and was sure I saw Maxentius leaning against the entrance to the administration building of the Northern Palace. His body was nearly hidden in the shadows, but I recognised his height and the tilt of his head and felt my heart thud. Following my gaze I heard Tobias suck his breath between his teeth.

"Scum." He hissed. Astonished I looked back at him and his face was contorted with anger.

"What?"

"He and his kind are scum, we should have killed them when we had the chance and thrown their bodies to the falcons. Why did you want to save them, they want us all dead."

"No they don't, they were here minding their own business, keeping an outpost of empire secure, protecting a trade route, you lot were the ones who barged in and attacked them." Mildly spoken, my words were pointed.

"They want to rule us, they want us as their slaves." I realised he might well have been right, but I stood by my words.

"I could not let you kill them, it would have been murder and you know that is against our laws. By the time you found them, the heat of battle had passed, they were unarmed and badly wounded and to have killed them would make you worse than they are. I lost one of them, he died as I held his hand, he died believing in the same basic causes that you believe in, you are not so different Tobias." My voice sounded harsh and uneven, I remembered Sergius' last moments, alone, save for Maxentius and I, away from his family, on an isolated rock in a savage desert. Tobias looked back at me then, his eyes searching my face curiously.

"You cared for this man who died?" Choosing my words carefully so as not to set him off again, I replied.

"Yes, as with any person who is sick, I do not care about who they are, what they have done or where they are from. I have to look passed this, for my job is to treat their sickness or their injuries until they are healed or until I can do no more to save them. Otherwise, I would not be true to myself or my calling."

Tobias studied me a moment longer and seemed satisfied with my answer. He leaned back against the wall relaxing in the warmth of the late afternoon. Silently sighing with relief, I sent up a quick prayer thanking whoever it was that helped me over that little hurdle and glancing back towards the other building I noticed, rather wistfully, that Maxentius was no longer there.

Chapter Twenty

A little while later, I dragged my thoughts back to the job in hand.

"Come on Tobias, you need to get back to bed and I must finish my chores." I held out my arm and we walked back to the ward slowly. Tobias seemed weary now' "I have kept you out of bed for too long, I am sorry." He smiled,

"I do feel rather tired, I'll have a nap before they bring food, hopefully I will sleep better tonight."

"You haven't been sleeping properly? Why didn't you tell me?" Chiding him gently. "I don't ask questions for the good of my health you know, but for yours."

"Sorry, you have enough on your plate, I didn't want to bother you." Exasperated, I squeezed his arm.

"Don't be silly, you must rest well, that it the best thing for healing" I will come later and give you something that will help." Guiding him to his cot, I helped him lie down. His pain seemed under control but only just. Touching the back of my hand to his head he wasn't hot, but still clammy. Covering him with a sheet and laying a blanket over the top, I smiled down at him. "I'll be back soon, try and eat something when they bring the food round, it will help too."

Taking a quick walk through the two rooms, I made sure the others were all resting comfortably before collecting up the remaining pile of sheets and bandages that needed to be washed. Crossing the plateau to the other palace, I went back to the laundry room. The metal bucket was bubbling nicely, so wrapping the handle with several pieces of cloth I heaved it up, pouring it all into the sink. Adding salt, lemon and vinegar, I swirled the whole lot around waiting for everything to mix in. The smell of hot lemon was lovely and cleared my head, which was beginning to ache from all my activities of the day. Once I was sure everything was nicely dissolved, I left them to soak and wandered slowly back to my little corner of the palace. Oh for a hot shower.

I had realised that hanging above my doorframe, was a very heavy curtain hooked back with a cord, a curtain that would give me some privacy if I let it swing down. Suiting my thoughts to action, I unhooked the cord allowing the rich, heavy material to block my doorway. Stripping off completely, I gave myself a thorough wash, rubbing some sweet smelling oil into my skin and finishing off by managing to wash my hair. I knew that there were two bath houses and a swimming pool on Masada, but didn't know whether any of them still functioned. The thought of submerging myself into a relaxing bath was almost too much, but I resolved to ask Maxentius, surely he would know.

Drying off and towelling my hair as best I could, I dressed in clean clothes. My shift was pale grey and my tunic a soft violet. I hunted about the drawers and found a belt I felt would be suitable and sat down to comb through my curls. I remembered Maxentius helping me after I had been unwell and wondered whether he would comb my hair, thinking how intimate that would be and then dismissed it as too fanciful. I knew I needed to go and check up on him and Marcus, but I felt shy suddenly and, to be honest, a little fearful that, after our revelations of the morning, he would clam up again.

Mentally shaking myself, I pulled myself together and tying the curtain back against the wall, allowing the draft to circulate, made my way to the next room. Both men were sitting in chairs that had been brought in from somewhere, chatting about whatever it was men chatted about. They glanced up as I came in and both smiled, Maxentius finishing his with a slow wink, it was all I could do not to blush, but I grinned back at them happily. I felt safe here in this room, with these two men, safer than I did with the men of my own culture. Odd that.

"I just wanted to ask, I understand that there is at least one bath house in this complex. Do you know whether I would be able to use either of them?" They looked at each, then back at me, then back at each other. I wasn't sure what was bothering them, but they seemed reluctant to speak. "What is it?" I looked over at Maxentius my brow lowering, not this nonsense again and, preparing for some kind of argument, I waited. Nothing.

"Oh, not again, now what have I done? I'm really tired and I've had a very long day. I've already had one fight with you…" Marcus looked at the two of us in confusion, "…and I'm not sure I can take another one. I've had to persuade someone else that killing you both is not very sporting and I just hoped I might be able to relax in a bath. Is that too much to ask?" I could hear my voice getting shrill, but I'd had it. Hours of treating injured men, changing beds, writing on wax tablets and worrying that more men might die on me, on top of it only being two days since I'd been so unwell that I could not get out of bed.

"No, no, its not that we don't want to you to use the bath house, but Raizel told us that they took Sergius to the small one on the lower terrace, which would be the most private." Maxentius held my gaze as he told me. I glanced at Marcus who had bent his head. I slumped onto the floor, ignoring Maxentius' invitation to use his chair.

"Oh I'm am so sorry, I never would have thought they would take his body there, why did they do that?'" My voice was hushed, sad.

"We do not know, they said it was cool and secluded, or maybe they just threw him over the edge, we have not been down to check."

"Ok, I need to find out what's going on." Dragging myself off the floor and brushing my clothes down, I started to leave; Maxentius stood too and caught my arm, pulled me to him, kissing me quick and hard. I heard Marcus gasp, but I could not stop the smile that lit up my face.

"It is a secret Marcus Aelianus, please keep it to yourself, for if you place this woman in any danger I will kill you." Softening his words with a grin and a wink, Maxentius released me, pushing me out of the door. As I floated along the hallway, I heard... "I will tell you later, for now just accept it and make no mention of it."

Quickly I made my way to the rooms I thought Aharon was using, calling his name softly as I reached the open doorway.

"Come." His voice invited me in and I entered a room full of light and colour. He had landed on his feet, I didn't know what this had been, but it was beautifully appointed.

"I just wanted to thank you for allowing Raizel to help me and, of course for carrying me to my room the other night." Rather embarrassed.

"It was nothing." Waving his hand. "You were unwell, you needed help, the tall Roman carried you, we merely made sure you were in no danger from him." Oh, so that's how it went was it, storing this little titbit up for later, I continued:

"Still it was a kindness..." pausing, "...would you mind telling me where you placed the body of the Roman who died? I need to make sure I cleanse his body so that infection cannot spread to others. He will need to be buried or cremated, I am not sure of their rituals."

"We took him to the bath house, the one at the bottom of this palace, it is off the courtyard and quite secluded. I cannot imagine anyone going to look."

"Would it be acceptable to you for me to purify his remains? It is of little matter to me, but it may give his comrades a little comfort." Aiming for ritual rather than grief, I hoped my apparent disinterest would sway him. It seemed it did for his next words opened the way for me.

"If you must, it is no matter to me, but be careful my sister, these Romans cannot be trusted."

"I do not fear them my brother, I have the treatments that cure them, which I can withhold if they disrespect me." This went down well, he nodded and we exchanged a few more pleasantries and I left him to what ever he'd been doing before I interrupted him.

Skipping a little at my victory, I went back to the two men and quietly told them what had happened. Marcus still looked a bit stunned from our earlier exchange, but did not refer to it.

"My brother has approved this and, I know I am tired, but I would really like to go now, please will you take me? It has been agreed that both of you may accompany me, which is a good job since I have no idea where it is." Taking a few moments to make sure they were warmly dressed, they also threw cloaks over their shoulders and pinned them securely. Maxentius' clasp seemed quite elaborate and its design teased at something in my memory, but I found I could not recall why. Ignoring it, and asking them to wait for me, I hurried back to my room and hunted out my mantle.

The little silver brooch I used to pin the edges together had bent under the weight of the material and I worried that it might not last much longer. Maybe I could find a spare one in one of the palace bedrooms. Rejoining my two guardians, I followed them through the passageways and stairwells of this incredible building. I peeked into some of the rooms on our way through, which although I imagined would be opulent, actually were stunning in their simplicity. We made our way down to the lowest terrace, where the view out over the desert to the Dead Sea was incredible.

"How did he build this? It is mind boggling."

"He had very clever engineers and although considered despotic, I think he must also have been a visionary. I have visited his palace at Herodium and it is just as breathtaking." I listened while Maxentius described this other palace, I'd heard tales of its beauty but did not know anyone who had seen it and, how would I have done, it was a ruin in my time. What an amazing world this man had seen.

"Here we are." Pushing open a wooden door, and leading us into a small building to the side of the courtyard, Maxentius stood to one side and let me pass, touching my arm as I did.

"It will be bad Hannah."

"I know, but worse for you two I think, allow me to make sure he is covered and as…presentable…as possible." Nodding he waited, Marcus came in last and stood with his commanding officer while I looked for where they had laid Sergius.

Surprisingly, they had not just tossed him in here; he had been laid at the top of the steps down to the bath, but tidily and with a modicum of respect. He was covered with a blanket and I praised whoever had thought to bring him here because it was very cool and the flies I thought would be surrounding him by now were relatively few in number. Cautiously, I lifted the blanket off his body, noting that his skin was already darkening in the dry air. His face seemed peaceful but his body was bloating with the gasses accumulating inside him. How did I explain this to the two men who were his friends? Laying the blanket back over him, I made my way back the entrance, raised eyebrows asked the silent question and I hesitated before gritting my teeth, they had to know, it was their right.

"His face looks quite peaceful, but his body is not something you should see, when a person dies, certain changes occur and they are…" searching for a less descriptive term, "…unpleasant."

"We have seen bodies on the battlefield, we know what happens, they blacken, balloon and are swarmed over by flies and maggots." Harsh, emotionless.

"Yes, but they may not have been those closest to you, more likely battlefield enemies, not like this man who saved your life and to whom you talked as he slipped from this world." I looked at them, touching their hands in my need to make them understand. "Death is ugly, it does not care for the feelings of those left behind, it ravages the body and desecrates it. I am not sure you wish to remember Sergius in this manner."

"What do you suggest my Hannah?"

"I think you need to leave him here with me for a little while, if you could wait in the courtyard I will do what I can to tidy him up and then tomorrow, I will bring ritual oils and rosemary to cleanse his body and we can either find a way to cover his body, or we can cremate him, as I do not think we will be able to bury him. The choice will be yours. You will not be able to return him to his family wherever they may be."

"I understand, we will do as you wish, Marcus and I will decide the best rite of burial for him." The two of them left the room and I turned back to the body on the floor.

"Oh Sergius I am so sorry I did not save you, I tried so hard." I'm not sure I believed in souls and heaven, but I talked to the broken body of the man lying in front of me as though I did. Removing the blanket completely and shooing away the flies, I tried to breathe through my mouth rather than my nose and began to prepare him for the funeral rites I felt would be appropriate. Unsure of what was required, I simply made sure he was lying properly and that all his limbs were where they should be.

200

Using the towel hooked through my belt, I soaked it in the water I found in a little round stone dish, which reminded me of a font, above the main bath. I cleaned his body as thoroughly as I could, wondering if there was a way of releasing the gasses filling the cavities of his body. I had no clue, so decided they would probably work their own way out. Since he had been lying there for a few days, the blood had dried and it took quite a while for me to get him to a point were I felt the other two could see him without immediately thinking of the manner of his death.

Coming across a large shell that I used as a scoop, I rinsed his hair, combing it with my fingers to make it look as normal as possible. His face I left until last, wanting to smooth his skin as much as I was able, his features no longer contorted in pain. My heart bled for this man whom I had known for such a short time, yet it had seemed like an age. Finally I was satisfied that I had done all I could this day and would come back in the morning before the sun was too high and use herbs I imagined would be appropriate to send him on his way.

Leaving him covered by the blanket, I went out into the courtyard where Marcus and Maxentius waited patiently. Looking up as they heard me come towards them. On reaching them they both touched my shoulder as if in acknowledgement of my actions. I was drained and finding it difficult to put one foot in front of the other. I looked up at the height of the precipice we were standing under, how was I going to get back up there? Daylight was almost gone we needed to get up before darkness fell because I wasn't sure if there were any lamps at these levels.

"Come on you two, we must return to the upper level, I don't think we have any torches or lamps down here." My voice reflected my weariness and Maxentius glanced at me in concern.

"Are you alright Hannah? Will you be able to walk back up?"

"I have no choice, I cannot stay here and there's probably a heap of things for me to do before I can rest."

"You have worked hard today and this care of Sergius Crispus is emotionally draining." How did he know how I felt? The men I grew up with generally did not care about women's feelings. His concern for me was a constant surprise; it was obviously unusual in my life, because I didn't know how to deal with it.

"Maybe so, but my day is not yet over and you two need food."

We made our way back up the stairs and levels eventually coming back out at the top, just as the last of the light faded from the sky. I walked with them to their room; platters of food had been left for them and a flagon of wine, with two goblets alongside. Lucky guys I thought, I was so hungry I could have eaten a horse. With a sigh that could have blown a lesser man over, I left them to their meal. Traipsing over to the laundry I checked on the sheets, they were soaking nicely, the water changing colour as the dirt came free. I knew I should probably change the water over, but I did not have the will. Next door in one of the kitchens, I heard movement and stuck my head through the door to see Raizel preparing dinner for her family. Noticing me she motioned me in.

"Here Hannah, there is enough for you to share." Passing me a plate of breads and hot vegetables smothered in olive oil. I thanked her and inhaled it, it was so tasty, the warm bread soaking up the oil, I ate it so fast some dribbled down my chin, making Raizel laugh as I tried to catch it with the bread.

Oh, thank you Raizel, that was delicious, I was so, so hungry. You are an amazing cook, Aharon is lucky to have a wife like you."

Grinning she agreed that this was indeed true and we chattered together for a little while. I started to relax and felt better once the food reached my stomach. I refused a goblet of wine, as I knew I needed to check on the men in the ward. Any alcohol now and I would be asleep in seconds.

A little while later, I thanked Raizel again and, picking up a lamp to help me see my way over to the other building, left her preparing the rest of her family's meal. As I walked over the open plateau, I realised that I'd forgotten to ask her about Tobias, never mind it would have to wait. I had not time for this tonight and I really wanted to feel Maxentius' arms around me again, even if it was only for a few moments, but that too would have to wait 'til I had finished my remaining tasks.

Fighting my exhaustion, I reached the Western Palace and made my way into the ward, all was quiet and, noting the empty platters all over the floor, it looked as though they had enjoyed their meals. I collected them up, piling them by the doorway to take with me when I left. Walking quietly into the anteroom, I picked up the flagon of the sleeping draft, which I had left on a high shelf, a cloth thrown over the top to keep the flies out.

Continuing through the far room I checked all my patients one by one, making sure that those men who seemed restless had enough to give them a more peaceful night. One or two had higher than normal temperatures, so I sat with them for a while, cooling their skin with damp cloths, checking bandages in case of seeping wounds. As far as I could tell it was just their bodies fighting the infection, their breathing and pulse rates were quite steady. I sat a little longer with Eli, he was so pale and quiet and his skin had lost none of its earlier clamminess. I worried I had missed something.

The outer room was also quiet, Tobias looked to be asleep and I was certainly not going to wake him by checking his pulse. His skin was still pale, but his breathing was regular. Maybe I was going to get to sleep sooner than I thought. I replaced the flagon back onto the shelf, checked to make sure that everything was stocked up and that there were enough bandages for me to treat anyone that might need it in the night. One last look and I slipped silently out of the door, standing for a moment to enjoy the solitude.

The sky was alive with stars, the moon just peeping over the mountain range in the distance. Everything was silent; I let it and the inky darkness cloak me, giving me respite from the chaos of the day. I heard movement behind me and noticed one of the other men, I thought his name was Simeon, walking in my direction.

"Hannah." Nodding as he made to pass me, I put out my hand to stop him.

"Are you on watch tonight?" He nodded again. "Please would you call me if any of the men in there," motioning towards the two rooms, "are in pain, or need me for anything at all?"

"I or Malachi will call you if you are needed, he will take the second watch."

"Thank you." I left him to his duties and trudged back to the two rooms in the Northern Palace, which had become my sanctuary in this isolated corner of the world.

Quietly I looked in on Marcus and Maxentius expecting them to be in bed if not already asleep, but they were still sitting up, talking in undertones. They looked up as I popped my head through the door. Maxentius asked if I would like some wine and I nodded gratefully.

"I'm afraid there's only two goblets, I will go and wash mine." Shaking my head, I took it out of his hand and using a clean cloth simply wiped the rim.

"Alcohol is a natural disinfectant, it would be unlikely that I would catch any infection from sharing this goblet. See, all the useless information you are picking up from hanging around with me." I was unable to stop a bubble of mirth as I said this. Oh dear, I could feel hysteria borne of tiredness building up.

"That's it, she is cracking up." Smiled Marcus. I threw the cloth I'd just used on the goblet at him, catching him right on the nose.

"Might be tired and hysterical, but I can still hit you." I laughed sitting down on the floor with my back against the wall.

"Hannah, have this chair." Maxentius stood up and tried to get me to move.

"I can't move, I may have to sleep here, my legs have given up on me. No its ok…" as they both moved to help me up, "…I'm fine, just ignore me. After what happened this afternoon, I wanted to check on you before I went to bed, but now you may have to put up with me until I can find the strength to move." I knew I was babbling, but I was powerless to stop the nonsense that was falling from my lips. "Sorry, so sorry, I'm very tired."

All I wanted to do was sleep, but I also wanted Maxentius to hold me close and in my befuddled state I knew I needed to shut up for it was highly likely I would actually ask him. I could feel my head drooping and desperately tried to wake myself up. Suddenly, I felt four strong arms lifting me, carrying me along the hall and placing me gently on my bed. Footsteps faded down the hall, I tried to sit up but simply could not do it. Falling back onto the pillow, I felt one solitary tear trickle down my cheek.

"Why so sad my Hannah?" I turned my head to see Maxentius sitting on my chair; he was the most welcome sight.

"Oh…you stayed." My eyes shone like the stars I had just been admiring.

"Of course, you are obviously not fit to be left alone quite yet, who knows what you would do if we didn't keep an eye on you" I saw him wink at me in the soft glow of the oil lamp.

"I really want you to hold me." Dreamily. "Please don't go."

"I am here my Hannah." Again I tried to rise, but he calmly pushed me back and leaning over me kissed me very gently.

Sitting back in the chair, he reached out and taking my hand, began to rub his thumb against my palm, and the exhaustion I had been fighting, finally won.

Nearly two thousand years away, another man watched over a woman, who lay, head bandaged, in a large comfortable bed in what looked like a medical centre. She was deeply unconscious, but had been agitated, muttering incoherently. He was holding her hand to his heart and talking to her softly. He could swear she kept saying his name but he couldn't reach her, couldn't get her to come back to him. She was too far away.

Chapter Twenty One

The next morning I woke early, to find that I had slept deeply and for once without dreams. Maxentius had gone, I had not heard him leave and I hoped he had also managed to get a decent night's rest too. The light suggested that it was not long after dawn. Moving as quietly as possible, I washed, dressed and went along to the next room. The two men were fast asleep and I stood for several seconds just watching them, they looked so peaceful. Without disturbing them, I checked that their skin felt cool and un-fevered, a light touch on their wrists confirmed that their pulse rates were steady and strong.

I gazed rather longer at Maxentius' face, wishing I could kiss him awake and have him caress me with his lips and his hands, teasing my senses into a whirlwind of passion. Sheesh Hannah…get a grip woman…I dragged my mind back to what I needed to do and quietly began to gather the oils and herbs I would need to cleanse the body of their comrade. I also needed to check on those maggots I had placed in Marcus's wound.

Going over to the laundry, I checked the sheets and bandages, which had been soaking overnight. Lifting them out and refilling the sink with clean fresh water, I dropped them back in piece by piece, swishing the cloth around to rinse each one thoroughly. Wringing them out, I carried the great pile over to the drying racks and neatly hung everything up. The fire was still burning; someone must check this during the night and keep it fuelled. Once that was done, I filled a large flagon with water and walked back to the treatment room.

Maxentius was awake when I re-entered the room, I smiled across at him and he grinned back, rather sleepily, I wondered how long he had stayed with me the night before. I went to re-check his temperature, resting the back of my hand on his forehead. He grasped my hand as I lifted it off his head, turning my palm to his lips. A tingle ran through me and, listening for the sound of anyone approaching, I sank down on the bed next to him, leaning in to kiss him soundly.

"Well, good morning to you too…" smiling his slow smile, "…although, I must say, that while, personally, I wholly approve of this method of waking your patients, I trust you aren't employing it with all of them."

Hmmm…well, it is a most effective way of checking someone's temperature." Innocently.

Chuckling he pulled me closer.

"Well, then you little minx, I would be most appreciative if you would check mine again."

"Happy to oblige sir." Enjoying the warmth of his hand on my back, I spent the next few moments employing those methods to good effect. Reluctantly I got up.

"I must get on, I have to take things down to the bath house and prepare the body of Sergius for his final journey and I want to check Marcus before we go."

"I will help you carry what you need to take down."

"If you are sure, I would rather you slept longer, I can come and get you when I'm ready.

"No, there is too much there for one small person to carry all the way down, give me a few moments and I will be ready."

Leaving him to his morning ablutions, I went back along to my room and found a suitable basket in which I would be able to lay my herbs and ointments. Realising that I probably didn't need too much of either, I decided on rosemary, frankincense and myrrh, all of which sat well in my head as oils I would use to prepare a body for burial or cremation. In modern times these last two were not inexpensive, yet there appeared to be plenty in my stock. I made a mental note to check the storerooms to see whether there was any more.

Going back along to the other room, I found what I needed and poured the oils into smaller bottles, making sure they were well sealed. Marcus was up and about now too, so I took the opportunity to examine the wounds with the maggots in. They had done their job, the infected areas were clean and the maggots fell into my hand replete. Fascinated by what had happened, Maxentius watched me clean, rub salve in and re-bandage the injuries and, I knew from here on in Marcus would be fine. Marcus himself was just thankful that he didn't need to have any more of those wriggly critters - his words - feasting on him any more.

It was still early and I doubted anyone else was up and about, so I knew we would be able to do this without drawing attention to ourselves and that I would be back to begin my usual tasks before anyone knew what had happened. Even though Aharon had given me permission, I was pretty sure that if the Zealots knew I was caring for the body of a Roman soldier, a sworn enemy, there might be repercussions and I didn't want to cause any further antagonism.

Gathering a couple of clean sheets, I asked the two men accompanying me whether Sergius had anything they felt he should be buried in or with. Marcus nodded and shot off round one side of the building returning after several moments with a small pile of clothing and what looked like a dagger lying on top. What was he thinking?

"Marcus, hide that underneath." I muttered. "If anyone sees that you're a dead man." Doing as I bid, he quickly slid it between the other layers of cloth. "Sorry, but that was a bit risky, why did you bring it?"

"It is his *pugio*, his dagger, it is fitting that he be laid to rest with this by his side." More than a little exasperated, but understanding his motives, I nodded and we carried on towards the terraces.

As we walked, I realised how intriguing this palace was.

"One day I would like a proper tour of this palace, in fact the whole citadel." I said. "It looks like a rabbit warren." Maxentius grinned and bowing replied,

"It would be our pleasure to show it to you, it is quite remarkable, Herod certainly knew how to impress." We made it to the bottom without incident, despite my concerns that I would trip on the hem of my tunic and spill everything. This time, I asked them to come in with me. I would need their help to move the body.

It was dim and cool, the room still in shadow, I lit an oil lamp perched on a shelf and a soft glow suffused the space. The light was kind, for despite the agonies of his death, Sergius looked peaceful. Moving the whole of the sheet from around him, I proceeded to anoint his skin with the aromatic oils and without conscious thought, began to sing one of the elegies I must have learned as a child. It was a mournful lament for the death of a soldier. I had no recollection of how I knew this, but it felt appropriate given the circumstances.

The two tall Romans watched me in silence and when I completed my task, they moved forward to help me lift the body onto the fresh sheets. Carefully dressing him in the clothing Marcus had brought, the last thing was to slip the dagger into Sergius' hand, bending his, now relaxed, fingers around the hilt. We fashioned a shroud from the two lengths of sheet and wrapped him tightly within them. This done I stood back and waited to see what his comrades would do.

"We are sorry we are unable to take you back to your homeland Sergius, honoured friend, We leave you here in this cool place, away from scavenging animals and those who would seek to desecrate your remains and hope you find safe passage with the ferryman." Placing a coin in his mouth, they each touched Sergius' head, then covered his face and tucked the cloth securely in. Moving away, they stood for a few moments lost in thought, then as if released from a spell, turned as one and walked quickly out of the door.

Giving them some space, I spent a little while tidying the room, collecting my things together and, rolling up the soiled sheet, placed it in the basket on top of the jars. This sheet I would burn, I did not have the heart to re-use it. Finally, I laid a spring of fresh rosemary on top of the sheet, blew out the oil lamp and left Sergius to his last journey. Coming out into the morning light, I noticed the sun was already lighting the sides of the rock, I guessed it be around eight o'clock. I should get back and start my day.

"What did you decide?" My question needed no explanation.

"We think we will leave him there, rather than burn his body or try to bury it in this dusty soil. We think he will lay undisturbed, only a few know where he lies and if they were going to despoil him, they would have done so already. He will be safe here." Maxentius words seemed ponderous and Marcus merely nodded, but I guessed they were probably struggling a bit. The last hour would have not only renewed their sense of loss, but also reinforced the realisation that they were captives of a desperate bunch of men who could kill them without compunction.

Making our way back to the top level, I left them to go and put the rolled up sheet on the fire in the laundry room and also to see whether any breakfast platters, had been prepared. I suddenly remember that I had forgotten to bring the platters over from the two wards, where I left them stacked last night. Ugh, any food would be stuck on and they'd be fly ridden - you are rubbish Hannah, I admonished myself. However, upon entering the kitchen, I saw a huge pile of platters drying on a table and realised that some kind soul had found them and washed them. Smiling gratefully, I located what looked to be likely prospects for breakfast, a pitcher of water, three drinking bowls and three platters standing at one end of a wooden bench. I found what appeared to be a tray of sorts and managed to fit everything on.

Walking carefully, I made it back over to the treatment room without dropping anything and placed the tray triumphantly on a small wooden table in the middle of the room and did a kind of 'ta daaaa' flourish, spreading my hands to show them what I had brought.

"For your breakfasting pleasure my lords." They both chuckled, Maxentius commented.

"I think you may be more in need of sustenance than we, you seem rather…errr…flighty." I grinned back at them. I did feel a sense of relief. It had been emotionally draining to work with a dead body and my responsibility to get everything right must have been weighing on me more heavily than I realised. I felt as though a burden had been lifted and that I would be able to continue my day with a lighter heart.

We chatted over our food after which, I collected the dishes and returned them to the kitchen, rinsing them clean and stacking them with the others on the table. Making sure the two Romans had everything they needed, I went over to the other building and began my examination of the other men under my care.

Entering the wards, I could see that most of the men were still sleeping, it was quiet and cool and for this I was very thankful. Softly walking to the anteroom, I made sure there was a fresh draft of the painkilling drink and that I had enough salve for those

212

whose wounds needed it. Glancing at the tablets I had conscientiously scratched the day before, I remembered Eli, who had looked so unwell and I went to check on him first. He slept still, so I merely checked his pulse and temperature, trying not to disturb him as I did so. He looked so young, nothing like I would have imagined a rebel warrior would look. Sighing with the futility of it all, knowing in my heart that I was treating these men, helping them to heal, only for them to die in the not too distant future.

The tenuous nature of life suddenly made me think of Max, my other Max, somewhere beyond time and wished I was with him. What was happening there? Where was I? What did they do with Naomi? Was anyone else hurt in that mad struggle? Was I doomed to die here along with the rest of these people, never to see my world again, but if I did how could I have come back to this rock so far in the future, surely this 'me' must live? Shaking my head, I brought my thoughts back to the job in hand, nothing you can do Hannah, except hope. Leaving Eli to wake up before I examined him, I made my rounds of the other beds. Save the very few who were concerning me, the majority had woken up and looked quite bright, their skin cool and eyes pain free.

"How about some fresh air this morning? I'm sure you would enjoy sitting in the sunshine for a little while, you're all looking a bit peaky." They grinned at me and seemed happy to fall in with my suggestion, so we made our way out onto the plateau. Some were able to manage by themselves, others were helped by their friends or comrades and I helped the rest. Eli still hadn't woken despite the racket the rest of them were making, which was rather worrying. So once the men were settled in the sunshine, close to shady spots in case they got too warm, I went back to check on him. He lay so still, I watched his chest rise and fall, his breathing was steady but his skin was clammy. Gathering my medicines around me on the floor and ensuring I had plenty of cloths and bandages, I carefully lifted the sheet and laid it aside.

Gently running my fingers over his skin, checking for abrasions I might have missed, I finally removed the bandage covering the worst injury. It was oozing yellow pus around the cloth I had packed into the gash. Frustrated at this ongoing damage, I peeled the cloth delicately away and pressed the sides lightly encouraging the pus to drain out. Wiping it away and making sure his skin around the wound was clean, I used my trusty salt and water solution to clean inside the cut. Looking closely at the insides of the wound, the skin seemed to be the proper colour; it wasn't white or necrotic, so hopefully the infection was contained to the deepest part. Not that this was particularly good news, but it meant I knew where to place the salve. Adding more frankincense to the mixture, I pushed it well into the gash, using my fingers to make sure it went in as far as it would go. It was a bit stomach wrenching actually, but I gritted my teeth and carried on - this man was not going to die if I had anything to do with it.

As I was finishing my rather grim task, I noticed Eli had woken up, no surprise given what I'd just put his poor body through and, was watching me work. I grinned down at him, hoping I looked more positive than I felt.

"Well now what some people will do to get my attention, just asking for me would have done it, throwing a temperature and providing me with an oozing sore is just plain greedy." He smiled back at me, but I could tell he was in pain. "Want some of the draft?" He nodded and I helped him drink enough to send him back off to sleep. "Don't you go showing off anymore, I've enough to deal with without worrying about you all day."

I cooled his hot face with a wet cloth and quickly, before he dozed off, I changed his sheets, which were soaked with sweat and now blood. Using another cloth I wiped his tangled hair off his forehead, so that any breeze that filtered through would cool his skin. He caught my arm and I had to bend close to hear him.

"I'm afraid. Am I going to die?" He was close to tears and my heart went out to him. By rights this young man, little more than a boy, should have been enjoying life with his mates, maybe doing some studies, not lying in a bed, on an desolate outcrop of rock, recovering from a terrible injury.

"Of course not, do you think I'd let anything happen to you?" I infused veracity into my voice. "You'll be up and about before you know it, no-one dies on my watch!"

Blatantly ignoring what had happened to Sergius, I gripped Eli's hand, squeezing it in an attempt to make him believe me and without thinking, dropped a kiss on his forehead. "Sleep now, I'll try and be here when you wake and tomorrow, maybe you can join the others outside." His eyes drooped and he slept. His pulse and heart felt steady and I watched as his breathing settled into a rhythm, hopefully I had caught the infection. I had done all I could for now. Waiting until I was sure he was properly asleep, I pulled a blanket over the lower half of his body in case he felt chilled and, took my leave.

Replacing my medicines, balms and the sleeping draft back in the anteroom, I checked the other beds, changing all those that required it and piling the dirty sheets by the door. I pulled the door between the rooms nearly closed leaving Eli to rest in peace and quiet, but opened the main door wide, letting the air circulate through. The breeze ruffled the edges of the sheets, so I knew it was strong enough to push out the old stale air. Happy with what I'd achieved, I went over to the men sitting or lying in the warm morning sun, asking how they were feeling, was there anything they wanted or needed. Other than my general enquiries, I avoided singling any of them out, especially Tobias, he unnerved me and I still hadn't asked Raizel what his problem was.

Leaving them to their chatter, I went back over the laundry with yet another pile of sheets to be cleaned. Honestly I felt less like a healer, more like an underpaid washer woman, come to think of it I didn't get paid either… ah, but at least I didn't have to go find a river and some rocks. Chuckling to myself at the image that conjured up, I got on with sorting out the bedding. The sheets, cloths and bandages on the racks were all dry, so I folded them into neat piles and hung anything left in the tub up, after wringing them out. Refilling the trough with hot water and my mixture of lemon, salt and vinegar I left them to soak.

Looking round, I felt like I'd earned a break, what I wouldn't give for a hot cup of coffee, did they even have coffee in this time? No, I remembered reading somewhere that it was discovered sometime around the fifteenth century. Dammit! Oh well, I searched through the stock in the kitchen and found honey, lemon and a flagon of something that smelt like red wine. I poured the honey and wine into a large goblet, adding hot water and some lemon. Not perfect, in fact it was rather like modern day cough medicine, but it was hot and seemed to quench my desire for caffeine.

Taking the goblet with me, I walked back over to the treatment room and saw that Maxentius and Marcus had brought their chairs out into the courtyard to enjoy the day. Going back in to fetch a chair for me so I could join them, I relaxed for a while, not talking, just listening to their banter, still marvelling that, for the most part, I understood them.

When there was a lull in conversation I broached the subject of touring the fortress.

"When do you think you'd be able to start showing me round this place?"

"Anytime you like, its not like we have other pressing matters we need to attend to." Smiling ironically, "I'll check our schedules, though, just to be sure." I chuckled at this.

"Can we start this afternoon? We could do it in small doses, so I can fit it in with my other chores."

"Of course, just come by when you're ready, I'm sure we'll be able to spare a few moments." Finishing my rather odd drink, I left the pair of them grinning at their wit and returned to the other tasks I needed to complete. Checking their bedroom, I changed the sheets here too and made sure the water in the pitcher was cool, all food platters had been stacked ready to take away, that the dust had been wiped from the shelves and the floor, swept. Satisfied that I had tidied and cleaned in here thoroughly. I carried the dirty dishes over to the kitchen and dropped the sheets in the trough in the laundry, what had I just said about being a washer woman…?

Quickly retracing my steps over to the other wards, I peeped in on Eli, he was still sleeping, but I thought the colour of his skin looked slightly better, the room was cool still and the air felt fresh. Hopefully he would pick up soon. The others were still lounging around in the open air, but had moved into the shade of the high walls. Someone had brought them food, water and wine so they were quite happy. I noticed Tobias watching me and to avoid any further resentment from his end, I smiled across at him as I left them to their afternoon.

"Be sure to go back in if you feel tired and I don't want to have to deal with an outbreak of sunstroke on top of everything else so stay in the shade."

"Yes Ma'am…"

"Of course my lady…"

"We promise…" …and other such exclamations reached me as I turned to leave, I simply waved my hand in the air and carried on, hearing chortles of laughter as I walked away.

Before rejoining my two Romans, yes I felt rather proprietary towards them, I quickly freshened up in my room, I felt sticky and hot from working all morning and it was nice to change into clean clothes. I ran the comb through my long hair, which seemed untameable, tied it back into its thick plait and went along to where they were still sitting in the courtyard.

"Do you think we'll ever be allowed to go back to our own rooms Hannah?" Marcus asked as I sank into the chair beside them.

"Were they in the barracks?"

"Well, mine were but Maxentius had quarters in the main palace."

"Not sure you'll be able to go back to the barracks - too close to weapons, but if there's a room near where Maxentius used to sleep, they may let you move there. They will want to keep you together so they can watch you. You may be my patients, but you are still captives, for little while longer at least. Now, are you ready to give me a tour? You can show me where Maxentius' rooms are and we can check to see if there is a suitable one close by."

Smiling down at them, as they drained the last of their drinks, they grinned back, relaxed and healing well. As they stood I noticed that Maxentius still seemed stiff, but I hoped it was just the bruising. "How do you both feel today? Before you sleep tonight, I will need to examine your injuries."

"You just can't stop yourself can you? Just when we think you've finished prodding and poking us around, you start again." Marcus chuckled, only half serious.

"So, sue me and preserve me from ungrateful patients." If I had been in my own time, I'd have linked arms with them as we walked, custom dictated that we did nothing of the kind and I kept my arms tightly at my sides. The afternoon was quiet, the palace seemed empty save for us.

"Where do we start?"

"I think this third level will do, just the palace though, we'll leave the storerooms and rest of the administration buildings for another day." Maxentius led the way, showing me through the building and onto the huge semi-circular balcony with its astonishing view. There were fewer rooms here than I had anticipated, not remembering that the Byzantine monks had added it to at a much later date and, I said as much.

"This was only for Herod and possibly one of his wives, the palace over on the west wall was the main centre for the business of state and receiving of visitors. I think this would have only been seen by a few very special guests." I leaned against the balcony, looking back into the room imagining all that had gone on here. Although to any of his wives who accompanied him here, it must have seemed like a gilded cage.

"Seen enough for today?" Maxentius asked softly. I sighed and turned to take one last look at the view.

"Yes, I probably should get back to my other jobs, those sheets won't clean themselves and I have other patients to check up on. Although I do believe that the room along from yours…" nodding at Maxentius, "…would be suitable for Marcus, if my brother and the other leaders can be persuaded that you aren't going to kill us in our beds…" hesitating a moment, "…you aren't are you?"

"Not for the foreseeable future at any rate." Maxentius smiled down at me.

"Well, let me see what I can do, I haven't got much influence but they might be happier with you over here, away from me and, you'd be far enough from the other men so as not to be coming across one another, which may not end well." I could see that

Maxentius hadn't considered this, but he accepted that they couldn't sleep in the treatment room long term, it had other uses.

"Well, let us know when they come a decision, I think we are well enough to move."

We walked back towards the administration block where we parted, they heading to their room, while I went back to the laundry to check the sheets. The fire was burning brightly and the water boiling, so I took the time to finish cleaning and rinsing them there and then, it was one less job to do later. Poking my head into the kitchen, I spotted Raizel stirring something on the fire, something that smelt so delicious, I began to salivate.

"Wow, Raizel, what are you cooking? It smells heavenly."

"Just some stew, it'll be ready for the evening meal, how are you today?"

"Tired, but I've been busy, I am worried about Eli, so I'm going back over there to check on him. He seems very weak still."

"Tell them I'll bring their meal over before it gets dark. I think they enjoyed the fresh air today.

"Hope so, its the best thing for them. Fresh air will help them sleep well and that is the greatest healer. I'll get them outside every day now if I can."

I was about to leave, lugging my inevitable pile of clean sheets, when I remembered,

"Raizel - what is with Tobias? He seems to think he has some claim on me. I do not like the feeling." Raizel stopped stirring for a minute and looked at me.

"You can't have forgotten?" Oh great there was something I was supposed to know.

"Humour me."

"He asked Aharon for your hand, but Aharon refused to give you to him, he said you were to chose your own husband." Now that didn't seem quite right, not in this time, women were chattels to be married off to the highest bidder weren't they?

"What? Aharon did not tell me this." Hoping it was true, or that if he had they would accept that with everything that had happened, I'd forgotten. "No wonder he told me he missed me, that he wanted me to sit with him." Inwardly groaning, I thanked Raizel and went back over to where most of the men were still sitting in the sun. The afternoon was cooling now and I didn't want them to get chilled.

"Come on you horrible lot, time to head back." Shooing them in front of me I corralled them into the building and along to the ward.

"Raizel tells me she will be bringing hot stew over with bread for your meal, but only those settled when she gets here will be getting any." Threat issued, I watched while they all did as I bid them, washing their dusty hands and faces in the large container at the door, before getting into bed and trying to see who could look most look angelic. I laughed as I watched them, for they were very amusing. Putting the sheets into the store cupboard in the anteroom, I went to check on Eli. He was awake and chatting to the man in the next bed, who I think was called Daniel. His skin felt better, the colour was definitely improving and he said he was hungry. Telling him that I'd be back before the last hour, I left him to it.

Walking out on to the plateau I stretched my arms above my head feeling my joints crack as they straightened out. I arched my back trying to loosen the knots I could feel there and daydreamed of a hot massage. Pushing these fanciful thoughts aside, I wandered over to the pomegranate tree and sat on the upturned jar - surely we could find a proper bench - and just let my thoughts wander, thinking about my life and what I had done over the past few days. I hadn't used the internet, watched any television, listened to any music or even read a book, oh and my journal, I missed my journal.

As I mused about the things in my modern life that I didn't really seem to be bothered about, I remembered that I still didn't know what I looked like and whether there was anything of the modern me in this other Hannah? What would happen to my two Romans? Did Maxentius and I have any chance of happiness together? What was going to happen would happen and maybe I would die here? And the ever present ache deep within, when I thought about my other life and my other Max.

Overwhelmed for a moment with the enormity of what was happening to me, I wanted to scream at the heavens, scream until I had no voice left, scream in the hopes that someone far, far away might hear me. How could I feel this way for two men, men who seemed to have so much in common, yet were poles (ok, yes and millennia) apart. I still believed it was as I'd explained it to Max; I was experiencing life through this Hannah. I wasn't actually her. I hadn't disappeared from the twenty first century, I was still there, I hoped, but for a little while my mind or my soul was here. This Hannah was doing all the work, I was just seeing it through her eyes, but my emotions were real. I was feeling all the things this Hannah was feeling, her passion for this Roman was the same as my passion for Max and in this we were the same. Maybe this was the connection and what, if anything, did all this have to do with my brooch, the one in a velvet pouch in a safe two thousand years away.

Sighing, it was all too hard. I pushed myself up and went back over to the kitchen, to see if Raizel wanted a hand dishing out the food.

Chapter Twenty Two

After helping Raizel sort out the evening meal and tidying up afterwards, I went to check on my patients one last time before finally having a break. They were settled now and beginning to drowse after being so long in the fresh air. They were all doing so well, I was quite proud of myself. Even Eli was brighter, although I did spend longer with him checking his wound and adding more of the salve. We chatted while I treated him and he told me about his family, left behind in Jerusalem and when I asked him why he had joined this band of rebels, his reply seemed to echo the feelings of everyone here.

"It's our land, its our home, we fought long and hard to get it the first time, we are not giving it back." Rallying cry of every disenfranchised group throughout the history of the world. Smiling at his fervour I suggested he channel some of that passion into getting better before starting another fight. Grinning he settled back on his pillows and after accepting a small dose of the sleeping draft, he closed his eyes and was asleep nearly before I'd stood up.

Final quick check to see whether Raizel needed any more help from me that evening, which she didn't, I wandered back across to my room. It was dark now, the night wrapping round us like a blanket, all was still and it was so peaceful. Quickly tidying myself up, I walked along to where Aharon and Raizel were ensconced and, after knocking, was invited in. I talked a little about the men, giving my brother an update of their conditions and he was happy with what I was doing.

He asked about the Romans and how they were healing and whether I had dealt with their dead comrade. I explained what had happened that morning and said that I hoped that leaving him to rest in the small bathhouse was acceptable. He didn't seem to care, so I moved swiftly on.

"I did wonder my brother, whether you think the two Romans could be moved to the main body of the palace?" He looked at me, questions in his eyes. I took a deep breath. "Its just that the room they use now is where I keep all my medicines, my herbs and oils, while it has been acceptable for them to stay there when they needed treatment constantly, now they are nearly healed, I would like the use of that room back as a kind of clinic."

"Clinic, what do you mean clinic?"

"Well, say someone is sick, or hurt and needs my help, this room would work as a treatment station, it is easy to find and close to the laundry and kitchens we use regularly, it is very convenient. The ward in the other building is fine for now, but is only any good if many people need beds. It is a long way to carry sheets, bandages, blankets and food, if there are only one or two people using it." Entreating him. "Please Aharon, they can do no harm, even if they escaped, where would they go? Set a sentry near their doors if you are worried, but I do not think we have anything to fear from them, they are only two against all these men. As captives, once they have regained their strength, maybe you can put them to work? I really want that room for other uses." I stopped speaking, aware I had probably overstated my case and waited quietly while he thought it over.

"Leave it with me, I will discuss it with the other elders, you make a powerful argument Hannah, but they are still an enemy, even if only two. I make no promises." Impulsively I jumped up and hugged him, not even knowing whether that was acceptable behaviour, but he seemed like a thoughtful, kind man and a man who cared about me, who in another time would never have been caught up in this craziness.

224

"Hannah!" Remonstrating with me, he gently pushed me away, but not before I noticed a smile teasing at the corners of his mouth and I did not imagine the quick squeeze of his returned hug.

Thanking them both, I bid them goodnight and quietly closed the door behind me. Running along to the treatment room, where Marcus and Maxentius were sitting enjoying a goblet of wine, I slipped in and plonked myself on one of the beds.

"I think I did it."

"Did what?"

"Got you your rooms. I've just talked to my brother and although he wouldn't give me any guarantees, he's going to talk to the other elders and see what they think. I told him I needed this room back and it was high time you were out of it. So fingers crossed..." they looked at me askance, "...oh c'mon, don't you guys know anything? Call yourselves worldly."

Sighing I proceeded to explain why I'd used that colloquialism, after which I sat back, resting against the wall, swinging my feet as they dangled over the bed. "Any more of that wine left?"

"Not sure wine would be a good idea, you seem rather...err, hmm...moonstruck."

"Hahaha, maybe so, but I'll chance it, I really need a drink." Oh dear, I realised that I didn't sound very 'era' appropriate, but quite frankly, I just wanted to relax with friends and not have to concentrate, if only for a little while. You can't do this Hannah a little voice in my head warned; even sitting on this bed is out of order. This was not where a single woman should be, on a bed in a room where two, presumably single, men slept. Sighing, I made to stand up.

"Sorry, I am behaving badly, it is not acceptable for me to lounge about here and it is your room." My words sounded stilted and, inexplicably, I felt disconsolate, I *had* no close friends, well except maybe for Raizel, but her husband was her priority, not her childhood playmate. Even though Maxentius and I shared something precious, were we friends? I wasn't sure. I had cared for them and treated their injuries and I think they liked and respected me, but I was a woman, friendships between men and women did not survive adolescence. It was not seemly for people of the opposite sex to gather round a table and chat about their lives and hopes and dreams. I felt a cold shiver pass over my shoulders, like the touch of a ghostly finger and I knew I was quite alone.

The two men were gazing at me in astonishment, I had gone from cheerful to sombre in the time it takes to pour a drink and they were floored.

"What is wrong my Hannah?" Quietly spoken, Maxentius studied my face.

"Oh you wouldn't understand." I knew I sounded petulant but I was unable to prevent myself. "No one would understand, its all a big huge mess and I just want everything to go back to where it was." My cheeks flared with a hectic colour I could not control and, shrugging helplessly, I turned to leave.

"I think we may need to take a walk, you need to clear your head and there is obviously something bothering you." Calmly and with complete disregard for etiquette, he took my hand and walked me through the door, across the courtyard to the main palace. "We will go to the balcony where we stood this afternoon, it is quiet and no-one will disturb us." Sulkily, I went with him, only because he would not let go of my hand.

"This is dangerous Maxentius, what if someo…"

"Shhhh, I will be careful, trust me." He said nothing else until we stood on the cool tiled floor of the balcony room. The night sky was spread out before us, the stars looked so close I thought I would be able to pull them down from the heavens. The dark shadows of the mountains rippled in jagged splendour, wave after wave of them as far as the eye could see. It was unbelievably beautiful.

"Now tell me my Hannah, what hurts you so much that your smile disappears in an instant?" I looked up at his face, this tall handsome stranger who had taken my heart, I wanted to tell him everything, but I knew he would not understand. I had not known him long enough and once he heard my story, he would withdraw from me, his eyes no longer lighting up when he looked at me. I would not see that slow smile warm his face, he would reject me and rightly so, I would seem taken with madness. I could not bear it. Yet part of me wanted to take that risk, to tell someone, it was a burden I was beginning to find too heavy. Wouldn't it be better to let it all out, to share this knowledge and my fears, could I trust him?

"Maxentius?" Hesitating. "Maxentius, do you trust me?"

"With my life. Why?" I took a deep breath.

"There are things about me you do not know, things, which if I told you would probably make you run from me. You would think me stark raving mad, but I fear that if I do not tell you I am hiding the part of me that makes me the person you say you care for." I didn't dare say 'love,' it seemed presumptuous.

"Unfortunately, I don't think you quite realise that there is no going back for me, I could not stop loving you even if you told me you had floated down from the moon." Little did he realise, I thought. "Trust me Hannah, I promise I will never leave you."

"You say that now, you don't know what I wish to tell you. That moon thing will seem like a walk in the park when you've heard what I am about to say." Trying for levity, I didn't quite make it and without warning a tear ran down my cheek…more with the crying…come on Hannah, get a grip.

He pulled me to him then and kissed me, his arms wrapping me close to his chest, his lips cool and hard, pressed against mine sending thrills of pleasure up and down my body.

"If you do that I'll never be able to tell you…" I muttered against his mouth, "…so - on second thoughts - keep going."

"Oh no my love, you intrigue me, I knew there was something different about you, things you say, the knowledge you have, seems somewhat…" searching, "…unconventional."

"I don't know whether I dare, if you turn away I could not bear it."

"I don't think you will be happy unless you tell me, I am quite worldly you know." Smiling.

"But this is way beyond what you will have ever had to see, hear or understand, even I struggle with it and I am living it." Holding me close again, his kisses raining down on my head and face, I felt safe, secure - please don't let me lose this.

"All right, but please don't interrupt me until I've finished, it will be hard enough. I'm happy to answer your questions later, but just for now, let me get through it." Taking another deep breath I held both of his hands and looked deep into his eyes, holding his gaze. "Maxentius, if you find what I am about to tell you too hard to comprehend, or if you think me deranged, please do not pretend you can accept it and then withdraw from me. That would be worse than death, for at least dead I would not have to endure your rejection. I need you to be honest, I can absent myself from your life, this rock is big enough for us to avoid any contact and would be more bearable than seeing you every day, knowing you cannot understand, or abide, who I am."

Maxentius looked back at me for a very long time, trying to disseminate what I was saying.

"I understand, but I cannot imagine anything you say would repel me."

228

"Then I hope you find that my words are true." Simply, quietly. "Are you sure you want to hear this?"

"Well if I wasn't before, I certainly am now."

So settling into one of the chairs, he pulled me onto his knee and although I didn't know whether this would be the best idea, at least I would have him close for a few more minutes. Slowly and hesitatingly, I began to tell him everything that had happened, taking care to try and clarify that the Hannah who was sitting on his knee was born in this time, not two thousand years in the future. That this Hannah was a healer, that everything about her was from this time, but that her descendent had somehow connected to her across the millennia. I explained about Max and Naomi and what had happened and that I had been working on the archaeological remains of this place, suddenly being part of the discovery of items I knew I had placed - well tossed - there.

As when I had told my other Max, it sounded utterly preposterous, but the more I talked, the better I felt, a weight was lifting and I knew that even if I had blown it, it had been eating me up inside - my relief was palpable. This knowledge that I had, that I could share, that would help him, needed to be told. Finally I came to the end and as my voice trickled to a halt, I did not dare look at him. Allowing my head to fall on my chest and my hair to cover my face, I sat like a stone, trying to stem the tremors running down my spine. Had he understood, was I clear enough? Maybe I should never had told him, I knew it was too much and thought it would be easier if I left him to his thoughts.

I began to get off his knee, head still bowed, but as he felt me move, he turned me to him and lifted my chin with a light finger so he could look into my eyes, the only sign of emotion, a muscle pulsing along his jaw line. I was sure he would be able to see my fear reflected there, but I held his gaze. The tremors had become shudders and, the silence went on for so long, I was certain he'd decided that I was indeed deranged. Tears ran down my face now, I could not stop them and just when I thought my heart would splinter, he spoke, his hushed words like a warm embrace.

"How could you have lived with this for so long and not told me? Your life has been turned upside down in ways I can never comprehend, yet you get up every day, to tend the injured, you dress wounds and make sure we are comfortable. You went of your way to make sure we were well treated, not thrown in an empty room and left for dead. You have cared for us in a manner I do not think my people would have thought to do. You even tried to save my friend, knowing he was your enemy and probably beyond help, then when you couldn't save him, prepared his body for the next life, all this without any recall as to who you were and why?"

Hope flickered as he continued, still in that soothing voice.

"I cannot imagine the terror you must feel, but you still found the courage to tell me and, although, I must agree that much of it is too baffling to fathom, I know you have no reason to speak in untruths. Your story is too complicated to be fantasy and I do trust you." Unable to tear my gaze away and not sure quite what he meant, I sat in his arms, mute, my body still shivering with dread, merely waiting. "Oh my Hannah." His head dipped and he kissed me, he kissed me so long and so hard I began to feel breathless, emotions roiled over me. I supposed this meant that he believed me, but did he still love me?

"Maxentius…what does this mean?" Confused with his reply and the kisses he would not stop covering me with, I tried to make sense of what he meant. Batting at him, to little effect, I questioned him again. "Are you saying you believe me?"

"Of course I believe you, what reason would you have for telling me an untruth?" Astonishment made my eyes go wide and my mouth formed an 'O'.

230

"B...b..but it does sound like I'm crazy, there's no 'of course' about it, even when I'm trying to explain it, I know I sound completely mad, how could I expect anyone else to understand?"

"Simple, you didn't have to tell me, you could have kept it secret, I would never have known, but you were prepared to risk everything, to tell me, that's why I believe you. Some of the words you use and some of your actions do not fit with this world. I had just assumed it was because you had had more freedom than most, that being a healer had afforded you a little independence. More, when we were first injured, there was a moment when, even though you had been treating us for quite a while, it was as though you had never met us, it was perplexing then, now it is clearer; part of you did not know us. Your explanation, while I can't believe I'm saying it, makes much more sense and, if you can spare a little more time, please would you tell me some more about your other life?"

I was stunned, this man was remarkable and he took it in his stride, even wanted to hear more. Nestling back against his chest, I asked him what he wanted to know. For the next hour or so we talked, I explained as much as I could without completely frying his brain. I told him of my first dream, when the fortress had been overrun and I had seen the three of them, wounded and bleeding, in a dimly lit room and that I thought we had made eye contact. He stopped me there and mentioned that he had heard a noise and glancing up had seen a shadowy figure in strange clothes in the doorway, but assuming it was his imagination had forgotten it. When I explained that the 'strange clothes' were modern day sleeping attire, his chest rumbled with laughter.

The longer we talked, the more he seemed able to process it, especially when I told him about the wads of bandages Nate had found in the ruin of the room they were currently sleeping in. I also told him about the pin, the one from my mantle that somehow got torn off, how, I did not know. Such little things, but the two were, so far, the only tangible link between the two me's.

Eventually Maxentius could see that I was tiring, we had talked for a long time and I was fighting to stay awake. Snuggling up against him it would have been easy just to fall asleep on his lap.

"We must go back Hannah, we do not want to get caught like this, we have been so careful."

"Will you still..." I still found it hard to say the words, so skirted right on passed them, "...be comfortable with me treating you after all of this?" He answered that with another long hard kiss, running his hands over my tunic, catching the skin on my arm and shaping me to his long length.

"I will be more than comfortable, I look forward to seeing you every day, that will not change and I will never stop loving you Hannah, never. Whatever else happens, that will be the one constant." Smiling up at him, I kissed him back, finding a gap in his tunic and brushing my fingers over his back, enjoying the feel of his skin against my searching fingers. He shivered and groaned "No, not fair, stop...urrrhhhhh..." as I caught the hollow under his arm, "...we must go." Knowing he was right I stopped, albeit reluctantly, as he lifted me off his knee. Once standing we made sure we both looked like models of decorum and, with one more lingering kiss, returned to the rooms in the other building.

He walked me to my room and after a glance around to make sure no-one saw us, kissed me again, deeply, tenderly and just enough to make that slow fire spark.

"Don't leave me."

"I'm just along here, you are safe." Dropping a last kiss onto the top of my head, he gently pushed me into my room, smiled that toe curling smile and went along to the room he shared with Marcus. The kiss, the action, the smile were all so familiar I had to blink to confirm I was actually still in the past, it was exactly what Max had done that morning when I'd been so angry with him. Oh my life…what a complicated, crazy, deliciously ludicrous mess. Changing into my night slip, I snuggled under the covers and dreamed very satisfying dreams.

Chapter Twenty Three

The next day was pretty much the same as all my others, I checked the other men, bathed and redressed those whose wounds required it, changed beds, washed sheets, the routine was becoming very easy, I had slipped into it as though I had been doing it a long time, which, maybe I had been! Maxentius behaved as if I hadn't told him anything the previous evening, when I'd gone to examine his and Marcus's injuries.

Both were doing very well, even Maxentius' bruising had almost gone. His wounds, especially the deeper gash were healing nicely, I felt that maybe I had managed to save them all. Later that day Maxentius asked if we could walk out to the pomegranate tree, I knew that the other men were relaxing at the far side of the Western Palace, so I thought we would be fine. Marcus had decided to go and check out the rooms in the other palace on the off chance they got to move over there.

It was nice, just us two, in daylight. We were, however, the souls of discretion, walking a few feet apart and no touching of hands. Following, just little behind, as his strides were too long for me to keep up with now he was fitter, I could study Maxentius without him or anyone else knowing. His hair was quite long now and he had taken to catching it back with a little strip of leather. His shoulders, broad and strong, his back straight and through the tunic he was wearing I could just about see the outline of his torso and the muscular shape of his legs. He certainly was huge this Roman, I kept forgetting how burly he was until he stood close to me. Watching him walk over to 'our' tree, I realised how impressive he would look in full armour at the head of a legion of soldiers.

After he had got settled…there was still no bench, I really needed to get on to that…he asked if I would tell him more about what would happen. After extracting from him his word that he would not in any way try to change the outcome and, making sure that he really did want to know how this would turn out and the consequences of that knowledge, I explained what would come. That Jerusalem would fall to the Romans, following which more rebels would find refuge here until the governor decided to quash this last little pocket of resistance and lay siege to Masada. That the Romans would send out a huge force and they would build a massive ramp up the side of the rock, which they would use to storm the fortress after protracted negotiations came to nothing. That when they reached the top, they would find only bodies for a number of rebels would kill everyone within before taking their own lives. I could see that this information was hard for him to accept, what about the two of us, did we survive?

"I don't know, I'd like to think so, for somehow I have descended through this Hannah's line, but I think we just have to let it run its course, we cannot change the future, I believe that everything is happening the way it should and we just have to hope that we make it. Although even if we did, I am not sure we could ever be together…" I trailed off, realising that even if we both survived, we would probably never see each other again.

"I will find a way to be with you my Hannah, I cannot lose you now." I smiled at him, hoping he could read in my eyes what I couldn't physically demonstrate.

"I know, the enormity of it is too much to try and get your head around, but you have given me your word, please do not try to alter what is already set down. I do not want to lose you either, but I cannot see how our relationship would be accepted. If I survive, I will be made a slave, you are a Roman general, there is no middle ground."

"Trust me Hannah." Confident in his abilities, he patted my hand and said no more. We dropped the topic then, to go over and over it would not change the outcome, we had to wait it out and see where life would lead us. I went back to my chores, he went over to see what Marcus had found and we rarely spoke of it again and I am sure he never breathed a word of it to his comrade.

My days began to settle into a routine. I carried on treating the wounded men in my care and, slowly but surely they all healed, even Eli. They started to spend some time working on the plateau, setting up their own living quarters, some used the barracks and the rooms of the smaller palaces dotted about the rock, others found it more comfortable to create living quarters within the casemate wall. Some went off and got involved in small skirmishes and raids against the Romans; whether or not they were successful I did not ask nor care. What I did care about was that I ended up treating them when they came back hurt, which although kept me busy did seem to be a waste of my time. No sooner had I dressed and bandaged injuries, than they were off again returning with fresh wounds or re-opened the ones I'd just fixed up, it was very frustrating.

Thankfully, some stayed on the rock, happily working the soil, such as it was and, helping to grow food. We had goats and chickens and the oxen, which were mysteriously added to now and again. I never asked, I did not want to know; neither did I want to know when they just as mysteriously disappeared. Marcus and Maxentius moved into the main part of the Northern Palace, the elders deciding that my plea to use the room as a clinic was agreeable. My two Romans healed well, Maxentius' bruising eventually went down and his ribs healed. It must have been hard for them knowing that those who had caused their injuries lived a hairs breadth away across the compound. I suppose on the other hand, these two had probably done their fair share of damage to

236

the rebels too. All in all, my days were full, I slept well and as a far as a person out of time can be, I was happy with my lot.

I had managed to avoid Tobias as much as possible, hoping that he would get the message without my having to spell it out. It was difficult and for a while he seemed intent on courting me. The only way I could handle it was to continue behaving towards him, as I thought I always had, giving him no cause to think he had a chance, but without hurting him. So, I treated him no differently from all the other men, with respect and from a distance. I talked to them, treated their illnesses, made sure that they kept a hygienic regimen and reminded them, constantly, to change their clothes.

I showed them where to put their dirty laundry, how they could help me by washing things through and either hanging them on the drying racks or laying them over the bushes, or walls. I made sure that the bedding was freshened regularly, but they had to pull their weight. They took it with good grace, knowing that, so far, Raizel and I were the only women on this fortress and we could not manage everything, further Raizel was pregnant again and so less able to help. We made a deal, if they cleaned their clothes, we'd make dinner. It worked. For a time everything settled into a comfortable routine.

I began to explore this rock called Masada properly. Marcus and Maxentius knew it well and they were good guides. I found the other bath house, which was still functional and I decided to use as often as possible, the storerooms, which were exceedingly well stocked, the cisterns where all the water was stored, the mikvah, or ritual bath and the many smaller buildings spread over this vast outpost. There was even a synagogue and although it had been damaged, eventually the rebels rebuilt it within the original footprint. The Western Palace took the longest time to become familiar with, for it was spread over an enormous four thousand square metres, a lot of ground to cover within its walls. I loved wandering through its halls, imagining Herod and his entourage entertaining people from across the ancient world, I didn't know whether he did, but it was fun pretending!

One day, in one of the rooms, a bedchamber, I found a large oval of highly polished metal, leaning on what appeared to me to be a beautifully carved dresser. Excitement touched me, for the first time since I had come to this place, I would be able to see my reflection properly, rather than a swirly image in water. It was a nerve-wracking moment, as now that I could actually see myself, I wasn't sure I'd be able to cope. I was certain I would look so different that it would freak me out. My two Romans who were with me, chuckled as I asked if they would think me vain if I looked in the mirror, assuring me that it would be fine.

Tentatively, I moved to stand in front of it and simply stared. The person looking back was, but wasn't, me. She was somewhat smaller than I am and I'm not tall and, I knew her hair was rich dark chestnut and curly, but I hadn't really registered how beautiful it looked. It was, surprisingly, in a fairly neat plait, which I had twisted up into a bun. Without thinking, I unpinned it, letting it fall across my shoulders and down my back. I heard Maxentius gasp as it swung free, its luxurious length fell in shining curls and I let it ripple through my fingers. It felt very sensuous and probably wasn't the most prudent thing to be doing in front of two hot blooded males, but whatever.

My skin was olive and my face, familiar. We shared the same facial characteristics, although this Hannah had finer more elfin features, very dainty yet determined and I knew the modern me would seem quite tall beside her. But it was the eyes that held me, they were the same green as my eyes in my other world and, I assumed would be very unusual in a Hebrew woman. I was inordinately pleased; I'd always thought my eyes were my best trait. I was also enchanted that there was an attribute that linked

238

us, that despite our obvious differences, we were connected. I knew this Hannah, she was part of me and I, her. I smiled and as my image smiled back, I felt that we had shared a very precious moment. Pulling a face at my whimsy, I tried to break the quiet that had descended while I had been studying my reflection.

"I suppose I'm not too plain and my hair's quite pretty, I guess." The two men just stared at me, nonplussed. "What, what did I say now?"

"You think you're plain, that your features are not pleasing to look at?"

"Well, duh...I've seen some really beautiful woman in my life and I don't even come close." I was not being overly modest, or begging to be admired, I was merely stating what I thought to be the facts. Yeah, my hair was a lovely colour and my eyes were interesting, but the rest of me seemed rather average. Now where had I heard that before? It pulled at my memory, but I couldn't place it. I continued. "I'm just average."

"I have also seen a lot of beautiful women in my life, which has been somewhat longer than yours, yet I have never seen anyone quite so exquisite as you." Maxentius stated this as though it was blindingly obvious and Marcus nodded in agreement.

"Agreed, you are by far the loveliest lady I have ever met and you are as lovely within. The beauty of many women is only skin deep, most are like empty vessels." I gaped at them, their expressions told me that they believed this to be true. Before this got out of hand, I muttered something about women and their appalling vanity and, blushing furiously, quickly moved off to the next room followed by the sound of gleeful laughter. It was a long time before I could bring myself to look in the polished oval again.

Many more days passed before I was confident I knew my way round just this palace, but I was determined, I wanted to know every inch of this fortress, its nooks and crannies, secret stairs and hidden entrances. You never know when that sort of information might come in handy.

I realised how long I had been here when my time to use the mikvah, a ritual bath for women after their monthly cycle, came round again and I suddenly worked out how many times I'd used it. I had been here well over a year, maybe nearly two and it seemed as though my place was now in this time. Maybe I would never return to my other world, my other Max and while I grieved, I was so busy, that I didn't really have time to mourn its loss.

Although my sleep was usually untroubled, I did dream of a white room, with a high bed and a man talking to the woman who lay on it. Surrounded by wires and tubes and flashing boxes, very pale and still, she seemed familiar and the man looked so sad my heart ached for him. I wanted to touch his face, to tell him it would be all right, but I couldn't reach him. These dreams often haunted my nights, they never left me, but I was at a loss to explain them.

My relationship with Maxentius, although still secret, continued to flourish. Occasionally he asked about modern things, but I think it mostly just messed with his head, so he didn't bother too much. Also I was starting to forget, no - not forget - more, no longer need and, to try and keep recalling what I could no longer access, upset me and was futile. Maxentius did watch over me and when he thought I was struggling to cope, or became overwhelmed with what I knew, made sure he was there to help me talk it through.

We were still models of decorum, we stole our kisses when we knew we were alone and every now and again we managed to go a little further, but consummation of our love was something we could not even think about. Although I had to admit I was finding it harder to hold back and, going by the changes in his body when we stood close together, Maxentius was too. I knew the risks of taking this to another level were high, but I wasn't sure how much longer I could behave like the young single women I was supposed to be.

My understanding of some ancient traditions and cultures was sketchy, but I was pretty sure marriage between a Jew and a Roman, a freeborn woman and a man who, although was a very high ranking officer of the Roman army, was now a captive, was frowned upon if not forbidden. I remembered something about a woman having to be a virgin and her suitor was supposed to offer a gift to the head of the household, which, in my case would be Aharon, as our father was dead, to seal the betrothal. Regardless of that, he hadn't even asked me, so what was I even thinking, thus we continued as we were.

I was still wary of Tobias who tried, not infrequently, to corner me. He had a proprietary air when he talked to me, almost as if he thought he owned me and I found it disquieting. I really did not want him to come upon Maxentius and I in a compromising situation, for who knew what he might do. However, he steered clear of the two Romans, his anger still very close to the surface and, eventually it seemed that he had accepted that I was not interested in being anything other than an acquaintance.

Marcus, it soon became clear, was adept at farming; he had grown up in a rural neighbourhood a few miles outside Rome and was a whiz at all things agricultural. Quite why he had joined the army when his skills would have been much better employed on a farm was beyond me, but who am I to question the whims of men. Even though many of the crops we were trying to grow were different from what he was used to, he had a knack for knowing just what to do. The elders allowed him to manage the crops and the animals, there was always a guard nearby, but as I'd said to Aharon long ago, even if they could escape, where would they go?

Slowly, very slowly, the Zealots came to respect his expertise and although I wouldn't say they ever became friends, their relationship took on a more cordial tone. He would never have risked being alone with them, but as long as Maxentius, the guard, or I were there, he felt safe. He loved being outside, he relished the long days and even began to learn Hebrew, so he could discuss what he was doing with those who worked alongside him.

Maxentius on the other hand seemed to be a born soldier, he had been in the army for ten years, since before he had turned twenty and knew no other life. At nearly thirty years old, he was struggling to find things to do that did not involve organising a campaign or planning battle tactics. I needed to channel his energy and it took me some time to come up with anything that I thought would suit him, too much time on his hands when he was used to being busy, was making him crotchety.

Until that was, I persuaded him to make some furniture. I was still desperate for a bench under our tree and wanted some better tables, bigger tougher structures than the fine furniture left by Herod, which for the most part had not had the best treatment at the hands of the subsequent Roman garrisons. I also wanted proper hospital beds, something that would stand higher than the pallets we had used initially. I preferred that air could circulate around my patients not just over them and if, as I suspected I was going to be dealing with more wounded men soon enough, I wanted things ready. Drawing what I wanted in the dust and telling him to use anything he wanted to make them, even if that involved breaking down other furniture, I left him to it.

It was like he'd found a new lease of life, he appropriated the tools from the armoury and storerooms and wood from who knows where and began to create the most amazing pieces. It wasn't enough for him simply to make a functional object, he wanted it to look good too, making sure the wood was smooth and the edges rounded, I was blown away. Kept him busy for months, although I did need to remove hundreds of splinters, clean many scratches and bind his thumbs and fingers after he'd hit them with what I assumed to be something akin to a hammer.

In this way they also contributed to the running of the enclave. As the situation in Jerusalem worsened, more and more people found their way out to this desert outpost. Numbers grew steadily and now there were whole families, women and children who had accompanied their husbands, we needed to feed and clothe and treat all of them.

My days now included dealing with childhood ailments and scraped knees, along with a plethora of adult maladies and quite a lot of malnutrition. Thankfully the storerooms were very well stocked and there looked to be enough food to feed several armies for decades. We were very careful with how we distributed it and, where possible, cooked for everyone in one of the bigger kitchens. This way we could monitor usage and try to restock those foods that seemed low. My skills were pushed to their limits, but I had realised long ago, that I could only do my best.

Chapter Twenty Four

One evening after a very long day, I was sitting under the pomegranate tree, on a new and very smart bench when Maxentius came over to join me.

"Hey beautiful, how was your day?"

"Very, very long and if I see one more child with sickness after over indulging on dried figs I'm going to scream. What is with them and their parents for that matter? Grrr...enough now!" Maxentius grinned at me, I loved his smile, it warmed me all over, I smiled back happily wishing I could lean into his shoulder.

"What have you been doing? More furniture?"

"We have finished that last table, so I think we have ten now." I had asked that the tables be long with folding legs so they could be stacked out of the way if we ever needed to, but we usually ate outside, the weather warm enough to do so and it made everyone join together. Each table could sit about twenty adults and lots more children. Several of the other men had decided to join in and help him so they had also made long bench seats to go with each table. I was endlessly amazed by what they had achieved.

"So what's next?"

"I'm thinking of making a set of open shelves for someone who keeps moaning that she does not have enough places to stack her medicines."

"Oh that would be wonderful and totally unprompted." Chuckling at his expression I leaned in quickly to kiss him on the cheek, he turned his head at the last minute and sought my mouth with his lips. I felt the inevitable shudder run through me and the little spark ignite in the pit of my stomach.

"We mustn't." I whispered,

"I know, but I can't help myself, I haven't seen you all day."

"I'm sorry I shouldn't have started this." Remorseful now, I gazed up at him, desperate to wrap my arms around his broad shoulders and hold him close.

"Its ok, welcome to my world. I have to watch you every day, talking and laughing with the others, many of whom are men who admire you and I am unable to claim you as mine." Casually he moved so his leg pressed against mine, anyone looking over would never know, yet to me it was deliciously sinful and a moment I could treasure when I was alone. I stood up,

"Well good sir, would you be so kind as to walk me back to my quarters?" Very business like, good effort Hannah.

"It would be my pleasure."

Smiling, he waited until I had gathered my basket up and walked alongside me over to my rooms. I had made the treatment room into a clinic and found another room just across the courtyard, near to the laundry, which acted as a mini ward. The beds that Maxentius had made stood proudly in a line, each covered with clean bedding and a blanket. No one required them at the moment, so my evenings were my own. The shelves he was talking about would stand in this new room, to hold pots and jars, bottles and flagons, so I didn't need to keep going back and forth all the time. At least I was efficient. Maxentius waved as he walked towards his rooms in the main palace and I went back to my bedroom, thinking I might change before the evening meal.

My clothes felt sticky on me and my mantle was covered in dust. I had just entered my room and was filling a bowl with water when I felt a draft and thinking maybe Maxentius had risked coming to see me. I turned with a smile ready on my face, to see Tobias, his hand holding back the heavy curtain.

"What on earth are you doing here Tobias, are you ill?"

"No, unless you call broken hearted, ill."

"What are you talking about, don't be daft, broken hearted, you had too much wine again?" Jovially.

"I know what you are up to, I've been watching you. You think you are careful but I know exactly what is going on." His voice was beginning to seem rather hostile, I watched him warily.

"What on earth are you prattling about, go on, off with you, I have enough to do without dealing with drunk men and what are you doing here in my room? You know perfectly well that you shouldn't be here."

"Oh, but I bet I know who you would prefer to have in here behind this curtain, how many times have you let him have you, this Roman scum?"

"Tobias, how dare you?" I raised my voice as loudly as I could without actually shouting, hoping someone would hear me. "What gives you the right to speak to me this way?"

"I asked your brother for you, years ago, he refused, said it was your choice, this is wrong, against our traditions, so I want to claim what is rightfully mine. No-one else has asked for your hand and you need someone to tame you, I am here to collect my due." Spluttering to get the words out, I was so angry, my voice became a shriek.

"Tame me…TAME me, get out Tobias, get out right now! Any rights you may think you had were lost the minute you said that…earned the right…by all that's holy leave me, or I will call for my brother." My thoughts were whirling, I hoped he would just leave, but he had a strange look in his eyes and I knew that my rooms were in a quieter area of the fortress, simply because the sick needed to be able to rest peacefully. I couldn't get past him, he was standing right in the doorway. I thought I saw movement beyond him, but no one came.

Panic was beginning to take hold and I tried again, concentrating hard, I began to reason with him.

"Well, why don't we go and talk to Aharon? He is just along there, he will be able to help, or one of the other elders."

"Why, so you can wriggle out of it again, if I take you now they will have to let me marry you." I didn't know whether that was right or not, but I wasn't about to give him the chance.

"You cannot be serious, you think you can force yourself on me and get away with it?"

"Oh yes, I am sure of it." He advanced slowly into the room. I screamed at the top of my lungs and tried to dodge passed him. He caught me by my cloak, ripping it off my shoulders, I heard the clasp ping as it hit the ground, oh no, he broke my pin - a distant memory flickered across my consciousness and was gone.

I swung away desperate to escape, but he was too strong, yanking me across to him he forced me back up against the wall. He had a knife - who carries a knife on an isolated rock? - in his hand and he held it up under my chin, his other arm holding me still, his knee up against my groin.

"One more sound out of you my girl." And he ran the knife along my throat, I moaned in terror.

"Oh, I like that, I like that I can make you moan for me." Oh God I could feel bile rising from my stomach I was going to be sick. Waiting 'til he relaxed his hold I tried again to wriggle out of his grasp, I couldn't do it, he grabbed my hair, pulling it hard and lifting his knife, said very quietly.

"Do you know what we do to Roman whores?" There was a long pause. "We scalp them." And, using his knife, proceeded to hack at my hair, the knife catching my neck in his frenzy, blood trickled down onto my shoulder.

I was screaming blue murder now, terrified that he would carry out this threat, never mind his other objectives. I fought with everything I had, but it just seemed to egg him on, he was enjoying trying to break me, it was part of his game. My hair floated to the ground in dark rivulets, but, writhing, I managed to stop him, by clawing at his face. He swore and slammed me back against the wall, my head cracking against the stone, while pawing at my clothes, he tried to get his hands under the material. Oh no, no, no, this couldn't be happening, please someone save me. Pushing up against me I could feel that he was completely aroused and that probably I had only seconds to try and get away, but I was tiring and very dizzy from banging my head, I knew his strength would win out, still I had no intention of giving in.

My legs were losing strength and I felt myself sliding down the wall, using this to his advantage, Tobias let me fall to the floor, dropping on top of me, holding me down with his weight. Finally, he got one hand under my tunic and slapped the other one hard over my mouth. Still screaming albeit muffled now, I tossed my head frantically trying to get him to let go. His hand was snaking up my legs, dragging at my clothes, tearing at the fabric and, pummelling at him, I kept trying to push him away, but I was totally ineffectual. Somehow in all of this, he had lifted his own tunic and I felt him against me. I could feel the bile rising up into my throat, gagging I tried one last time to free my mouth and, just as he got my clothes up over my hips, I threw up all over him - it didn't even slow him down, he simply smacked me hard across my face with his fist and grabbed both of my flailing hands in one of his, holding me fast.

Ah - but at least now I could scream again and did so at the top of my lungs, I just screamed and screamed and screamed, my voice becoming hoarse with the effort. I felt the edge of his knife against my side, its point jabbing me and, just when I thought he would actually penetrate me, with more than just his knife, there was noise outside my room and several men burst in all at once. Hauling Tobias off me I heard Aharon roaring like a wounded bull, Maxentius and Marcus tumbled in next followed by at least two others. Oh praise every god under the sun I'm saved. Panting I tried to get up, but found I didn't have the strength, I knew I needed to cover myself up, all these men, but couldn't seem to pull my tunic back down over my hips, I tried to ask for their help, but the words wouldn't form. The dizziness that had come over me after Tobias had slammed my head into the wall, returned and I promptly fainted.

I was only unconscious for a minute or so, but by the time I came round, I was lying on my bed, covered with a warm blanket, surrounded by a group of very anxious looking men. Glad that they I had found me in time I was still embarrassed that they had seen me in such a state of undress and could not prevent the hectic colour flare up my cheeks. Maxentius leaned forward as if to touch me, then thought better of it and simply asked:

"Hannah, what happened, did he…?" Unable to finish the sentence he hesitated and Eli, oh bless his heart, bookish Eli had come to my rescue too, spoke.

"I don't think he did, I think we arrived just in time. What on earth made him do this?" Groggily I tried to tell them.

"He thinks I should be his and that he needs to tame me." I giggled, hysteria playing at the edges of my senses.
"Tame…me…" I spluttered unable to stop the laughter that was bubbling up. I knew it was reaction, but that didn't mean I could control it.

I took several deep breaths to try and calm myself - it helped.
"Where's Aharon? What will he do?"

"He dragged him off down the corridor, I have no idea where he took him, or what he will do, it is better that I do not know." I could see that Maxentius had himself under tight restraint and thanked whoever it was who had told Aharon, so he got here first.
"Do you think you can tell us what happened?" Trying to sit up, I felt woozy again, but they helped me and propped me up against

my pillow. After a little while, I felt more comfortable and pulling the blanket right up to warm my now shivering body, I told them what had happened, leaving nothing out. They needed to hear it all, I wasn't letting Tobias get away with it.

"He said that if he took me, Aharon would have to let him marry me." Mortified, I could feel the sickness rising again and motioned for a bowl. "So, sorry…" wiping my face on the cloth one of them handed me, "…oh dear what a mess." With this massive understatement I calmly threw up again and quietly asked for some water. My throat was sore from screaming and my voice was hoarse. I ached all over and really really wanted a bath and to burn everything I was wearing. Then I remembered my hair and lifted my hands to feel my head. "Oh my hair, my hair, how bad is it?" Beseeching them, I knew it wasn't good, their faces reflected their shock as they took a good look at what Tobias had done. "He called me a Roman whore and told me this is what you did to Roman whores." My voice was sorrowful, but I refused to cry - no more, I would not cry over this man's treatment of me, I refused to give him that satisfaction.

"Is my face bruised too, what about my neck, I felt blood?" Then, unable to help himself, Maxentius leaned over and gently touched my face.

"It is rather swollen, I think you may have a black eye tomorrow, there is a cut on your neck, it has stopped bleeding." The others looked at him askance, but I put my hands out to them.

"Please, say nothing, let me deal with it." They nodded, confused about what was going on here, sensing there were undercurrents, but weren't sure what they meant. "I need to change my clothes and wash off his touch, if I don't, I think I will start screaming all over again. I will use the mikvah for my wash, it will cleanse me. Please will you help me up?"

They gathered round me and lifted me off the bed. Aching all over, I staggered to my feet, the four men helping me walk out through my door. I wasn't even sure I could ever sleep in that room again. They came with me over to the mikvah and then left me to my ministrations, where I noticed that the knife had also nicked my side, but thankfully didn't seem too deep. I would have to dress it though. Someone had found a clean outfit for me as well as a cloak for warmth.

It was nearly dark, the night was cool, everything was quiet and it was as though nothing had happened, which was weird, for surely the world should have been tilted off its axis with all that trauma. I realised that my hair was all lop-sided, so I walked over to the kitchen, found a sharp knife and cut the rest off so that it was almost even. It was so short now, barely touching my shoulders, but at least I wasn't scalped. I casually dropped my tattered clothes onto the fire and stood watching while they burned, the flames leaping as the material caught, casting shadows on the walls.

Now I really did need a drink. On one of the benches stood some wine, I was too tired to find a goblet and so I simply drank straight from flagon. I knew I should try and speak to Aharon, but I couldn't find it in me to go to him, I was afraid he was still with Tobias and him I could not face, ever again.

I walked over to my clinic and sat on one of the beds so beautifully made by Maxentius, what did I do now, should I tell Aharon? My head was swirling with images and I kept shuddering as the events of the evening kept repeating themselves. Suddenly both Marcus and Maxentius came in.

"Why are you in here? We've been looking for you, you should not be alone, you need to be with those you trust."

"I don't know, but I cannot go back to that room, I need to speak with Aharon, but I fear he is still with Tobias. I am so, so tired, but I am frightened to close my eyes. What do I do?" I looked at them and my face must have looked full of despair, for they both moved towards me as one.

"We are here for you my Hannah, come we will go to Aharon, I will check that Tobias is gone before you need enter the rooms."

I nodded absently and went along with them to my brother's rooms. Knocking quietly, Maxentius opened the door at Aharon's invitation. Going in, I heard a murmured discussion and then he came back for me.

"We have her here, she is in shock, be gentle with her." I registered that Maxentius was talking about me to Aharon in a very familiar manner, but I couldn't process it. Raizel was there too; she came and helped me over to a chair. I felt detached from the proceedings, as though watching them from outside my body.

"What happened Hannah?" Raizel's soft voice penetrated my thoughts, her lovely hands were massaging mine and she was smiling into my face. So for the second time that night, I told my story, my words were stilted and formal, my voice still hoarse and, full of unshed tears, sounded harsh, but I was still determined not to cry. As I had with the other four men back in my room, I told them everything. Every word, every insult, every threat, every action. My head was beginning to throb and my face hurt from Tobias' fist. I was going to be such a sight the next day.

When I finally wound up, I sat for long while, waiting for the verdict. Was it my fault, had I asked for this? Aharon's voice, when he eventually spoke, came from a long way off and I found it hard to concentrate on his words.

"My sister, you have been dealt a great wrong. I have spoken to as many of the men I can find at this hour to ask them if you have ever shown him favour. They all agree you have treated him with respect but nothing more. I know he asked for your hand some years ago, but I thought him a boorish youth who would not be a suitable husband for you. This, tonight, has proved that I was correct. I regret, my sister, that he has done this to you, he will be dealt with. You do not need to be afraid that he will ever be able to touch you again."

His words although formal were spoken kindly and when I raised my head to look at his face, he leaned down and placed his hand on my shoulder, squeezing it very gently.

"I am so sorry Hannah." I wanted to cry then but found I couldn't. I nodded and thanked him, my words emotionless and, slowly stood to take my leave.

"I don't know where to go, I don't know where to sleep, that room…" shaking my head, bewildered, "…I cannot sleep in that room. I fear I may never sleep again, yet I am so weary. What do I do now?" They all looked at me not knowing how to offer any comfort. Raizel stood and hugged me close.

"We will work something out my sister." Her lovely voice was like a balm.

"The guard is still over near our quarters, maybe you could sleep over there, I can share with Marcus for tonight and you will have a sentry to watch over you" Maxentius was taking a huge risk suggesting this, but it seemed as if he and Aharon had come to an entente, for Aharon nodded.

"It is a suggestion with merit, Raizel will come over with you to make sure everything is in order. I hope you are able to sleep my sister, you need to rest." Thanking him again, I walked out trancelike, across to the upper tier of the palace. Raizel checked the room and found it to be suitable, she waited for a few moments to make sure I was settled.

Marcus moved a pallet into his room and the two men, after asking the guard to call them if he was worried about me, wished me goodnight and left me to my thoughts. I could tell that Maxentius wanted to stay with me, but it was not possible. I closed the door and walked to the bed. How does one deal with this? I thought. I was so thankful that he had been stopped before actually taking me, I couldn't bring myself to use the other word, but I had still been abused, I had cleansed my body, but how do you cleanse your soul?

I had no night slip, so having divested myself of my clothes I slid, naked into the huge bed and felt warmed under the luxurious bed coverings. Closing my eyes I tried to sleep, but my dreams were tormented and I kept waking up terrified that Tobias had found a way to get back to me and finish what he'd started. I got up several times and wandered the room, I could look out of the window and see the stars but even their beauty was of no comfort this night. Eventually I fell into a restless slumber, I tossed and turned and somewhere around dawn, exhaustion took over and I slept.

Across the vast expanse of time, a pale, slender woman in a white bed, seemingly in a deep torpor suddenly became very distressed. The man watching her hoped this was the sign they had been waiting for, that she was waking up. She muttered his name, her voice, hoarse from lack of use; he held her close and spoke to her willing her to wake up. Crying out she thrashed her arms as if trying to fight something, then just as suddenly quietened, drifting back to wherever she had been. The man bent his head and whispered softly,

"Please Hannah come back I need you."

Chapter Twenty Five

When I finally woke, the sun was still climbing to its zenith and it took a few minutes to remember where I was, then it all flooded back. It must have actually happened, it wasn't just a very bad dream. Nobody had come to get me, so they must have decided I needed to rest. Finally, I had made them understand that sleep was a great healer, well that was something anyway. This bed was very comfortable, I lay for a long time, enjoying the feel of the sheets and the warm coverlet, far more sumptuous than mine, this must be the deluxe suite I thought, giggling a little at my nonsense. It was lovely just to lie here, nobody wanting ointments or balms, or something to stop them being sick, or to help with a headache. I lay for so long I fell back to sleep and dreamed of the lady in the white bed again, she seemed distressed and the man was calling to her, it was odd, he was using my name.

I must have slept for another few hours for the sun was high overhead and the light in this room was enchanting. I looked around properly, it was magnificent, simple black and white tiled floor, but there were beautiful frescoes on the walls and, the fluted columns, supporting the ceiling were also decorated. The furnishings were elegant and seemed to be made from very high quality wood and marble, I decided it must have been either one of Herod's, or one of his wives' bed chambers. Still I really shouldn't stay in bed all day; there was probably something I should be doing.

I found a washstand, which held a large bowl, a pitcher of water and a towel. I freshened up and then spotting one of those polished metal mirrors, examined myself thoroughly. The cut in my side wasn't too bad, but would need cleaning, who knew where that knife had been, I checked the shudder that ran through me, but was determined not to let it get to me, I was stronger than this. I could tell the wound on my neck was superficial but quite long, stretching from my hairline to my shoulder, it could have been so much worse.

My face sported a beautiful black eye and my cheek was puffed up. Gently pressing around the area I thought I had avoided broken bones in my nose and cheek, but it would need some ointment to reduce the swelling and bruising. The rest of my body was also bruised where he had held me, my arms, my legs, and my chest all looked like I'd been in the boxing ring and the back of my head had a lump the size of an ostrich egg, ok well that may be a bit of an exaggeration, but it felt huge and was very painful. However, I thought that in light of what could have happened I had come out of it relatively unscathed.

Dressing in the same clothes I had worn last night I ventured, reluctantly, out of this gorgeous room. The sentry was still there, bless him, who told me that the two Romans were out on the plateau and that Raizel had left food for me in the kitchen and would I like him to go and fetch it? Sweet! I told him, I'd be fine to go and get it myself, but he followed me discreetly, I'm not really sure whether it was for my benefit or he had been instructed to do so, but it was rather comforting having a body guard.

I found the platter and nibbled at the breads and fruit, not really hungry but my brain told me I needed to eat. I made myself a hot lemon drink, which was soothing and warmed me, then I walked over to my treatment room, where I mixed up some of the salve I had used when I was looking after patients, it seemed so long ago now. Cleaning both of my wounds with saline, I hoped I'd removed any lingering dirt, but it was difficult to see either of them.

I knew I should call Raizel to help me but I was feeling stubborn, I wanted to do it on my own. Eventually, after twisting myself into all sorts of weird shapes, I was satisfied that I'd cleaned them thoroughly and finished by rubbing salve into the cut on my side and wrapping a bandage round to keep it clean. Locating the arnica I had used on Maxentius, I mixed it with some oil and rubbed it in to my poor bruised skin, the scent was rather pungent but I didn't really care.

All this effort had tired me and I wanted nothing more than to go back to bed, but I needed to feel fresh air on my face and the warmth of the sun on my body. Straightening my shoulders and making sure I looked tidy, I went out, my guard still following me at a discreet distance. It was so strange, nothing had changed, life was continuing here as it had the whole time I'd been here, but everything seemed different, I felt detached, adrift. Gazing out across the plateau, I watched people going about their daily business, what ever that was, noticing that Marcus was over in the veggie patch. He saw me walking over and waved, dropping his tools he came to greet me.

"Hannah, should you be up? We thought you might prefer to stay in the room and rest."

"I do not want to be alone with my thoughts Marcus, they are too dark."

"Maxentius will want to speak to you, he did not sleep much last night." Join the club I thought.

"Well he knows where I am. I'm sure he will find me when he's good and ready." I knew my words were cold, stilted, but I couldn't help it. Marcus looked at me weighing up whether it was worthwhile saying any more, but he erred on the side of caution and merely talked about the vegetables and fruits they were trying to grow.

After a few more minutes, I took my leave, telling him he was doing a fine job, even to me I sounded withdrawn. He watched me walk away, concern all over his young face. I walked over to the Western Palace and took a little time in the quiet of the rooms there, but being alone bothered me, I was not comfortable being so far from the others, so I did not stay long. Back in the sunshine, my ever present guardian shadowing my steps, I made my way over to the bench under the pomegranate tree, from here I could watch everyone and they would see me, near enough if I called out, but not so close to make me feel hemmed in.

I wondered again what they had done with, or where they had put, Tobias, he must still be in the fortress somewhere, was there a guardhouse? Or just a locked room? Unbidden, images streamed through my head from the previous night and again, I pushed them back, I did not want this to change me, but I was afraid it already had. I felt hard, cold and emotionless, had he ruined everything for me? Would Maxentius even want to be near me after what Tobias had done? I had been violated, no man wants another's leftovers. Maybe that was it, maybe this was what finished it for us, we had tried so hard to keep it going against all the odds, but maybe this was just too much. I would understand if he was repulsed by me now. I knew I should feel very sad, but I just felt empty.

I realised that I did not want to deal with anyone, so returned to my room, or at least the room I was using. Allowing the drapes to fall across the windows darkening the room, I went back to bed and slept. Raizel came in with some food, she sat with me for a little while, but I found it hard to talk. She hugged me before taking her leave, but I could not return it. I remained in my room for several days, never opening those heavy curtains, only leaving it to go and redress my wounds. They healed quickly, the bruising started to fade and the swelling in my cheek went down. Still I shunned company, I didn't know what to do, or say, or how to behave. I wasn't sure I could face them; they would all know what had happened, gossip travels quickly in a small community and they had little enough to talk about as it was.

I missed Maxentius, but as he hadn't been to see me I assumed he had decided that I was damaged goods and better avoided. What I did not know was that he had come into my room every night while I slept, with the guard of course, to make sure my dreams were untroubled. That he had spent hours talking with Aharon, explaining what had started to grow between us, trying to persuade him that our relationship was serious and that he would do what ever it took to protect me. Suspicious of his motives and struggling to trust this man, an enemy, who through circumstance had become part of this stronghold, working within our little community to help provide what was needed, Aharon had eventually capitulated, but said that anything further would only happen after talking with me. That he constantly asked Raizel how I was and whether he could see me. She had said that it was better to let me come round of my own volition, that I would rejoin them when I felt ready. What she didn't know was that I didn't think I would ever feel ready.

Then one day, I'd had enough of moping about, I needed to get back to doing what I did best, which was treating the sick and injured, although I hoped there was none of the latter. I felt motivated, something I hadn't felt since that night and so I got up, washed and dressed, again something I hadn't bothered with for a while. My hair was ratty, so I rinsed it properly and rubbed some sweet oil through it. Although it felt strange being so short, it was light and bouncy and I didn't need to plait it, or twist it up into some elaborate bun. I found clean clothes, a dark blue tunic over pale blue shift, cinched at the waist with a blue and white belt. Slipping my feet into sandals I realised I actually felt quite normal for the first time in many days.

I ate my breakfast looking out of the big picture window, after which, I went to the clinic, no-one there yet, but I spent a little while tidying up the jars and flasks and restocking shelves. Satisfied that it was as prepared as it could be, I decided to go and enjoy the sun. Inevitably, my feet took me to the bench under the pomegranate tree. I sat down and ran my fingers over the carved wood - Maxentius had done me proud - it was perfect. I leaned my head back and closed my eyes, enjoying the peace. For the first time since that night, I started to feel relaxed.

After a while I heard footsteps coming towards me and glanced up, unable to prevent a flicker of fear threading through me, but it was Maxentius, he walked slowly as if unsure of his reception and smiled. That slow, toe curling, stomach flipping, spark igniting smile and I felt my heart thud in response. It was still there, I still loved him, but what were his feelings? He asked if he could sit beside me, I nodded and waited for him to speak.

"So my Hannah, how do you feel this morning? Raizel tells me your cuts and bruises are nearly healed and I can see that the swelling on your cheek has gone." He lifted his hand as if to touch my face but thought better of it and dropped it back onto his leg.

"I am...better...I did not feel that I should show my face after what had happened and my body ached from the bruises. Though I fear I will never be able to rid myself of the smell of arnica. Maybe that is what kept you away." Aiming at levity, I failed my voice was bleak. He looked at me in puzzlement,

"Why on this good earth do you think anything could keep me away, let alone the smell of bruise ointment?" His hand moved towards mine, which were clasped tightly together on my lap.

"Be careful Maxentius, someone might see." Still in that emotionless little voice.

"I think I am passed caring, if I had had more courage, you would not have had to suffer what you did that night." I looked at him then, my eyes cloudy with bewilderment.

"How could you have stopped it? If not that night maybe the next or the next, maybe today, maybe tomorrow, maybe next week, he seemed determined to take me."

"Yes, but if I had spoken to Aharon sooner, maybe I could have prevented it happening at all."

"Spoken to Aharon, what do you mean spoken to Aharon?" Maxentius seemed to choose his words carefully, as though anxious as to how I would interpret them.

"I had already had some private discussions with him over what they intended to use me for, if they were to keep me alive..." a tremor ran through me at the thought of him dead, "...and it seems I may be of use as a negotiator, should one be required, with the Roman governor, or, if they send one, an army commander. After all..." his head lifted a little, proud of his position, "...I am also a general of the Roman army. Thus, after this happened to you, I felt that if they trusted me to accomplish this for them, maybe I could be trusted to take care of you."

Shocked, several things ran through my head at the same time, yes I knew that there would be great need for a negotiator, but would have preferred that Maxentius was safely away from here by that point. But more than this, he had risked everything to talk to Aharon about me. My brother, or any of the elders could have chosen to kill Maxentius on the spot, no questions asked, for what he had asked, so what could this mean? Was there any chance for us? I hardly dared ask.

"What did Aharon say?" My voice was not much more than a murmur, everything I had ever hoped for was tied up in his answer but did I really want to hear it? The cold hard lump that had formed around my heart seemed to soften, but if this were not the answer I wanted, it would quickly freeze back over.

"He said he needed to discuss it with you, that although he agreed that I had a persuasive argument, it was up to you." I gazed at him for a long moment, reading his eyes, trying to make sense of his words.

"Are you telling me that my brother did not say no?" Astonished, my voice warming a little, I just sat there, not really knowing what to do or say.

"That is what I am telling you, do you think it is still something you might want?"

"I might want? I want this more than anything in the world, but I feared that you…" unable to say what I truly did fear I trailed off.

"That I what, Hannah? That I wouldn't want you? That I had stopped loving you?"

"Well I haven't…you didn't…I thought…" I struggled to find the words, still unsure of how he felt.

"Did you think I would abandon you? I, in company with your guard, checked every night to make sure you slept and I asked Raizel every day if she thought I would be able to see you. She felt that you were better left alone, as you had much to recover from."

"I would have healed more quickly if you had been close." Shyly, smiling at him from under my lashes, I felt the lump soften a little more.

"I was unsure you would be comfortable with any man being near you after what Tobias did, I could not risk causing you more pain." Again, carefully chosen words, but not what I wanted to hear.

"I presumed that you had decided I was sullied and that it was easier just to finish things, rather than keep fighting against all the odds for us to be together." I sounded very prim, but part of me,

262

ok all of me, wanted to hear that he loved me beyond reason and would never give up on me.

"Hannah! After everything I've said to you, after all we've been through, after what you told me about yourself, how could you, for one minute, think that?" He was appalled and I knew I needed to explain.

"Max..." using the diminutive, made me feel closer to him even if we couldn't touch, "...Max, when a woman is...abused, violated, she somehow feels to blame, even though she knows that she did nothing to cause the attack." Deep breath, "I come from a culture which does not usually give women the benefit of the doubt. If he had not been stopped, Tobias would have raped me." A reflexive movement from Maxentius made me falter, but placing my hand on his knee, I continued. "He was determined to break me, to tame me, he considered me to be his by right and if he had taken me, would almost certainly have had to marry me. He was going to make me his one way or another. I would have had no say. I am very lucky that my brother is more opened minded than most and even more grateful that you all found me when you did." Pausing. "How did you know by the way?"

"Know what?"

"That Tobias was..."

"Attacking you? Marcus was walking back to his room, when he heard you shouting, he ran down to Aharon and then came to find me. Eli and Daniel just happened to be with your brother."

"I had thought I'd seen the shadow of someone passing, but since no-one came, I assumed I'd imagined it. As much as I would have much rather it was you who saved me, I am glad Marcus went to get Aharon first, at least that way Tobias had no grounds for his accusations."

"Its a good job Aharon found you before I did, I'd have ripped his head off, then crapped down his neck." Which, not only sounded very amusing, was also - I learned a very, very long time later - a favourite army expletive.

"Marcus had to hold me back, I was so angry I could barely see." I smiled at him then and squeezed his hand and without thinking said,

"I love you Max, I will always love you." Embarrassed, I started to withdraw my hand, my face flaming - way to be forward Hannah. Maxentius was having none of it and caught my hand in his.

"I love you too, more than I can ever express in words, I hope that your brother will allow us to marry so I can show you just how much." The cold lump shattered, my heart warmed as my body responded to his words, tears trickling down my face. I couldn't stop them, the dam broke and I began to sob uncontrollably.

Maxentius let me cry, but when it seemed as though I was on the verge of hysteria he shook me, not ungently.

"Hannah, you need to stop now, you will make yourself ill again." Untucking the inevitable towel from my belt, he wiped my face. Then tenderly: "You need to take a deep breath and calm yourself."

"What I need is for you to kiss me." I whispered, hiccupping from the onslaught.

"Not long, come." Catching the last of my tears with the corner of his robe, he helped me up. "Let us go and talk to your brother, I understand once things are agreed, the formalities are short and can be done quickly."

"I should talk to him alone first, then maybe we can speak to him together, that might be easier for Aharon to handle."

Maxentius nodded his agreement and we walked over to the wing where my brother's rooms were. I was invited to enter and we spent a long time talking, first I had to persuade him that I was indeed getting better, and that my injuries were healing. I convinced him that I was ready to resume my duties and thanked him for being so patient. Then I broached the subject of Maxentius and explained that I knew they had been in discussion about many things, including me.

"I know it is hard for you to accept and to believe my brother, but this man is my world, he means more to me than anything and I know he feels the same about me. He would never hurt me or treat me badly and he would give his life protecting me. I know he is a Roman and technically your sworn enemy, but we have been living on this outpost for years now and never once has he, or Marcus for that matter, done the wrong thing or tried to escape. If you think anything of me, believe what I am saying, you can trust them and you can trust that Maxentius will be a very suitable husband. You should be more worried about me being a suitable wife." I added this last bit with a rueful grin, hoping to make Aharon, who had remained very stern throughout my speech, smile just a little.

"So you truly believe that this man would be a satisfactory husband?"

"I do and you know I am not your typical Hebrew maiden. I am hoydenish, stubborn, headstrong and recalcitrant, pity the poor man who wants to take me on, for it will not be an easy life.

"Yet you are also, caring, understanding, kind and have infinite patience with anyone who needs your help. These are admirable qualities my sister, your Roman is a lucky man." I blushed at his words.

"Aharon, I did not realise you saw me this way, I imagined you still think I'm just your bratty annoying sister."

"Oh you are most definitely still that, just a little more gown up." He smiled one of his rare smiles and I hugged him.

"Thank you my brother, you will not regret this decision."

We called Maxentius in and the three of us and then later, when Raizel joined us, four of us discussed the marriage. Since we were in strange times the traditional rituals would not be tenable, things were managed differently. So it went something like this, I told Aharon that I had chosen Maxentius as my husband. Then Aharon spoke with Maxentius, explaining that, traditionally he needed to pay the bride price, or dowry, however, as these were unusual circumstances, he just needed to be sure that Maxentius could support me? He said he could. So far so good!

There were other customs as well, such as consummating the marriage in the father's home, so that proof of virginity could be established, or in our case, here in Aharon's rooms, but I decided that there was no way that was going to happen. Maxentius declared that he promised to love, support and protect me, I agreed to be as dutiful a wife as I could possibly be, given all that I'd said to Aharon and, that I would love him and always have his back, which made him laugh. Nice and personal I thought.

I did discover at this point that Maxentius' full name was Lucius Maxentius Valerius, which did have quite a flourish. My name, Hannah bat Avigail, seemed much less interesting, so I thought I might take his. In the end it was all signed, sealed and delivered very quickly and without much fuss. Suddenly we were married.

Chapter Twenty Six

Unexpectedly, I felt shy, this man whom I had loved for so long was now my husband, in my culture, he owned me, but I wasn't sure about the status of wives in his. We thanked Aharon and Raizel and taking my hand Maxentius led me out.

"That was…errr…quick." I said, "I didn't think it would happen like that. I imagined it would take longer, that they would give you time to consider your decision. I am sorry."

"I am not, there was never any decision to make. Now I can show how much I love you without worrying that I am behaving in a manner unacceptable to your people. Now, I can shout it from the top of the watchtowers if I so choose. I am also very much looking forward to demonstrating to you, how happy I am that we are married." He grinned as we walked slowly over to the palace.

I suddenly realised I would have to go to my old room, my stomach knotted.

"Ummm…would you mind?" Motioning in its general direction. "There are things I must get and I need you to come with me, I cannot bear to go in on my own."

"It is nothing, come, we will collect everything now and you need not go back in at all." We walked into the room of my nightmares; it took nearly everything I had to step across the threshold. The room was still in disarray, left exactly as it had been so many nights ago, it chilled me and my skin crawled. Maxentius put his arm around me and held me close for a moment, then I pulled myself together and began rifling quickly through my clothes, in the end just grabbing a whole pile to take over to his rooms, which would now be ours. That had such a lovely sound, 'ours.'

I remembered my pin, the one that had been snapped in the struggle, dropping the pile on the bed I tried to find it, scrabbling about in the corner where I thought it had landed. The memory flitted through my mind again, but I couldn't hold onto it.

"What have you lost Hannah?"

"My pin, the one that held my mantle, it was pulled off the night…that night and I wanted to find it, it is my only pin." We both looked, but could not locate it, eventually giving up. I was saddened that it seemed lost, but there was nothing I could do, I might try again another day, knowing, even as I thought it, that this was unlikely. Between us, we gathered my heap of clothes and the few other things I would need and walked over to Maxentius' rooms. I tidied my things up, and made it look as though I hadn't just got out of bed.

The room itself was huge, not only a sleeping area, but there was a small living space which held a marble table with two ornate chairs, a divan, several oil lamps and some marble statues. It was one of the most beautiful rooms I had ever seen, something I had only barely registered before now, despite spending nearly two weeks in here. Unable to deal with the light, I had left the drapes closed for most of the time and they had kept the room cool and dim.

Eventually however, I could do no more tidying, Maxentius was sitting in one of the fine chairs watching me, a rather amused expression on his face.

"What is it my Hannah?" My hands fluttered.

"I'm nervous, I've wanted this for so long, but now I'm nervous. I don't know what to do."

"That is not a problem, I do." He got up and walked over to me and in gesture I found hauntingly familiar, but couldn't place, he curved one hand round the back of my neck, tilting my head so he could look down at me and breathing my name, bent to kiss me.

Gently, tenderly his lips sought mine, teasing, tasting, I felt the spark ignite and the flame begin to burn.

How long we stood there just kissing I do not know, strangely, even though I could tell that Maxentius wanted me, he went no further. Puzzled I pulled away searching his face and echoing his words of earlier I asked.

"What is it Maxentius?" He looked down at me, his eyes concerned.

"I do not want to hurt you, or frighten you."

Frighten me? How could you possibly fright…" then I realised what he meant, he feared that any more than this, very delightful, kissing, might make me recall what Tobias had done. "…oh my love, you could never frighten me." Leaning up I kissed him again, letting my hands roam over his body, he sighed and kissed me back, less tenderly now, our passion rising, heartbeats quickening, fingers - stroking, feeling, learning. I moaned under his kiss causing him to shudder and kiss me even harder, his hands rough from working outdoors ran over my body, touching every part of me, our clothes were getting in the way, yet he still seemed strangely reluctant.

Pulling away from him I stood and very deliberately removed all of my clothing. His eyes darkened when he saw my injuries and nearly healed bruises, but I did not give him the chance to say anything, merely walked back into his arms and kissed him again. His hands roved over my skin, he cupped my breast, running his fingers around the dark aureole at the peak, following up with his tongue, I could feel heat coursing through me and pushed against his body, desperate to feel him. I fumbled with his clothes but in my flustered state, I couldn't work them out.

"Max, please get out of these clothes, please, I need to feel your body, all of it."

"Hmmm…begging me now are we? Rather like that in a wife." I bit him on the earlobe, "Ok, ok." He slipped out of his garments and I gaped, I had seen some of him when I was caring for his wounds, but this was all of him, all at once. "Not quite the reaction I was expecting." He muttered, trying to pull me to him.

"No wait, I want to look at you, this is now all mine, I want to see what my bride price got me." Grinning up at him as we stood facing each other. "No…" as he reached for me again, "…not yet." Standing on tiptoe, I ran my fingers up his arms, along his shoulders, describing gentle loops through the hollows at the base of his neck and down the middle of his chest. A smattering of dark hair nestled there and I twisted my fingers through it, and outwards to brush his nipples, he groaned and I could see just how much he wanted me.

"Nearly…" I whispered, sliding my finger down his flat stomach, tracing the scars from his wounds and finally down to caress him, teasing, feeling the throb of his muscles as he tried to contain his desire.

"Oh, by all the gods, Hannah, what are you doing to me?"

"Hmmm…me? Just checking out the goods, they seem eminently suitable, I may just keep them." And twirling my fingers back up his body, I kissed his chest, which was about my eye level and drew little circles with my tongue. Swearing, he swung me up and onto the bed.

"No more my girl, now it's my turn." He proceeded to discover every single part of my body, every nook, every hidden place, his fingers and his mouth were relentless until I was crying out for him to take me, I needed to feel him inside of me, I wanted to consume him, the whole of my body was on fire.

"Max please…"

"Hmm…are you begging me my love?"

"I am be…e…gging you…" my voice stuttering with the intensity of my emotions, "…ahhhh…ahhh." I arched my back trying to get closer, lifting myself to his tongue, which was flicking up my leg towards my inner thigh, this wasn't enough it would never be enough. I was almost sobbing now, so desperate was I, still he held back, his tongue continued its magical adventure, his hands stroking over my breasts and my stomach and tremors rippled through me.

Just as I thought, seriously, that I might pass out from desire, he moved to lay on top of me, kissing me deeply, he ran his hands down my body and sliding between my legs, entered me. There was a split second of discomfort, immediately forgotten as he took me to heights I never imagined possible. The pleasure that exploded through me again and again was indescribable. I wrapped my legs across his back, pulling him in deeper, waves of ecstasy crashing over me. A slow crescendo began surging, he let it build slowly, deliciously, though how he was able to make it stretch out I have no clue, until finally we reached a peak and I erupted, I swear my veins were molten lava.

Breathless I clung to him, my Roman, my husband, my love. Running my hands through his hair, I pulled it out of the leather strip that held it so neatly, letting it fall free around his neck, bringing his face close to mine so I could kiss him with everything that was in me. Slowly our breathing settled, I could have stayed like this forever, him lying on top of me his arms wrapped around me, our bodies, slick with sweat, touching.

"My Hannah, my Hannah, I am so glad you are mine." He lifted his head to look down on me; I smiled up at him, my eyes sparkling.

"Oh, sir, I think it is the other way around, you are in fact, mine." I winked at him, bringing my hand up to caress his face, he kissed my palm and I felt an immediate spark in the pit of my stomach. I felt him move within me and gasped as new sensations raced along my body, he rolled over placing me on top this time. I raised myself so I was almost sitting, hooking my legs under his and holding his hands with mine I began to move rhythmically over him. His eyes widened as he realised what I was doing and lifted his hips to match my movement, it was slower more leisurely this way but no less intense. Releasing Max's hands I leaned forward and used my tongue to great effect over his skin, my hands stroking along his sides, gently teasing the swell of his buttocks before dragging my nails slowly up his back, making him groan and, cupping my head he brought my face down to his mouth.

Kisses deepening our slow rhythm increased, becoming more frenzied and I could feel the climax approaching. As I arched my back and Max raised his hips higher he sent me beyond the millions of stars sparkling above us, my body felt as though it was shattering into tiny pieces, before eventually floating back to earth on a euphoric cloud, to be made whole again in the arms of this man. Breathing ragged and hearts drumming in time, we held each other close waiting for the earth to slow down around us. I never in my wildest dream thought I would know such joy; neither did I ever want this moment to end.

"Promise me you will never stop doing this." I whispered against his chest, my fingers renewing their circular design over his warm skin.

"Hmmm…well, I'm not sure." Lazily. "I got the distinct impression you were pretty indifferent to the whole thing." Indignantly I sat up ready to give him what for, until I noticed the expression on his face.

"You bloody bugger." Ignoring the fact that this term may not even be in use yet, I tried to pummel him with my fists, which proved completely ineffectual as he just held them tight, then

272

pulled me down on top of him, wrapped his arms right around me, crushing me to him. Spluttering, I tried to wriggle free, feeling a rumble of laugher shake his chest. Loosening his hold, he rolled me onto my side facing him, scooped my legs around him and, taking his time, gently and tenderly made love to me all over again. It was utterly blissful.

We dozed, but on waking we simply continued where we'd left off. At some point Maxentius went to get some food bringing back all sorts of delicious nibbles, along with a flagon of wine. It felt very decadent, eating in bed, sitting wrapped in a blanket, amongst ridiculously luxurious coverlets and sheets, eating bread dipped in oil and vinegar, some cold roasted vegetables, grapes and figs. He had also found a pomegranate, the trees on the plateau were laden at the moment, and they were delicious. We shared it, devouring the sweet pulp, the red juice dribbling down our chins. Trying to keep if off the bedding was a nightmare, although Maxentius found a novel way of stopping it…no, that's my secret…suffice it to say it worked.

Then, we snuggled back under the covers, I lay with my back to Maxentius' chest and he curled up around me, wrapping me in his embrace. I felt cocooned and safe here, nuzzling my head under his chin. I relaxed settling against his body as if I had been lying this way forever. Still dozing occasionally, we mostly just talked until the dawn broke the night's grasp.

Chapter Twenty Seven

Much as it would have been lovely to spend long hours in our quarters, we both had chores and jobs to do, so the next morning, granted maybe a little later than usual, we washed, dressed and, trying to behave as nonchalantly as possible, got on with our day. I had a queue of families waiting at the clinic, mainly children who had over indulged, but a few had minor scratches and cuts that needed a little more attention. One of two of the men had slightly more serious injuries from not taking enough care with their tools, but I got through everything fairly quickly.

Maxentius was still working on some furniture, so I didn't disturb him. Later in the morning, I went over to find Marcus, who was surrounded by children wanting to help him planting vegetables. He had so much patience it astounded me, I would have gone bonkers with all that jumping and chattering going on around me. He smiled at me over their heads and shouted that he'd be with me in a minute. I watched as he set the little ones various chores and then, after making sure they understood what he wanted, left them to it. He sauntered over to where I was resting on the ubiquitous upturned pot and grinned.

"So Hannah, what news do you want to share with me?" Blushing, I stammered a bit, took a breath and tried again.

"Well, its like this, yesterday, I, we, he, Aharon, errrmm…we…" oh goodness this was going to be harder than I thought, I could not get my words in order, another deep breath. "…right, so yesterday after some long discussions, Maxentius and I were married. I'm so sorry we did not let you know beforehand, but it happened very quickly and was kind of over before we realised." I spoke so quickly, I was amazed he understood half of what I was gabbling about, but he didn't even seem surprised.

"Well it's about time, wondered how long you two could go on the way things were especially after what happened to you. Maxentius was incandescent with rage; he would have killed Tobias if he'd had the chance. I knew it was only a matter of time before he decided to risk talking to your brother."

"Thank you my friend, it would have been nice for you to be there with him, but it sort of just happened. I rather think Aharon was pleased to hand me over to someone else's keeping. I think I am a bother to him."

"No, I don't think that is the case, he obviously cares deeply for you, when he saw what Tobias was doing to you, he was more angry than Maxentius and I would have thought possible. None of us would ever want you be hurt Hannah, the other men have been devastated by what happened, they would never disrespect you so."

"That is one of the nicest things anyone has ever said to me, you are a true gentleman Marcus and don't ever let anyone tell you otherwise." He bowed and chuckled.

"Why thank you kind lady."

"Will you join us for dinner this evening? It would be so nice for us to enjoy a meal together and just talk and, now I am able to do so, with the two of you without raising eyebrows or suspicions."

"It would be my absolute pleasure." Smiling he took my hand and pressed it gently, "I am happy for you Hannah. Now if you could just find me a good woman…" leaving his sentence dangling and, dropping me a cheeky wink, he went back to his crowd of youngsters, crouching down to help them with their very important jobs. I smiled at the scene; he was like the pied piper. That thought pulled at a memory, who was the pied piper and why was I thinking of him? I mulled it around my head for a while, but couldn't work it out, another time maybe.

Later that day, when Maxentius had finished his furniture building and I had completed everything I had been avoiding for the last week or so, we met and took a walk round the fortress. I asked to go though the Western Palace, it had become my favourite place to wander and I liked that the others rarely ventured in further than the first few rooms, which were used for administrative purposes. It was so huge and opulent and I think it unnerved most of them.

We walked through rooms, along hallways and into courtyards, it was so peaceful. The throne room was magnificent, I felt like a princess just walking into it and despite the fact that it was decades since Herod had died, the beautiful soft furnishings remained and were for the most part undamaged. I loved running my hands over the drapes and cushions and taking off my sandals to walk barefoot over the exquisite mosaics, tracing their patterns with my toes. Much of the wooden furniture had been commandeered now by Maxentius and those helping him, to build more practical household equipment, but they had left some, deemed too delicate or small to be of any use.

At the back of the main palace was a set of storerooms, which held costly items including such luxuries as cosmetic oils and flasks of perfume. Since there were not many women on the plateau and those who were here were not usually interested in this type of frivolity, I occasionally 'acquisitioned' one or more jars, it made me feel special to be able to rub sweet oil through my hair, or soften my skin with aromatic ointments. We were on our way across to the particular storeroom where these things had been accrued, when I noticed a large room off to our left that I didn't think we'd been in. Dragging Maxentius towards it, I asked him whether he'd been along this wing of the palace.

276

"I must have been, we have been all over the fortress, we needed to know every inch in case there were places, or areas, should we ever get ambushed, that our attackers could hide. If only we had known." He grinned at the irony of his words. "I think this is one of the administration offices." We walked into the room, it was beautifully appointed, with several pieces of furniture scattered around. A marble bench stood against one wall, on the top of which stood several oil lamps. Opposite this, was what I could only describe as a book case, or shelving unit and, between them had been placed a desk, with two chairs, one in front and one behind.

There were lots of pots leaning up against the walls in a haphazard fashion and several scrolls lay on the shelves, but they were so dry, I did not dare unroll them. A thick rug on the floor was covering a mosaic and suddenly I really wanted to see it, the pattern running round the edge seemed familiar, but I didn't know why. Bending, I started to roll the rug off and, seeing what I was trying to do, Maxentius helped me.

"Why do you want to see this Hannah?"

"I don't know, its just that…" my voice died away as we rolled the rug rolled away from the last section and stared at the design, it had swirls of vine leaves surrounding colourful blossoms and at the centre, a tree laden with fruit. "Oh, its a pomegranate tree." I whispered. "I've heard about this before."

A conversation with someone I used to know, someone who was important to me, telling me about a mosaic with some sort of tree in its centre. Head whirling, I sat down in one of the chairs. Maxentius came and knelt beside me and holding my hand asked what I meant. I gazed at him, confusion clouding my eyes. "I'm not sure, but I think someone told me about this, when they were excavating it."

"What, you mean this is known by the other Hannah, the other you?" I loved that he didn't even seem phased by this statement, which, if anyone else had heard would sound ludicrous. I nodded and dredged through my memory for the conversation, finding it and telling Maxentius about the discovery and the excitement of the archaeologists.

"So you're telling me, that this floor is cause for great excitement in about two thousand years?" I nodded again.

"Well then, maybe we should make sure it remains protected for as long as possible." So, very carefully, we rolled the rug back over the beautiful mosaic and moved the desk to stand over it, effectively hiding it and quietly left the room. I hoped it would be enough.

That evening, the three of us enjoyed a lovely meal, relaxing around the low table in our rooms. I had noticed that there was a wide curtain, which if unhooked, would fall right across the sleeping space separating the two areas of the room, giving both a sense of privacy. I found that I needed to delineate our private and public living areas. Unlike some on this outpost who appeared quite complacent living cheek by jowl, I would never be comfortable sharing our sleeping space. It was nice to have such a separation, made it feel homely.

We chattered about many things, our lives, how they had changed, especially for my two Romans, they were virtually honorary Hebrews now; they even dressed like our men did. I knew many would find it hard to accept that Maxentius and I had married, but it had been approved by the powers that be and that was all I cared about. At the end of the evening, Marcus returned to his rooms and we sat awhile enjoying each other's company. Suddenly, I remembered there was something I had forgotten to ask Maxentius the day before.

"Oh, I knew I should have asked this before we…you know…but I wondered, that is I thought you may, err…well…I hope you don't have a lady waiting for you back home, or maybe you are already married?" Maxentius guffawed at my question.

"Do you think that if I had a wife, even if she was many, many miles away, that I would marry someone else?"

"I don't know," plaintively, "I just knew I should have checked and I didn't and then I thought maybe I shouldn't, but I had to."

"No, Hannah bat Avigail Valerius, I have no other wife, no lady waiting for me, just you. Until I met you I thought to remain unmarried, for I could not imagine caring enough about another person to want them to share my life." And picking me up out of my chair, he carried me through the curtain and illustrated exactly how much he cared. I was getting to like this.

As before, our days fell into a pattern, Maxentius would work on anything that was needed for the growing community of refugees and I would care for anyone who was unwell or who had hurt themselves. The days were long and busy, but they were fulfilling and we went to bed tired but happy. We were a partnership, Maxentius did not try to own, or tame me, we shared everything and treated each other as equals. I never saw Tobias again and I did not ask what had happened. I did not want to know, I was just happy that he was out of my life. We got occasional news from Jerusalem and it did not bode well for the Jews, the Romans were intent on taking the city and I knew eventually, they would have their prize.

Time passed, the seasons changed, some winters were harsh and cold with torrential downpours, but the water from the storms filled our cisterns. Some of the summers were scorchers, but for the most part the weather was pleasant, warm to tolerably hot days with cool clear nights, until one day I realised that I had been here for nearly four years. Even though I had accepted that my life was now here, I still worried about what I knew was going to happen. If I had been here all that time, Jerusalem was about to fall and the survivors from the conflict would end up here at Masada.

I explained this to Maxentius one afternoon while we were sitting under our favourite tree and told him that soon he would probably be called on to negotiate with the Romans who were going to lay siege to this rock.

"You need to find a way to escape before the end my love, I cannot bear to think what might happen if you are here when this fortress falls.

"I refuse to leave you Hannah, you know that without you I have no reason to live." It was the same argument, every time we discussed the scenario; we came round to the same problem. How to get away, or how to keep each other safe and we never got anywhere.

Now we had a new problem, one we could very well have done without. I had noticed that I had not needed to use to mikvah for a little while and my belly was beginning to swell. In my very limited experience, I gauged that I must be about three to four months pregnant.

"There's something else." I looked him straight in the eye. "Its really bad timing, knowing what I know, but what can you do."

"What Hannah, what is it?"

"We're going to have a baby." I whispered the words, unsure whether he would want to be a father; we had never talked about having children.

"We're what?"

"You heard me, I wasn't sure, but…" I never finished my sentence, for I was suddenly swung up into his arms and kissed very thoroughly, my heart flipping over and a warm glow suffusing my being. He ran his hand over my stomach feeling the changes there.

"Oh my Hannah, I'm going to be a father? Best news I've had since you told me you loved me."

"That was just this morning, silly." Grinning down at him, running my fingers through his hair and kissing him back, I was relieved.

"Just the same...are you alright? Should I be holding you like this? Maybe you should be lying down. How did I not notice this change in you" Laughing I put my finger on his lips.

"You were too busy doing other things." Dropping a lascivious wink. "I'm fine, I'm just pregnant and hundreds of women give birth every day, its quite natural." What I didn't tell him was that many women died in childbirth, so my chances weren't brilliant, but I was healthy and my husband would be with me to make sure I didn't overdo things.

Maxentius was ecstatic, he was the one who told those closest to us, and everyone seemed pleased, especially Marcus, who claimed the title of honorary uncle. Life continued; my pregnancy developed, as normally as I could hope and, as we were so busy with everyday chores, it seemed to pass very quickly. In my spare time, I spent hours making baby clothes out of old tunics, the soft material perfect for delicate infant skin, while Maxentius made a wooden cradle with little rockers underneath, it was quite beautiful. All the while, he was very attentive and I, of course, enjoyed his vigilance.

During this time, we heard that Jerusalem had fallen to the Romans. Emperor Vespasian's son had led the assault and they had sacked the temple, with countless deaths. The rebels here at Masada were devastated at this catastrophe, but they were impotent in the face of such power. The numbers of Roman soldiers far outweighed those of the Jewish fighters. Eventually the survivors made their way across the desert to join us, led by a fearsome Zealot called Eleazar ben Yair, a nephew of, the now dead, Menahem and a very distant relative of Raizel. He was a charismatic man and held many of the Zealots in his thrall. I hated him with a vengeance, he had taken our safe, quiet existence and thrown it into turmoil, it was he who would bring the wrath of the Roman Empire down on us.

His talk of reprisal attacks were just that, talk. If he went anywhere near Jerusalem he would be assassinated, but many held onto the hope that they could win and so believed his rhetoric. As far as possible I steered clear of him, as did both Maxentius and Marcus, they did not need to come to his attention. I told them both that the Romans would not want there to be any pockets of resistance and that they would eventually find us, Marcus did not seem surprised that I knew a little of politics and they both entered into discussions with Aharon and those few elders who were not under Eleazar's spell to try and come up with a strategy.

Soon, I came to term and, early one evening I knew I had reached my time. I admit to being absolutely terrified, but incredibly, my labour did not seem to last for too long. Raizel and a couple of the other women assisted me. Around dawn, less than eight hours after my first contraction, I gave birth to a baby girl. Nothing in my life could have prepared me for the feelings that washed over me when I looked into my daughter's face. To me she was the most beautiful thing I had ever seen and I knew right there that I would kill to protect this tiny bundle of joy.

Maxentius was over the moon; I don't think he came off cloud nine for a good week. Our friends and my family were very happy for us and they along with Marcus were constant visitors. Aharon's children, Efraim and Liora were very excited about having a cousin to play with and couldn't understand why they couldn't take her off with them immediately. Flouting Roman naming traditions, we named her Claudia after Maxentius' mother and the day after her birth, while I was nursing, my husband gave me a most precious gift.

Pressing it into my palm he said softly.

"This was given to me by my mother who had it made for my entrance into the army. It was blessed by one of the three major *flamines* - an important priest in my world - and has held my cloak securely for many years. Now I want you to have it, it will replace the pin you lost and be something you can pass onto our daughter when she is old enough to know our story."

It was the clasp I'd seen on his cloak, the morning we'd farewelled Sergius. It was quite remarkable, a rich red stone, dark at the centre, paler at the edges and its shape was not quite oval, not quite teardrop, somewhere in between. It nestled in an intricate surround, a gold coloured metal, which had been swirled and twisted round the stone. Such a tactile clasp, I kept rolling it around in my fingers, tracing the delicate, yet surprisingly strong design and, when I looked at the stone, it seemed to glow.

Unbidden, a phrase popped into my head, something about a gift from a grateful soldier. Puzzled, I searched my memory trying to place it, but was unable to. I stored it away with all those other things, whose meanings, I struggled to remember.

"Max, this is too much, it is gorgeous, how could you part with it?"

"It is something I have wanted to give you for many moons, but I did not want to remind you how you lost your other pin. This very auspicious occasion called for something extraordinary and I want you to have it." Reaching my hand to his face I stroked his cheek. Smiling up at him.

"My love, how did we get so lucky?" He turned his head to kiss my palm, then bent closer to brush my lips and, sat with me while I fed our child. He did not seem in the slightest bit embarrassed by me breast-feeding and I rather liked his presence. I was utterly content, I knew that we still had a little time before all hell would break loose and I intended to make the most of it.

We spent many hours together, the three of us, I still worked at the clinic and often if I was very busy and to save Claudia from being exposed to infections, Maxentius took care of her. It worked well and although I imagine it was not what many men would have wanted to do, Maxentius thrived on it. What news we got was sketchy, brought by people who had fled the city to find refuge at this outpost, but rumblings of reprisals were growing and I knew it would not be too many more months before we would see the dust kicked up by the feet of thousands of soldiers intent on our destruction.

Millennia away a weary looking man, placed a strange looking red clasp into the hand of the woman asleep in the white bed.

"Maybe this will help Hannah, if I can't reach you, maybe this will bring you back." As he folded her fingers over the brooch, she murmured and brought her arm up onto her chest. Her eyelids fluttered for an instant, but nothing more. Hope flared in the young man's eyes. There was still a chance.

Chapter Twenty Eight

It did not seem as though we had very long left at all, although it was not quite a year later before we heard the distant rumble of thousands of marching feet. Claudia was crawling and trying to talk, she was a funny little scrap, always laughing and had everyone in our small circle wrapped round her chubby little fingers. Raizel's mother, Aliza, had managed to find safe passage through the desert a few months previously and had taken on the role of grandmother. She rarely had a moment's peace with not only our daughter, but also Aharon's two children and many of the others living on the plateau constantly dragging her in to their games and high jinks. Although, to be fair Claudia just went along for the ride, being a little too young to be the cause of any mischief.

Eleazar was still whipping up the rage of the men stranded here, and they often disappeared for days on raids, giving me plenty to do when they came back battered and bruised. Did they not realise that going up against the might of the Roman Empire was never going to end well? I kept warning those closest to me what would happen, I refused to leave without Maxentius, Marcus and my brother with his family. They refused to abandon the others to their fate. Moreover, we had been here for several years now, it had become our home and many thought that the Romans would not bother with a few rebels so far out in the desert. We were deadlocked and I knew we would all be here until the bitter end.

One morning, after I had finished at the clinic, I had decided to take a walk over to the huge balcony in the upper tier of the Northern Palace. It was a beautiful day, the sky was clear and the most incredible cerulean blue, the air was still cool and you could see right out across the desert. In the far distance the Dead Sea sparkled, I breathed a sigh of utter contentment. Maxentius had seen me walk over and followed me; Claudia was napping, watched over by Aliza, so it was just the two of us, bliss! He came up behind me, wrapping his arms around me and resting his chin on my head. I leaned into him, feeling the spark ignite at his touch, as it always did and turning to face him, we enjoyed a long, deep and tender kiss.

Breathlessly, I pulled away, looking up into his eyes, inviting him, he responded and we swayed together, letting our hands work their magic, our passion rising, we simply let our emotions lead us. Some time later, our clothes flung haphazardly over the floor, we lay naked in each other's arms. I gazed at this man, whom I loved beyond reason, trying to imprint his features onto my brain, I had now known him for around six years and we had been through so much, I was so afraid that soon we would lose each other. He smiled his slow, toe curling smile and hugged my tightly.

"Please don't ever let me go." I whispered.

"Never my Hannah. Trust me." He kissed me and, made sweet tender love to me all over again. I clung to him as though I was drowning, willing this to go on forever.

As we dressed and made to go back to our work, I glanced out across the desert and blinked, rubbed my eyes and looked again. What was that in the distance?

"Maxentius, I think there is a dust storm coming, look." Pointing out towards the horizon, he followed my finger and squinted in the sunlight. We watched it for long moments before Maxentius spun on his heel and grabbing my arm to bring me with him, said urgently.

"We need to see Aharon, now." I ran with him across to the offices where many of the Zealots spent their days. Aharon was talking to a few of the others when we burst in without knocking

"Aharon, gather your men, we need to talk now." Aharon had looked up at our rather unceremonious entrance, the reprimand on his lips dying as he saw Maxentius' expression.

"Go Daniel, call the others, I will report to Eleazar when I have heard what Maxentius has to say." Daniel dashed off; Simeon, Ari and Benyamin remained while we waited for Daniel to come back with the few men Aharon felt he could trust.

"Now, what is it Maxentius?" Aharon asked, as they all pushed into the room.

"The Romans are on their way, they are marching towards us, they can be seen in the far distance. I think they will be here before nightfall the day after tomorrow." I looked at him horror struck, no, no, not yet, please not yet.

"How can you be sure?"

"Hannah thought there was a dust storm approaching, but as I watched I realised the dust was rising, not rolling, it is being kicked up by the feet of thousands, not whipped up by a desert wind. Believe me, I recognise the signs."

Aharon listened while Maxentius went on to explain what would happen. The soldiers, along with auxiliary units and probably slaves would set up camp around the base of the rock and most likely lay siege. Negotiations were possible, but until he knew who their commander was he was not sure what the outcome would be. I bent my head, I did know what the outcome would be, but my voice had to remain silent. They would not believe me even if I told them.

"What can we do?"

"I would suggest you make sure that the fortifications can hold and that where you think they may breach the walls that there is another wall built up behind. Rocks, mud and wood can make a very strong barrier if constructed correctly."

They talked a while longer, I slipped out of the door leaving them to their discussions there was nothing I could do to help. I worried now about him and Marcus, they would be seen as traitors, aiding and abetting the enemy. I started to think about ways they could escape. Walking over to the vegetable patch where Marcus was working, teaching yet another group of youngsters about farming techniques, I asked if I could have a moment of his time. He came over, and I walked him out of earshot of the children.

"They are coming Marcus, Maxentius says they will be here in two days." He knew exactly what I meant.

"How can he be sure?"

"We saw the dust from their feet in the far distance this morning, he is telling Aharon and the others now." Marcus looked stunned,

"I never thought they would bother us here."

"Neither did I, I fear what will come Marcus, you and Maxentius must get away."

"He will not leave you."

"Then somehow you must make him. It is better that you are handed over as captives than found here and treated as traitors." He knew my reasoning was sound, but he also knew what Maxentius' reaction would be.

"I will do what I can, I make no promises." I squeezed his hand,

"Thank you Marcus, that is all I ask."

I smiled and left him to his class, hurrying back over to our quarters to check on Claudia. She was waking and when she saw me come into the room, her face lit up stretching her arms up for me to lift her out of bed. Aliza said that she had slept well, I thanked her for taking care of her and she nodded and left us to it. After feeding Claudia, we played for a little while and then I carried her out onto the plateau.

"Look at this my precious girl, this was your home, I want you to remember it this way, for soon it will be gone." Claudia merely gurgled and pulled my hair, uncaring of my words, just wanting to get down and try to walk on her chubby little legs. I placed her carefully on the ground, making sure she was steady before I let go. She held onto my hand and we walked at her pace to the Western Gate. I stood for a long time gazing at the column of dust moving inexorably closer. Oh god, if this is to be my end, let it be quick.

Glancing down at my daughter I felt a spark of anger stir, no one was going to hurt this little girl, not if I could help it. I already knew I would die for her, but I did not want her to be saved, only to live as a slave. I had to make sure we got through this, but how? I waited for Maxentius to finish his meeting, which had gone on for a long time and joined him when he came back out into the sunshine. He explained what they had decided. They would fortify the wall where needed, prepare for a long siege and hope that whoever was in charge would be open to negotiations, at least they maybe able to save the women and children.

"But won't they simply enslave them? They will not be allowed to go free?"

"It is likely, but at least they will be alive."

"I'm not sure life as a slave is preferable." I sighed. "Oh Max, this is such a mess." He lifted Claudia nestling her on his arm and putting the other one round me, held us close.

They did arrive within two days, the noise was deafening, sounds of metal clanging, raucous voices shouting and the constant hammering. In what seemed like the blink of an eye, but was actually over several weeks, eight camps appeared around the base of Masada, accommodating, Maxentius reckoned, at least ten to fifteen thousand people. Then they built a wall right round the base of the rock. How could we ever hope to face them down? There were less than a thousand of us including women and children and, even if we managed to flee the citadel, the wall would prevent us getting any further, especially as guards were placed at regular intervals.

Their commander was the Roman Governor, Flavius Silva, Maxentius knew him a little, they had met on a previous campaign and he knew him to be a determined soldier, one who would not back down. Believing he had some hope of saving the women and children, he somehow managed to set up negotiations with Silva, who probably assumed they were to discuss terms of surrender, but it was a start. Maxentius explained that he had been captive along with a comrade since the garrison had fallen and convinced Silva that he had obtained inside knowledge of the Zealots' plans. While these negotiations were continuing, Silva instructed that a ramp should be built up the incline alongside the Northern Palace, it was a massive undertaking and the Romans forced thousands of Jewish prisoners do the work.

Meanwhile inside the fortress, the rebels built another barrier inside the casemate wall, to fortify it. It was a sensible move, for several months later, at the completion of the ramp, the Romans moved a great battering ram into place against the outer wall, but although they managed to break some parts of it, the newly constructed inner wall held. They also erected siege towers from which they could shower all manner of stones and arrows at us. It was terrifying, nobody could walk across the plateau for fear of being taken down by a missile, we spent our days like moles, hidden from view within the buildings and if it proved necessary to go outside, we had to hug the casemate wall, which at least offered some protection.

The tension inside the fortress was extreme; the men were caught between a rock and a hard place. They wanted to kill the Romans, but knew they were outnumbered. At the same time those who had them, wanted to try and save their families, aware that this meant surrender, which they could not countenance. All the while Eleazar kept ranting on about what would happen if the Romans got their hands on us. It was a nightmare of horrific proportions, even more so for Maxentius and myself, for I knew exactly how this was going to end. And still the ceaseless noise, it was a never ending cacophony, all day and all night, which in itself was enough to drive anyone to surrender.

Inevitably, it became obvious that negotiations were going to fail. One evening, I gathered Maxentius and Marcus together and quite seriously informed them that they needed to leave.

"The next time you meet with Silva, you must go down the ramp with him, I don't care how you do it, but you must leave. I know how this will end, we are all supposed to die and if you stay they will find a way to kill you too. However, I think I have a way by which I can avoid what is to befall this citadel. Eleazar is going to persuade everyone to die by their own hand."

Maxentius started to interrupt.

"No my love, I have absolutely no intention of letting this man take my life or our daughter's, but I cannot let him or anyone else know this. I have a plan, I think it will work, but I refuse to tell anyone, not even you Max, you will try to stop me. Believe me when I tell you that I can and I will survive this, but you must be among the first to come back up with the Romans when they breach the defences. They will send fire over the wall; it will burn the newly constructed inner defence and weaken the whole structure. They will retire for the night, then resolve to mount a final onslaught early the next morning."

Marcus was looking at me aghast, how did I know all this and how did I imagine I was going to escape.

"Do not question how I know this Marcus, my friend, just accept that it is true. Maxentius, I will make sure that I am wearing my clasp, the one you gave me. If necessary, tell them I am your slave, that may at least keep me alive long enough for you to find me." Maxentius was not happy with me, but I could tell that my words made sense to him. If they stayed we all died, this way there was a chance. "It will not be long now, they have the ram, they have the siege towers and the talks have collapsed. Eleazar is becoming more frenzied, the end is close and this fortress will not prevail."

We talked long into the night, but as dawn's fingers began to creep across the mountains, I knew I had persuaded them. We made our plans; I suggested that when they came for me, to look in the cisterns. They were the only places I could think of that no one else would go and, the only places safe from fire.

The time came, Marcus and Maxentius left to try one last time. Silva met them on the ramp as usual, they talked for an age, when suddenly four soldiers came up and grabbed my two Romans, marching them down to Silva's camp at the bottom. I hoped that they were safe, but I had to look after Claudia and myself now. Eleazar had called everyone together, thankfully he did not seem to notice, or care that their supposed captives were not among the throng gathered round him.

I stood at the very edge, partly hidden by a doorway. I did not want to be part of this, but needed to hear his words. He exhorted everyone to consider what would happen if the Romans breached the wall. They would kill all the men and take the women and children as slaves. They were not going to let us survive, we were the last pocket of resistance. He railed on and on about the iniquitous Romans and what they had done to Jerusalem, most of which was quite true to be fair, but he took it a whole new level.

By the end of the speech he had nearly persuaded the crowd that honour killing was better than being taken. The men would kill their wives and children, and a select few would kill them and so on until we were all dead. I ran my eyes over the group, the women were terror struck and some of the men looked less than convinced. Most still did not realise that death was imminent, one way or another and could not bring themselves to hurt their wives and children.

Behind us I could hear the ram battering at the wall, its powerful thud causing tremors to shake the plateau. Burning torches were hurled over the top, most landing on dry dust and going out, but some falling into the wooden inner wall. This was where it was weakened; this was how they would get through. I motioned to Aharon who came over.

"Look at this, the wall will not withstand a fiery onslaught, although we have enough water to dowse the flames, by the time we get it here another volley will have landed. We need to get out or surrender now." Aharon shook his head.

"I love you my sister, but I am not leaving my wife and children to be taken prisoner or worse. If this is where we die, I will take them with me as painlessly as possible. I am willing to include you and Claudia if you chose." I stared at him, tears filling my eyes.

"You cannot mean that, your children…" I shook my head trying to rid myself of the image that formed.

"It is the way it must be, God is waiting for us, we have done all we can, there is no escape from this mountain." He hugged me briefly and nodded to a few of his friends who went to try and remove the torches.

I felt hopeless, but resigned. As dissension grew among some of the men, Eleazar mounted what would be his final speech; it was a masterstroke of eloquence. Exhorting their loyalty, their courage, their desire to protect their loved ones, honour of those who had already died for the cause, that it was better to walk free with God than live as a prisoner of the Romans. He railed on and on, now soft and persuasive, now loud and stentorian, he certainly knew how to get under your skin. If I hadn't hated him so much, I might have been convinced myself. He went for what seemed like hours, by which time, it seemed as though the fire had blown back on itself and would burn out and he had everyone, except me, in the palm of his hand.

Chapter Twenty Nine

The plan was set, the die cast, this was it. The men would kill their wives and children, then they would draw lots to decide which ten would kill the remaining men, with one man chosen to kill this last ten and then himself. Long after this day, I did not know how they had the courage to carry out their plan, it was barbaric, but I supposed that the alternative, to them, was much worse. Also, they may well have been right and Eleazar was nothing if not ruthless, he was determined that the Romans would find nothing but death and destruction. He and some of his cronies entered the storerooms and set fire to many of them, so that if the Romans did breach the wall, they would find nothing to plunder either.

Families had set their things to rights and tidied up their living areas, something I found heartbreaking, why did they care whether they looked tidy in death? I ran back to our rooms, Aliza was there with Claudia.

"Have you heard Aliza, do you know what they intend to do?" She nodded petrified. "If you think you can keep quiet, I can save you from this, do you trust me?" She nodded again. "I cannot let Aharon kill his children, they deserve a life. If I can persuade him to hand them over to me, will you help me with them? They will need to be like mice, no sound at all." Aliza nodded once more, incapable of speech. "Stay here, find some warm clothes, wear several layers if you have to and a winter mantle. Do the same for Claudia, do not answer the door to anyone, pretend there is no one here." I held her by the shoulders and looked her straight in the eye. "Do you understand?"

Finding her voice at last Aliza replied.

"Yes, go, fetch the children, I will be ready when you return."
I slipped silently out of the door and along the walls hidden by the
smoke billowing across the fortress. The smell was acrid now and
there was a sense of utter terror pervading every corner. I found
my way without incident to Aharon's rooms and without
bothering to knock, went in. He was standing with Raizel; they
were holding each other and their children, unaware of what was
to befall them, played happily with some toys. Aharon looked up
as I entered. His smile was full of sadness. I walked over to the
two of them.

"My brother, my beloved brother and my beautiful sister, I
know of your decision, but I am here to beg you to give me Efraim
and Liora. Please let me take them with me. I intend to survive this
massacre and be reunited with my husband. No one will notice if I
am not among those to be killed, for since Maxentius was taken, I
am without husband here and I have avoided Eleazar as much as
possible. I know I can save your children. If you will let me take
them, I promise you I will give them safe and happy life."

They looked at me and then at their children. Raizel started to
speak, then found she couldn't.

"This is a huge risk my sister…" said Aharon, "…what if you
are caught?"

"I have no intention of being caught, the only thing your
children have to do is be silent. I wish you would come with me,
but I respect your choice. Please let me take them, I will love them
as my own." They gazed at each other for a long moment, their
expressions, agonised. It was all I could do not to cry. Finally,
they both turned to me and said they were in accord, I could have
the children.

Releasing a breath, I hadn't realised I was holding I hugged
them both tightly.

"I love you Aharon, I love you Raizel and I will miss you more than words can say. Be at peace." We kissed and gathering up the two children, I told them we were going to play a game called hide and seek, but that they had to be like mice and make no sound at all. Liora did think she might like to squeak like a mouse, but her mother persuaded her not to. Trying not to instill fear into their offspring, Aharon and Raizel gave them a big hug and, then kissing them, said to have fun with Aunt Hannah. We waved and as we walked out, I sent a look of heartfelt thanks over the heads of their unsuspecting children, to my brother and his wife, tears pouring down all of our cheeks and then we fled.

Back through the smoke, we ran, quietly as we could. I realised that the wind had changed; this would mean that if the fire hadn't burnt itself out, it would reignite along the inner defence. We only had a few hours. Reaching my rooms, we went in and, I could see that Aliza had readied herself and Claudia. I found some warm wraps suitable for Efraim and Liora and, although Efraim thought he was too much of man to need one. I managed to persuade him that he should carry it for his sister in case she got cold.

"Right, now I'm going to go and get some food, we might need a midnight snack." I smiled. "Stay here and pretend to be asleep, when I come back there will be a treat for the one who stayed quietest the longest." Nodding at Aliza, I went in search of food that would keep us full but would not be too much to carry. I picked up flat breads and dried fruit. Water would be plentiful so I didn't need that and, I found some sweetmeats for the children. That would have to do. Wrapping everything in a piece of cloth I had found lying on a bench, I found my way back to my quarters, detouring into the clinic to collect a small jar of the sleeping draft, just in case. The smoke was thicker now, but it was a good shield. I wondered, briefly, how Maxentius and Marcus were doing.

Back in the room, the vapours were beginning to filter through the window and under the door, if we didn't go soon, we would likely suffocate. The littlies were curled up on my bed, sleeping quietly, I looked at them for long moments, bless their hearts, they didn't ask for this.

"Aliza, we do not have long before the Romans breach the wall, there is fire everywhere and the smoke gets thicker. We need to go now, but we need to be very careful, if we are spotted they will surely kill us like they are killing everyone else. You need to be brave with me, I cannot do this on my own." She nodded and patted my hand.

"I am with you Hannah you can rely on me." I hugged her and between us we woke the two older children.

"If you can carry Claudia, I need not wake her, I will manage both Efraim and Liora." Aliza scooped up Claudia and I wrapped a mantel around Aliza's shoulders, then dipping some fine linen in water and squeezing it out, I draped it over Claudia's face, protecting it from the smoke. I did the same with the other children, before handing Aliza a cloth for her face. Tucking mine in my belt, I checked that we had everything, my clasp...grabbing it from the table, I used it to pin my mantle closed, making sure it was very secure. One last look around the room, and we were ready.

"Now remember, quieter than mice, we're going to find a really good place to hide." They nodded and we crept out of my room like ghosts. It was horrible, thick smoke, sounds of sobbing, the clash of metal, I did not want to think what that was and, still the noise from the encampments below. They sounded like they were having the party to end all parties. Good for them I thought cynically. Liora kept pointing out places she thought would be good to hide in, but I shook my head and ushered them onwards.

We had to get across the front of the Hanging Palace, round the administration block, passed the storerooms and into the cistern, near the casemate wall, close to the snake path. I just hoped that Maxentius would know where to come, that our hours and hours of exploring this fortress would pay off. It was hard not to cough, the acrid smoke was getting thicker by the minute, as although I was not yet aware, Eleazar and his men had already set fire to a substantial amount of the compound. By the time the Romans did break through, much would be damaged beyond repair.

We managed to avoid being spotted by the Zealots sweeping through the rooms, smashing what was in them, leaving nothing for the Romans and setting fire to anything that would burn. I wondered about all my herbs, balms and oils, they'd most likely also be destroyed, all my hard work, wasted. Hugging walls and doorways we moved slowly and carefully towards my goal, but unbelievably, as we were easing our way, I spotted two more children wandering alone in the courtyard, wailing disconsolately, no sign of any adults with them.

Unable to abandon them to certain death and without considering the risks I was taking, I sprinted across to them, hauling them into my arms and getting back as quickly as I could, I didn't even recognise them, they were covered in soot and what may well have been blood. How had they escaped and whose children were they? With no time to ponder this, I hushed them, hustling them along with the rest of our intrepid band.

Would I be able to keep seven of us quiet? I could only pray. As we crept around the outside of the palace, we had one very hairy moment when I was sure we were caught, a group of men came inexorably towards us, through the thick haze, intent on their quarry, who, I assumed, was us. Terrified, I quickly quieted the children, pulling everyone in against the wall and hiding our faces, thankfully they turned before they reached us and headed out over the plateau. Breathing a very shaky sigh of relief, I hurried everyone along the edge of the buildings and, after what seemed like an eternity, we found the steps leading down to relative safety.

It was one of the smaller cisterns, it had not been topped up lately, so there wasn't too much water and a kind of shelf ran along one end under the steps. If we sat there, anyone glancing in would not see us, they would have to come right inside. It was our only option. The large cistern, which would have offered much better protection, was at the far end of the plateau and I did not think our chances of getting all the way across without being seen were very favourable. The children were little angels, a most unusual trait. Claudia had slept through the whole thing and, although I could see that Efraim and Liora were tiring, they seemed to know the other two. They were both girls, whose names I discovered were Gavriella and Sarah and, the four of them were chatting excitedly, but quietly, about midnight feasts. Oh the innocence of the very young.

We snuggled them between us and dropped their mantles over their little bodies. Aliza looked exhausted and very upset, so I took Claudia off her.

"Close your eyes Aliza, I will keep watch." She smiled gratefully and lifting her cloak up to her shoulders and leaned her head back against the wall. I didn't think I would ever sleep again. My heart had just about slowed down to its regular rhythm, but until we were safe with Maxentius, my fear would keep me awake. Claudia stirred in my arms, but I rocked her back to sleep, gazing down at her infant face, praying that we would survive this.

We sat in utter silence for hours, occasionally I heard the sounds of feet running over head, shouts from the men, but eventually all fell quiet and even though it was night, the light from the fires lit the sky. Still we waited. I hoped they hadn't set

300

fire to the trees, especially our pomegranate tree - that would be so sad. The children slept peacefully, unaware that their world had fallen apart, Aliza slept peacefully aware that I was watching over them. I on the other hand could not have slept, even if I wanted to, so I spent the time thinking about my life. I ruminated about the other Hannah, the one who seemed so long ago, yet was still here in my head, she was the one who knew about this event, the one who had given me the knowledge that would save us.

Suddenly, like a light piercing the gloom, I realised that she was the woman in the white bed, the one I saw in my dreams. We were still connected this woman and I - I needed to survive for her. I fingered the clasp that Maxentius had given me, staring into its deep red depths; it was like my talisman, the one thing that just might protect us, if he wasn't the one who found us. It seemed to be glowing, but that was just my fanciful and overwrought mind, imagining things, or and much more likely, it was the glow from the fires catching the facets. For no apparent reason, I kissed it, whispering that if there were such a thing as magic, invoking it now would be much appreciated.

At some point during that long night, the children woke and we gave them their 'midnight feast,' although it was probably well after that when we were eating. Very afraid that they might not go back to sleep, I added a tiny drop of my special sleeping draft to their water. It did the trick; they were soon back in the land of nod, thinking that this was all a great game. Aliza and I talked for a little while, in low voices, so as not to disturb the children, or bring any unwanted attention to us. Aliza asked, tiredly, if we should go up and check whether it was safe, but, determined not to go up those stairs until someone I trusted came down them, I persuaded her that it was probably better to wait here a little longer. She merely nodded and, wrapping herself back into her cloak, dozed for another hour or so.

Around dawn, I heard a new noise, it was the sound of the battering ram, I knew it would breach the defences this time; the fire would have made their job so much easier. Romans in full armour would spill into the fortress, moving into the buildings and spreading out over the plateau. They would search every quarter of Masada, finding nothing but death and destruction and at some point they would find us. I knew this because the other 'me' had read about it millennia away and had somehow entrusted it to me, knowing that I could have changed history, but having faith that I wouldn't. I hoped she was right. Rocking Claudia, my arms weary from holding her, but unable to risk placing her on the shelf next to me, I waited.

It was full daylight outside, before I heard the sounds of voices from right above us and, although our hiding place was still dim, I moved us all along to the darkest corner of the cistern, behind the steps, putting my fingers to my lips to ensure the children stayed quiet. Straining to hear, I tried to discern who was issuing, or rather barking, orders, but it was a voice I did not recognise. There were others too, but none sounded familiar, then, after what seemed like a lifetime, I heard someone calling my name.

Unwilling to risk leaving the safety of the cistern, I listened for a while longer, I needed to be certain who was speaking, especially as whoever was yelling sounded hoarse, maybe from the smoke, maybe from all the shouting. After the silence of the night it was ear splitting, not helped by the fact that the walls of the cistern acted like an echo chamber. The waiting was agony, but I was too afraid to do anything other than cower in the gloom. Claudia was awake now, as unsurprisingly, the cacophony had disturbed her. She tilted her head to look at me and the voice was still bawling my name. She put her hands out of the blanket she was wrapped in and chortling with glee shouted back.

"Papa." Petrified I shushed her, turning her face into my chest, hoping no one had heard. The sudden silence above us was deafening. Then there was the sound of scrambling feet and several men in full Roman armour, appeared at the bottom of the stairs, led by Marcus and Maxentius, I could scarcely believe my eyes, they were here, right in front of us. I tried to stand but found my body had stiffened up from sitting in the same position for so many hours. Liora and Efraim had no such problem, recognising the two men, they ran out from the corner, pulling the other two with them and hurled themselves into their uncles' arms, shrieking about being mice and midnight feasts and sleeping in a well, words tumbling out so fast they made very little sense.

Aliza stayed with me, I was frozen to the spot, not daring to believe we were safe. Marcus came towards me and grinned, giving me a hug as he went to help Aliza up the steps, still I did not move. Claudia was wriggling, wanting to be put on the floor so she could go to her father, absently I put her down and she toddled across to the tall man who was staring at me over the heads of the people milling around us.

"My Hannah." My whole world was in those two words; it was like the whisper of angels. Tremulously I smiled, exhausted beyond reason, but nothing could have stopped the happiness bubbling up from the centre of my being. Maxentius smiled back, his familiar slow, toe curling smile. I finally moved, running to him to be lifted and crushed against his chest, held so tightly I couldn't breathe, but I didn't care, he was here.

He held me for a long time, my Roman, just held me, whispering my name over and over again and showering my face, which must have been very sooty, with feather light kisses. Liora, Efraim and the two little girls had gone up with Marcus, but Claudia clung to her father's leg, desperate for him to pick her up. Eventually, he released me to collect his daughter in his arms and then pulled me back into his embrace, the three off us stood wrapped together, in a dark cistern, under a decimated fortress, in the middle of the Judaean Desert.

Chapter Thirty

Eventually, we walked up the steps into the sunlight; it was another beautiful day, in complete contrast to the horror that met my eyes, as we walked back across the plateau. The fire had indeed destroyed many of the buildings, but had somehow missed others, burning out before doing too much damage. There was still smoke billowing out of the ruins of the makeshift defence wall and those buildings that had been torched. Here and there, I noticed bodies through doorways, but could not bear to look too hard.

"Maxentius?" My voice quivered, he looked down at me. "Please, I have to check on Aharon and Raizel." Wordlessly he nodded and gripping my hand we walked towards what had been their rooms. Marcus, who had been waiting close to the entrance to the cistern came towards us and I asked if he would take Claudia just for a minute, neither she nor Liora nor Efraim needed to see this. He carried her off to join the other five who were sitting in the sun with some food, being watched by one or two of the soldiers. I hoped they were there for support not repercussions.

Maxentius and I carried on into the building, the stench from the fire and burnt flesh was dreadful, my stomach churned and I knew this next few minutes would be harrowing. We entered their rooms, which surprisingly, were not too badly damaged, in fact the fire had barely reached beyond their door, it was just very smoky. On the bed at the far side, lay my brother and his wife, in each other arms. They looked so peaceful; it was hard to believe they were not simply asleep. Moving closer to the bed, it was clear they weren't, but I hoped it had been quick, that they didn't suffer too long. I leaned down and kissed them both, touching their cold faces with my hand in a final goodbye, then unable to leave them like this, found a sheet and covered them with it, offering them some dignity in this most brutal of deaths.

Maxentius waited until I had done this, then left me for a moment, understanding my need to be on my own with the last of my immediate blood kin. How would I explain this to Liora and Efraim? Would Maxentius be happy to take on not one but two children from another family, my family yes, but still…did I dare even to ask? What about Gavriella and Sarah, would I be able to find their kin, if not what would their fate be? Questions, always questions and I had no answers today. Dragging myself away, I closed what was left of the door and left them, maybe the Romans would allow us to bury them, or maybe they would not condone such ceremony for seditious Zealots.

These questions too would have to wait for another day. I needed to wash, I smelt of smoke and fear, I needed to find clean clothes, some food and I needed to know what would happen to us. Would the commander accept that I was Maxentius' wife? Would we all be allowed to go free, there were seven of us that was a big ask. Would the word of two soldiers, held for six long years be enough to prevent the Roman Governor, this Flavius Silva, from handing us to the nearest slave trader? My fear partially dampened by our rescue started to rear its ugly head again, had I completely misread this situation and placed us in more danger?

"What will happen Max? Do you think there is any hope of us being allowed to go free?" Maxentius glanced at my face, still streaked with soot, my hair all tousled, falling out of its plait and grinned.

"Well if you go and meet him looking like that there's every chance he'll think you're some kind of fire sprite coming to reek vengeance on all these lost souls, so maybe we should try and find somewhere you can have a wash." I nudged his arm.

"Its no laughing matter my love. He may not accept that Claudia and I are your daughter and wife and what about the other five, I couldn't let them die but I hope I haven't saved them just to face a worse fate."

"I believe it will work out, Marcus and I explained your role in saving our lives and the time you spent trying to save Sergius. That you and I are married and that Claudia is my daughter, although technically as a soldier I am not supposed to marry, the circumstances were extraordinary. I am sure that, if we speak for Aliza and the other children we will be able to persuade Silva that they come under our protection. Liora and Efraim and their little friends are now orphans and too small to be classed as rebels or Zealots and, I think Aliza is too old to be considered a threat to anyone. Yes, it will be complicated and may take much discussion, but leave it with Marcus and me, we will talk with Silva." I leaned my head against his chest, too weary to care.

"I need to sleep Max, I have not slept for more than twenty four hours and I'm struggling to stand, but I really want to be clean first, is there any water left anywhere on this fortress, other than the cistern you found us in? I don't think I can face going back down there." Shuddering as I recalled the horror of the previous night.

"Let's find the others and see what we can do." Making our way back over to where the others had been waiting, I looked out over the plateau, Roman soldiers were everywhere trying to extinguish the fires, starting the long job of removing the dead and returning the citadel to some sense of order.

Marcus had been doing a sterling job of keeping four small and energetic children from running amok. The few soldiers, who had been standing with them, were also getting involved in silly games, happily playing with the children of their foe. Aliza was watching Claudia who was toddling around. Smiling my thanks as we joined them, we had a brief consultation about our need for clean water. One of the soldiers went to check the kitchens and another headed over to the Western Palace. I spotted an upturned bench and righting it, sank onto its dusty seat.

Almost immediately the man who had gone to the kitchens came back to tell us that yes there was water, it was a bit dangerous accessing it, due to fallen masonry and wood, but if we were careful we could manage it. A moment later the other soldier returned to say that the Western Palace was not too badly damaged, but he hadn't been able to find any water. I knew I could probably find some in the service wing, but we were closer to the Hanging Palace. The kitchen it was. We trooped over, taking care not to trip over, or bump into, the debris littering the floor.

The Zealots had done a good job; this would require a huge repair effort. Incredibly, despite the destruction all around, the fire had not touched the kitchen itself, or my laundry next door. There was water, admittedly, with a layer of ash floating on it, but that was easily removed. I washed the children by dint of placing them bodily in the sink and rinsing the soot and dust off them. Digging through my pile of cloths to find the cleanest ones, I towelled them off.

While I'd been doing this, Maxentius had gone back to Aharon's rooms to find Liora and Efraim some fresh clothes and then onto what had been our room to collect the same for Claudia. They looked almost human again by the time we'd finished and they went off happily with Marcus and the two soldiers, whose names I hadn't registered yet. Aliza went next, while Maxentius and I went back to our rooms for me to see if I had any clothes left. Again, amazingly, not much damage, very sooty, but that was all. Everything would need a good scrub but it was habitable.

Pushing my worry about what might happen to us to the back of my head, I worked out the logistics of sleeping arrangements until we knew which parts of Masada were able to be used and which parts too damaged. Picking out clothes that smelled the least smoky, we went back to the kitchen where I managed to remove most of the grime, rinsed my hair several times and miracle of miracles found some of the lemon I'd used when I did laundry. Not ideal, but I massaged it into my hair and over my skin, hoping the aroma would clear my sinuses. Finally, I felt presentable and went out to join the others.

Maxentius and Marcus along with their two comrades were discussing repair strategies, with a larger group of soldiers. Other men were carrying pieces of equipment through the charred hole in the casemate wall, it was all movement and noise, but this time it seemed more cheerful. Despite being surrounded by the utter devastation of both lives and buildings, there was a sense of positivity about their actions. Soldiers are always happiest when they have something to work towards. A pragmatic bunch, most probably had no real argument with the people who took this fortress, just their ideologies and, now just needed to get on with the task at hand.

Maxentius came over to me and took my hand, I didn't want him to let go - ever and, gripping it tight asked whether it would be a suitable time to talk to Silva and get this over with? He had a quick conversation with Marcus who motioned towards the Western Palace; apparently, the Governor had already appropriated Herod's old throne room for his temporary office.

Without disturbing the other children and Aliza who were resting in the shade, we made our way to where Silva was directing operations. Waiting the few minutes to be admitted, my anxiety reached boiling point, I was trembling all over and my hands felt clammy. Get a grip Hannah I admonished myself, you need to appear in control, this man will not abide weakness. Inhaling deeply, I straightened my shoulders and tried to calm my fear, it didn't really work, but the breathing helped. Eventually we were summoned to Silva's presence. Not very tall, both Maxentius and Marcus towered over him, his dark hair framed a rather unprepossessing face, but he had a dignified bearing that demanded attention and when he spoke, I recognised authority in his voice. This was not a man to be messed with.

Maxentius explained who I was, that I was the woman who had saved him, Marcus and Sergius from being put to death many years ago and had treated their injuries. That eventually he had taken me as his wife and we had a daughter, one of the five children rescued from the cistern. Marcus briefed the governor about the other children and Aliza, that they were kin of mine whom I had secreted away, unable to sanction their deaths. They discussed the situation for a long time, I think I heard them mention Sergius but I could not be sure, they were speaking too fast for me to understand everything. I concentrated on staying awake, which was a real struggle now. After what seemed like hours, there were nods all round and the governor came over to me where, somehow, I had remained standing a little way from their group.

"It is an honour to meet the person who saved my commander and his comrade. I thank you for your courage and also for your efforts in trying to save the life of Quintus Sergius Crispus. For these acts, I am empowered to grant you all your freedom. A legionary cannot legally marry and his wife and any offspring are not classed as citizens, however, Lucius Maxentius is a commander and took you as his wife in a bid to protect you. These have been extraordinary circumstances and as such I am taking the extraordinary step of granting all of you citizenship as a reward for your service to the State of Rome."

310

I must have looked confused, for he smiled gently and continued. "For saving the lives of my soldiers." I gazed at him for a few moments and, dipping a low curtsey, which I felt appropriate under the circumstances, I beamed at him, my smile lighting up my tired face.

"Thank you sir. Thank you from the bottom of my heart. I am indebted to you." He nodded, accepting my appreciation and saying something quietly to Maxentius, dismissed us. We walked from the building, into the sunshine. I had no idea what would happen from here, but we were safe, all of us, we could make plans and have a life, hopefully, a long and happy life. There were still things we needed to deal with, but not now, now I wanted to sleep.

"Max, please, I must rest, but I don't want you to leave me, can you come?" He nodded, Marcus said he would keep an eye on the others, maybe get the children over by his beloved garden beds, they could spend the day getting dirty all over again. I hugged him, thanking him for everything and then my Roman and I strolled to the Hanging Palace, passing by the balcony room to our little corner of the world. Entering our haven, we closed the door and stood in each other's arms.

Utterly exhausted, yet supremely happy I leaned against his chest. Maxentius tilted my chin and cupping one hand round the back of my head, whispered my name and kissed me slowly and tenderly, while divesting me of my clothes with the other. He lifted me, laying me on our bed, removed his own armour and tunic and then laid along side me pulling the coverlet up. He pulled me into his chest and kissed me again on the nose.

"I think we made it my Hannah." I smiled, nodded and kissing him back, snuggled into his neck and we fell asleep wrapped together - finally safe.

Epilogue

I have no idea how long I slept, but it was dark when I awoke, the only light, a dim lamp in the corner of the room. I stretched, and tried to kick the cover off, but it seemed heavy and I was still too tired to bother very much. I sensed movement from next to me and heard a low voice.

"Hannah, are you awake? Please tell me you're awake." The voice was like the promise of a warm summer breeze, distant yet exquisitely familiar, but I struggled to place it. Turning my head I noticed a tall, very weary looking man sitting next to me, the bed seemed very high and his chair unusual. This wasn't my room, confused and not a little panicked; I tried to sit up but didn't have the strength. My head hurt and when I raised my hand to touch it, felt cloth. What on earth was going on? Where was I? Images flashed though my mind - death, fire, ruins, Romans, Zealots, a tall soldier, a small child - but I couldn't process them.

"Hannah, look at me, do you know who I am?" Trying to quench my alarm, I studied the man who was speaking, he was so handsome. A memory tickled at me, I knew this man, I knew him very well. His face was etched with sadness and I felt I should understand why, but I didn't, what had happened to him? He took my hand, it felt so natural, he turned it through his and held it against his chest and I could feel his heartbeat, strong and steady.

"Can you remember what happened at the fortress?" Well of course I can, I haven't been asleep that long, I wanted to say, but I couldn't form the words. Panic flickered again and I tried once more to sit up. This time, he helped me and lifted the pillows so I could lie back against them comfortably. I looked at him again, his clothing seemed strange, yet I felt it shouldn't be.

This bed was not mine, the pillows were too soft, like clouds and the sheets were so white, everything in this room seemed to be white. There was a tube in my arm and a box with numbers that were lit. Wait…a white bed, tubes, flashing boxes…the memory coalesced and came into focus, could it be? I tried to speak, my voice sounded hoarse, as if it hadn't been used for a long time. I tried again.

"Are you Max?" I questioned tentatively. His smile told me, a familiar slow, heart warming, toe curling smile.

"Oh Hannah," his voice was gentle, enfolding me, "you have no idea how long we've - I've - waited for you to wake, to hear you speak. I was afraid it might never happen." Still unsure of what was going on, I just gazed at him, trying to pin down the kaleidoscope of thoughts and images swirling through my head.

"I'm sorry."

"Why are you sorry? It wasn't your fault."

"What wasn't my fault?"

"You don't remember?" I shook my head slowly, willing myself to understand what was going on. "You were pushed down a flight of steps, cracking your head on a rock when you landed. You have been deeply unconscious for several weeks." Puzzled I looked at him, well that couldn't be right at all.

"What steps?"

"It was late in the day, you came looking for me, but Naomi followed you and she went a little, errr…crazy and shoved you down the steps by the middle terrace." Naomi, I rolled that name around my mind for a while, Naomi - a tall grey eyed woman with long curly hair, holding my arm, saying that Max was hers. I sighed; it was so hard for me to keep focusing, just when I thought I'd grasped something, it skittered off. Other images kept fighting for dominance, the tall soldier and the little girl. Was I going mad?

"I can't seem to hold anything steady in my mind, I keep seeing a very tall dark haired man, you remind me of him and, a little girl maybe two years old. What happened to them?" Embarrassed, I felt a tear roll down my cheek; suddenly I was bereft, as though I lost my whole world. Yet something in this man's eyes told me I was *his* world. He brushed my cheek with his free hand, his touch a caress, like velvet. I lifted my hand, the one he wasn't holding and nestled within it was a clasp, a deep ruby red stone surrounded by an intricate web of burnished metal.

I traced its shape, memories bubbling up, a gift from a grateful soldier, a gift for a young woman from her long dead grandmother. I looked up at the man whose eyes had not left my face, startled, this clasp was mine. I had been given it twice. Once in this life and once in another, on an isolated rocky outcrop in the middle of the Judaean desert. All at once the images stabilised and became a coherent picture, I remembered a girl, working on a dig, finding artefacts she already knew about, that same girl becoming part of a rebellion and its catastrophic finale that happened nearly two millennia ago. Two lives, connected, intertwined, yet separate. Had I come home?

I smiled at this man, this man whom I had seen in my dreams, this man who had watched over me, calling me back, I knew I loved him, I knew that, in this life, he was everything to me.

"Max." I breathed his name again. "Thank you for waiting for me." My voice was still scratchy, my throat, dry.

"I knew you would come back, you just needed time."

"For a while there I didn't think I would or even could. So much has happened and I need to tell you everything, but maybe not just yet, for now there is something I would really love you to do."

"What's that sunshine?'" His pet name nearly undid me, but I was determined not to weep, I could guarantee that when I told him my tale, there would be tears enough, but not tonight.

"My throat is so dry and my mouth feels like its full of sawdust, am I allowed a drink, then maybe a hug?" Smiling across at him, I winked and he grinned back, his face lighting up.

"Two ticks…" There was already a full glass by my bed, which he handed to me, while he rooted around by a basin in the corner of the room, coming back with some mouthwash and a small metal bowl, saying, "…thought this might help too." Having downed the water, I swished the minty wash around my dry mouth, it was so refreshing. Max placed everything back on the little table beside the bed and came back to sit next to me. "I should call the doctor, he'll want to check you over"

"Not just yet, I don't think I can deal with anyone else yet."

Feeling so much better, I gazed at him, he took my hand and as I pulled him close he curved his other hand around my neck to make sure I didn't hurt my head and leaning in, kissed me, his lips cool and firm, I trembled as a familiar flame started a slow burn in the pit of my stomach.

"Hold me Max, please hold me." I whispered.

"Are you sure? I don't want to hurt you, you've been very sick."

"I don't care, please, I need to feel your arms around me, don't let me go." Sitting on the bed and, taking care not to dislodge the tubes I was still attached to, he wrapped himself around me.

Enveloping me in his arms, his heartbeat was quicker now, as was his breathing. My arms did not seem to have their usual strength, but determined, I returned his embrace as best I could, letting my emotions wash through me. "Stay with me Max, will you stay?"

"I haven't left you yet, why should tonight be different, I don't intend to lose you again." Scooching me over to the other side of the bed and drawing the duvet up, he lay, fully clothed, alongside me.

"You can't possibly be comfortable." Sleepily.

"I'm fine sunshine, go back to sleep." Being so well behaved, I did as instructed.

Several days later we were standing on the top of Masada, the excavations had been completed for this season and most who had been working at the site had already left, although a few remained to catalogue all the finds. It had been very successful. Nate had worked out that the cloths were indeed bandages, balled up and forgotten about. There was still some confusion over the fact that some of the shards of pottery he had found may have contained herbs, oils and balms, but I wasn't about to enlighten him. Some things were better left unsaid.

After her breakdown, Naomi had been taken for assessment and it turned out that she had been in a very abusive relationship and fixated on anyone who was the antithesis of her partner. Max had just been in the wrong place at the wrong time and I was simply collateral damage. The afternoon of my accident, Naomi had asked Max to accompany her to Ein Bokek, for the evening and he had declined, telling her that he was spending the evening with me and suggesting she ask Tom. For whatever reason, it had been enough to make her flip out, but she had, at least, written to apologise for what she had done, which I appreciated.

My head had healed, there was a very nice scar and my hair was slowly going back, thank goodness for my floppy hat. My shoulder had been pushed back into its socket that first evening and seemed fine although a little tender. The damage to my back had turned out to be bruising, painful but nowhere near as scary as broken bones, it would just take time. My body felt very weak, having been so long in bed and it took me a little while to feel able to do anything without help. During that time, I had told Max everything, even what Tobias tried to do, that was hard for both of us, but it needed to be explained, it had affected who I was.

My story, my life was convoluted, I knew that, but I tried to explain it as best as I could, that it was not me as such, more, being involved in events as they unfolded, through another's eyes. There were, as I had predicted, many tears. I had, after all, lost six years, a husband and a child - a whole life - yet here, in this time, I was only a few weeks older. I explained how Maxentius had seemed so very familiar, not necessarily, as was with the other Hannah, in looks, but in mannerisms and characteristics, except for his eyes, his eyes were exactly the same. That for a long time I was torn because I was one person in two bodies, in love with two men.

Funnily enough one morning, a day or so later, we discovered that there was, in fact, a connection. I was writing in my journal, trying to record everything while it was still fresh. As I was noting down the names of my ancient counterparts, Max, who was watching, spotted Maxentius' full name and commented that his family name, Vallier, was the modern equivalent of Valerius - neither of us even seemed surprised. The circle was complete.

Aware that I needed to time to readjust, Max was attentive, without being over protective, staying close without monopolising me, his strength and love, a balm to my aching soul, which I feared would take longer to heal than my head. I had asked to take a last walk round the fortress as we were leaving the next day. Although the doctor had pronounced me fit enough to go home, Max had decided we would travel slowly, in stages, doing some sightseeing on the way. I hoped to come back some day to this stark, beautiful, harsh yet beloved outcrop that I was connected to in so many ways, but for now I needed to say goodbye.

I took Max through the two ruined palaces, explaining what they had looked like, weaving a picture for him of my everyday life, where I had worked and slept. By chance we ended up in the room where the mosaic was that he had been working on, the centre of which they had not yet uncovered, work had stopped on the day of my accident, the rest was for another season. Now I told him about this room, what had been in here and, finally, that the tree in the centre was actually a pomegranate. We stood and admired the beauty of the design and, as the sun filtered through the protective canopy, I could see the room, as it had been, the desk, the shelves and the papyrus, it was a poignant moment.

Then we left the past behind, going back onto the plateau and I dragged Max over to one of the pomegranate trees growing between the two palaces. Standing in its shade, I turned to him.

"This was about where our tree was." I felt him inhale sharply as I said 'our.' I placed my hand on his arm. "It wasn't really me Max, I never left you, but this is the only way I can explain it. Don't fear something that happened a world ago."

Drawing him close, I kissed him, letting my body tell him how I felt, he shuddered and responded. So far he had been very loving, gentle and tender, yet something was holding him back, as if unsure of my reaction, but today his lips crushed mine, his kiss claiming me, branding me. I ran my hands up his back and moulded myself against him, this was what I had been waiting for, I was afraid I had scared him off with my story, that he would not desire me in the same way as before, I knew he loved me, but I wanted this passion.

The spark flared and ignited, heat shooting through me, as Max let his cool fingers roam, touching, teasing and stroking, rediscovering my body. I clung to him, pushing my hands under his shirt, feeling his skin tremble as I traced his muscles, breathing raggedly he caught my hands, holding them behind me while he

318

continued to bruise my lips. Wriggling free I brought my arms round his neck my hand curving round his head matching him kiss for kiss.

How long we were there I cannot remember now, but it was as though we were exorcising the ghosts of my past, the longer we kissed the further away they seemed. Slowly, we came back to reality - thankfully there was no one around - I grinned at Max, my eyes shining from happiness, he smiled back, eyes still dark with desire. Leaning back in against him, I sighed against his cheek.

"Soon."

"Now that's a promise I intend to hold you too."

Smiling, we stood together under the shade of the pomegranate tree, gazing out over the vast expanse that was the Judaean Desert, the sun sparkling on the Dead Sea in the distance. Nearly two thousand years away, a very tall man and a small woman - sitting on a rather scorched bench, in almost the same place, watching a group of children play in front of them - smiled back.

In my hand was the clasp and lifting it so that the blood red of the stone caught the sun, suddenly I knew...

...It wasn't over.

Made in the USA
Charleston, SC
08 February 2016